ESSENTIAL LIBERTY

A Thriller

ROB OLIVE

This book is a work of fiction. Names, characters, places, and incidents either are products of the author's imagination or are used fictitiously. Any resemblance to actual events or locales or persons living or dead is entirely coincidental.

First Revision, December, 2012

ISBN 978-0-9859020-2-5 (hardcover)
ISBN 978-0-9859020-0-1 (paperback)
ISBN 978-0-9859020-1-8 (ebook)

For all those who've served and sacrificed so that this
Grand Experiment in Liberty may remain ongoing

Preface to the First Revision

The first draft of *Essential Liberty* was completed in 1999. At that time, the Bureau of Alcohol, Tobacco and Firearms (ATF) was part of the U.S. Treasury Department. In 2003, the law enforcement functions of ATF were transferred to the Department of Justice under the Homeland Security Act and the name was changed to the Bureau of Alcohol, Tobacco, Firearms and Explosives (though it is still referred to as ATF). In the first edition of my novel, I describe ATF as being part of the Treasury Department. In this revision, I have changed that to reflect the current reality. As a result, Treasury Secretary Martinez has become Attorney General Martinez. I have also deleted one spurious quote that I had incorrectly attributed to Thomas Jefferson and I want to assure you that misattribution is a literary sin I will never again commit. The practical effect of these changes upon the story is negligible, but I wanted to be forthright about them. All other changes in this revision are minor corrections in form, rather than substance.

Rob Olive
December, 2012

"Those who would give up Essential Liberty to purchase a little Temporary Safety, deserve neither Liberty nor Safety."

—Benjamin Franklin

ESSENTIAL LIBERTY

Prologue

"Good intentions will always be pleaded for every assumption of power; but they cannot justify it, even if we were sure that they existed. It is hardly too strong to say, that the Constitution was made to guard the people against the dangers of good intention, real or pretended."

— Daniel Webster

HE HAD NEVER been so scared in his life. Drained from fear and exhaustion, he could only dread tomorrow, when he would either get his life back or lose it for good.

The old story about the boiling frog came to mind, that if you put a frog in water and heated it slowly, the damn thing would allow itself to be boiled to death. Whether or not the story was true, it was a metaphor for his life: the water around him had begun to boil. How could he and millions of other Americans not have seen this coming?

He lay on a decrepit bed in a filthy motel room, staring at the water-stained ceiling. Paint was peeling off the walls, the carpet was a mess, and the disgusting odor from God knows what turned his stomach.

The owners of this place had long ago quit caring. When it was fresh and new, it must have been a source of pride for them, but at some point they began to let the little things slide, until the little things became too big to deal with. Now it had been neglected for so long, it no longer appeared worth saving.

In a moment of insight, he realized that the same could be said of his country. Until three weeks ago, he'd never questioned the integrity of his government. Liberty was a grand eighteenth-century concept justifiably taken for granted in twenty-first-century America. Now, hunted by the same government he had always trusted implicitly, he was testing the boundaries of the concept so beloved by the Founders.

1

"Tyranny, like hell, is not easily conquered; yet we have this consolation with us, that the harder the conflict, the more glorious the triumph."

—Thomas Paine

Portland, Oregon
Monday, April 7

THE MAN KNOCKING on the front door was dressed in a blue suit and had close-cropped hair. "Mr. Schmidt?" he asked when the homeowner opened the door.

"Yeah, what can I do for you?" Schmidt didn't see the other four men hidden on both sides of the porch, weapons drawn.

"Sir, I'm with the Bureau of Alcohol, Tobacco, Firearms and Explosives," the stranger replied as he flashed a badge. "Our records indicate that you own a number of illegal firearms. Additionally, you have failed to turn in those firearms during the six-month grace period allowed by law. I'm here to confiscate those weapons and to place you under arrest."

Schmidt stared in wide-eyed disbelief. He'd thought all the talk from the government was just "saber rattling"—there was no way they'd ever *actually* go door to door. "Wait a minute…you've got to be kidding me!"

"No sir, I'm not," the federal agent answered as he pushed past the man and entered his home. The other four agents immediately came into view and followed him inside. The homeowner, who appeared catatonic at this point, seemed to barely notice as two of them handcuffed him and began to walk him out to their waiting vehicle.

"Who is it, honey?" Schmidt's wife asked from the kitchen table, surrounded by four children in the middle of dinner.

The lead agent froze and turned back toward the door. "Hold on. At least let him say good-bye to his family, for God's sake."

* * * * * *

The soil this high in the mountains was full of rocks, which made digging damn tough. It was also still partially frozen. But Mike Niculescu owned his own construction company, which meant he had access to heavy equipment—a necessity for the large hole he was digging. Mike was on his parents' vacation property deep in the Cascade Mountains of Oregon. The remote property was a much better choice than his own for what he had to do.

Never in his wildest dreams had Mike imagined himself doing what he was doing. When he'd heard about others doing it, it had struck him as ridiculously paranoid. Maybe that's what he was, Mike thought as he worked the backhoe. Then, as quickly as the thought had entered his mind, it was gone. He was a lot of things right now: resolute, determined…and pissed off; but he was not paranoid. Paranoid people wrung their hands and worried, but didn't try to correct the situation that made them anxious. He was a man of action—even when the action required was as distasteful as what he was doing now.

After he finished digging, Mike carefully squared the edges of the hole with a shovel. Then, using a combination of rebar, stainless steel sheet metal, and foam, he created an underground vault. It wasn't airtight, but it didn't need to be.

He had meticulously preserved and prepared nearly his entire collection of fine firearms for long-term storage. "Caching" was the term commonly used to describe the process and it was tedious. Every firearm had to be individually treated with a corrosion inhibitor and sealed in a specially made, multi-layer poly/foil bag, then vacuum-sealed. The final step was to arrange the long guns and handguns so that they fit—without the potential for damage—into polyethylene tubes, called Mono Vaults. He then placed desiccant packets in each of the tubes and screwed on the end caps, which were sealed with a rubber O-ring. With this preparation, Mike's firearms could last for decades...though he hoped they wouldn't need to. Not if the American people came to their senses.

As immigrants from Communist Romania, Mike's parents had instilled in him a great love for the United States of America. The striking differences between the country of their birth and their new home were never lost on them. The Niculescus believed that most Americans took liberty for granted—and therefore seldom even noticed it. To George and Ana Niculescu, however, individual liberty had the same effect that a powerful drug might have. They noticed it almost daily; everywhere they turned, it stared them in the face. They would never get used to it because they'd had far too much experience with the alternative.

Ana Niculescu had made the journey from Romania pregnant with the only child they would ever be blessed with. In his parents' homeland he would have been "Mihai," but his father insisted on Michael: his son was a United States citizen and he should have an American name.

Because of his parents' love for the country that had offered them so much freedom and opportunity, Mike felt a tremendous sense of both patriotism and responsibility. He believed that the U.S. Constitution deserved and required constant and vigorous defense. These deeply held beliefs were what drove Mike to seek a commission as a second lieutenant in the Marine Corps immediately upon graduation from college.

He loved being a Marine, but civilian life eventually called. He wanted to be there for his parents (though they'd have never asked him to) and he also felt the need for a family to share his life with—something often difficult for an active-duty Marine to achieve, unfortunately. It turned out to be the right call, though he would always miss the Corps.

Mike carefully arranged the large plastic tubes in the vault, rolled a piece of foam insulation across the top, and put the stainless steel cover in place. Sure, all the metal he'd used in the vault's construction would make it easy to detect, but he figured the remoteness of the property offset that fact—and he liked the extra protection it offered his prized possessions. After covering the vault with three feet of soil, he spread the rest around the property, put the backhoe on the trailer, and collected the rest of his equipment. Then he sat down and thought about what he'd just done. It was an extreme step, to be sure, but he was convinced that it was necessary.

Mike wondered whether the Feds would be coming for him. He'd been afflicted with a love for firearms at an early age, ever since his father presented him with a single-shot .22 rifle for his tenth birthday. To both of them, it was a symbol of what it meant to live in freedom; owning a gun would have been impossible in his parents' homeland. Always practicing discipline and safety with that rifle and every other gun he'd owned since, Mike took very seriously what he saw as a sacred right guaranteed to every American.

He also felt there was a reason for the place of honor that firearms held in the minds of those who had founded this country. It had nothing to do with hunting, or even protection from criminals. Instead, it had everything to do with holding in check the very government they were creating. Rather than the people counting on the government's benevolence, the government was supposed to fear becoming anything other than benevolent. Mike couldn't help but laugh at *that* thought, in light of current events.

Of course, the mere mention of such historical facts these days could very well result in one being branded a "right-wing extremist." Mike was always dumbfounded by the fact that the words upon which his country was founded were now considered "extreme." Even if the necessity for such desperate measures seemed unlikely in this day and age, the need for proven safeguards would always be there. Every dictator in history had had to disarm his people in order to subjugate them. How that wasn't obvious to *everyone* was impossible for Mike to understand.

What if they *did* come for him? He'd never thought about it as a real possibility, but one thing was certain: he would *not* meekly comply—not when the issue was something this important. What about his family, though? *This should not be happening in the United States of America!* It was exactly this kind of thing that his parents had fled from.

Worn out and filthy, Mike headed back down the mountain toward home that evening and called his friend Don's cell number as soon as he had reception, but got no answer. He wanted to meet Don for lunch tomorrow. He really needed to talk to someone about this and although they often disagreed on political matters, Don was a good friend, someone he felt he could trust. A few minutes later, he called Don's home number.

Jenny, Don's wife, sounded her usual bubbly self, telling him that Don wasn't home from work yet. "Is something wrong, Mike?"

"No, everything's fine," he lied and hung up. The truth was that everything had not been "fine" for the past four years or so. The political ball had begun rolling soon after President Nichols' election. There had been a rash of shootings in schools and workplaces and gang violence had begun to encroach on the suburbs. *That* was the last straw for many. It seemed as if the lead item in every nightly newscast was some type of tragedy involving the use of a firearm.

The fact that prisons were overflowing to the point that violent offenders were often turned back out onto the streets within a matter of weeks (or even days) of their incarceration was too complicated an issue for politicians to deal with. Firearms were much easier to wrap their heads around. Many politicians and others chose to exploit these tragedies for their own purposes and the American public seemed ripe for demagoguery.

At the center of the debate was presidential candidate Nichols, who had campaigned vigorously on gun control. He'd advocated the registration of every handgun in the United States and the licensing of all current owners and future purchasers. These steps had seemed reasonable to far too many people, in Mike's opinion. "After all," Nichols had been fond of saying, "why should a license and registration be required to drive a car but not to operate a deadly handgun?"

Facts and logic mattered not at all, as many firearms rights supporters quickly discovered. When emotions ran as high as they did on this issue, there could be no true debate. There had not been this kind of attention focused on a single social issue in the United States for decades. The resulting pressure on Congress became more than most legislators could stand and gave many of them the way out that they needed to back the President's plan. Within six months of his election, the President proposed and Congress passed a comprehensive bill mandating the registration of all handguns, as well as the licensing of all handgun owners. It was far too easily accomplished.

In spite of all its "hard work," though, the Administration was stunned by how few firearms were registered and by the small number of current owners who voluntarily submitted to licensing. Many gun owners felt there was really no way for them to be identified and, as a result, saw no justification for relinquishing their privacy and their constitutional rights.

As if to prove them wrong, two years later the Nichols Administration proposed the much more ambitious Family Protection Act. They'd done everything possible to stem the "proliferation" of guns, the President had lamented, but it wasn't enough. The only remaining course of action was to take away the privately owned firearms already in circulation. The centerpiece of this legislation was a complete ban on the ownership of all handguns and most types of rifles and shotguns by civilians. All existing firearms affected by the ban were to be "collected," one way or another. More than just a matter of semantics, it was determined through focus groups early on that the word "collection" was more palatable than "confiscation."

Additionally, the manpower of the Bureau of Alcohol, Tobacco,

Firearms and Explosives (ATF) was to be increased by several thousand agents, in order to enforce the new legislation. A few lawmakers dared to question the need for such a huge expansion of a federal law enforcement agency already known for some rather questionable tactics, but in the end they were drowned out by a strong majority of their colleagues and the media. It was unimportant that the rights of what was fast becoming a marginalized subculture were infringed upon in the process.

Though he shouldn't have been surprised by it, one of the things that bothered Mike the most was that all of the advocacy groups normally championing individual rights were silent on the issue. This, in spite of the fact that many saw the potential for the newly strengthened ATF to become the proverbial "secret police," known to most Americans only through Cold War novels. The reason for this failure to speak out against the legislation was its obvious primary purpose. Second and Fourth Amendment considerations aside, "taking guns off the streets" was *always* a good thing. Such groups were hypocritical pretenders, as far as Mike was concerned. They chose to narrowly interpret the Second Amendment while going to great lengths to protect the rest of the Bill of Rights. It was preposterous and Mike was convinced that it would have sickened the Framers of the Constitution.

Every court in the land seemed to march in lockstep with the Nichols Administration on the issue and a decision by the Supreme Court was touted as "the final nail in the coffin of the embarrassing Second Amendment" by the Editorial Board of the *New York Times*. In reality, the Court's decision was made possible not by anything written in the Constitution, but rather by the fact that President Nichols had made the most of his two opportunities to appoint justices to the High Court.

The reaction of many gun owners was one of slack-jawed disbelief, at first. While they were still trying to figure out what had hit them, the media began its editorial barrage, demonizing anyone who owned a firearm and was reluctant to turn it over to the federal government.

In the end, the legislation passed both houses of Congress and was signed by the President in a lavish Rose Garden ceremony, complete with a number of police chiefs, schoolchildren, Hollywood stars, and representatives from every gun control group in existence.

In spite of the pressure on them not to do so, many congressional representatives and senators *did* oppose the Family Protection Act. One of those was Congressman Tom Skiles of Oregon, Mike's representative. During what little debate there was over the legislation, Congressman Skiles was vocal in his opposition and became nationally famous (infamous, in some circles) because of it. When the news outlets needed a comment from "the opposition," they usually contacted Skiles. The conventional wisdom was that his opposition would cost him his job when elections were held later that year. Taking such a stance required guts. Not bad for a Democrat, Mike thought. He had never voted for Skiles before, but that would change this year.

Of more immediate interest to Mike, however, was the fact that the confiscation of guns was now actually under way. He'd heard a report on satellite radio this morning that Collection had begun to take place across the country. Though he was very much a realist most of the time, Mike had had a hard time believing that the ATF would break down the doors of regular people to confiscate firearms. He was obviously wrong.

Rather than comply with what they felt was an unprecedented soiling of the Constitution, Mike and many other die-hard firearms enthusiasts had made the decision to hide their banned guns and ride out the storm until common sense prevailed in the nation's capital. Their hope was that bureaucracy would be their saving grace—that records were incomplete, that the mechanics of Collection would be too overwhelming to carry out effectively, and that the odds of an individual gun-owner being targeted were still relatively low.

It was wishful thinking and not realistic. Unfortunately for them, information obtained over several years through the background check, registration, and licensing processes made it fairly easy for the

ATF to compile "Collection lists," even before registration became official policy. All of this data was compared to the "voluntary submission" listing, which had been compiled during the amnesty period. The difference between those who had the contraband and those who chose to turn it in became known as "The List."

The ATF was very secretive about how complete The List was, leaving the average American gun owner to wonder whether or not he was on it. The reality was that The List was *very* complete and the powers that be at ATF were surprised by how many formerly law-abiding citizens had refused to turn in their firearms. What they found, in general, was that the guns turned in were those purchased during the "registration" period. Many of those who had bought their firearms prior to that time maintained a false sense of security.

It was now obvious to Mike that a number of unlucky people just like him would serve as an example to all those who hadn't complied. How long would the rest hold out after seeing their "brothers in arms" hauled away from their families in handcuffs? His head told him that he *had* to be on The List, but his heart held out hope that he wasn't. Following his heart, in this case, was made easier by the fact that some of the Internet chat, along with other information he had received, indicated that The List wasn't nearly as complete as people had been led to believe.

Mike hadn't purchased a single firearm since registration went into effect. Since he'd also declined to submit to the licensing process, he liked to think that he was invisible to the ATF. It was this sliver of hope that persuaded him to hold out. He knew it probably wasn't realistic, but he also knew it was the right thing to do…probably. Of course, Sarah, his wife, thought he had turned his guns in. After all, he'd told her he had and he'd never lied to her before.

* * * * * *

The buzzing startled Don Williams out of his meeting-induced haze. It had been an especially long unit meeting this afternoon and his mind wasn't yet back in gear. He punched the speaker button on his phone, allowing his secretary's voice to intrude upon his end-of-the-day reflection.

"Don, it's after five. I'm going home and I think you should too."

Don smiled. "Okay, Jean, see you in the morning." He didn't mind the gentle nudging, especially when she was right. Jean knew his family well, after eight years as his secretary, and considered it part of her job to see that he got home to them at a decent hour as often as possible. He also desperately needed to start exercising. That would mean either getting home earlier or getting up earlier, neither of which was an attractive option. Being over six feet tall, Don could hide a multitude of sins. Still, he'd just turned forty and the weight of *that*, combined with the little paunch he'd begun to develop a few years earlier, made him look and feel less healthy than his ego told him he should. Lately, he'd been getting home between six thirty and seven o'clock, after his thirty-minute commute, and that had to stop.

Don considered it a manager's duty to arrive early and leave after everyone else. As the divisional claims manager for a major insurance company, he supervised over two hundred employees and he felt a responsibility to each one to set an example. Jean was right, though: his family was important too.

Don's life had been a well-thought-out plan. He believed there were rules to follow, both written and unwritten, and if a person followed those rules, things tended to work out. Don had always been considered "sensible" by those who knew him well—one of the highest compliments a person could earn, as far as he was concerned. He believed that if everyone got up early, worked hard all day, did their best to raise a family, and obeyed the law, this would once again be the country that it used to be.

His house was very nice without being pretentious. Tucked into a modest-size lot in a large subdivision, it was not unlike every third or fourth house on his street or, for that matter, on any other street in his neighborhood. It was also absolutely the most house he could afford and still manage to meet every other financial obligation he had.

Proud of himself for getting home by six, Don set his bulging briefcase down while he unlocked the front door. "Daddy! Daddy!" greeted him as he stepped inside and a blonde five-year-old attached herself to his knee. Troy was standing back, watching with a scornful eye as Stephanie mauled Dad. He was eight now and trying very hard these days to act grown up. Even so, it didn't bother him that Dad gave him a bear hug as he passed.

"Where's Mom?" Don asked.

"Hello," his wife called from the kitchen. "To what do we owe the honor of your presence this early?"

"Oh, I didn't have too much work piled up, so I figured what the hell, may as well go home to the old ball and chain," Don whispered as he walked up and hugged Jenny from behind. Jenny Williams was a beautiful, petite brunette, with a personality that made everyone want to be her friend.

"Hey, watch out, mister, it doesn't take much to turn on an old ball and chain."

"Promises, promises," he teased back. "Where's Clay?"

"Out exploring the world on his bike, which is about all he wants to do lately," Jenny answered. "Should a twelve-year-old be that independent?" Don's only answer was a shrug.

Don insisted that the family communicate with each other at the dinner table. As they settled in to eat after blessing their food, Jenny started the conversation. "By the way, I forgot to tell you Mike called just before you got home. He sounded a little…distracted. Anyway, he wanted to make sure we're still going over there on Saturday."

Clay looked up from his plate. "We are, aren't we, Dad?"

"You bet we are, buddy." Clay idolized Mike and had become great friends with his son Brett, who was the same age and had many of the same interests.

Don had many acquaintances, but few close friends. Of those, Mike was by far the closest and always the one Don turned to when he wanted to talk about something important, or on the rare occasions when he allowed himself to ask for advice. They had met a few years before and quickly became good friends. The funny thing was that they really didn't have much in common except close families and a tremendous work ethic. They'd also both recently turned forty—something they'd commiserated about more than once.

After dinner, Don sat down on the couch, turned on the television, and found one of the cable news channels. "In various parts of the country today, ATF agents made numerous arrests for failure to comply with the gun control measures enacted six months ago as part of President Nichols' Family Protection Act," the news anchor began.

"You have *got* to be kidding me!" Don bellowed uncharacteristically at the television.

"Among other things, the law required owners of most firearms to turn them in to an ATF Collection Station within six months of the date on which it was signed by the President. Those who complied were compensated with fair market value in exchange for the weapons. Some of those who did not were paid a visit today by federal agents. The Attorney General issued a statement at a press conference a short time ago."

Jenny and Clay came into the room and stood behind Don as the camera switched from Atlanta to Washington, D.C. Attorney General Charles Martinez, former governor of New Jersey and good friend of the President's, cleared his throat to speak. "Today, on my order, federal agents began to execute warrants for the arrest of those suspected of being in possession of illegal firearms. Those arrested have been given every opportunity to turn in these weapons. Rather than comply with federal law, however, these individuals chose to knowingly violate the law."

Immediately, Don thought about Mike. "I can't believe they did it," he muttered.

"Who?" Jenny asked. "The guys who didn't turn in the guns, or the police?"

"Both, I guess...I mean, it *is* the law now. I can't see how anyone would risk so much just to keep their guns. Still, I can't believe the

Feds actually arrested them. You'd think there'd be a million or so *actual* bad guys out there to keep them busy."

Since Don had never had any use for guns, the new law didn't affect him. Mike, on the other hand, apparently owned several that had been banned. He was pretty carried away with all this Second Amendment stuff. Mike had said several times that he would never give up his guns and there was no talking any sense into him. Don thought confiscation was a little fascist, but there really was no need for firearms like the ones Mike had. They had talked about it only a couple of times since the law was passed and Mike had told Don that he'd finally bitten the bullet and turned over his guns. Don was relieved that his friend had been sensible.

He called Mike and left a voice mail. Since watching the newscast, he had a strange feeling that he should talk to him as soon as possible, but tomorrow Don had work obligations from early morning into the evening. He'd try to catch him during the week, but if all else failed, they'd see each other on Saturday.

"They probably thought either they wouldn't get caught or it was important enough to stand up for," Jenny said, as they were getting ready for bed.

"Yeah, these guys must have figured they were safe from Big Brother," Don answered, not even considering the second possibility that his wife had offered.

2

Portland, Oregon
Monday, April 7

Deputy Marshal Scott Keller pulled his U.S. Marshals Service (USMS) pool car into one of the last remaining spaces in the newly paved parking lot. The building in front of him said a lot about the recent shift in thinking within the federal law enforcement community. With the passage of the Family Protection Act and subsequent buildup of the ATF, no other federal agency was as high profile. For a Marshal, this was a little hard to swallow. Competition among the various agencies was always an issue—at least unofficially. Lately, ATF was getting a lot of media attention.

At thirty-three, and in only his third year with the Marshals Service, Scott Keller was known as a rising star. His ability to pick up on details and clues that others missed was acknowledged by his peers. Scott loved to sink his teeth into a case, outline the mission required to solve it, and then execute to perfection.

He had always enjoyed being in the thick of the action. Upon graduation from the Naval Academy, Scott had taken the "Marine option," much to the chagrin of his father, who was also an Academy graduate. Ron Keller had stayed with the Navy, retiring as a Rear Admiral. Scott entered the Marine Corps as an infantry officer and, as soon as possible, applied for the Marine Corps Forces Special Operations Command (MARSOC). Though lesser-known outside military circles than other Special Operations Forces, MARSOC performed similar missions.

What made MARSOC Marines, Navy SEALs, Army Special Forces, Air Force Pararescuemen, and all other Operators different from the average Marine, Sailor, Soldier, or Airman was the Operator's ability to be flexible and adaptable. The mental aspect was what separated them from conventional forces. Scott didn't see MARSOC as "elite"—just different. Not everyone was cut out to operate within the parameters that Special Operations units did.

Scott had as bright a future as any young Marine officer could have, but it was soon time to decide which direction his career and life would take. As a result of a lot of serious thought, Scott decided he didn't want to make a career out of the Marine Corps. He had thoroughly enjoyed his job, but felt there was something else out there for him.

So, at the age of thirty, Captain Scott Keller, USMC, became Deputy Marshal Scott Keller, USMS. The transition had been surprisingly easy. Both positions required diligence, hard work, aptitude, and intelligence in order to succeed. Both also required an ability to put up with some in positions of authority who possessed none of those traits.

Of all the things Scott had done right so far in his career, the most important had to be realizing early on that he wasn't as smart as he'd thought he was. As a member of a team of Marshals hot on the trail of an escaped fugitive, he was sure he had the guy nailed. He was so sure that he disobeyed an order from the team's senior Marshal, following his own youthful instincts instead. In the end, Scott was shot and nearly killed. Instead of the manhunt ending then and there, it would be almost another week and countless man-hours before it was over—luckily, before anyone else was injured.

That senior Marshal, who, to this day, was the best bloodhound Scott had ever seen, forgave his cockiness. He chalked the mistake up to a dangerous combination of youth and talent. Time would prove the older man right. Scott turned out to be one of the best he'd seen in over thirty years. The lesson learned was invaluable and this great

Marshal became a very important part of young Scott Keller's life—as well as his father-in-law.

As in the Marine Corps, Scott wanted to push himself as hard as possible within the Marshals Service. That desire led him into the Marshals' Special Operations Group (SOG), a tactical unit deployed for especially sticky and high-profile cases. Like most other members of SOG, Scott carried out his normal duties most of the time, while on call twenty-four hours a day for SOG missions.

Scott knew that this latest assignment, which was what brought him to the new ATF complex, would be far different from anything else he had ever done. As both a Marine and a Marshal, he had always believed in the objective. There were specifics about some missions and cases he may not have agreed with, but overall, the objective had always been worth pursuing. The lack of a noble purpose now caused him to feel queasy about doing his job for the first time in his life. Scott was one of many in the law enforcement community who believed that the process of confiscating firearms from and arresting people who had otherwise been law-abiding citizens was both fraught with peril and less than morally or constitutionally right.

He was here because the powers that be had decided that each ATF Field Division Office would work with one of the best the Marshals Service had to offer. Due to their experience in apprehending fugitives, the Marshals were to assist the ATF with Collection. It was assumed that there would be a certain percentage of Collection subjects who would flee and that was how Marshals made their living. Specifically, each of the six new ATF Hazardous Operations Teams (HOT) would be assigned a Marshal from SOG. This made sense, as the training and abilities of both units were similar. Mostly against his wishes, Scott had been selected to fill that slot for HOT (Northwest).

His boss, the U.S. Marshal for the District of Oregon and a man whom Scott respected greatly, saw this as an excellent opportunity for a bright young Deputy Marshal. It was not for this reason, however, but because U.S. Marshal Doug Filson had personally asked him to that Scott had accepted the assignment. Blind faith had nothing to do with it. Filson was well aware of Scott's reservations about Collection. The bottom line was that both of them knew Scott was the right man for the job.

It was with all of this running through his mind that Scott approached the large glass doors of the beautiful six-story ATF office. Behind the building were forty security-fenced acres. This was the headquarters and training facility for the ATF's Hazardous Operations Team (Northwest). One of only six such facilities in the country, Scott reminded himself. He supposed he ought to feel lucky to be assigned here.

"Thank you," the guard replied as he held out his credentials for inspection. "You'll find the Commander's office on the sixth floor."

Scott moved toward the heavy steel security door. The guard on the other side tripped the electronic lock on the door with a button under his desk. After showing his credentials again, he was allowed to proceed to the elevator. As he stepped out onto the sixth floor, it was obvious that this was where the boss lived. Some in positions of authority preferred to keep a low profile, while others wanted the world to know how important they considered themselves. HOT Commander William Payne was obviously a member of the latter group. The hallway and entry into his office suite was lavishly decorated and photos of him with various important people began just outside the elevator. Scott was trying hard not to immediately dislike the guy, but it was becoming increasingly difficult the closer he got to Payne's private office.

"Marshal Keller?" inquired the Commander's very attractive secretary.

"Yes, I have an appointment with Commander Payne."

"Yes sir, if you'll have a seat, I'll let him know you're here," she replied, looking him in the eye and smiling. The smile seemed to last a very long time. It also seemed to have a message in it. Scott got that from women a lot. He returned the smile and walked across the vast reception area toward a gorgeous overstuffed leather couch against the far wall.

Sinking into the couch, he thought he'd never been so comfortable in his life. The thing must have cost a small fortune. In the reception area, VIP power photos gave way to upscale artwork. The wallpaper was stunning, the carpet thick. The overall feel of the sixth floor so far was one of opulence and power—more like the Oval Office than an ATF Field Office. There was the obvious touch of a very good, and very expensive, interior decorator. And that was something he wasn't used to seeing in a law enforcement field office of *any* kind.

On the mahogany coffee table in front of him was a selection of every newsmagazine available. Scott picked up a copy of *Newsweek* and lazily thumbed through it. After about twenty minutes—too long to keep an appointment waiting without explanation, unless a message was being sent—the secretary's phone buzzed.

"Marshal Keller, the Commander will see you now." Scott stood and followed Victoria (he'd learned her name from the brass placard on her desk) to the extra-wide door to Payne's office. The thing looked like a five-hundred-pound piece of solid walnut. She ceremoniously opened the door for him and waved him through.

Commander Payne had his back toward the door as they entered, apparently finishing up something on the computer behind his desk. "Excuse me, sir, this is Marshal Keller," Victoria announced after several seconds. Her boss continued typing and spoke over his shoulder. "Have a seat, Marshal. I'll be with you in just a minute."

Scott thanked Victoria, who smiled at him knowingly, and approached one of the two leather armchairs across from the desk. After an appropriate delay, Payne pushed away from the credenza and spun his large executive chair around slowly. It was all about showing the Marshal who was in charge.

Payne's private office was even more ornate than the waiting area, except for the adornment of the walls. Instead of tasteful, upscale artwork, this inner sanctum displayed a continuation of the "power pictures" he'd seen in the hallway. There he was shaking hands with President Nichols, the Attorney General, the ATF Director, and many other obvious VIPs. Like everything else about this man, his surroundings were meant to intimidate.

Payne stood and, rather than walking around the huge desk, extended his hand across it. In his mid-forties, he was shorter than Scott, though not a small man. His temples were beginning to gray and he had the look of a man who tried hard to stay in shape, despite the fact that he carried a small paunch.

"Good morning, Marshal. I'm Commander Payne." Scott took Payne's hand and shook it firmly, resisting the temptation to squeeze harder. *Knock it off, Keller.*

"Good morning, sir," was all he could muster. Both men sat back down and eyed each other. Scott realized that he was being evaluated. Actually, "sized up" was probably more accurate.

"Well, Marshal Keller, out of respect for those in Washington who think we can't complete this mission without the assistance of the Marshals Service, I suppose we ought to agree right off the bat to get along with each other, eh?"

It was absolutely the most in-your-face greeting Scott had ever experienced. He'd always taken pride in his ability to work well with other agencies. He had a great deal of respect for the job every law enforcement agency did and that came across loud and clear most of the time. But he'd never run up against anyone quite like Bill Payne.

"I don't see why that should be a problem at all," Scott lied. "I'm simply here to assist you in any way I possibly can." He could see Payne relax—the words had exactly the effect he wanted. In dealing with people like Payne, he'd learned that they were least dangerous when under the impression that they were in control.

"That's good," Payne quipped. "I'm glad you have that attitude." Imperceptibly, Scott took a deep breath and told himself to maintain his composure. Payne continued. "I have been asked to address an ATF convention on Monday in D.C. Every Division Director and, of course, Director Mullin and the Attorney General will be present. At that meeting we will discuss some of the specific actions required to deal with Collection on a widespread basis. These guidelines have been determined by the Collection Operations Committee, which I happen to chair."

Scott's face registered genuine surprise. "Is something wrong, Marshal Keller?" Payne prodded.

"Well, I guess I'm a little confused. Obviously, the Collection process is already under way and I assumed that the 'specific actions required' would have been determined and agreed upon by now." The point was pure common sense, which is probably why it pissed the Commander off so thoroughly.

Payne's face flushed. "Look, Marshal, if you're trying to imply that the process wasn't well thought out beforehand, you couldn't be more wrong. What we need to discuss further are the specific methods required to address the various tactical situations we might encounter, especially vis-à-vis the six Hazardous Operations Teams."

It suddenly became clear to Scott what Payne was saying, though he didn't allow his face to reveal that understanding. He wanted to force the man to continue.

"We know that a certain percentage of those guilty of illegal firearms possession will not allow our agents to carry out their duties without resistance of some sort. Of course, a mission like this also requires that I and others in my position be given substantial flexibility in determining the best course of action under specific circumstances. The outcome of this meeting will *not* be to eliminate that flexibility."

Translation: How far would HOT be allowed to go when they had reason to believe that the "bad guys" were likely to shoot back? The truth was that ATF had been pushed into this operation so fast, there hadn't been time to think everything through completely. Procedures were being amended and, in some cases, invented "on the fly." The six Hazardous Operations Teams in particular seemed to be poised for something not yet encountered. Patterned after such groups as the FBI's Hostage Rescue Team and the Marshals Service's SOG, the HOT units were almost militaristic in their approach and they were reserved for "special operations." Scott wasn't sure exactly what that meant yet, but he was afraid he had a very good idea.

Up to now, HOT had been used no differently than any other ATF Field Division Office: knock on the door, arrest the homeowner, and confiscate the guns inside. The first round of arrests and collections had been based on "no-brainer" listings—people who had purchased their firearms *after* registration and licensing went into effect. These listings were compiled at ATF Headquarters in Washington and distributed to the Field Division Offices (FDO). From here on, individual FDOs would have the ability to run their own lists. Then, theoretically at least, what they'd begun to call "Hot Cases" (appropriately enough) would be kicked up to HOT, at the various FDO's discretion. That "discretion" bothered Commander Payne. He wanted more control and was determined to get it.

Scott had Payne fired up and decided to redirect. "I think I understand now. I certainly didn't mean to imply a lack of preparedness on your part, Commander." Payne waved off his apparent concern and the Marshal continued. "It's my understanding that this facility is occupied solely by HOT, is that correct?"

"Yes, it is," answered Payne. Scott knew that Payne would embellish and he wasn't disappointed. "It was determined that ATF's mission couldn't be accomplished without a very special unit to carry out operations not within the parameters of our normal activities. Through the input of myself and a handful of others, the HOT concept was established and put in place. We are made up of exceptional men and women who are totally dedicated to our mission."

Scott was aware of the rigorous training HOT members endured. ATF seemed obsessed with "outdoing" the other federal agencies, in terms of training their new special unit. He also knew that many of those making the cut for HOT were former Special Operators. This was a justifiable point of pride among team members and a potential cause for concern to people like Scott, who had serious doubts about the Collection process. A greater cause for concern, however, sat directly across the huge mahogany desk from him. He realized how big of a mess this could become if guys like Payne were allowed too much "flexibility."

"I assume, Marshal Keller, that you're attached to my command exclusively...that is, you have no other 'Marshal duties' for the time being?"

Scott gritted his teeth. "This is my only assignment at the present time."

"Good. I'll be leaving tomorrow for a series of meetings in D.C. prior to next Monday's convention. While I'm gone, I'd like you to become acquainted with my people and our procedures. There are a total of ten squads. I'll be briefing them upon my return on Tuesday afternoon and I'd like you to be present. Deputy Commander Burke would normally brief you and show you around, but he happens to be in D.C. himself at the moment. He'll be back on Saturday, but in the meantime, you can report to squad room seven on the fourth floor to get set up. Squad seven is one of our best and you'll be training with them this week. Agent Myers, the squad leader, is waiting for you now. Any questions?"

"Not at this point," Scott answered.

"Well, then," Payne said as he stood up and extended his hand, still not bothering to walk around the desk. "I'm glad to have you on my team."

Scott moved toward the door. Waving at Victoria on the way out, he received another knowing look. It was hard to believe the poor thing could put up with her boss on a daily basis.

He was a little upset with himself. He had let Payne get to him and that didn't happen very often. He'd have to force himself to tolerate the man. Scott had never suffered fools well, but he was normally capable of dealing with them. He speculated that Payne might turn out to be his greatest challenge yet, in that regard.

Scott got off the elevator on the fourth floor and found squad room seven. Opening the door, he felt instantly more comfortable. It was much more akin to what he was used to: professionals doing their jobs. "Excuse me," he asked a passing agent. "Where can I find Agent Myers?"

"Over there, the one leaning over the desk," the agent replied, pointing to the far corner of the room. There, a large and very fit-looking black man had both hands flat on a desk, leaning down and looking directly into the eyes of a young agent to whom he was obviously trying to make himself perfectly clear. Scott smiled. He had a feeling he was going to like this guy.

"Agent Myers?" he asked.

"I am, and who might you be?" Bobby Myers answered gruffly.

"Scott Keller, Marshals Service."

"I thought so," Bobby answered, extending a huge hand. "Been waiting for you. Bobby Myers. How are ya?"

"Not bad. I just spent a while up on the sixth floor getting dialed in."

"Well, then, I'm sure you understand your position in the food chain a little better now, don't you?" Bobby whispered. Scott just nodded his head.

After introducing Scott to the members of his team, Bobby gave him a tour of the building. There were ten very large and well-equipped individual squad rooms spread out over floors one through five, all identical to squad seven's. Each of the twelve squad members had a cubicle with a desk and phone and each of the ten squad leaders had a private office.

All the rooms were set up to be fully self-contained bases from which to operate, complete with secure phone and computer systems. Each had a small briefing area, with a rectangular conference table, television, and whiteboard on the wall. Finally, each of the ten squad rooms had a large secure area in the back. These spaces had an electronically locked outer "safe door," which remained open while the squad room was occupied. Past this door was an open staging area of about three hundred square feet, followed by a steel cage with another electronic lock. Inside the caged area were a variety of tactical weapons, shields, battering rams, and other items used to conduct "special" ATF operations.

In addition to housing squad rooms one and two, as well as the heavily guarded entrance, the bottom floor included one huge conference room, complete with equipment for conducting video conferences, and two smaller conference rooms. All in all, the building bespoke efficiency and thoughtful design. Scott wondered if the USMS could borrow their architect the next time it designed a field office.

* * * * * *

Portland, Oregon
Friday, April 11

Scott had really enjoyed the past week—certainly much more than he could have imagined after leaving Payne's office on Monday. Of course, this applied to some activities more than others. All week long, they'd trained hard. Bobby Myers pushed his people, both mentally and physically. If they failed, it wouldn't be because they were unprepared.

Scott enjoyed pushing himself physically more than most, but he had to admit that pain was still pain. They were in the middle of HOT's brutal daily Crossfit routine and Myers seemed to be *enjoying* it! Members of the Marshals Service's SOG were expected to maintain excellent physical condition and virtually all of them did. Still, there was a difference between voluntary conditioning and the mandatory regimen of a unit like this one, which did physical training together nearly every day. The pace was always faster with the members of a team pushing each other. Though Scott kept himself in very good shape, this was something he hadn't experienced in a while.

He'd let Bobby know at the beginning of the week that he expected to be part of the team in every way possible. The squad leader liked the attitude and welcomed him aboard. Because of his built-in competitiveness, though, Bobby also wanted to show the Marshal just how good HOT really was. The rest of the team members figured as much; there had to be *some* reason their boss was setting the pace that he was.

As they finished, Scott forced himself to control his breathing. His burning lungs and muscles made that awfully difficult. Bobby approached him with a smile that Scott was unable to return with any conviction. "Well, how do you feel?"

"Like I just woke up…not even warmed up yet," he lied, hands up high on his hips to give his lungs room to expand.

"Good, glad to hear it. Hey, we're going to get showered and move into some drills at 0900. I assume you're up for it?"

"You bet," Scott managed to croak out. His breath was starting to return, thank goodness. "I do this for a living, you know."

"Yeah, I know…been a while since you went that hard, though, huh?"

"Been a while."

The rest of the day went well. Scott had to admit that he learned a couple of things during the drills, just as he had all week. Bobby was very good and HOT's tactics were solid. These people were ready. It was what they were ready *for* that worried him.

The most enjoyable part of the past week, for Scott, had been getting to know Bobby Myers. The two men had really hit it off and both felt as if they'd known each other for a lot longer than they had.

After squaring his gear away near the end of the day, Bobby had what he thought was a great idea and walked over to the desk they were letting Scott use. "Wanna grab a beer?"

"Sure," Scott answered.

* * * * * *

Bobby headed for a quiet corner booth in the bar. As the two of them scanned their menus halfheartedly, Scott saw nervousness in the other man that he hadn't noticed before. He decided to break the ice. "So, I've had the privilege of meeting Caesar. How about his next in command—what's he like?"

"Who, Burke?"

"Yeah."

"He's pretty much a lapdog for Payne. He *is* smart, though—real good with numbers and computers."

"You got two real winners running this show, huh?"

"Hey, what can I say? The Commander handpicked his deputy.

Don't tell me the same shit doesn't go on over at your place."

"Oh, it does," Scott admitted. *But I've never seen it this bad*, he didn't say.

They ordered some appetizers and a pitcher of beer and Bobby leaned forward, his massive forearms covering half the table. "So, Scott, now that you've spent a week with us, tell me what you honestly think of our little dog and pony show over there."

"I'm impressed…really."

"You're not real convincing."

Scott saw a small opening that told him he could confide in Bobby. "Look, I think your people are solid. You guys know what you're doing, without a doubt. I guess…what bothers me a little, though, is that when you get to strut your stuff, you'll be doing it mostly against guys whose only 'crime' is standing up for what they *thought* was a constitutional right." He paused for a moment. "I assume you wanted an *honest* answer?"

Bobby smiled. "Yeah, you can always assume that." The look on his face told Scott he wanted to say more, but wondered whether he should.

Scott prodded him. "That honesty thing goes both ways, you know."

Again, a smile from Bobby. "Keller, you just may be too smart for us to keep you around."

"Good. Maybe I'll get to go home early."

The waitress brought their beer and, as she moved away, Bobby leaned forward again. "Well, I was going to ask you what you thought about this whole Collection thing…but I think you just answered my question."

Scott wondered how far he should go. Although he'd known Bobby Myers for only a few days, his intuition said he could trust the man completely. "Is this a test, Bobby?"

"No, it's a question…man to man, off the record."

Scott knew he meant it. "Well, then, my answer, man to man, is that it makes me sick. I don't believe for a second that it's the right thing to do. I've always liked shooting and having guns around. And I don't believe that guns are society's biggest problem—not even close." Bobby's dark eyes stared unblinkingly at him. For a moment, Scott wondered whether he'd read Bobby right.

"Why are you over here hangin' out with us, then?" Bobby asked.

It was a fair question. "I don't know. My boss thought I was the right guy for the job and that it would be a good career move. I guess he was right. This thing's going down with or without me. I guess I felt like, if I was involved, at least I might be able to control what happens to some degree. Sounds like a load of egotistical bullshit, huh?"

"Nope. I know exactly where you're coming from."

"Bobby, which branch did you serve in?" Scott was sure Bobby had been in the military. He definitely had "the look," but they hadn't had much downtime during the past week to talk about such things.

"Army. Why?"

"What unit?" Scott pressed.

"Rangers…how about you?"

"Marine Corps, MARSOC."

"Oo Rah," Bobby chimed in.

Scott cracked a smile and continued. "In all the time you served, did you ever doubt that you were doing the right thing?"

"No, I didn't."

"Then I've got an 'off the record' question for you: Do you doubt that you're doing the right thing now?" The pause was so long it was uncomfortable.

"Yeah I do…and if you ever tell anyone else I said that, I'll deny it and dedicate my life to making yours miserable," Bobby said, smiling and draining the rest of his beer. He re-filled both glasses and looked Scott in the eye.

Both men knew that a bond had just been formed. Neither took lightly the fact that they had opened themselves up to being ostracized by the "true believers" in Collection (of which there were many). The operation had become almost a religion among politicians and law enforcement alike. Some of the best in ATF had resigned over the policy. Others stayed on because they couldn't afford not to. And some, like Bobby Myers, stayed, at least partly, to see that things didn't get out of hand. Yet there was a relatively small group who seemed to truly enjoy what was going on, the best example of which was Payne. These were the people who would not tolerate dissension.

"Scott, I watched some good friends of mine take off when this thing came down and I thought about doing it myself. In fact, if guys like Payne were all that was left, I would have. The thing is, there are a bunch of good men and women who stayed on because this job was all they knew—and all they had. You know, decent money, good benefits…I know, it sounds hollow. Fact is, you can talk about 'honor' all you want, but when you've gotta choose between pulling the rug out from under your family and doing a job you don't like, the call ain't so easy to make.

"To tell you the truth, that was a part of it for me, too. You do something long enough, you start to doubt whether you can do anything else. The HOT thing was an ego trip at first, too. But the main reason I'm still hanging around is to do what I can to keep things from getting out of hand. Believe me, I've got no delusions of grandeur about this. I just want to do what I can to keep my people in check. Make sure they don't get hurt, or hurt anybody they don't absolutely have to."

Bobby took another long pull on his beer and looked hard at Scott again. Scott had the feeling he wasn't finished yet.

"I haven't been crazy about this job for a long time. The Paynes of the world have been doing things for the wrong reasons forever. You know he was involved in Ruby Ridge *and* Waco? And instead of being run out on a rail, he gets promoted! Don't think for a minute I haven't thought about putting in an app for the FBI or the Marshals. You know, be a big shot like you. Who knows, maybe I will someday."

Scott cracked a smile. "Yeah, well, I hope you set your sights higher than me. Besides, like I said, it's not like a lot of the same shit doesn't happen everywhere."

Bobby polished off the rest of his beer. "Yeah, I know. What's eating me alive, though, is that I used to really believe in what I was doing. You know, going after *real* bad guys...the kind you never had to wonder about. Maybe a gunrunner funneling guns into the inner cities, just to make a buck. The kind of guys who wouldn't think twice about blowing some kid away, without worrying for a second about how many lives they might be fuckin' up in the process.

"This is different, though. We've made a few busts already and... I feel like I'm arresting guys that don't deserve it. I've never had that feeling before. Up till now, in the Army *and* ATF, the bad guys have been easy to spot. I never really questioned what I was doing. Now I do and I just don't know how long I can keep it up."

Scott stared at the man in front of him. "Jesus, Bobby, how long have you felt this way?"

"Ever since about the second arrest. I figured the first one was a fluke."

"Have you told anyone else?"

"Just my wife."

"Why me? I mean, we just met a few days ago."

"I don't know, Scott. Maybe because you're not part of our little world, or maybe because I feel like I can talk straight to you. Or maybe a little of both."

"Listen, Bobby, I'm convinced you'd be a credit to the FBI, the Marshals, or anywhere else you decided to go.

"First things first, though. We're both committed to seeing this thing through for now. We also feel the same way about Collection and we've both been around long enough to know that we're gonna be in the minority. Let's ride it out for a while. I still want to believe the people in D.C. will come to their senses and call this thing off."

Bobby looked at Scott as he might a child. "Yeah...sure they will."

3

Portland, Oregon
Saturday, April 12

EVERY TIME DON drove to Mike's house, he was struck by the degree of isolation that his friend enjoyed. Unlike Don, who preferred neighbors around him to interact with regularly, Mike liked having his own space. It wasn't that he was antisocial; in fact he and Sarah were on very good terms with all of their neighbors. There were times, though, when Mike wanted privacy and the design of his property allowed for that.

To those whom he liked and trusted, there was no better friend in the world than Mike Niculescu. It simply took time to gain the required trust and respect. Mike guarded his privacy and, because of that, he allowed few people to get close to him. Part of the reason may have been the stories that his parents told him about life in Romania. Mike grew up hearing that the government would try to take what a person had and that even your "friends" would gladly give the government information about you in order to curry favor.

This attitude struck Don as more than a little paranoid, but he was smart enough to realize that a person's perceptions are formed by life experiences and Mike's parents had endured things in their lives that many would not have held up under. Don had a tremendous amount of respect and affection for them. He also felt privileged to have been so completely accepted into Mike's world. Whether you agreed with everything he believed in or not, you couldn't help but admire the man.

The family that Mike and Sarah had made together was a special one. The kids were polite and fun to be around and they seemed to have Mike's sense of honor and strength of character. Spending time around them was something that all who knew them truly *wanted* to do.

Don turned off the county road and proceeded down the quarter-mile-long driveway. Because of the large trees on the front of Mike's property, a first-time guest might have wondered whether it was inhabited at all. You couldn't see the house until you were virtually on top of it. Only then did you realize the beauty of the home and it never failed to impress. Not only was the house itself large and well designed, but there was a huge shop and other outbuildings as well. Mike had built it himself, after working hard for many years building custom homes for others. Don knew that Mike felt blessed to live in a country that allowed him to achieve what he had, but the truth was that hard work and self-denial had played a large part in what he had accomplished.

Three generations of Niculescus waited to greet them as Don and his family got out of the car and it seemed like thirty minutes passed before all of the hugs and handshakes were out of the way. Later, while Mike cooked the hamburgers and hot dogs, George and Ana Niculescu fawned over little Stephanie as if she were their own grandchild. It had been a while since Mike's kids were that age and it brought back fond memories for him to watch his parents being mesmerized by the youngster.

Everyone found something to do. Mike's daughter Lori tried to talk "grownup" with Jenny and Sarah. Clay and Mike's son Brett discussed their latest collections of whatever it was that twelve year-olds collected these days, while Stephanie continued to entertain George and Ana. Even Patton, Mike's huge Chesapeake Bay retriever, seemed to be enjoying himself. The dog always kept a watchful eye on everything going on. Now he was lying in the grass watching everyone and taking in the last bit of sunlight that this unseasonably warm Oregon April day had to offer.

Everyone except Mike talked as though they hadn't a care in the world. Meanwhile, Mike, usually easygoing, shifted his eyes around the property as if he were scanning the tree line for threats. Don knew that something serious was on his friend's mind, but he also knew that it would be a mistake to bring it up in front of everyone else. They'd played "phone tag" during the week, but hadn't spoken to each other.

Finally, everyone had their fill and the children once again dispersed. Clay and Brett headed off to explore the "back forty" while the rest went inside. Mike seized the opportunity to ask Don to help him with something in the shop. The two men kept walking, past the shop and toward the road. As always, Patton followed closely behind. Mike, his hands shoved into his pockets and his head down, was searching for the words to begin the conversation when Don broke the ice.

"I assume you've caught some of the news over the last week?"

"Yeah, I have," his friend answered.

"Well?"

"I didn't sleep five minutes last night."

"After Jenny told me you called Monday and how you sounded, I figured you were pissed off about the arrests," Don responded.

Mike stopped walking, his eyes still on the ground. "You really don't get it, do you?" he asked. Struck by the tone of the question, Don didn't immediately respond. Mike continued. "It's not a matter of me being 'pissed off.' In fact, it's not about *me* at all. I know you think only wackos talk like this, but what they've done is rip the foundation out from under this country."

"Now come on," Don said. "I'll admit it was a little weird to see regular guys being arrested on the news, but who's going to be hurt by *not* having millions of handguns and assault rifles on the streets?"

"This isn't about *guns*, damn it!" Mike roared. Then, catching himself, he continued more calmly. "You know what, Don, I'm not going down that road with you again. I'm too tired and there are more important things on my mind right now than giving you a history lesson."

It suddenly became crystal clear to Don exactly what *was* on his friend's mind. "Holy shit, Mike—you didn't turn in your guns, did you?"

"Of course not. Did you really expect me to?"

"Yes, I did! Look, I know you're really into this whole constitutional thing, but in case you haven't noticed, these people are serious…and your family could end up paying the price for your stubbornness!"

"Don't lecture me, Don! I don't get mad easily, but you're pushing a button."

"I'm pushing a button because I *give* a damn!" Don snapped back.

Mike paused for a few seconds before speaking again. When he finally did, his strong voice was barely above a whisper. "Don, some things are important enough to stand up for. I refuse to roll over and let them turn this country into something it was never intended to be."

Don was exasperated. "Look, I know you're serious and I know your mom and dad's experiences have a lot to do with the way you feel. But this is the twenty-first-century United States, not Communist Romania. Besides, it's not like the only people in favor of confiscation are Nichols and Martinez. Look at the polls; most people agree with it. That's what a democracy is all about."

"Thank you, professor, but we're supposed to be guided by our *Constitution*, not polls. I know it's not cool to talk about these days and I know it's outdated and all. But it's worked pretty well for over two hundred years. Call me a nut, but before we chuck it, we'd better be prepared for what comes next."

Mike took a deep breath and continued. "I also find it interesting that the 'majority' you're talking about think they can pick and choose which rights they want…like it's a damn fast-food menu! Well, it's NOT! It's an all-or-nothing deal."

Not even attempting to consider what his friend was saying, Don tried to redirect the conversation. "Mike, what are you going to do? Maybe it's not too late. Take your guns to one of their 'Collection Stations' and go on with your life. Next election, if enough people feel the way you do, vote 'em out of office—but let the system work!"

His plea was met by a shake of the head and a solemn expression. "What you don't seem to understand is that the 'system' has become so corrupted that *it's* as much a problem as some of the people in it."

Mike paused. He sensed that he was wasting his breath and had no desire to do so any longer. "Anyway, there's a good chance I'm okay. I don't think their records are nearly as complete as they say they are."

"And you're going to take that chance?" Don asked incredulously.

"Listen, they'd never find them now anyway, even if they *did* come looking."

"I can't believe this," Don muttered, half to himself. "I don't want to know any more."

He turned away, facing west. Tonight's sunset was going to be awesome. "Mike, one of the things I admire most about you is that you're unflappable. I've never seen anything rattle you. But aren't you even a little scared right now? I am and I haven't done anything wrong!"

"Neither have I, Don."

Don shook his head slowly and continued to look away. They could hear the sound of the kids playing out back, thankfully oblivious to all that was going on. Mike had to try again to make his friend understand. "Sure I'm scared, but I made one of the most important decisions of my life based on *principle* and I'm not going to back away from it now. I want my kids to be able to look back on this and say they're proud of what I did."

"Even if they're saying it through two-inch-thick prison glass?"

"Yeah…even then."

By the time they made it back up to the house, the kids were settled in watching a movie on Mike's big-screen television and the adults were in the living room having coffee. Mike grabbed a couple of beers and the two men sat down by their wives. Don still looked shell-shocked and the "what's wrong?" expression in Jenny's eyes was met by a quick shake of his head.

As usual, Sarah was first to pick up the conversation after the guys sat down. She always enjoyed talking, especially with Don and Jenny. Sarah was as gregarious and easy to talk to as Mike was strong and silent. That balance was one of the many reasons for the strength of their marriage.

"We were watching the news while we cleaned up. It looks like the ATF arrested more people today. Honey, I know how you feel about it, but I'm so glad you turned your guns in." Unable to face her, Mike patted his wife on the knee to let her know he understood.

Don stared at his untouched beer bottle, not daring to look up for fear of being overcome by the urge to tell everyone exactly what was on his mind.

George sat in a rocking chair, looking down at the cover of a book on the coffee table and trying to find the right words to use. After many years in the United States, his mastery of the English language was good, but he was still self-conscious when speaking. As with everything else having to do with his "Americanism," he wanted his speech to be perfect. He had legally changed the spelling of his given name from "Gheorghe" soon after arriving in his new country and always insisted on speaking English, even when the conversation was only with his wife in the privacy of their own home. Ana was not quite as dedicated to assimilating into American culture. Though she could be described as fiercely patriotic, she also liked to hold on to aspects of their Romanian heritage. A prime example was her insistence on referring to their son as "Mihai." George was sure his wife did this only to irritate him.

After an awkward silence, George felt the need to say something. "All of this we see in last few days makes me very sad. I must say, I never thought I see something such as this in America. It brings back to me old memories. Looks like *Securitate* going door to door. Next thing, they will check papers at street corner!"

Because of the mood he was in, Don's first thought was "the nut doesn't fall too far from the tree," but then he remembered how much respect he had for both these men. Still, they were wrong about this. They *had* to be.

The somber conversation was interrupted when Clay and Brett burst into the living room with their latest "great idea."

"Mom, can Clay sleep over tonight?" Brett asked hopefully.

"Well, it's okay with me if it's okay with his mom and dad," replied Sarah.

Jenny was about to agree when Don broke in, very unexpectedly and awkwardly. "*No*...uh, I don't think so, buddy...not tonight."

"But Dad, why not?" came the anticipated objection. Jenny and Mike noticed how sharply Don's answer had come, with Jenny wondering why and Mike knowing the reason.

Jenny joined in the objection. "Honey, it's okay, isn't it? I mean we really don't have anything planned for tomorrow. I have to run by the mall anyway, so I could come by and pick him up on the way home." Don uncharacteristically glared at his wife.

Mike put his head in his hands. The realization that his friend had doubts about his son's safety was especially hurtful, since protecting those he cared about was one of the things he took the most pride in.

Brett then petitioned Sarah, who assured Don that it was fine with her. Finally, Don realized he couldn't deny them without telling everyone what was on his mind. "I guess it's all right," he relented, sending the two boys whooping and hollering all the way upstairs to Brett's room.

"Well, honey, we probably ought to get going," Don said, interrupting the silence created by the boys' sudden departure.

This time it was Sarah who foiled his plans. "Oh, come on, you guys. It's still early and we've hardly had any time to visit."

"Yeah," Jenny chimed in. "It's not even eight o'clock yet. You're not getting old on me, are you?"

Give it up. This isn't the time or place to cause a scene. "Yes, I am," Don answered. "But I guess even old people can stay up past eight every now and then."

Under any other circumstances, Jenny would have had to drag him out of Mike's house. With the night's revelations still fresh in his mind, however, Don just wasn't in the mood for conversation. At the very least, he hoped they would turn to another subject.

That hope was dashed when Ana spoke. "I do not say much about politics of America. But I see my son fight for this country and love it so much. Then these people make him into criminal. This makes me feel very…ashamed. He would die to protect this country and they do this. It is not right!" she exclaimed, nearly in tears.

"Mama, it's okay," Mike tried to assure her.

"But Mihai, in America, a good man should not be afraid of government. The President should not be feared, as in Romania. Police should *protect* good people, not break in their home and take them from family." George reached over and patted his wife on the back to comfort her. It was obvious she had spoken her piece and would say no more on the subject.

Don felt a reflexive desire to speak up—to tell Ana she was wrong. However, something inside him wouldn't allow him to do it. He knew instinctively that she was wrong, but he felt unqualified to tell her so. The same was true for George. Don had been raised to respect the experience that came with age and, particularly in the case of the Niculescus, that respect was both genuine and intense.

Sarah picked up the conversation after a brief but awkward silence. "Papa, can you *really* compare what's happening here with what you saw in Romania? I mean we do *elect* our leaders, which means we can vote against them the next time around if we don't like what they've done."

Finally, Don thought, *someone else is going to help me out on the reality front.* Before George could answer his daughter-in-law's question, Don jumped into the fray. "I have to agree with Sarah. The fact that we *elect* our leaders makes us very different from what you experienced in your country. I understand how you could see similarities at a time like this, but I really believe—"

That was as far as Don got before George broke in and silenced him. "Excuse me, Don. I know it is not polite to interrupt, but I must correct you. *This* is my country. With respect, I came here before you were born. Also, you do not understand something. The bad part of communism is not 'leaders,' it is what happens to the people. They must allow it."

Don could not hide his lack of comprehension. "George, I'm afraid I don't understand..."

"Papa," Mike said, "do you mind if I try to explain?"

"Please yes, I am not so good at speaking my ideas sometimes."

"Don, what he's trying to say is that leaders, even in communist countries, come and go. The real damage isn't done by them, but by a majority of the population that allows itself to be conned into believing that giving up freedom and control over their own lives will be good for them in the long run—that they'll be safer or more secure. Ben Franklin warned us a long time ago that anyone who'd give up liberty for safety deserves neither. I'd say the old man was right.

"The bottom line is that the *citizens* are to blame for letting these things happen to them—for failing to stand up and put a stop to it—whether it's communism or this nonsense we're going through now in our own country. Sure, power-hungry politicians are also to blame, but it's not their *fault*, ultimately.

"Does any of this make sense?"

Don felt drained. As a result, he was slow to respond and, when he did, the answer was surprisingly non-combative. "Yeah, I understand where you're going with this. I don't necessarily agree, but I do see your point."

They were all spared the need for further discussion by Stephanie's screaming in another room—a sure sign that she'd "hit the wall" and was ready for bed. This prompted the Williamses to begin the packing-up process.

Soon they were heading home and a look into the backseat after a few minutes revealed that Troy and Stephanie were already asleep. There was total silence in the car until Jenny could no longer stand it. "Honey, what was wrong with you tonight? It seemed like all you wanted to do was pick fights and you could hardly wait to leave. You just didn't seem yourself."

There was no sense in beating around the bush. "Babe, Mike has gone off the deep end."

"What do you mean?"

"Well, you're not going to believe this, but the fact is he did *not* turn in his guns! He's convinced he's right and he's taken all this 'communist conspiracy' crap completely to heart!"

Don expected Jenny to display the same shock and anger he felt. Instead, his outrage was met with a quiet reply. "I guess I'm not surprised."

"Why do you sound so calm about it?" Don hissed.

Inside the dark vehicle, they couldn't see each other's faces very well, but Jenny looked over at her husband and began to speak. "Honey, you've always thought the world of Mike, right?"

"Yeah, and I still do, but this is different."

"Oh, really? For a long time now, I've heard you say that he's smart, honest, has great instincts, always seems to end up being right, and on and on. Is he suddenly an idiot?" Jenny had been thinking all this through while everyone else argued in the living room. Don's silence meant she was getting through, so she pushed on. "Don't you think there's a chance he may be right about this? Maybe this law *is* stupid and unconstitutional."

"That's for the courts to decide," Don shot back.

"And meanwhile, ordinary people are being hauled out of their homes to prison," she countered. "Honey, how would you feel if you became a criminal overnight, without doing anything differently than you always had?" Again, silence. "I know you could care less about guns. Lord knows I don't want anything to do with them, but it seems like this is about something more important."

Don was frustrated. He knew she was at least partly right, but he'd spent his entire life believing that there was no excuse for not playing by the rules. Without rules and laws there was anarchy and that would serve no one well, except the lawbreakers. "Well, what am I supposed to do, help him dig a bunker where we can all hide and wait for the cops to come get us?" he asked sarcastically.

"Honey, I haven't gotten that far yet. Maybe you could write letters to our congressman or senators. Maybe you could call them, or even go to their offices and see them in person. I'll admit I don't know much about this kind of thing."

"Look, Mike and a lot of other people tried all that before the law was passed. It didn't work then and it sure won't work now that they've hired several thousand more federal cops to enforce Collection. These people have too much of a vested interest in seeing it through."

Jenny was experiencing an epiphany. "Don, doesn't *that* scare you? The idea that the momentum is too great to stop…that they'd rather arrest average citizens than admit they made a mistake gives me chills. All of a sudden, everything George, Ana, and Mike were saying tonight makes perfect sense!"

Don was pulling into their driveway now. He put the car in park and looked over at her. "Honey, I wouldn't go that far. Look, you make a good point. I'll think about what I can do to help Mike, but this may be a case where he has to clean up his own mess."

"Do you know of a single case in his life when he *hasn't* taken care of things himself?" Jenny asked. The question stung and brought nothing in response. "There may not be anything you can do to help besides supporting him, but I think you at least owe him that much."

Don looked at his wife in the semi-darkness. Her eyes conveyed the compassion that she was well-known for. She was his best friend and confidante, as well as the person he cared most about in the world. He'd always known that she was bright and insightful, but she surprised him tonight. He nodded his head and leaned over to kiss her. As he pulled away, Don assured her that he would be there for his friend.

* * * * * *

It was only mid-afternoon on Saturday, but Ray Burke's body was still on Eastern Time. Having spent the last few days in D.C., he felt as if he already needed dinner. He had flown in around noon, Portland time, went home to spend a couple of hours with the family, and then hustled down to the office. There was a sense of power in having the run of the place and now, except for the duty guard crew, he did.

Payne had sent him to Washington for two reasons. First, he wanted to make sure that the final software package was what they expected—they both hated surprises. Also, he wanted a working copy of the categorization program before anyone else in the field received it. Burke's trip had been successful on both counts. He was now in the process of installing the program on HOT's computer system and things were going so well it was scary. The system was just finishing a successful search of a test database.

The six HOT units had "master systems" capable of accessing and searching data from any geographical area of the country. Field Division Offices had the ability to access only their own territories. As the protocol was currently defined, however, only the FDOs were authorized to develop Collection listings. As he logged on to the Portland FDO's system, Burke wondered briefly just how much trouble he was stirring up by doing so. Hopefully none and, if someone found out, he was only following orders. Before long, Payne would see to it that they could pull their own targets from the FDO systems anyway. Burke was just getting a head start.

He plugged in the search parameters and linked the Portland area database to the new software. This was no longer a test. It took only a few minutes to search the Greater Portland area. Just like that, Burke was staring at two listings, each with several hundred names. Each search could have been broken down into infinite subgroups if necessary. For his purpose, though, Burke would start with the complete level-two list.

This was the fun part. A relative handful of members from this list would become HOT's "first contestants." He entered the necessary keystrokes, sat back, and smiled to himself. He really did love his job.

4

Chesapeake Beach, Maryland
Sunday, April 13

BILL PAYNE RELAXED in the splendor of the limousine's backseat. He wasn't accustomed to being chauffeured, but was convinced that he could get used to it. ATF Director Mullin had sent the car to his hotel for him. A nice touch, Payne thought. Tonight's gathering at the Director's home had been something of a last-minute idea, but it would serve nicely as a chance for Payne to renew his all-important political connection to the top man. Not surprisingly, Payne hadn't seen much of Mullin since he'd become Director. Though he wouldn't be alone with Mullin tonight, he would make sure that he was the *last* one to leave. The Commander had an important pitch to make.

Being a friend of the Director had its advantages when you were an ambitious member of the Bureau of Alcohol, Tobacco, Firearms and Explosives. They'd gotten to know each other several years before in Texas, where Payne was Assistant Special Agent in Charge (ASAC) of the Dallas FDO and Mullin was Deputy Assistant Director for Field Operations.

Their relationship was a quirk of fate. Essentially, Payne had brought the ATF great public relations exposure on a high-profile case. This made Mullin look very good in the eyes of his superiors and, unlike many others in Payne's experience, Mullin never forgot it. Though it was obvious to everyone that Mullin was on the way up, Payne never would have guessed back then that John Mullin would become Director of the ATF. It proved once again that it always paid to hitch your wagon to the right horse.

It had been Mullin who'd requested that Payne address the convention. The purpose of Payne's speech was to outline recommendations for dealing with the various threat levels that ATF might face in the Collection process. Payne was to outline a series of proposals developed by the Collection Operations Committee, which he chaired. This committee consisted of eighteen up-and-coming Special Agents in Charge (SAC) from around the country, as well as the six HOT Commanders.

They had developed a system for categorizing Collection subjects to assist ATF Field Offices in deploying agents as efficiently as possible. Additionally (and most important to Payne), the committee had established guidelines for the proper use of HOT. Payne wanted to have a say in how his team would be used and it looked as if he was going to. Most of the SACs, as well as three of the other five HOT Commanders, had objected repeatedly to his "suggestions." They felt that Payne was making a power grab that could lead not only to bad PR but to an unnecessary number of civilian and ATF casualties as well.

The committee members had agreed at their last meeting to present their proposals to this convention and to solicit input from all attendees. Payne wasn't in favor of that idea, but he felt as if he had to give a little ground—or at least appear to. Not wanting to preside over a free-for-all tomorrow, however, he made the decision to personally discuss *his* plan with Director Mullin tonight. He would much rather announce the decision to implement a specific strategy than listen to the grandstanding that would surely take place if all of the committee's proposals were brought up before the convention one by one for discussion. Payne had a crystal clear vision of what he wanted to achieve. His immediate goal was to ensure that the Director shared that vision.

The ride was so comfortable that Payne was almost sorry when the driver pulled up in front of Mullin's beautiful home. He waited for the driver to hustle around the car to open his door, only slightly surprised at how natural it felt to do so. The Director greeted Payne warmly at the front door and ushered him inside.

John Mullin was a fairly thin man of medium height. While not large in physical stature, he moved with the grace of a man who was confident in his abilities. Only in his mid-fifties, Mullin had begun his career as an ATF Special Agent and a meteoric rise through the ATF organizational structure had followed.

A highly intelligent man, Mullin knew that a large part of the reason for his success had been good luck: he was always in the right place at the right time. Of equal importance was the fact that he always seemed to have just left the *wrong* place at the right time. The best example was his promotion (and subsequent transfer) just prior to the Waco debacle. Mullin considered Waco to be the most dangerous bullet he had ever dodged in his thirty-year career. Had he not been promoted beforehand, the whole mess would have gone down on his watch and right under his nose—though he liked to think he would have done a few things differently. While it may not have ruined his career, Waco probably would have knocked him out of the running for Director.

Everyone who "climbed the ladder" knew that you typically needed a sponsor to do so. When Mullin's friend Charlie Martinez was appointed Attorney General, he had his sponsor. Within a few months, Mullin was appointed Assistant Director, Field Operations for the ATF. The agency's Director at the time was not in favor of Mullin's appointment. He had his own people in mind. Of course, in the end, Martinez had the final say, but not without creating some highly visible bad blood within the Bureau.

Not coincidentally, just prior to the ATF's expansion, Martinez determined that the incumbent Director ought to seriously consider retirement. He simply wasn't the right person for the job. Not only was it well known within the Bureau that the Director did *not* believe in the concept of Collection, but he had been fairly vocal about it as well. Martinez needed someone who would "play ball" enthusiastically. The President agreed and the decision was made. Mullin's confirmation was only a formality.

Mullin's wife Joan gave Bill Payne a hug, just to be polite—she'd never liked the man. Be that as it may, her husband's job, now more than ever, required her to "kiss the right cheeks." Payne put his coat away and moved into the living room, where everyone had gathered. Present were all the Deputy Assistant Directors; the Executive Assistant, Field Ops; and the Assistant Director, Field Ops.

It wasn't lost on Payne that he was the lowest-ranked man present. The HOT (Northeast) Commander had been invited as well, but was unable to attend. Mullin wanted only token representation from HOT tonight, given the fact that the entire concept was still a little controversial—even within ATF. With that in mind, Payne was the logical choice. He would be addressing the convention tomorrow and had played a major role in the formation of HOT. Payne was perfectly comfortable being the unit's sole representative. One with less confidence in himself might have been intimidated by the company, but not Bill Payne. Instead of feeling diminished by those in attendance, he was buoyed. He knew there was a reason he'd been invited.

As confident as he was, he also understood that this was a test. He had to be not only credible but also commanding in front of those who outranked him in order to be a candidate for promotion. It wasn't enough for the *boss* to like you. You had to be accepted by at least a majority of the management structure as well, since there would be times when the Director wasn't around. With that in mind, Bill had to admit that few in the room—with the exception of the one who counted most—were truly on his side.

The mood over drinks was particularly carefree and jovial, in spite of the fact that virtually the entire upper management of ATF's highest-profile division was in the Director's house. No spouses were present. This convention, and therefore this dinner, was a *working* event. Joan Mullin had excused herself after everyone's arrival and was nowhere to be seen.

Payne had a feeling that the lighthearted mood would change

over dinner. As he suspected, due to the drinks beforehand and the lack of mixed company, opinions began to flow like the wine right after dinner was served—though everyone present was careful not to step on the boss's toes. Mullin had a reputation for listening to all points of view, until he had made up his mind. After that, he expected support, not dissension.

Eventually, one of the other dinner guests addressed Payne. "So, Bill, why don't you give us an idea of the contents of your report." It was Assistant Director, Field Ops Sam Kerr—a man not to be trifled with. Although he never let on publicly, it was widely rumored that Kerr was not in favor of Collection. Even more important to Payne, however, was the fact that Kerr had been completely against the formation of HOT. Payne knew to be careful here.

"Well, sir, essentially, the committee recommends that we categorize all Collection subjects into three levels, according to the degree of threat they represent."

"Will one of these 'levels' automatically trigger the use of HOT?"

It was a question with a hook in it. *Damn it!* Payne knew he'd made it crystal clear to the other committee members that not a word was to be spoken of their plans prior to his address to the convention. Also, it was well known that the committee was to report only to the Director and that Kerr was pissed off to no end over *that* fact. Payne had wanted to do the unveiling himself, but now it was obvious that someone had gone to Kerr (and who knew how many others) with specifics.

None of these thoughts were betrayed by Payne's poker face, however. "Actually, sir, the committee does feel that *all* level-three threats may require a highly trained and specialized unit, such as HOT, to deal with them."

"Exactly what type of 'threats' might those be?" Kerr persisted. Obviously, he knew about the plan and had an ax to grind.

Mullin decided to break in and save Payne. "Rather than have Commander Payne go over all the details tonight, I think we should wait until tomorrow and hear about the committee's plan in full."

The Director's comment, combined with the fact that he pushed his chair away from the table and stood, signaled to all present that dinner was ended. Mullin didn't offer after-dinner drinks—a hint that he didn't want after-dinner guests. Payne was beginning to wonder whether he would have the Director's ear tonight and was relieved when Mullin approached him quietly and asked him to stay after the others had left. Each of the other dinner guests said their good-byes to the Director while Payne remained in the background. He was sure they would snipe at him behind his back, but he was used to that.

The Director had a passion for good cigars and fine brandy after dinner. Payne didn't, but figured he ought to take advantage of the hospitality offered. As they sat on the Director's second-floor deck overlooking Chesapeake Bay, Mullin turned to his ambitious underling. "Well, Bill, I see you survived the evening's festivities."

"Yes, sir. It wasn't so bad, actually."

"Bill, tell me more about the 'third level' we discussed tonight. I know you've got Kerr and some of the others worked up into a frenzy over it."

"Well, sir, we're convinced that some level of specialization will be required to deal with a certain percentage of our operations. That's really the reason for HOT's existence in the first place." Mullin was famous for not interrupting, not needing to take notes, and soaking everything up like a sponge. He remained silent and Payne took that as a cue to continue. "We've run detailed background checks and developed computer models that will assist us in identifying level-three threats. These would include former military personnel and members of certain organizations. These and a variety of other characteristics and demographic factors have enabled us to compile reliable data that should serve us well." Mullin smiled to himself. Payne's ability to articulate exactly what others wanted to hear had not diminished one bit.

"Uh, there *is* one other item, sir." Payne paused before going further. What he was about to do would infuriate his committee counterparts. "I feel that a certain amount of flexibility is paramount to the success of HOT. Of course, full and regular accountability to Assistant Director Kerr and yourself is a given. However, I do *not* believe that the individual FDOs should be required to verify and approve of each of our operations."

"Bill, don't you think they should be aware of what's going on in their own backyards?"

Don't panic, Bill. "Oh, of course, sir! My point is simply that those SACs have their hands full already. Also, those of us at HOT are more aware of our capabilities than the FDOs are. It really is more a matter of efficiency than anything else." Payne held his breath.

"Are you looking for a green light from me?"

"Well, yes sir, I suppose so. It's a small but important detail in both the interface of HOT with the FDOs and the entire three-level categorization process."

Mullin looked hard at Payne. He sensed that some, and maybe *everyone*, on the committee disagreed with Payne about this, but he also felt that the points he had just heard were valid. "How much dissension is there within the committee over this, Bill?"

"To tell you the truth, sir, I'm not sure that committee could come to agreement on *anything*." Payne hoped he hadn't shown too much frustration. "It would probably be accurate to say that opinions are mixed on this point, as well as on most others."

"Well, I guess we ought to be discussing this with Sam Kerr present, but I can go over it with him later. I think what you're saying makes sense. We may have to modify the process after we gain some experience, but for now, let's do it your way." The Director knew that what he'd just done might not have been politically smart, but he considered it a "field decision." You made them based on instinct and without the luxury of endless pontification. He'd been dreading the upcoming convention for days, specifically because he knew that every point would be talked to death. Even then, in the end, *he* would have to make the final decisions. *Might as well get one of them out of the way tonight*, he thought. Where Collection matters were concerned, the buck didn't stop until it got to his desk.

Payne nodded. The importance of this victory could not be overstated. He outlined the rest of the plan to be covered in his address and touched on a couple of other jurisdictional issues that had come up before the committee. There was nothing else controversial, though. In the end, Payne received a green light on the entire proposal. "Well done, Bill. You and the rest of the committee have done some very important work. I expect you to stay in touch with the other members and monitor the process as we move forward."

"You bet, sir."

"Bill, you do realize that Collection *has* to succeed, don't you?"

"Of course, sir. It's the centerpiece of the Family Protection Act."

Mullin leaned forward and set his brandy down on the table between them. "Of course it is, Bill. But perhaps more importantly, you and I are inextricably tied to it…for better or worse. Do you understand me?"

Payne swallowed hard. "Yes sir, I do."

"Good. I want you to keep me posted as we move forward. I'm giving you a lot of leeway, Bill. I want you to be aggressive but not stupid. In other words, don't make any messes you can't clean up."

* * * * * *

Washington, D.C.
Monday, April 14

Payne looked carefully in the bathroom mirror at his freshly shaven face. Mullin's words last night had been sobering, but they also hardened his resolve. Collection *would* succeed and so would Bill Payne. There was every indication that today's meeting would be extremely important to his future. As far as Payne was concerned, everyone who mattered at ATF would be listening intently to what he had to say this morning. It was an extraordinary opportunity. He felt completely confident in the content of his speech and his delivery had never let him down. The final ingredient was to look the part and, examining himself in the mirror, he was satisfied that he did.

******

The hotel's grand ballroom was full by 7:30 a.m., though the meeting didn't begin until 8:00. All of those present were very interested in what was to be discussed. To this point in the Collection process, ATF had been floundering a bit—though that never would have been admitted publicly. This convention was seen by many as a forum to provide the clarification they'd been looking for. As with any other large organization, some within ATF craved the spotlight that leadership brought, but many (if not most) simply wanted direction.

"Well, Bill, are you prepared to enlighten us?" Payne knew the voice. He gritted his teeth and turned around to smile at his counterpart, Commander Stan Collier of HOT (Northeast). Collier was looking at Payne with his usual mocking smile, arms folded across his huge chest. The two men had crossed paths several times over the years and Collier had always intimidated him. The guy looked like a bodybuilder and was tough as nails. Collier had boxed his way to an Olympic silver medal and he carried himself with tremendous confidence. Payne knew that Collier despised him and the only response that came naturally was to hate him back.

Stan Collier was a "player's coach," in the best sense of the term. He was well thought of by his subordinates *and* very effective in managing them—an unusual combination. This made him everything that Payne wasn't and led to their distaste for each other.

Collier saw Payne as a pandering ladder-climber who would do virtually anything to advance his agenda. His first reaction to Payne being named HOT (Northwest) Commander was utter disbelief. The man had always been more a paper pusher than a field guy. Tactically, he would probably end up getting people killed. Then again, it made perfect sense when held up to the rest of Payne's career. HOT was the most high-profile unit ATF had ever fielded and Payne was smart enough to surround himself with a few people who really knew their business, just to keep himself out of trouble. The bastard would probably end up being made Director before this whole thing was over.

Collier had no such ambitions. He had risen further than he ever thought he would, given his propensity for speaking his mind. The reason he had come so far was that he was good at his job. Anyone worth his salt in upper management knew that they needed a few guys like Stan Collier around when it hit the fan. This, in addition to his proven field worthiness, made him one of the most logical choices for an HOT Commander.

From the beginning, exactly how HOT would be used had been unclear and Collier had been apprehensive about how things might unfold. Philosophically, he thought the idea of confiscation was ridiculous. First of all, he knew it wouldn't reduce violent crime. That had been his job for twenty years now and he knew you couldn't accomplish it by taking guns away from the good guys.

He had accepted the HOT command for only one reason: because Sam Kerr had asked him to. Kerr was opposed to Collection and wanted someone he could trust at HOT. Collier also didn't believe it would be any worse than anything else he could be doing at ATF these days.

"I'll do what I can to enlighten you, Stan," Payne shot back, replying to his rival's sarcastic question. "Of course, some people are beyond help," he added, with a sense of confidence that he didn't feel. "I was surprised I didn't see you at the Director's house last night."

"You know, Bill, dinner parties are just more important to some people than they are to others." Payne looked like he wanted to reply, but was unsure of what to say.

Collier knew this was pointless, but it was so much fun. Enough was enough, though. "Anyway, I hope you're going to make it clear that HOT won't be acting on its own…that all level-threes will be confirmed and okayed by the FDOs."

This was going to be delicious, thought Payne, but he was a little nervous. He was glad there were lots of other people in the room with them. "Actually, Stan, we've decided not to go that route."

Collier stared at the man in front of him, his eyes narrowing. "Payne, I know you're waiting for me to ask this, so here it comes: *Who* decided not to go that route?"

"Director Mullin and I."

"I oughta kick your ass right here and now!" Collier seethed. "You know we were supposed to present our recommendations to everyone here and solicit input." Several of those around them turned to see what the commotion was about. Collier moved to within inches of the shorter man's face and lowered his voice. "I cannot believe what a fucking weasel you are, Payne. You'll pay for this." He turned around and stormed off.

Payne looked around nervously, trying to get an idea of how many others had seen what went on. No matter, though. With ATF's renowned rumor mill, it wouldn't be long before everyone knew. That was fine with him. No one had heard specifics and it might even help his reputation to have gotten into a scrape with Collier. The Commander poured himself a cup of coffee and headed toward the front of the large ballroom.

* * * * * *

Director Mullin cleared his throat into the microphone. "Now that we've been updated on the status of the Collection process to this point, I would like to bring up the chairman of the Collection Operations Committee to spell out our plan for categorizing Collection subjects. We feel that this process will make it easier for each of you to discharge your duties. As you all know, Bill Payne is the Commander of HOT Northwest. He is also a man in whom I have great confidence. Please welcome Commander Bill Payne."

Amid mostly polite applause, Payne approached the podium and settled in. "Thank you, Director and good morning to all of you. As we've heard this morning, since the first arrests last week, some suspects have chosen to turn themselves in, either at our Collection

Stations or local police stations. Their number, however, is extremely low, relative to the number of illegal firearms we *know* to still be out there." Payne wanted to mention this right off the bat. Some of those who were "soft" on Collection, such as Sam Kerr, were pointing to these surrenders as cause for rethinking the process that was already under way. That was ridiculous, of course. The Bureau had devoted far too much time and resources to seeing this through. Besides, it was ATF's resolve that had led to these people "seeing the light" in the first place. That resolve *had* to remain strong.

"With that in mind, I would like to discuss the categorization process that the Director referred to. We've determined that there will be three levels of Collection subjects. This is necessary for the safety of our agents and for the sake of efficiency.

"The first level will include those not likely to offer any resistance. Virtually all of those who've surrendered their illegal firearms in the last few days would fall into this category. Level two consists of those individuals whom we feel have the potential to flee and/or hide the contraband, even in the face of certain arrest. The parameters used to establish these first two levels have been integrated into a software program, which will be used by FDOs to run searches of their respective geographic areas. In fact, the software packages will be waiting for you upon your return.

"This brings me to the third level. Individuals so designated will have both the means and the will to offer armed resistance. In other words, they're more likely to fight than run. These subjects are potentially the most dangerous and must be handled with the utmost care. The decision has been made, therefore, to deploy HOT for all level-three threats. The training and unique abilities possessed by HOT will provide for the highest probability of success in these cases." Again, the Commander paused. There'd already been an uproar once this morning over what he was about to say and it could happen again.

"The process for determining level-three threats is a bit more involved than for the first two levels. Because of that, and the fact that FDOs will have their hands full as it is, we have determined that the six HOT units will review level-two listings from each FDO in their region in order to sift out level-threes. HOT will then deploy teams for Collection. Of course, we'll stay in close contact with each FDO while working in your area."

About a dozen rows back, a hand shot up. It was Chris Mills, the SAC from Houston and fellow committee member. Payne thought about saying that he would wait till the end to field any questions, but figured he may as well get it over with. "Yes, Chris?"

Mills looked shell-shocked. "Bill, the committee decided that HOT and the FDOs would review all potential level-threes jointly. There was supposed to be agreement reached on *every* level-three classification!" Wherever Stan Collier was, Payne was sure the arrogant bastard was trying hard not to laugh out loud.

Payne took a deep breath and forged ahead. "You're correct. Those *were* the committee's recommendations. After taking them into consideration, however, Director Mullin made the decision, for the reasons I've already outlined, to handle it in the manner I just described."

Pausing for effect had never seemed more appropriate to Payne and it had the desired impact on the audience. He finally asked, "Are there any further questions on this matter?" Silence. Even for a man skilled at hiding his true thoughts, it was tough not to smile like a Cheshire cat. This was the ultimate victory and it came to him in front of everyone who mattered in his world.

5

Portland, Oregon
Tuesday, April 15

NOBODY HATED "tax day" more than Mike Niculescu did. The thought of having to tally up how much he'd paid this corrupt institution last year and now (as always) having to pay even more by midnight tonight, was especially bothersome in view of the way his money had been spent lately. The irony of filing this particular tax return hit him especially hard—it was as if he was footing the bill for his own prosecution.

Not only did Mike feel like his own tax dollars were being used directly against him at the moment, but in a broader sense, he believed that income taxation itself—like gun control—was an example of the U.S. government sapping freedom from its citizens. Obviously, the federal government required revenue. Just as obvious, however, was the fact that both "tools" had been misused by governments throughout history to control and subjugate people.

Mike sat in his home office after his usual morning workout, mentally preparing himself to seal his return and drop it in the mail. It was almost seven o'clock and he needed to get moving. He was usually at the job site by now and he hadn't even showered yet.

Mike's home office was his haven—he couldn't imagine having to go to work in a sterile office environment somewhere else. Usually, his job took him out of the house, but whether he was at a job site or here at home, he never felt the constraints that an "office" environment placed on the people who worked in them. He honestly didn't know how Don did it.

As he leaned back in his swivel chair, Mike looked over in the opposite corner of the room at his two huge safes. Sarah wouldn't allow them anywhere else inside the house, but this was *his* room. Formerly, they'd both contained a variety of firearms. Though many who chose not to own guns might have found it hard to understand, Mike had always taken great pride in their ownership. Few material things in life were more pleasing to him than a fine firearm.

Now, the few remaining in his safes were all "legal." In fact, he had only two "contraband" items in the house. One was a Vang Comp Systems custom Remington 870 12-gauge shotgun with extended magazine, Surefire forend light, and several other custom touches. This one was kept loaded with 00 buckshot and stored in a safe in the master bedroom closet. The other was a Glock 34 he kept in the nightstand for his primary home defense weapon. Since Mike didn't believe in keeping an "unsecured" gun anywhere in the house, this one was locked in a Gun Vault gun safe. The nifty little steel box had an easy-to-use keypad and held one handgun, with room for a spare magazine. It was totally secure, yet provided almost instant access.

He liked Glocks in general and this one in particular. The 9 mm caliber was very effective when the right loads were used and the slide and barrel on this model were slightly longer than on other Glocks, offering an improved sight radius and better recoil control. He'd installed Trijicon night sights, an Insight Technology weapon-mounted light and an unobtrusive Crimson Trace Lasergrips module that allowed him to project a red laser dot for use in close quarters and low light—perfect for home defense. The magazine held seventeen rounds, so, with a loaded chamber and spare magazine, he had a total of thirty-five rounds available to him.

"Why would anyone *need* that many 'bullets' in a gun?" went the familiar old question. Mike's answer was always the same: one never knew the type of threat he might face. Home invasions had become all too common since the Family Protection Act was passed. These crimes usually involved gangs of armed men breaking into occupied homes and stealing anything they could easily carry—often raping women and beating or killing men in the process. The rapid increase in the number of these attacks coincided with the announcement of the new law. Apparently, Mike wasn't the only "criminal" who watched the nightly news. The consensus among the various television talking heads was that the criminal element in society wanted to grab as many guns as they could before Uncle Sam confiscated them, so all the more reason to get them off the streets quickly. The fact, of course, was that the "criminal element" knew that law-abiding citizens were now largely unarmed—and easy prey.

Sarah had practiced enough with the Glock to become fully comfortable with it and Mike was confident in her ability to use it properly. Of course, one never knew how a person would perform under the stress of real world conditions. Everything was different when the light was dim and there was a real person in front of you. All you could do was prepare. Mike had been there before, with human beings at the end of his gun. It had been a long time ago, but he'd gone "downrange" and gotten the job done. He was confident that he'd perform well if required to again.

Mike had been worrying a lot more than normal over the last couple of days. He worried for his family and he worried for the future of the country that he loved so dearly. What he saw happening was more troubling than anything he'd ever witnessed, or even read about, in the history of the United States—and his concerns weren't limited to the Second Amendment. Society was rotting at its core and nobody seemed to care. There were probably a number of reasons, but the one that kept popping up in Mike's mind was that people no longer cared about the rights of others, if trampling on *those* rights didn't impact them personally.

Politicians were making a living by pitting various groups against each other, creating crises, and proposing what previously would have been unthinkable solutions to them. They were taking full advantage of the public mood. Yet government wasn't completely to blame.

After all, the government really was "of the people." Though it was fashionable to smirk at that statement these days, he truly believed that we got the government we deserved.

Far too many "gun rights people" focused on the gun issue alone, which was shortsighted and selfish, not to mention hypocritical. Freedom was freedom and it had been slipping away in this country for much of the twentieth century. Sure, there had to be a balance between freedom and order. Never had an American citizen had the right to do *anything* he wanted. On the other end of the spectrum, perfect order could be achieved only through the surrender of virtually all individual rights. Mike would always believe that, although the price to be paid for living in a truly free society was often very high, it was far preferable to the alternative. If a society had to err on one side or the other (and it always did), it should err on the side of freedom.

Yet, We the People had been surrendering our liberty willingly for decades. The concepts of self-reliance and rugged individualism that had made this country unique, and arguably the greatest in history, existed now only in theory. Mike knew it was a cop-out to point an accusatory finger at the government without first looking in the mirror.

This whole gun "collection" business really was symptomatic of a larger societal problem. People were disconnected from what went on in Washington, D.C. and in their state capitals. This was understandable, to a degree. Everyone was busy, had families to raise and lives to lead. But didn't we also have the duty to stay informed enough to make intelligent decisions when it came time to vote? People had divergent political views, but Mike felt strongly that they should at least be able to articulate them. Far too many got their "opinions" directly from the nightly news or their favorite talk radio show—regurgitating what they heard or read without processing it. This tendency led to the things Mike was worrying about these days.

His tax return was ready to mail and it was 7:15. Time to get a move on. As he was straightening up his desk, his cell phone rang. The caller ID told him it was Don.

"What are you up to?" Don asked.

"Just finishing up my friggin' tax return."

"Nothing like waiting till the last minute. I had mine in over three months ago...already got my refund back."

Mike shook his head. "Why doesn't that surprise me?" He couldn't help himself. "You know, Don, when you get a refund, that means you overpaid the U.S. Treasury, which means you lost the opportunity cost on that money until your government graciously decided to return it to you."

"Yeah, well, I'd always rather get a refund than have to pay at the end of the year."

"Again, why am I not surprised," Mike jabbed.

"What's wrong with you, Mike? You're even more of a smart-ass than usual."

Mike looked up at the ceiling and took a deep breath. "Sorry. It's a combination of things, I guess. It's tax day for one thing and I've also got a couple of fairly major problems on my main job right now," Mike said, trying to excuse his mood.

"How about the other thing we discussed over the weekend—that bothering you any?" Don asked.

"Nope. Never gave it a second thought...what do you think?" Mike asked sarcastically.

"Yeah, I thought so. Listen, how about lunch today? I'll meet you at Campbell's. That'll help your mood. See you there around twelve thirty?"

"Sounds great. I've never been one to turn down lunch, especially when you buy. I'll see you then." Mike gathered up his tax return and headed upstairs to shower. He really did have a couple of problems to address this morning at the job site.

* * * * * *

Don arrived at the restaurant at 12:20 and was lucky enough to grab a booth. The place was generally packed at lunchtime and for good reason. It had the best barbecue in town. It wasn't fancy, but the food was good enough to have turned Don and Mike into regulars.

Don had thought a lot about what Jenny said. Mike was his best friend and he at least owed him moral support. No doubt Mike felt like the whole world was against him. What he needed was someone on *his* side. Don's reservations hadn't disappeared, but that wasn't the issue. It was Don's responsibility to do whatever he could to help his friend. Jenny had made him realize that.

The truth was, Jenny had made him realize a lot of things since the day they first met. Having grown up in a home where emotions weren't displayed and feelings weren't discussed, Don had a lot to learn in those areas. His parents were good, hard-working, sensible people; but they were like bank vaults when it came to getting emotion, affection, or praise out of them. Don had always tried hard to avoid those faults and sometimes his wife's gentle nudging helped him do so.

A few minutes later, Mike showed up. He tried to make small talk after they ordered, knowing that wasn't his strong suit. Finally, Don could take no more. "Mike, I'm sorry for the way I acted at your house the other night. You caught me off guard and I acted like a damn fool. I know I came off rude to your mom and dad too and I hope you know that's the last thing I ever want to do."

"No need to apologize. I've been far from easy to get along with for the last week or so. We've both got strong opinions and things like that are bound to happen from time to time. Don't worry…my parents thought nothing of it."

Don took a deep breath. "Listen, I can only imagine what you must be going through. You're watching good people being arrested for doing nothing more than living their lives the same way they always have. They're not hurting anyone, yet they're being blamed for society's ills. Am I on target?"

Mike looked shocked. "Well, yeah. What's the reason for your sudden change of heart?"

"It's not a total change of heart. I still think you're wrong about a lot of things. I'm just trying to look at this mess from your perspective.

I still don't have a big problem with their ultimate goal, but I've come to believe that the way they're going about it leaves a lot to be desired."

"Don, how many different ways are there to take freedom away from law-abiding citizens? I mean, they either trust us to live freely, or they don't. I'm not trying to convert you and I'm not asking you or anybody else to believe in the same things I do. I just want the room to do my own thing. That's what this country used to be about."

"Mike, let's not go there again. Why don't we just agree to disagree about some things, okay?" Mike put his hands up in an unusual gesture of surrender, prompting Don to continue. "Anyway, I want to help—however I can. Do you think it would do any good for me to call Congressman Skiles' office…or maybe even go see him?"

"Don, thanks…really." Mike looked drained, both mentally and physically. "I just don't see what good that could possibly do. No one is more against what's going on than Skiles. He just doesn't have enough pull to do anything about it. Then again, at this point, I'm not sure *anyone* does."

Don was really starting to worry now. He'd never seen his proud and stubborn friend like this before. "I assume you're not budging on this, so I've got to ask: What do you really think the chances are that they're going to come knocking on your door?"

"I don't know. I really don't. A lot of people have been coming forward over the last few days to surrender their guns. I've heard some talk that the Feds might rethink the whole thing. Maybe they're softening up on Collection," Mike added hopefully.

"Well, what if they're not?" It was a question to which Don knew no answer would be forthcoming. "Jesus, Mike, I think I'm more worried about this than you are!"

"Don't bet on it."

* * * * * *

"You must be Marshal Keller," the stranger blurted out as he approached Scott, hand extended. "I'm Deputy Commander Ray Burke."

Scott had entered the conference room and was looking for Bobby Myers, or anyone else he knew. So far, he'd spent time only around squad seven and he looked forward to getting to know more people, since he knew he would have to work with other units. Scott had just spotted Bobby and was headed his way when Burke intercepted him. "It's a pleasure to meet you, Commander. I hear you've been in D.C. for a few days."

"Yes, I have. I always enjoy going back to Headquarters," Burke added proudly. "I understand you've been training with squad seven."

"I have, and I must say I'm very impressed—especially with this guy," Scott said, pointing with his thumb to where Bobby was standing a few feet away and making sure he said it loud enough for his new friend to hear.

"I agree. Agent Myers is about as good as they come."

The last thing in the world Bobby wanted was to chitchat with Ray Burke, but he excused himself from the conversation he was in and did so anyway—for the simple reason that he liked Scott Keller. "My ears were burning over there," he joked as he approached the two.

"You know it was all good stuff, Bobby," Burke answered, smiling.

"Oh, yes sir, I'm sure. So, Scott, are you ready for your first full HOT meeting?"

"As ready as I'm going to be."

Burke chimed in. "I've heard Commander Payne has some good scoop for us from the convention." Both Scott and Bobby had to fight the urge to look at each other. It was highly unlikely that Burke had not already been briefed on the "scoop."

At that moment, Commander Bill Payne strode confidently into the large conference room. He was back on *his* turf now—and it showed. Payne had never felt more important in his entire professional life. He'd played a major role in setting policy not only for his command but also for the entire Bureau of Alcohol, Tobacco, Firearms and Explosives. Now, like a victorious general returning home to his loyal and adoring troops, he was about to address his people.

Immediately upon Payne's entrance, Burke made his way to the front of the room, letting everyone know that it was time to come to order. The members of all ten squads were present. This was a very big deal in the brief history of ATF's Hazardous Operations Team.

Payne went straight to the podium and began shuffling through his notes. Within a matter of seconds everyone had taken their seats and the room was silent. This was a disciplined and serious bunch, thought Scott, who had grabbed a seat next to Bobby. Payne cleared his throat. "As you know, yesterday in Washington, I addressed a convention of all SACs and upper management, including the Director and the Attorney General.

"At that meeting, we hammered out what will become the final draft, if you will, for the Collection process. More importantly to this unit, we also determined the specific situations in which HOT will be used. In a nutshell, HOT will deploy teams to various geographic locations based on their respective jurisdictions. We will touch bases with each area's FDO, but will be fully autonomous in terms of our operations." Scott and Bobby glanced reflexively at each other at that statement.

"Furthermore, we will determine who our subjects will be through the use of a new software program that will be discussed with the squad leaders following this meeting. The bottom line is that we will in no way be dependent upon FDOs for support, briefings, intel, et cetera. All of our gear will travel with us, which means we will be fully self-contained.

"More details will be forthcoming, but I hope you all have a basic idea now as to how you will be used to accomplish our mission. You are the most important tool our government has at its disposal to accomplish what the President of the United States has declared to be in the best interest of this country.

"There is simply no room for doubt about what we're doing. It is not only necessary, but also right. At the risk of being blunt, I must be crystal clear about this. Dissension in any form cannot be tolerated. If you have doubts about our mission, you're in the wrong place. There is no room for discussion on this point. It is vital that you bear this in mind as you carry out your duties." With that, Payne was finished. There would be no questions asked directly of him in this venue. Everyone knew better. Instead, it would be left to Burke to field questions from the squad leaders, who would then relay the answers to their troops.

This guy is completely full of shit, thought Scott. He also had the feeling, however, that a surprisingly large number of those in attendance bought this nonsense hook, line, and sinker. It was all a matter of perspective, he supposed. As everyone stood, he looked at his squad leader. "Sounds like you've got a meeting to get to."

Bobby rolled his eyes. "Sounds like it."

"Well, I guess I'll head back to the squad room and dig into the Playbook some more," Scott said, referring to the Tactical Field Manual for HOT. Bobby had run his team through several drills over the last couple of days and had included Scott in each of them. This helped a lot and much of what he'd seen was not unfamiliar to him. Nevertheless, he was smart enough to know that it took more than a few dry runs to learn this business. "I feel like I need to be a lot more comfortable with at least all the basic scenarios before I'm anything more than a liability," he admitted to Bobby.

"Don't worry about it too much. The drills will take care of that. Besides, at the risk of inflating your already over-inflated U.S. Marshals ego, you *do* pick up on this stuff pretty fast."

"I bet you say that to all the guys," Scott whispered.

They were cracking up as Burke approached them. "Well, I'm glad to see Marshal Keller is fitting right in." The mood instantly changed. Burke sensed this and continued quickly, looking at Scott. "I've spoken to Commander Payne and he feels it would be to everyone's benefit for you to familiarize yourself with as many of our people as possible. We'd like you to head over to squad room five and get to know those folks. You'll be training with them for the next week or so. Squad Leader Dennis Hatcher will be right over after our meeting. It shouldn't run more than an hour or so."

"Uh…you bet," Scott answered, somewhat taken by surprise,

though he shouldn't have been. He knew it made sense. Shooting Bobby a quick glance, he excused himself and headed for the elevator. He wanted to ask him about Hatcher, because he'd come to trust Bobby's judgment. Then again, he knew he was better off forming his own opinions.

* * * * * *

"Ray, I want you to narrow the list down to the Greater Portland area. This one is way too long to be manageable." Payne was looking down at a very thick listing of level-three Collection subjects from the entire state of Oregon.

"Sir, I have that listing right over here," Burke assured him, reaching for a shorter yet still surprisingly large list. A significant percentage of Oregon's population *did* live in the Portland area, after all.

"That's still a ton of names," Payne objected. "Is it broken down by zip code?"

"No, sir. But I can run another search if you want a particular area."

"No. That'll do for now. So, how do we go about filtering the list to come up with, say, the top ten prospects? Our first series of collections needs to have maximum impact. I want the rest of them to see this happening on the evening news and be scared to death."

"Well, sir, I've been thinking about that. I do have a set of criteria that might achieve the result you want, but there's something else I think we ought to consider as well. I think it might be a good idea to include Keller in this conversation…if for no other reason than to be able to say we did."

Payne smirked. "That's ridiculous, Ray. I'm not going to let Keller stick his nose that far into the inner workings of our operation. He can train and work with some of the squads on specific assignments, but I don't want him involved in developing the big picture. Did you move him over to Hatcher's team?"

"Yes sir, I did."

"Good, I'm more comfortable with *him* keeping an eye on Keller than I am with Myers doing it."

Burke could see that he was going to need to come at this from another angle. Keller was going to have to be involved at a level higher than a mere squad member. The USMS was hardly going to lend some of its best agents out as rent-a-cops. Word would get out, if that turned out to be the case, and that could create more interference from Washington than Payne wanted. The Commander's jealousy of other federal agencies wouldn't let him see this now, but in the end he would agree with his deputy. Burke's primary but unwritten responsibility was to make his boss look good.

"Sir, please bear with me for just a moment." This was an art form that Burke had mastered long ago. "If there is at least the *perception* that Keller has had input, he'd be somewhat culpable should something go wrong…would he not? Besides, his involvement might head off any unwanted interference from Headquarters." Silence was critical here. Payne had to process the information and come to Burke's conclusion himself.

"Maybe we should involve him to a small degree…in an 'advisory role' only, though! Nothing is going to go wrong, so I don't want Keller standing by to steal the show after we've done the hard work."

"Don't worry, sir, his role will be purely superficial."

* * * * * *

Scott wondered what Payne wanted with him. He found it hard to imagine a reason why the Commander would want a Marshal around. He returned Victoria's wave and smile. "Go on in, Marshal Keller—they're expecting you."

"Thanks." He knocked lightly first, then opened the door. He noticed Burke sitting at a small table on the other side of the room.

"Ah, Marshal Keller. Good to see you," Payne said, meeting Scott halfway across the room and shaking his hand. "I hear you've been doing extremely well training with our people." He gestured for Scott to be seated at the small round conference table in the corner of the office. The two ATF men sat across the table from him.

"Well," Scott responded, "as I told Commander Burke, I'm very impressed with the level of professionalism they display, especially squad seven. I haven't met Hatcher yet, but I'm sure his people are very sharp as well."

"You'll meet him tomorrow morning. He's working on some things for me this afternoon. I'm sure you'll agree that he's top notch," Burke interjected.

"I have no doubt. What can I do for you gentlemen today?" Scott wanted to cut through the bullshit and find out what they were up to. He was also curious by now why Burke (and, he assumed, Payne) was so high on Hatcher.

Payne wanted to limit Keller's involvement in the process as much as possible, while making him feel privileged to be included. "Marshal Keller, we think you should become a bit more involved in this phase of our operation."

Scott was tempted to assure them that his present level of involvement was sufficient, but thought better of it. Marshal Filson *had* been fairly specific about the fact that Scott was to assist ATF in perfecting their "apprehension strategy." "Obviously, I'd like to help out however I can. What did you have in mind for me to do, specifically?"

"We're at the point now of selecting specific level-three subjects for Collection operations. We'd like your input on the particular characteristics you feel we should use in prioritizing the level-three listing, as well as your thoughts on determining which subjects are most likely to flee. We'll then take your input into consideration in determining the final criteria we'll use in the Collection process." With that, Payne made it quite clear that Scott was wasting his time. It was obvious that his opinion was being solicited for the sole purpose of satisfying a bureaucratic requirement.

He was aggravated because he didn't like having his time wasted. Still, he wondered if he could at least inject some sanity into this process before it was too late. "What is it you want to accomplish with the Collection operations?" It was a simple question, but also one that he felt sure would irritate Payne. The Commander was not used to being quizzed by someone he perceived to be a subordinate.

"I would think the answer to that question is obvious. What we hope to 'accomplish' is to remove dangerous and illegal weapons from circulation."

Scott felt like pushing it a little. "And that's *all*?"

"What, exactly, do you mean by that, Marshal?"

"I'm just curious as to whether the primary objective is ridding the country of illicit firearms or intimidating those who would question the authority of the federal government." Burke saw that Payne was about to explode and decided to intercede on his behalf to keep that from happening.

"Marshal Keller," Burke broke in quickly, "may I remind you that these people are felons?" He continued before Scott could answer. "In your duties as a U.S. Marshal, have you always extended the same level of compassion toward felons as you seem prone to do in this case?"

"No, I haven't. It's just that I've been under the assumption that there's a difference between the people you're after and murderers and bank robbers."

Payne was seething. "I'm sure the work of the Marshals Service is far more serious and important than ours here at ATF. Nevertheless, the President of the United States has determined that these people represent a great threat to our nation's security and he has charged *this* agency with eliminating that threat. If you have philosophical leanings that will impair your ability to discharge your duties, perhaps you should discuss them with Marshal Filson."

It was a power play and one that Scott wasn't surprised by. He'd clearly and intentionally pushed Payne's button when he shouldn't have. He knew better, but lately, it seemed, he didn't have the ability to hold his tongue, even when he knew he should. Maybe he was already getting too old for this. As his dad used to say, there was a proper time and place for everything. Right now, it was time to back off a little.

"Commander, I'm simply trying to prioritize your objectives.

That will help me accurately assess the level-three subjects, as you've asked me to do. I didn't intend to be accusatory. I can assure you that I'm fully aware of the importance of ATF's mission." It was a lie and the two ATF men knew it. Nonetheless, it did take some of the wind out of their sails.

Burke decided to jump in again. "Of course our ultimate goal is for those still possessing these firearms to realize that it's in everyone's best interest to turn them in. Having said that, we're all big boys here—not to mention experienced law enforcement officers. It's a fact of life that it's sometimes useful to 'intimidate'—to use your word—those breaking the law into complying with it. Life then becomes easier for everyone." Keller held his tongue this time—it wouldn't have done any good anyway. "Our *immediate* goal, however, is to physically collect these firearms. Philosophy aside, that's a reality that shouldn't be overlooked. Does that answer your question?" Burke stared into Keller's eyes.

"Yes it does." *Time to wrap this thing up and get out of here.* "Based on what I've heard, I think you should look for characteristics that would indicate a tendency toward self-reliance, even to the point of being outwardly 'anti-government.' This could manifest itself in a number of different ways."

"What specific characteristics would indicate those tendencies, in your opinion?" It was Payne this time.

"Well, first of all, I would cross-reference the level-three listing with IRS records. Look for a variety of things that generate red flags. IRS people can help you out a lot in that area. They've got the ability to sift through incredible amounts of information in a matter of minutes."

"We thought about the IRS angle, but decided that information wouldn't relate directly to what we're trying to accomplish." Payne was lying, of course.

"On its own, I think you'd be correct, but when that information is matched up with those already selected as level-threes, I believe it would narrow your list down. I'm not talking about absolutes here. There's no such thing. You just put together a puzzle, piece by piece."

He knew that the lecture would piss them off and didn't care. He was getting tired of this.

"You might also want to check on membership in various 'anti-government' groups. The FBI would probably be able to give you more specifics in this area, but I think any matches between these groups and your level-three listing would be very solid, in terms of what you're looking for.

"The only other thing I can think of—and I'm sure you've already considered this as well—is to cross-reference military records. Specifically (he hated to say this), I'd look for those with a Special Operations background. There won't be too many, but the few there are could create problems."

"What kind of problems?" asked Burke, though he already knew the answer.

"They're likely to fight back."

"Nothing we can't deal with, I'm sure," Payne asserted—fully aware of Scott's background. "I suppose you'd be careful of all ex-Marines as well?"

Scott smiled. "It couldn't hurt...and it's 'former.'"

"Pardon me?"

"*Former*...there's no such thing as an ex-Marine."

"Oh...thank you for the clarification," Payne mocked, pushing his chair back and standing as he spoke the words. Scott happily did the same, more than relieved to have this meeting over. "As I said, we'll carefully consider your input when we determine the final criteria."

Scott was moving toward the door. "Let me know if I can do anything else to help." He was curious about what had gone on in the squad leaders' meeting and was anxious to talk to Bobby. That would have to wait till the end of the day, though.

* * * * * *

Scott saw the big guy come into the bar and waved him over to the corner booth. "How am I supposed to maintain my razor-sharp edge when you keep dragging me into taverns?" Bobby asked with a smile.

"Yes, I've noticed how hard I have to twist your dainty little arm in order to achieve my dark purpose—that being to dull your 'razor-sharp edge.'"

Bobby exhaled sharply as he sat down. "Well, I spent most of the afternoon listening to Burke describe the software package in *excruciating* detail. I guess he wants us all to know how smart he is."

"I was hoping you got some good scoop. Sounds like you just got bored."

"That's it, man. How did it go up in the Ivory Tower?"

Scott shook his head. "Every time I'm around these guys, they surprise me. I thought I had both of them figured out the first time I met them, but once again they exceeded expectations."

"Went that well, huh?"

"Those two scare me, Bobby. They just seem to be enjoying this too much...especially Payne. What worries me most about Burke, though, is that I'm convinced he'll do *anything* to make Payne look good."

"I'd say you've got 'em both pegged."

"Listen, like I told you, I've seen guys like this before. The problem in this case, though, is that the bad guys they're after aren't all that bad and they still want to use the biggest hammer they can find!" Bobby didn't say a word. He wanted to hear all the Marshal had to say.

Scott pushed on. "To tell you the truth, I'm getting more and more squeamish about this whole process every day and it sure doesn't help my mood any to spend time with those two. Like I said before, I keep hoping the Powers That Be will change their minds on this." Bobby just shook his head and Scott continued. "Failing that, I'm starting to hope the 'bad guys' give up and turn their guns in—just so we can avoid what I'm afraid is coming."

Scott took a gulp of beer and a deep breath, then leaned forward and lowered his voice. "Then again, a part of me hopes that they look Nichols straight in the eye and say 'fuck you.' The more I think about this whole thing, the more wrong I think it is. Go back and read the Federalist Papers, the Constitution, the Declaration of

Independence…any of 'em. They all have the same message. It was exactly *this* kind of stuff that those old guys were afraid of."

"So, what are you saying, Scott…do you want out?"

"Yeah, I think so. I just don't think I can do this. I'm not going to call my boss tonight and tell him I don't want to go to work tomorrow. I've just got serious doubts, that's all. Next time I talk to him, I think I'll ask him to start working on a replacement. Our relationship's good enough that I can do that."

"You gonna take me with you?"

"Sure—There's got to be *something* we can find for you to do."

"Brother, I can't say I blame you a bit," Bobby admitted. "I wouldn't put up with this either if I didn't have to."

Scott decided to change the subject slightly. There was no sense in causing his buddy to hate his job any more than he already did. "Hey, tell me about Hatcher."

"Oh, that's right, you get to hang with him for a while, don't you?"

"Yeah, I 'get to'."

"Basically, Dennis is an okay guy. His biggest problem is that Burke was really high on him from the beginning. This, of course, led to Payne being really high on him and that's a double curse. Dennis is a tough, serious guy, who plays by the rules—no matter what. He's like a robot. Whatever they tell him to do, it gets done. I guess you tend to like guys like that when you're in management. I wouldn't call him a kiss-ass, though."

"What *would* you call him?"

"Let's just say he's real eager to please. Look, I shouldn't be so down on him…must just be my mood. Like I said, he's a pretty sharp dude. Give him a chance. You'll probably get along just fine with him."

* * * * * *

Payne and Burke called their wives to say they wouldn't be home until very late and ordered up food from the cafeteria. They wanted to get cracking on a list of names to present to their squad leaders.

Burke had inputted the search criteria he had in mind before they'd called Keller in and their meeting with the Marshal hadn't given him any reason to modify the search. Now they were looking at the names of real people, none of whom knew they were being targeted by the ATF. "Let's look at one of these guys a little more closely," Burke suggested, randomly selecting a name halfway down a page. "Let's see what *his* story is. No criminal record...lives outside town—wow!"

"What is it?" Payne asked.

"This guy has a *ton* of firearms."

"Good," the Commander answered.

******

Scott was still trying to figure out what quirk of fate had stuck him with his present assignment, as he pulled into his driveway and hit the garage door opener. It wasn't fate, he decided; it was the U.S. Marshal for the District of Oregon.

He could smell his favorite pasta dish simmering as soon as he opened the door. His wife was standing at the stove, determined not to let the sauce burn. "Glad to see you forced yourself to come home. Let me smell your clothes," Meg Keller insisted as she hugged him tightly and took a deep breath. "Let me guess...Jake's?"

"Yeah. It was a tough afternoon, sweetie."

"Is Bobby doing any better?" They'd talked about how much the ATF agent hated what he was doing and, although Meg had yet to meet the man, she felt as if she knew him.

"Seems to be. He's pretty much the strong, silent type, though, so it's hard to tell."

"Oh I wouldn't know anything about men like that." She winked at him. "Between you and Dad, I wouldn't have known men even *had* emotions if it weren't for television."

He had to admit she had a point. Scott scooped her up in his arms and walked to the couch, laying her down gently. "I love you, Mrs. Keller. You know that?"

"Yes, and I love you, too, Mr. Keller." Moments like this were all too rare lately.

Scott put his hand on her stomach and rubbed it. "How do you feel?"

"Are you talking to me, or the little one?" Meg was fourteen weeks pregnant with their first child and both of them were giddy with excitement. They'd been married for a little over two years and Meg had recently turned thirty. Both knew they wanted children and, though there was no such thing as a perfect time to do it, everything felt right. One consequence of her pregnancy was that Scott's normally strong protective instinct had gone into overdrive. Meg was convinced that he was going to drive her nuts over the next six months.

"I was talking to *you*, but maybe you can answer for both of you."

"We're both doing fine, thanks for asking, but I'm starting to really feel pregnant. Guess that's a good thing, huh?"

"I think it's an unfortunate but necessary side effect of being knocked up, sweetie. You really do look great, though. I know it's a cliché, but you've got a glow about you." Meg rolled her eyes. "I mean it...I've never seen a woman in my life more beautiful than you are right now."

"Thanks honey. I love you. You'd better go stir your sauce, though, or we're going to have frozen pizza for dinner."

As Scott inhaled the rigatoni with tomato cream sauce a few minutes later, Meg asked him about the day's adventures with ATF. "Well, I got called up to the principal's office today."

"You mean this Payne guy?"

"Yeah, he and his little henchman summoned me to 'ask for my assistance' in separating the bad guys from the *really* bad guys. I think I pissed them off when I questioned their motives in this whole thing."

"What do you mean?"

"I think those two are enjoying this way too much and that could lead to some bad things. Marshals put their *own* lives on the line all the time to protect scumbags who don't deserve it. Now I've got to watch Payne and Burke endanger the lives of people who, for the most part, have never done anything wrong. Basically, their targets woke up one day and were told they were felons if they didn't give up the right to do something they'd done their whole lives."

Meg looked surprised. "You know, I haven't really stopped to think about it that much and this is the first time we've talked about it like this." Scott tended to go about his job without saying much. It wasn't that he didn't want to include his wife. He really enjoyed talking to her about things that were important to him. He just assumed that she didn't want to hear all the details, having grown up with the U.S. Marshals Service. She continued. "Is that what you really think of this law?"

"Yeah, honey, it is."

"Why don't you ask Marshal Filson to replace you, then? It's pretty important for you to believe in what you're doing, isn't it?"

"Yeah, it's pretty important."

"Sounds like you being there is a sham anyway. Obviously, you don't think Payne and this other guy are even interested in your opinion, right?" Her husband nodded. "So, why are they asking for it?"

"First of all, they pretty much *have* to. This is a 'joint task force,' even though we're only tokens. Also, I think they want as many other people around as possible to point their bony little fingers at when it hits the fan."

Answering Meg's questions really *did* cause Scott to wonder why he was still reporting to ATF every day. "I do think I'm going to talk to Filson. He's on vacation for a few days right now, though."

"Must be nice," she smiled at him.

"Yeah. He needs it."

"Honey, we need it too," his wife gently reminded him.

"I know. There'll be a lot more time off after the baby's born," he promised, not realizing how naïve that sounded. Meg just nodded. She knew they needed time for *themselves* also and there would be a lot less of that after the baby came. There were some things that men just didn't get!

She knew it would be a continuing battle to convince Scott to take his allotted vacation every year. Meg understood her husband's driven personality; it was one of the things she loved about him. It was also something she was used to, having grown up in the same kind of environment. She wasn't really worried, though. She knew her father loved his family and that Scott would love his. Still, Dad hadn't been around to tell them often enough. She'd have to work on that with Scott.

"So you're going to talk to him when he gets back…promise?"

"Promise."

6

Portland, Oregon
Wednesday, April 16

SCOTT SHOWED UP in squad room five at a few minutes before eight o'clock. He'd considered getting there by seven so he could take part in the squad's Crossfit workout, but decided instead to go for a run at home and come in "late." Even though he was trying to keep an open mind about Hatcher, he had little desire to impress the man.

The squad room was empty at the moment, so Scott grabbed a cup of coffee and sat down with a copy of HOT's Tactical Field Manual. He'd worked hard to familiarize himself with it—even taking a copy home. Although he had serious doubts about the Collection process, it was in Scott Keller's nature to excel at every task he took on.

"You must be Marshal Keller." The door to the squad room had been propped open and Scott hadn't heard anyone come in. He'd forgotten how easy those soft-soled "combat boots" made it to sneak around. His own pair, along with the ATF-issue black fatigues, was still in his locker. He'd worn a coat and tie this morning and, having missed PT, hadn't bothered to change yet.

A smiling Dennis Hatcher extended his hand as Scott stood. "Hi. Scott Keller."

"Morning, Scott...Dennis Hatcher."

"I thought so. Nice to meet you, Dennis. Heard a lot about you."

"I'm not sure whether that's good or bad," Hatcher responded matter-of-factly.

Scott smiled. "All good, especially where it counts. The Commander and Deputy sure do think highly of you."

Hatcher looked slightly embarrassed. Whether it was right or wrong, being the "boss's boy" wasn't looked upon favorably—in the ATF or any other law enforcement agency. "Well, the Commander and Deputy think highly of all of us. We're a pretty efficient team here. We work hard and it pays off."

Scott wondered briefly how Hatcher could know yet that their training 'pays off.' "Yeah, I got to know some of your team members yesterday. Everyone I've met since I got here last week really does seem to be top notch," he replied.

"Looks like we're going to go live in a couple of days. In fact, we're getting our Collection assignments this afternoon," Hatcher announced excitedly. "It's about damn time."

How do you look forward to something like this? Scott wondered for the umpteenth time since he'd joined this outfit. "Yep, it's about time." He had absolutely no idea what else to say and didn't feel like engaging Hatcher in a philosophical discussion right now. What he *did* feel like doing, as soon as possible, was calling Marshal Filson.

"So, Scott, are you going to run drills with us today?"

"Yeah, if you don't mind. I've been working with Bobby's crew for the last few days. I'm starting to get the hang of it, I think. I'll go get changed and meet you back up here in a few minutes, okay?"

"Sounds good. We ought to be ready to roll about 0845. I'll see you back here in a few."

******

Impressive, Scott thought as he watched squad five run through its drills. He was sitting this drill out, along with six team members. The other half of the squad was running a split-team drill, meant for occasions when the full twelve-member squad wasn't needed.

HOT obviously believed there was a good chance that they would face well-prepared and well-armed opposition in the Collection process. Scott had his doubts. Try as he might, he couldn't imagine their subjects putting up much of a fight—especially to the degree that HOT seemed to be expecting. He was sure the holdouts were sitting in their homes, afraid of Big Brother's knock on the door. Nevertheless, someone besides Bill Payne believed otherwise. ATF had obviously allocated a big chunk of its new budget to the HOT concept. Sure, when the Collection process was over, there would still be *some* need for an ATF Spec Ops unit such as this one, but it was clearly *this* process for which it had been created.

The jarring sound of a flash-bang grenade going off in the mock house being assaulted shook Scott out of his daydream. This was followed by shouts of "ATF, DROP YOUR WEAPONS!" Bursts from the squad's M4 submachine guns punctuated the short pause following those words. Just like that, the drill was over. If HOT was right, Scott thought, these "level-three" guys were in a ton of trouble.

* * * * * *

Bobby Myers was among the last of the squad leaders to arrive in the small conference room. There was an open seat next to Dennis Hatcher and Bobby strode over and sat down. All else being equal, he normally would have chosen someone else to sit next to, but since Hatcher had been working with Scott, he wanted to pick his brain. "Hey, Dennis, what's up?"

"Oh, not much. I feel like a kid at Christmas, man!" Suddenly it was clear to Bobby why he usually looked for someone else to sit next to. "You looking as forward to this as I am?"

"Absolutely!" Bobby lied. "How's Keller working out with you guys?"

"He's sharp. Seems to have good instincts. I've really worked with him for only a couple of hours, though. I guarantee you one thing: based on the way he watched what we were doing, the Marshals' 'Special Operations Group' doesn't have a thing on us!"

"You know, I don't doubt for a second that you're right, but I can also tell you that Keller would be the first one to admit it."

"Yeah, right. You think he'd give us that much credit?"

Bobby knew Hatcher found the thought impossible to believe because he himself would never give an inch to another agency. "Yeah, I do," he answered. *Every time I start to give this guy another chance, he reminds me why I don't like him.* Luckily, Payne's entrance into the conference room excused him from having to continue the conversation. It also quieted those in the audience as quickly as if God himself had appeared before them.

Payne sat on the corner of a desk in the front of the room. Burke busied himself immediately by handing out packets marked with the squad number and squad leader's name. "Deputy Commander Burke is handing out the packets with information pertaining to your first assignment." Payne paused and waited in semi-disgust as each of the squad leaders opened their packets as they received them. *Why couldn't they wait until they were told to open them?* Finally, all ten had been distributed and opened.

"As you can see, there is a listing of the level-three subjects assigned to each squad. However, more importantly, there is detailed information relating to Friday's assignment. For the time being, I want to focus on those subjects only. One very important piece of information is the aerial photograph. These were taken over the last week and, especially in certain cases, should help greatly in planning the specific action required to accomplish your mission.

"All subjects in this first round are no more than a hundred miles from our location. I want to get a few of these under our belts before we venture too far from home. I've reviewed each of your cases myself. I want the element of surprise on *our* side, whenever possible. The stronger the initial show of force, the less likely resistance will be in future operations.

"Beyond that, I'm giving you a certain amount of latitude in determining the best course of action for your team. We will be meeting again briefly at 1500 tomorrow afternoon to answer any final questions. That will still leave each of you plenty of time to assemble your team and hit the road.

"This afternoon, I want you to have individual meetings to bring your people up to speed, followed by sessions with your team leaders to determine the best plan for the subject you've been assigned.

"Any questions?" Silence. "Very well. I'll be available throughout the night on Friday. I'll be here for advice and to answer any questions you might have. Do not hesitate to call. I also want to be notified *before* you go in and *after* you come out. I want the total number of collected firearms and an injury report. Everything else can wait till Saturday morning. I want us all to meet back here at 0800 Saturday morning to debrief. This is the big time, gentlemen. I'll probably be briefing reporters before lunch on Saturday and I want to have something positive to tell them.

"Oh, one other thing. Deputy Commander Burke will be going along with squad five. It's important that we understand how things are working at the field level firsthand." Bobby fought the urge to chuckle. *Scott's gonna love that!* "If there are no questions, then, go ahead and meet with your squads and I'll see you back here tomorrow at 1500 hours."

The room began to clear quickly, but Payne wanted a word with Hatcher before he left. "Agent Hatcher, I'd like a minute with you, please."

Hatcher put his notebook back down and approached his boss. "Yes sir?"

By now, only Payne, Burke and Hatcher remained in the conference room. Payne leaned against a desk and spoke quietly. "Dennis, I want to make an impact with this first round of Collection operations."

"Yes sir, I understand."

"I hope you do, Dennis. I know I can trust you to do what's necessary." Hatcher looked puzzled. "What I'm telling you is that your subject has been carefully selected, based on his background and the number and types of firearms he's refused to surrender." Hatcher still looked puzzled, so Payne pushed further. "Dennis, I want you to go in hard on this guy. I want you to bring the full might of our Hazardous Operations Team to bear on him. Understood?"

Hatcher swallowed hard and looked Payne in the eye. It was now crystal clear what Payne was telling him to do—kill a man...and maybe other members of his family. Hatcher knew where Payne was coming from and understood how important it was for Collection to succeed. He also hoped that, at the end of the day, *he* would have some measure of control over the outcome of the op.

"Sir, I do understand and I'll get the job done."

Payne smiled broadly and put his hand on Hatcher's shoulder.

"Dennis, you've got a very bright future at ATF. I want you to know that."

"Thank you, sir."

"Deputy Commander Burke will spend a few minutes with you going over some logistical details," Payne added before gathering his notes and leaving the room.

As he strode down the hallway to his office, Payne felt pleased with how well the briefing had gone. His squad leaders appeared to be extremely confident and ready. It never occurred to him that their silence might have been because some of them had serious doubts about Collection and were literally sick to their stomachs over the prospect of breaking down doors to enforce it.

Payne had verified earlier in the day that no other HOTs would be conducting operations before next week. He wanted to make sure he wasn't going to be upstaged by anyone, especially Stan Collier. The timing of HOT's first action had been discussed with the Director and Monday was the *unofficial* "go date." Payne had replayed that conversation in his head several times, however, and could think of no reason to wait until then if his people were ready to go earlier than that.

******

"Each of your packets contains photocopies of the information on our first assignment, as well as an aerial photograph of the property. Go ahead and open them up. In fact, let's take five minutes to briefly familiarize ourselves with the subject."

Hatcher paused to let his team read. All of them were sharp enough to scan the information in that short period of time and form an initial impression. He'd given them four and a half minutes. Time to quiz his two team leaders. "Sykes, what jumps out at you?"

"Well," Jamal Sykes began, "former military, business owner, no prior record. Looks like a guy who's been around the block. Seems like a pretty serious dude."

"Yeah, so serious that he failed to turn in a total of *at least* twenty-three illegal weapons. Obviously, a guy with that many that we know about probably has a lot more. Lynch, how about you?"

"Boss, the guy's got a virtual compound here. The aerial shows six outbuildings. Those structures should make it easier to approach the house unseen."

Hatcher nodded, "Good point but we're going in after dark, so that's less important than it might otherwise be. Any questions?"

A hand from a team member. "Do we have a feel yet for the general scenario we'll be facing?"

"Not yet. I'm going to be meeting with Sykes and Lynch for the rest of the afternoon to develop the tactics we'll use. We'll review them tomorrow morning at 0800. Anything else?"

Another hand. "Looking at the list of contraband and taking the subject's military background into account, it appears that this could get real nasty, real quick. I know you haven't finalized a plan yet, but have you discussed the rules of engagement with Commander Payne?"

"Yeah, we covered that. Each squad has a certain amount of flexibility in determining the best course of action for its particular case. The bottom line is that we're authorized to use any and all means of force necessary. If hostilities commence, we end them as quickly as possible, so as to minimize the danger to all parties."

"How about his family? Says here he has two kids." The questions were flowing more freely now, to Hatcher's growing annoyance.

"The one thing I *have* determined is that we'll go in early a.m., with a dynamic entry. That way, the risk to children—and to us—

should be minimized. Now I'd like to meet with the two team leaders to hash out the rest of the details…oh, and one more thing," Hatcher added, as if it were an afterthought. "Deputy Commander Burke will be accompanying us. They want to get a firsthand feel for this type of operation at the field level." He knew that wouldn't go over well and was in the process of standing up when Scott Keller cleared his throat and began to speak.

"Excuse me. I'm assuming we don't know things like the locations or number of bedrooms, correct?"

Hatcher was beginning to understand why Payne and Burke weren't so high on this guy. "Ah, that's correct, Marshal."

"Agent Hatcher, with all due respect, why don't we just pick this guy up on his way to work and be done with it?"

The question, in front of the entire team, infuriated Hatcher. "Look, Marshal, our subject is the one who put his family in danger, not us. Picking him up outside his compound could endanger the lives of innocent people."

Scott was dumbfounded and refused to let it go. "Okay, well then why don't you monitor the family's activities and pick a time when the house is empty? Then you can 'collect' your firearms, wait for him to come home, and arrest him."

The rest of the team looked back and forth as each man spoke. Hatcher sensed this and realized his authority was being dangerously undermined at a time when unit cohesion had never been more critical. "Listen, Marshal Keller, our timeline doesn't allow for that. Furthermore, I am not going to sit here and justify this operation to you. I'm under the impression that you're attached to our team and will be going with us Friday night. If that's the case, please keep your reservations to yourself and let us do our job."

Hatcher *had* to say what he'd just said. Still, he realized that at least part of the reason he was in such a foul mood was that he knew Keller was right. They *were* rushing into this. He'd been caught up in the excitement of it himself, but had begun to have doubts. To make matters worse, Payne and Burke had essentially told him how to conduct the op and Burke would be riding shotgun, which meant Hatcher was merely a puppet—and *that* pissed him off. The difference was that the Marshal was in a position to speak out about it and Hatcher wasn't. Somebody had to get the job done.

Scott stayed seated while Hatcher, Sykes, and Lynch left the room. The rest of the team members scattered to the outskirts of the squad room as quickly as possible, putting maximum distance between themselves and the outspoken Marshal. The last thing they wanted to do was raise the ire of their boss. Scott looked around and figured out quickly that he was alone—in more ways than one. That was fine with him. Marshals did some of their best work that way.

* * * * * *

"Bill?" Judy Payne said as she waved her hand in front of her husband's face. "You haven't heard a damn thing I've said!"

Payne had been completely lost in thought. He and his wife were having dinner at a restaurant, a rare occurrence, and he knew he owed it to both of them to try to make the most of it...even though there were a million other places he'd rather be.

They'd met when Payne was a young, hard-charging agent and Judy's father was a Texas congressman almost certain to become the state's next senator. Soon after the Paynes' second child was born, however, the congressman was caught up in a sex scandal and his political career came to a screeching halt. In retrospect, it was the only major miscalculation of Bill Payne's career. Judy was an attractive woman and a good mother, but she and Bill didn't like each other very much.

"Yeah...sorry." Payne shook his head, as if that would clear the thoughts that were keeping him from giving his wife the attention she demanded. "Did you call the kids today?" The Paynes' son and daughter, both in college at the University of Oregon, were the last bits of glue holding Bill and Judy Payne's marriage together. They were only a couple hours' drive south of Portland, but it seemed that they chose, more and more, to stay at school for the weekends.

"I talked to Alison, but I had to leave a message for Matt. He's quite the man-about-town these days," she said. Alison was a senior and very much an adult. Their freshman son was a different story entirely. "Ali's doing fine—said she thinks she has a good chance at straight A's again this term."

"Do you think Matt's going to make it through school?"

"I don't know. I keep hoping he'll grow out of this wild phase. He's probably not any different than most boys his age, though."

"I know," Payne conceded. "Did Ali say any more about sending out résumés?" She'd hinted at the possibility of going to graduate school. Her dad thought she should go out into the world and make some money of her own first. Two kids in college at the same time was financially devastating and he had serious doubts about his ability to string it out for an additional two years.

"She was going to send out a few next week. Sounds like she's scrapped the idea of graduate school for now." Payne was relieved—that would be one less thing on his very full plate.

* * * * * *

The phone rang six times and Scott was about to hang up when a breathless voice answered. "Hello?"

"Bobby?"

"Yeah…who's this, Scott?"

"Yeah. You sound out of breath. What are you doing, chasing your wife around the house naked again? You know, Bobby, 'no' really does mean 'no.'"

"Yeah right. Not a lot of that going on. I was out in the garage taking care of my honey-do list. Got a feeling this weekend is gonna be pretty busy at work."

"I get that feeling too. Hey, I won't keep you long, but I've got a question for you."

"Shoot."

"What's your subject like?"

"Man, I've been trying not to think about that," Bobby answered. But he continued, as Scott knew he would. "Former Navy SEAL. Thirty-four, two kids, fourteen illegal firearms—how much else do you need to know?"

"Just this: How do you feel about having to bust in on him in the middle of the night?"

"Seriously, Scott? First of all, I'm not gonna 'bust in on him in the middle of the night.' The plan is to knock on his door while the sun's still up with a half-dozen well-armed agents standing behind me. What are you trying to do, make me feel worse about my job than I already do?"

He was exactly right and Scott knew it. As a Marshal, he could run away from this mess anytime he wanted to (he hoped). Bobby, on the other hand, was pretty much stuck with it. "I'm sorry. No, that's not what I'm trying to do. I just wanted to see how you were going to handle your bust, that's all."

"Why?"

"Because Hatcher's going to get someone killed, that's why."

"Talk to me, Scott."

Scott had thought a lot that afternoon about going over his concerns with Bobby. He didn't want to be an alarmist, but his experience told him that Hatcher, Payne, and Burke were dangerous. Maybe they weren't out to gun people down, but their attitudes could easily lead to that. It wasn't hard to see. Scott was trained to notice things and this was as obvious as a body in the middle of the floor. "Bobby, I didn't get all the details, but what I *do* know is that we're going to *dynamically* enter our subject's home in the middle of the night. Oh, and did I mention the fact that he has two kids and that we have no clue who's in what bedroom...or even where the bedrooms *are* in the house?"

Scott let his words sink in. He knew it would take Bobby only a few seconds to process the information.

"That's the plan?"

"In a nutshell. Like I said, I didn't get all the details, because Hatcher took his two team leaders off to work on specifics, but he went over what I've told you before they left. He had that much already worked out before he told any of us who we were even *after*!"

"Scott, you're not going to like my answer. Listen, I've got enough on my own plate to worry about without second-guessing Hatcher. Like I told you, the guy's not my first choice to have a beer with, but he knows his stuff. This thing will probably go off without a hitch. I don't blame you for being spooked, but we've got to trust the process."

Bobby didn't believe a word of what he'd just said and Scott knew it. He also knew there wasn't a damn thing his friend could do about it.

7

Portland, Oregon
Thursday, April 17

ALL THE TEAMS from HOT (Northwest) met with their squad leaders at 0800 for final briefing on the plans for Friday's Level Three Collection operations. The rest of the morning would be spent drilling. In the afternoon, the team's equipment would be prepped and checked. This was not an inconsequential task, given the amount of gear that traveled with them. Everything *had* to work. That was why the final checks were performed today, rather than on the day of the operation. If there were any problems (and there usually were), it was better to find out now and have twenty-four hours to secure a replacement or make repairs.

Scott sat in complete silence throughout the briefing. There really was nothing for him to say anyway and he didn't want to put any more doubt in the squad members' minds than he knew already existed. He'd learned that lesson the night before during his conversation with Bobby.

As squad five performed its drills, Scott went through the motions but found he had a hard time concentrating. They were running the same drill repeatedly now, in preparation for tomorrow night, and this nightmare had suddenly become all too real. At first, he had decided to view his assignment to HOT as a break from the regimen he'd followed for the last three years. He'd hoped to use the time away from the USMS to look back on his Marshals career and reflect upon his future. Now he was preparing to do something that he hated the thought of. The only bright spot to this otherwise dreary day would be his afternoon appointment with Marshal Filson.

* * * * * *

Scott's mood improved with each step as he strode confidently through the U.S. Marshals Service Oregon District Office. The waves, hellos, and handshakes did great things for his spirits, especially after having felt as if he'd been put through the wringer for the last ten days. *Has it been only ten days?*

"Well, well...look what shows up when you don't have a gun!" It was Kathy's favorite greeting and, as the Marshal's secretary, she could get away with it (as well as just about anything else she wanted to). It was also music to his ears.

"Ah, you know you love me," he jabbed back at her.

"Scotty, you've figured me out. But we'll have to make sure Meg doesn't find out. You know how mean pregnant women can be."

"Mean as snakes," he whispered back.

"How are things across town?"

Scott rolled his eyes and shook his head. "You don't want to know."

"He's expecting you. Go on in."

Scott ducked his head inside the open door and knocked lightly. U.S. Marshal Doug Filson of the District of Oregon (D/OR) was leaning back in his chair with his hands locked behind his head, cradling the phone between his right shoulder and his ear. Obviously trying to terminate the call, the Marshal waved Scott over and indicated that he take a seat. After a few minutes, he hung up the phone, exhaled loudly, and stood up to shake his deputy's hand.

"Scott, how are you?"

"Do you really want to know, sir?"

All of a sudden, Scott felt like a whiner. *Should I really make a formal request for a change of assignment?* After some small talk, he didn't want to put the subject off any longer.

"Boss, I've been dreading this for one reason: the last thing in the world I want to do is sound like a whiner. You know how I feel about this whole 'Collection' business, so I'd be lying if I told you I didn't go into this thing with a bit of an attitude. But I really tried to give the ATF guys a chance. I figured they were just doing their job. They obviously had nothing to do with the politics of it."

Filson knew this wasn't easy for his deputy. The one thing the kid had never been was a complainer. But this might be good for him. The Marshal knew that a law enforcement career required a lot of a person—including having to do things that were distasteful from time to time.

Scott continued. "There *are* some sharp guys over there. In fact, I really hit it off with one of the squad leaders I've been working with. As I see it, though, they've got two major problems. The first is their mission. I'll never believe they're doing the right thing. But the second is a lot worse: a couple of people in positions of authority seem like they're enjoying it too much."

"Yeah, I've met Bill Payne a few times and I can picture him being pretty gung ho about an 'opportunity' like this."

"It's not just Payne. His deputy's a carbon copy and the squad leader I'm working with now seems like he's almost giddy about the idea of breaking down doors. Sir, these guys are going to get someone killed! They've got a recipe for disaster on their hands and nobody in a position to do anything about it seems to care."

"Scott, I know you're pretty pumped up over this, but are you sure it's that bad? You've only been over there for what, a week and a half?"

"Let me put it this way. Tomorrow, in the middle of the night, we're going to raid the home of a decorated veteran to take his guns away. We know he has kids, but we don't know who sleeps in what bedroom. In fact, we don't even know where the bedrooms are. *Why* don't we know where they are? Because no one has reconned the area. *Why* haven't they? Because their 'timeline doesn't allow for it.' *Their timeline doesn't allow for it!* That's a direct quote! Do you see where I'm coming from, sir?"

Filson put his head in his hands and rubbed his temples. "You know there's absolutely nothing I can do, Scott. This is ATF's show."

"Yes sir, I realize that." He paused. *Man, I hate doing this!* "What I'm asking you to do is transfer me back over here." He noticed a strange look on his boss's face and continued to explain. "I just can't be a part of what's going on over there, sir. Maybe you'd have another deputy volunteer for it."

"What if I don't, Scott? There's got to be a reason given for the switch. Should I just say that you're 'philosophically opposed to their mission'?"

Scott was both hurt and slightly pissed off. "When have I ever asked for special consideration of any kind, sir? I don't think the Marshals should be involved in this mess at all, but since we have to be, I know for a fact that *I* can't do it. In the military, following an order in combat that you know to be illegal and morally wrong can get you court-martialed. I think time will prove that's exactly what we're being asked to do here."

"You know this might not help your future plans in the Marshals Service any, don't you?"

"Sir, I honestly don't care. I'd rather be able to live with myself."

"I know, Scott. That's one of the reasons you're as good as you are. I'll get to work on this as soon as I can. It might take a little while, though."

Scott knew that was true, but dreaded the thought of one more day at HOT. "I understand, sir. I'd appreciate anything you can do. I *really* would."

* * * * * *

"How're you holding up?" Don inquired as Mike sat down and motioned to the bartender that he would have the same thing Don was having. Mike had called earlier and asked him to meet for a drink at one of their favorite watering holes. Even though he was buried with work, Don accepted. He'd come to realize how much his friend needed him these days.

"I'm actually doing pretty well…really," Mike tried to assure him. A lie and Don knew it. In truth, Mike had found it increasingly harder to concentrate on his business and he felt as if he was shutting his family out—especially Sarah. That couldn't happen; he wouldn't let it.

Seeing that Don was unconvinced by his assurance, he continued. "Look, I've only got a couple of 'illegal' guns in the house. Besides, I've been hearing more and more about ATF plans to pull back on their operations." In fact, Mike had heard very little to that effect; he just wanted to keep Don calm so that Sarah wouldn't find out what he'd done… or failed to do. Never having lied systematically to anyone before, Mike was very uncomfortable doing so. This wasn't the first time in his life he'd discovered that a lie could perform a "greater good," yet he would still tell his children until the day he died that it was *never* okay to lie. They would find out soon enough, on their own, the realities of life.

Don still hadn't bought it, but decided to let it go for the time being. He could tell that Mike had something else on his mind that he was having a hard time bringing up. "Mike, there's something else, isn't there?"

"Well, yeah, but it's got nothing to do with this other mess. Sarah and I have been talking a lot about who we would want to be guardians for the kids if anything happened to us. We've had a trust set up for several years now and my parents are the current guardians. The only problem is their age. They wouldn't be able to keep up with the kids," Mike added with a smile. He hated doing this kind of thing. In fact, he'd never been good at opening up to *anyone* except Sarah. "We'd like you and Jenny to be the guardians and trustees. Of course, this would come into play only if something happened to both of us at the same time. I mean, we're talking *highly unlikely*."

Don was stunned and it showed. Mike pounded down the rest of his beer and signaled for another. "Well," Don began, "I guess the first thing I would say is that this is all kind of creepy, in light of what's been going on over the last week or so."

"Don, one has nothing to do with the other." That was at least partially true. Mike had always been concerned about what would happen to the children upon his and Sarah's simultaneous deaths, as unlikely as that prospect might have been. He also wanted to see that his assets went to his *kids*, to the greatest extent possible, rather than to the government threatening his freedom. His estate was large enough to make that a potential issue. Mike had done a superb job of saving and investing and his estate was set up to minimize the effect of taxation upon it. He'd also been a believer in life insurance since the minute he found out Sarah was pregnant. Responsibility was part of Mike Niculescu's DNA and it was apparent in every aspect of his life. "There would be plenty of money available, too, so you wouldn't have to worry about finances," he assured his friend.

Waving that off, Don said, "Mike, we'd be honored." Don knew there was really no one else for them to consider. Sarah's parents were older as well and neither of them was in great health. "Just let me talk to Jenny about it first. I can let you know first thing tomorrow, okay?"

"Sure, that's fine," Mike answered, thankful to have that conversation over with.

* * * * * *

Washington, D.C.
Thursday, April 17

Attorney General Charles Martinez leaned back in his chair and stretched. It was late and he was still working—again. There were many facets of this job that demanded his attention and he enjoyed most of them. Reality sometimes reared its ugly head, though, and he had to prioritize. Lately, the number one priority had been the firearm Collection process underway over at ATF.

Martinez had played a major role in convincing the President that confiscation was the right thing to do. Though not his idea originally, he came to embrace the concept early on. From a political standpoint, it had legs. Many people were convinced that it was a necessary step in stemming the tide of gun violence in the country. Up until now, though, the American public had been unable to bring themselves to do what *had* to be done to solve the problem.

The idea began as a "brainstorming" policy discussion and gained momentum from there. After a lengthy public-relations campaign, polls indicated that this was the direction in which the public wanted to move. That was the easy part. The hard part had been putting the mechanism in place to accomplish it.

What Martinez had found, however, was that his ATF personnel were absolute professionals. There was very little he needed to worry about personally. John Mullin and his people went to work and got the job done. Always one to reward loyalty and hard work, Martinez promised himself to do everything within his power to see those people advance. The Collection process was divisive and even within the ATF he knew that there were some who disagreed with the policy. But those who had the proper levels of faith and obedience would be well taken care of.

Martinez *was* a little apprehensive about the nuts and bolts of the process, however. As fully behind this as the public appeared to be, he knew full well that the Administration was only one "accident" away from losing that support. Every poll supported what they were doing, but the same polls also showed no sign of a tolerance for body bags. Wasn't that just like the American people? They wanted results but didn't have the stomach to do what had to be done to achieve them.

President Nichols had nominated Martinez for Attorney General for a variety of reasons. He was bright, capable, and a minority. As a bonus, Charlie Martinez was both handsome and charismatic, two traits that had benefited his political career greatly. More than a few rumors were floating around New Jersey (and now D.C.) regarding his "extracurricular activities." Thankfully, none of them had stuck. Martinez, and nearly everyone else, figured that if he could keep his nose clean, there was no end in sight for his political future. Many members of the media in the know had already begun to discuss him as a potential presidential candidate. He liked the sound of that!

The Attorney General had been in close contact with Director

Mullin since the Collection process began and he knew that, so far, things had gone exactly as planned. There had been a lull in the action for a week or so following the initial raids, but according to Mullin, things were going to heat up again starting Monday. That was probably a good thing. Despite the contingent at ATF (as well as among the President's advisors) that wanted to take the process slowly by letting people "come to their senses" and turn the guns in themselves, Martinez understood that doing so would accomplish nothing more than display a crippling lack of resolve.

* * * * * *

Portland, Oregon
Thursday, April 17

Don didn't tell Jenny that he had something important to discuss with her until after the kids were in bed. Prior experience had taught him that she would drive herself crazy wondering about it if he had. This was their "quiet time"—an hour or so at the end of their day to really talk to each other without interruption. Their children were the most important things in their lives, but they'd always recognized the importance of staying connected to each other as well.

Don turned the television off as Jenny came downstairs from Stephanie's bedroom, shaking her head and smiling. "I swear, that little stinker is so cute, sometimes I can hardly stand it."

Don nodded his head. "I know...and sometimes she's just a little stinker." His wife laughed and piled onto the couch beside him.

"How was Mike doing when you talked to him tonight?"

"Okay, I guess. He's still not himself though...not that I can blame him. I couldn't do what he's doing. Can you imagine having the urge to look over your shoulder every five minutes?"

"No, honey, I can't. I feel so sorry for him."

"I do too, but let's not forget the fact that he *did* bring this on himself."

"Oh, stop it. Let's not go through that again."

Don raised his hands in surrender. "Okay, okay. Anyway, he laid something pretty heavy on me this afternoon. He and Sarah want us to be guardians for the kids." Letting that sink in, Don waited for Jenny to make the same connection that he had made initially.

"Good Lord, what does he think is going to happen?"

"That's what I thought. He says they're just updating their trust."

"Don't you think the timing's a little funny, with what's been going on?"

"Yeah, I do, but I guess it doesn't matter. They really want us to do it. He said his and Sarah's parents are too old and they aren't that close to anyone else."

"What did you tell him?"

"That I needed to talk to you first and that I felt honored to be asked."

"No kidding. Well, obviously, we say yes, right?"

"Yeah, I think so. I mean, the chances of it ever becoming an issue are almost nil, but I do think we should step up to the plate."

8

Portland, Oregon
Friday, April 18

Meg Keller decided to take part of the morning off from work to stay home with her husband. Neither could remember the last time they'd had breakfast together on a weekday, so it felt a little strange. Still, especially for Meg, it was nice. The further her pregnancy progressed, the more important little things like this were. Scott had been told, along with the rest of squad five, to come in at 1:00 p.m. They would have a team meeting to work on the details of the activity planned for that night. After that, whoever was able to would catch a couple hours of sleep.

Unable to help himself, Scott still rolled out of bed at five and ran three miles. After his run, he hit the weight machine in his garage for another hour. *Might as well get a good workout in.* It was likely to be a long and stressful day. While her husband showered and dressed, Meg made his favorite breakfast: bacon, eggs, and home-fried potatoes.

Sitting down at the kitchen table with a cup of coffee and a huge breakfast in front of him, Scott thought that he could really get used to this. "This is great, honey!" he said between forkfuls.

"Thanks. I do try to please my man," she added, smiling half-heartedly.

"Uh-oh, what's wrong?" Meg just shook her head and wiped away a tear. "Honey, what…?" And then the tears began coming in waves. Now truly confused, Scott put his fork down and pushed his chair back. Reaching out to her, he guided his wife to his lap and held her tightly. All his instincts told him to keep his mouth shut and just hold her.

After less than a minute, Meg pushed away from him and sat up, wiping her eyes with a napkin. "I'm sorry," she said. "I know you've been in a lot more dangerous situations than this before, but...I don't know, maybe it's because of the baby, but I'm just really worried."

Trying to think of something to say to comfort her, Scott came up with, "Look, sweetie, this is probably one of the *least* dangerous things I've done in a long time." He meant it, too. But Meg wasn't buying it.

"Oh, yeah? Then why do you have to go busting in there in the middle of the night?" The question was met by silence. "I'm not stupid, Scott. Remember, I grew up around this stuff. I just don't know if I can get through this for the next twenty-five years...not with kids in the picture. It really makes me appreciate what Mom went through for so long."

Life had changed for Scott Keller the moment he married Meg (for the better, to be sure). As it does for every man, marriage meant that Scott now had to consider someone else's feelings and that didn't come easily. When she became pregnant, however, things changed again—this time exponentially. His life was no longer his own, to do with as he pleased. Other people counted on his being there for them...every day, not just from time to time.

Afraid of making promises that he knew he couldn't keep, Scott filed the matter away for future consideration. He *would* think about this later and give it the attention it deserved. Nothing was worth jeopardizing the well-being of the woman he loved and their new baby. For now, though, he didn't need any more to think about than he already had on his mind. He really wasn't worried for his own safety tonight. There was no need to be. Instead, he was worried about squad five's subject and *his* family.

"Sweetie, listen to me. This guy's not some psychotic escaped felon or anything. It'll be a piece of cake compared to what I'm used to. I promise."

"Well, then, why are you *treating* him like a psychotic felon?"

Scott was stunned by the accusation. "*I'm* not treating him like that!"

Meg hadn't intended to insult him; she knew how strongly he felt about what was going on. Still, she felt that her question deserved an answer—from *someone*. "I know you're not. I didn't mean that. But I do think people like you should be screaming at the top of your lungs to let everyone know how wrong this is."

She was right—again. The American people had developed a wolf-pack mentality. The rabid many were running down the scared few and it was something that wasn't supposed to happen in the United States of America. This was madness and someone *did* need to stop it. But it wouldn't be him and it wouldn't be now.

"Honey, I *have* to go tonight."

"I know you do."

* * * * * *

Mike was poring over a house plan spread out over the hood of his pickup truck when his cell phone rang. Uncharacteristically annoyed by many things these days, he grabbed the phone and looked at the caller ID. When he saw it was Sarah calling, it took the wind out of his sails immediately.

"Hi there…got good news for you," she announced. "Your mom just called and offered to pick up the kids this afternoon and take them to the cabin. That means you and I will actually have some time alone." George and Ana had bought the cabin several years before as a place to escape to. It was a scenic hour-and-a-half drive from their home in Portland. Going to the cabin meant total relaxation—there wasn't even a telephone, which was just fine with them.

"That'll be nice," Mike said honestly. He felt he hadn't been paying enough attention to Sarah lately.

"I thought so too. Anyway, I was going to go out and pick up some steaks for dinner to have with a bottle of that good cabernet we've been saving."

"Sounds great. I'll make sure I'm home by five. Oh, I almost forgot. I heard from Don this morning and they agreed to do the guardian thing. I called the attorney and they're going to have the amendment ready this afternoon. Can you get by there today to sign the papers?"

"Sure. I hate thinking about this stuff any longer than I have to."

"I know, but at least it'll feel good to have it over with. I'll swing by and sign today too. I love you."

"I love you too," she answered, smiling to herself. He sounded so much more relaxed than he had lately. Tonight was going to be special.

******

The HOT (Northwest) Headquarters had been a beehive of mostly meaningless activity in the early afternoon. As was always the case, nervousness and self-doubt caused a certain percentage of those in charge to obsess and over-prepare. As evening approached, however, things began to heat up. By eight o'clock, two squads had completed their missions and returned to headquarters; and by the time squad five left at midnight, three more had returned—including Bobby's squad—all without incident, Scott was happy to hear. In each case, the squad leader was summoned to the sixth floor to be debriefed by Commander Payne.

The inevitable stories ensued. Those who'd already done it let off the steam of relief and those who hadn't yet "been there" tried to convince themselves that everything was going to be all right. There were high-fives, jokes, and (Scott noticed as he glanced around the room) several cases of agents mocking their subjects by holding their hands up in the classic surrender pose. It wasn't that he begrudged these people letting off steam after a job well done—he'd done so himself, more than once. The problem he had was reconciling the specifics of what they'd done with the fact that they laughed about it. Tonight was going to be a long one.

******

True to his word, Mike turned into his driveway a few minutes before five. He was looking forward to a nice quiet evening with his wife, a huge rib eye steak and a great bottle of wine. In that order.

Sarah was making a salad when Mike walked in. "Hey there, sweet thing," he said, smiling as he came into the kitchen.

"Hey there yourself," his wife replied, hugging him tightly. "It's been a while since you came home from work in a good mood. How were things at the job site today?"

"Things are really starting to come together pretty well. Looks like we'll come in right on schedule and I don't think the cost overruns are going to be nearly as big a deal as I did a couple weeks ago." He looked her in the eye, brushing her hair away from her face, and kissed her gently. "I guess I've also started to realize just how much I've got to be happy about."

"Yes, you do…and so do I." She looked up at her husband and kissed him passionately for a long time. "Wow…if someone doesn't throw some cold water on us, we'll never get to dinner."

"Problem is, there's never a guy with a bucket of cold water around when you need one, but you'd better save your energy for tonight, lady. You know how my thoughts turn to love after I get a belly full of wine and red meat."

"Yeah, I know," Sarah answered with a devilish smile. "That's when I like you best!"

Mike truly enjoyed grilling. They cooked out often and it was always relaxing to him, especially when the weather was nice. They'd built a huge patio and they really got the most out of it. With the smell of sizzling steaks behind him and a glass of Woodford Reserve bourbon in his hand, Mike surveyed his property from the patio. It occurred to him that this was the most relaxed he'd been in months. He really was fortunate (not lucky—there was a difference) to have the things and the family that he had. Patton came up and nudged his leg. "Hey, boy, sorry we didn't get a steak for you." The dog, as always, had his nose in the air to catch every whiff he could of Mike's cooking. "Don't worry. I guarantee you Mom won't eat all of hers."

Dinner was perfect and they made it most of the way through a second bottle of wine. Relaxing on the couch together afterward, Sarah looked up at her husband. "Honey, have you ever thought about what you want to do when you quit building?"

"Sure. I plan on sitting back and living it up on Social Security. Why?"

"Somehow I don't think so," she said, smiling. "I don't know. I just wonder what it will feel like when the kids are grown up and…"

"You're scared it's going to be boring, aren't you? What's the world coming to when a guy can't sit around the house for the last twenty or thirty years of his life in his underwear?" Mike asked, nibbling her ear.

Sarah turned serious. Taking her husband's face in her hands, she looked deeply into his eyes. "I'm the luckiest woman I know. I want to spend the rest of my life with you, being as happy as we are tonight. Now make love to me."

He did, after ceremoniously carrying her to their bedroom. Good thing it was downstairs! With as much alcohol as he'd drunk, he had serious doubts about his ability to climb stairs *alone*, much less while carrying his wife. It had been a while since they'd felt so close to each other. Tonight had been the kind of "quality time" both knew they needed more of. Times like this couldn't wait till the kids were grown up. Besides, Mike reminded his wife, by that time he'd be too old to participate in the festivities. Drifting off to sleep in each other's arms, they were more content than they'd been in a long time.

* * * * * *

There was very little nervousness apparent among squad five's members, Scott noticed. They were efficient, professional, and confidence-inspiring. Then again, perhaps that was all a matter of perspective. He supposed that a Collection subject would view them as cold, detached, and ruthless. Of course, the "bad guys" were *supposed* to be scared of the good guys, weren't they?

He watched as the team members readied equipment and staged it near the squad room's entrance. Once all the gear was ready, a final assignment briefing was held in which Hatcher made sure there was absolutely no confusion regarding duties and responsibilities.

Burke showed up with a bagful of gear just in time for the briefing. It was understood that he would observe and act as "Auxiliary Scene Commander," but nothing more. It would make no sense for him to enter the subject's residence, they were told. He hadn't trained with the team and that could create timing problems. *Or worse*, Scott thought. He had a feeling there was more to the story than that. It was probably safe to assume that Ray Burke had *not* been made Deputy Commander because of his tactical abilities.

HOT "squad vans" were impressive vehicles indeed. Studying the well-thought-out design in detail for the first time, Scott couldn't help being envious. As with nearly everything else having to do with ATF's elite unit, no expense had been spared in providing for their transportation. Based on extra-long, heavy-duty box trucks and powered by huge turbo-diesel engines, each vehicle was outfitted to carry one fully equipped HOT squad. Along each side of the cargo area was a row of comfortable bench seats, with room for six. There was also room for a passenger up front, giving the hybrid vehicle a seating capacity of fourteen. Behind the passenger area were racks and cabinets, up both sides and along the ceiling as well, holding everything from weapons to battering rams. These trucks had been designed so that HOT could carry out virtually any potential mission without having to return to headquarters for additional equipment.

The one thing they were *not* designed to do was carry prisoners. For that, a "chase vehicle" (in this case, a Chevrolet Suburban) would always follow, usually carrying two of the team members. Tonight, however, Deputy Commander Burke would drive the chase vehicle alone. Burke had insisted on it, telling Hatcher he should ride with his team so he could spend every possible moment going over the plan with them.

It was midnight, time to move out. The drive was about forty-five minutes at this time of night. They would park a short distance away and make any necessary final preparations there before moving toward the subject's residence on foot. The men around him were solemn and serious but not nervous or scared. Scott felt a burning in the pit of his stomach that he'd rarely felt before. There had almost always been a healthy mixture of adrenaline and excitement as operations began, but this time it was different. The excitement had been replaced by dread.

The driver pulled the squad van over into a gravel turnout along the deserted county road, about two hundred fifty yards from the subject's driveway. A few final questions were answered and the team members checked their equipment. Finally, Hatcher gave the "lock and load" order. Scott gripped his M4 tightly, puzzled by the way he began to feel as he did so. The sickness in his stomach was dissipating, at least partially, as his professional instincts took over. Developed over years of military and law enforcement training, these were the instincts that kept people like Scott from receiving posthumous awards. They *were* critical to his survival, he reminded himself, though this was something he didn't want to feel comfortable doing.

It was time to go. Not a word was spoken as the back doors were opened and the team members filed out. The time for talking was past. Slowly and silently, according to plan, the squad spread out and began to move toward the residence, working its way through the timber that screened the house from view.

A hundred feet from the house, half of the squad moved around toward the back and positioned itself near the sliding glass doors. The other half stationed itself in front. Two of the team in front moved directly in front of the huge plate glass window looking into the dining room, while the rest lined up behind those with the battering ram at the front door. All were linked by headset microphones.

It was at this point that a dog began barking wildly from a large chain-link dog run about fifty feet away from the agents in back of the house. Quickly, one of the agents ran toward the barking dog and fired three suppressed and well-aimed shots. The dog yelped once and lay quiet. "What's happening?" demanded Hatcher from the front.

"It's under control, sir. The dog's down."

"Roger that. Two ready?" "Ready," came the reply from Jamal Sykes in back. "One ready?" "Ready," answered Wayne Lynch at the front window. "Okay, we're a go on my three-count."

******

Normally a light sleeper, Mike was slow to sit up when he heard Patton's barking. *Way too much alcohol*, he admitted to himself. Slowly, the fog of sleep began to lift as he sat on the edge of the bed. There wasn't much that would make his dog bark like that. Every now and then a deer would come out of the timber and into the yard, but when that happened, Mike usually had to go out and chase the animal away to make Patton stop barking. *Did he yelp before he went quiet?* Wait a minute...he was sure he just heard the sound of someone stepping on the gravel between the house and Patton's dog run! *What the hell?* he wondered as he reached for the keypad of his Gun Vault safe.

******

Almost simultaneously, two agents slammed the battering ram into the front door and glass shattered at the rear of the house. The front door required two more hits before the hinges gave, making that group of agents the last to enter.

Immediately, the alarm system's deafening siren kicked on, but Mike didn't even notice it. The Glock was out of the safe now and Sarah had just sat bolt upright. Instinctively, Mike grabbed her and rolled both of them off the side of the bed opposite the door, just as a black-clad figure appeared in the doorway. Mike raised the Glock from behind the bed. With no time to activate the weapon's light, he trained the laser on the threat entering their bedroom. *He's got a gun!* Mike centered the laser's red dot on the man's face and pressed the trigger twice. The body slumped to its knees and then fell over backward, out of the doorway.

Sarah was screaming now, crouching in a ball on the floor. Mike glanced toward her and then caught movement out of the corner of his right eye. Before the dead man's body had hit the floor, another was in the doorway. "NOOOOOO…!" he screamed at the invader as he moved toward his wife.

Up came his pistol again, firing repeatedly as he covered the few feet between Sarah and him. The figure in the doorway staggered backward a step and returned fire as Mike fell on top of Sarah. All he could think of was to cover her. *I can protect her from this!*

Searing pain shot through every inch of his body as he lay there, unable to move. His eyes were turned away from the bedroom door and toward his wife's blood-soaked face. He'd done it. He'd made it to her. She'd be all right now, he thought, as his eyes closed.

"Clear!" Wayne Lynch screamed from inside the doorway, his smoking M4 still trained on the two motionless forms. "Clear!" came again from behind him. All lights were switched on. Less than sixty seconds had elapsed from the time of entrance, though it would always seem like much longer to those involved.

* * * * * *

Scott was with team two, which had entered through the sliding glass door at the back of the house. Following the plan, *that* half of squad five moved quickly through the kitchen and family room and then began to ascend the staircase, with Scott bringing up the rear. He'd just set foot on the second floor when he heard the first shots below them.

* * * * * *

Burke had, of course, caught bits and pieces of what went on over his headset. After the alarm sounded and the first shots were fired, he quickly radioed Payne and advised a call to the county sheriff's office to notify them that it was an ATF operation. They'd have to be prepared for that in the future. Most of these subjects were likely to have alarm systems and that meant local law enforcement rushing onto the scene, creating all kinds of potential problems. The Commander also reminded Burke that, based on the way things had gone down, he had an important task to carry out before leaving the premises—something Burke didn't need to be reminded of.

* * * * * *

Two agents checked the subjects for a pulse and took the pistol from the dead man's hand, while two others quickly moved to their friend and partner, who lay lifeless on the floor. "Roberts is gone, sir," announced one of them, looking up at their squad leader.

"Damnit!" Hatcher screamed.

"What's your situation?" It was Burke's voice buzzing in his ear.

"Roberts is dead, sir. Both subjects are as well and there's no one else in the house. One other agent took shots to the plates. He's fine."

"I'll be right up. Have everybody hang tight *inside* till I get there!" Burke ordered.

By now, the entire squad had moved into the huge master bedroom. Scott noticed first the dead agent on the floor. Sean Roberts was the youngest member of squad five. He'd turned twenty-four a couple of weeks earlier and had a fiancée that he'd talked a lot about. Then Scott's eyes were drawn beyond the king-size bed. As he moved to the foot of the bed to get a clear view of the carpeted floor on the other side of it, the picture became eerily clear to him.

He saw a tall, muscular man, with numerous bullet wounds, draped over the body of a woman. *His last act was to protect her... how could this have happened?* Then he noticed something. It was a strange thing to focus on, with all that had just occurred, but his eyes were drawn to it. On the man's right shoulder was a slightly faded tattoo, the familiar eagle, globe, and anchor emblem, right under the letters USMC. "Semper Fi, brother...Semper Fi," Scott whispered to himself before turning to walk out of the room.

Scott kept walking. He needed air—quickly. He walked out into the cool breeze and looked around at the house and yard. It was absolutely gorgeous…the kind of home everyone dreamed of someday being able to afford. Scott knew very little about Mike Niculescu, but he had a feeling that none of this had been given to him. *They have kids too. Thank God they weren't around to witness this—but where are they?* He thought of Meg and their baby…and, for the first time in a long time, tears began to flow from Deputy U.S. Marshal Scott Keller's eyes.

He stood there looking up at the stars and thinking. After a few minutes he wiped his eyes and turned to head back into the house. He wanted to get a better feel for the people who had just died defending their constitutional rights. Fifty feet or so to his left, Scott heard a noise from inside the shop, as if something had been knocked over. Looking in that direction, he saw a flashlight beam through a shop window. *What the hell?* Scott brought his M4 to the low ready position and approached the shop carefully. He had no idea who was making the noise, but he would take no chances.

******

As soon as the squad had moved out toward the house, Burke had opened the back of the Suburban and pulled out a fairly large locked, rectangular plastic case that he'd brought along without anyone else's knowledge—the reason he'd insisted on being alone in the chase vehicle. After he'd called Payne with the sitrep, Burke grabbed the heavy case and double-timed it toward Niculescu's shop.

Always prepared to accomplish whatever task he was given, he'd brought along the necessary tools to pick deadbolt locks, which he used to gain access to the shop in just a few minutes. Then it was a matter of finding a suitable spot to hide the case. Burke knew he didn't have much time before Hatcher and his men got antsy and would wonder where he was. They'd want to begin searching the premises and Burke wanted them to…just not until he'd given them something important to find.

After a couple of minutes looking around the shop with a flashlight, Burke decided to hide the case inside the closet of the shop's small upstairs apartment—not the best spot, perhaps; but it could really be anywhere on the premises to serve its purpose. Burke hustled back down the stairwell and turned toward the door. As he turned, he brushed against a shovel hung on the wall, knocking it to the floor. The clattering when it hit the concrete seemed as loud as the premises alarm had been. Burke nervously reached down, grabbed the shovel off the floor and carefully put it back on the wall. He calmed himself and moved toward the door again.

* * * * * *

Scott approached the door of the shop just as a man was pulling the door closed with his back to him. Scott knew the squad was inside the house and he had completely forgotten about Burke. He threw up the M4 and hit the flashlight switch on the vertical foregrip, nearly blinding a shocked Ray Burke as he turned around and looked directly into the 200-lumen beam of light.

Scott had just started to blurt out, "Don't move," when he saw who it was and lowered the carbine.

"Jesus, Keller. What are you doing?" Burke stammered, almost certain he'd soiled himself.

"I heard a noise and investigated. Isn't that what we're supposed to do?" Scott asked disgustedly.

"You were *supposed* to wait inside as I instructed," Burke answered, trying to sound authoritative. *Had Keller been standing there for a while, or did he just walk up?*

"Yeah, well, I didn't get that memo," Scott shot back. He was in no mood to take shit from Burke. "Besides, what were you doing in the shop?"

Burke fidgeted. "I…uh, was just trying to get an idea of where his safes might be. Turns out there's a huge one out here," he added unconvincingly.

"Why didn't you turn the lights on instead of sneaking around with a flashlight?"

"I wasn't 'sneaking around,' Keller, and I don't have to explain myself to *you*. Now let's get inside. I need to talk to the entire squad for a minute." Scott grudgingly obliged, but not before glancing back at the door of the shop as they walked away and wondering what Burke had been up to.

Burke wondered whether or not Keller could have seen what he'd been doing, but then realized he had other things to worry about right now—like how bad a mess he had on his hands. The agents assembled in the bedroom grew considerably more quiet upon his arrival. After surveying the scene and asking a few questions of various squad members, Burke pulled Dennis Hatcher outside the bedroom to talk privately.

"All right, listen. I want the house and outbuildings turned inside out looking for contraband. Just so we're on the same page, the subject killed Roberts *before* his wife was shot, right?" Hatcher was slow to respond. "Look, Dennis, these are likely to be the first fatalities in the Collection process. The way things are handled could have a lot to do with the level of public support we maintain."

"Yes sir," answered the loyal squad leader.

Burke nodded his approval and led them back into the bedroom. "Okay, people, I want every square inch of the house and *all* outbuildings searched. I mean open every drawer, cabinet and closet in the place. Also, get the two safes open in the room down the hall, as well as the one out in the shop. My guess is they're full. This man had a large number of illegal firearms and I want them collected." He paused for a moment. "And one other thing—I don't want you discussing the details of tonight's action with *anyone*. Is that clear?" Heads nodded all around.

Burke turned to walk out of the house. He had to get back to headquarters. There was a lot to discuss with the Commander before tomorrow's news conference. Scott had slipped out of the bedroom just before Burke finished handing down his commandments and was waiting near the front door. The look on his face made Burke more than a little uncomfortable, knowing what the Marshal may have witnessed. For that reason, and the fact that he didn't care for the man at all, Burke walked past him without saying anything.

"Commander Burke?"

"Yes?" Burke answered, turning partially around to face the Marshal and very clearly annoyed.

"Was it worth it?" Burke gave him only a puzzled look, so Scott pressed him. "Tonight. Was it worth it?"

"I don't know what you're talking about, Keller. Now I've got to get back to headquarters." It was another attempt to sound confident and in charge, though it struck Scott as neither. As Burke slammed the door of the Suburban, he thought about what a pain in the ass this guy might yet turn out to be.

* * * * * *

The van was tomb-like on the ride back, the silence nearly overwhelming. Part of the reason was fatigue, but the primary cause was a collective state of shock. They had helped load three dead bodies into ambulances. Tonight would leave a mark on every one of them. Not only had they lost a friend and partner, but they'd also caused the deaths of two people who, until just a few months ago, had probably never broken a law in their lives.

Worse yet, to Hatcher's chagrin, only two illegal firearms were collected, including the one taken directly from the subject. On the other hand, a large amount of homemade explosives was discovered in the apartment above the shop.

9

Portland, Oregon
Saturday, April 19

PAYNE AND BURKE both looked like zombies. Burke hadn't slept a wink yet and Payne had managed only about two hours' worth. The Niculescu raid had been the only one conducted that had resulted in fatalities. Shots had been fired in two of the other nine operations, but no HOT agents were hit and the two subjects involved had suffered relatively minor wounds.

Last night was a milestone for the ATF and the Hazardous Operations Teams in particular. In Payne's mind, it sent the message that they were serious about collecting illegal firearms. No longer would the ATF be taunted and dared.

Still, he was savvy enough to know that the potential for negative fallout existed. He'd called the Director very early this morning and he was sure that by now both the Attorney General and the President knew as well. That was fine. Payne just needed to get the facts straight in his mind in order to deflect the inevitable criticism to come.

Things like this were bound to happen. These operations didn't go on in a vacuum and a criminal's actions could never be predicted. His people had done well—exactly as they'd been trained to do. Nobody had better make this Niculescu character a victim, especially in view of the fact that he'd killed one of Payne's men...a man sent there to collect illegal weapons that a *law-abiding* citizen would have turned in. No, neither Payne nor his men had committed an error of any kind. They were doing nothing more than the job the American people had asked them to do and Niculescu was no less a criminal than a drug dealer, rapist, or armed robber was. There would be a press conference in a couple of hours. Public opinion would not be changed one bit by last night's events. Payne would make sure of that.

In the meantime, though, the Commander was positively irate that there'd been only two illegal firearms collected. "One dead citizen per gun is not a good ratio, Ray!"

"I realize that, sir, but we had no way of knowing what we'd find."

Payne knew he was right about that, but there were a couple of other issues to resolve. "So, the bottom line is that we did nothing overly aggressive. We were fired on and we fired back. We were right, they were wrong. Period. I can sell that," he added, as if to convince himself of it.

The other issue was potentially more problematic. Payne had come up with the idea of planting homemade explosives if things got out of hand. Burke had reluctantly conceded that the plan had merit and time had proven him right. There was a good chance that public sentiment would turn the wrong way if people began to weigh the death of a husband and wife against the possession of only two illegal firearms. They had to be guilty of something worse.

The more he thought about it, the more certain Payne was that they'd made the right decision regarding the explosives. They had access to plenty of it in their lockup and it wasn't easily traceable. The bigger picture had to be kept in mind. With that being the case, Payne knew that what the ATF was charged with doing and what he and Burke had done were both right and necessary.

This had been the first full-scale HOT operation and it was critical to keep *everyone* on their side—from the President on down. The less gray things were, the easier that would be. Black and white was much simpler and when dealing with politicians or the average American citizen, simpler was better.

"Now, as to the other matter, Ray, let's quit wringing our hands…

do you think Keller saw what you were doing?"

"No, sir, I don't think he did. My guess is that he was just approaching the doorway as I was coming out. He might *suspect* something, but I don't think he saw anything."

"Good. I think we can deal with him, then. Now I've got to work on a statement for the press conference. Some of those reporters can be as much of a pain in the ass as Keller is."

* * * * * *

Washington, D.C.
Saturday, April 19

President James Nichols sat at the breakfast table as the steward carefully placed the grapefruit and whole wheat toast before him. As with every meal he ate, this breakfast would be *just* enough to relieve his hunger, but not a bite more. Having always had to battle a slight weight problem, the President knew he couldn't get away with overdoing it for long. Regular exercise helped as well and even allowed him to sneak dessert from time to time. He was a reasonably fit man for his age, with just the right amount of gray in his hair to lend a distinguished air, yet not so much as to make him look older than he was.

Across the board, Jim Nichols was not a man given to excess of any kind. Major decisions were made very deliberately and only after the careful consideration of all possible angles and ramifications. Nichols relied heavily on input from his advisors, though he was careful to keep that fact from becoming common knowledge. In his mind, it was a sign of weakness. In spite of a long and fairly distinguished career as a U.S. congressman and senator, he simply did not have the self-confidence to make high-level decisions on his own without first running them by others whose judgment he trusted. Often, after doing so, Nichols would modify his original decision to reflect the opinions he'd received. His advisors knew of this tendency and some were said to have taken advantage of it repeatedly.

Other side effects of the President's indecisiveness were his insistence on floating one trial balloon after another through the media and his seemingly endless use of focus groups and polling. Even then, his administration's proposals tended to be "small-time," according to his critics—more like those that a governor, or even a mayor, would make.

The Family Protection Act was different, though. It was lauded by most inside the Beltway as a bold and gutsy stroke of political genius. Out in the real world, it was seen as just the kind of political leadership voters had been waiting for. Polls had Nichols up by fifteen to twenty points over his rival in the upcoming election, due largely to the FPA. It *was* out-of-the-box thinking for him, precisely because it was perceived as being so politically risky. Yet the data indicated that the majority of the public would love it. The President and his advisors felt that they had a sure thing…bold *and* popular. Perfect.

Still, President Nichols was worried. The FPA was the only real leap into the unknown of his lengthy political career. There were constitutional issues involved and, although it was popular among a sizeable majority of the American public at this point, minority opposition was stronger than any he had ever encountered. These people were nuts! He knew enough to understand the role guns had played throughout the history of the United States, but this was the twenty-first century, for heaven's sake! What possible need was there for *any* guns in this day and age? Times had changed and the Nichols Administration would see to it that the country's policies changed with them.

It looked to be a beautiful spring day in the nation's capital, he noticed as he stared idly out the large window to his right. Though it was Saturday, the President had still awakened before six o'clock. After his customary morning workout, a shower, and breakfast, he was ready to take the day's pulse, as he liked to put it. That involved scanning several newspapers and watching CNN. It wasn't unusual for him to find out more from doing that than he did in his daily briefings. Since it was near the top of the hour, he started with CNN.

"Our top story this morning involves the first deaths due to the federal government's firearm Collection efforts. Apparently, a late-night raid by the Bureau of Alcohol, Tobacco, Firearms and Explosives' elite Hazardous Operations Team near Portland, Oregon resulted in the deaths of a man and a woman, as well as one ATF agent. For more, we go live to Kathy Winters, from our affiliate in Portland. Kathy, what else can you tell us about what happened out there?"

"Well, Dan, though we can't see the house from this side of the police line, behind me is the property of a man named Michael Niculescu. Although the police haven't released any names yet, we can assume that the deceased are, in fact, Mr. Niculescu and his wife. We have also learned from the ATF officer in charge at the scene that there were what appeared to be homemade explosives found on the premises." Then, reaching over to her right, the reporter pulled a very tired-looking man to her side. "This gentleman is Mr. Niculescu's neighbor. Sir, what can you tell us about Michael Niculescu?"

The man was obviously not enjoying the attention, especially at 5:00 a.m. Pacific Time. "Well, first of all, I have a real hard time believing Mike was involved with any kind of explosives or bombs. He just isn't the type. He's…was…the most solid and decent guy I've ever met. I mean that. I just can't believe this happened!" Seeing that she needed to take control of the situation, the reporter interrupted him.

"Sir, what about the firearms he owned? This was an elite ATF unit involved here last night and we're told that they are only used on the most potentially dangerous Collection subjects. Do you know how many firearms your neighbor owned? And was he ever reckless in any way with them?"

"Reckless? Mike? No…never once in all the time I've known him. I guess they've killed Sarah too? Jesus, what about the kids? Were they in the house?"

"We don't know that at this point, sir." It was clear the neighbor had gone beyond the point of being useful to the reporter. "Thank you very much for your time," she stated flatly and moved away from him. "Again, Dan, at this point all we know is that an ATF agent as well as a civilian man and woman were killed here last night and that there appears to have been a large quantity of homemade explosives found on the premises as well. Back to you."

It was not as though the President thought something like this would *never* happen. In fact, the possibility had been discussed in one of their policy meetings when the FPA was being formulated. Still, hearing about it on CNN and hearing the man's neighbor talk about him the way he did, was a jolt to Nichols. Having just been thinking about his lead in the polls, he wondered how *this* would impact the electorate's mood. It was also hard for him to believe that people would actually fight back against such overwhelming odds. *Turn the things in and stop endangering your families!* Maybe he should address the nation and say exactly that. He would need to talk to Charlie Martinez—soon.

The President still looked as if he'd had a bucket of ice water dumped on him when the First Lady joined him at the breakfast table. Barbara Nichols was a graceful, attractive woman. She had a warmth and gentleness about her that made everyone she met feel comfortable, yet she was also shrewd, insightful, and very protective of her husband. It was obvious that Jim Nichols had married well and just as obvious that his wife had been a huge asset to her husband's political career.

"Honey, what's wrong?" she wondered. After telling his wife what he'd just seen, Nichols looked to her for the reassurance that he knew would come. "Jim, those people made the decision to break the law; it wasn't as if they didn't have plenty of warning. Besides, you said an ATF agent was killed too. They were obviously dangerous. With all the explosives ATF found, this guy might have been planning another Oklahoma City or something." There was no significant response from her husband. "I guess I don't understand why you'd be so affected by this. What makes them different from anyone else who breaks the law? It sounds to me as if the ATF did its job and lost one of its own people in the process. I'm sure most voters out there will feel the same way and the gun nuts are going to hate you no matter what."

She was right, of course. At his core, he knew that. Still, he'd seen the fickleness of the American people. Whipping them into a frenzy for military action had never been too difficult, especially if it had been a while since they'd had a taste of it. Let a few body bags started coming back full, though, and their appetite always disappeared. "I know. I'm just being paranoid. The FPA is the centerpiece of everything we've tried to do in this first term. You know that." She nodded with complete understanding, but remained silent. "I can just see us being in the middle of a huge mess when the convention rolls around in August. The election's just around the corner!"

"Jim, you *will* be re-elected—because you deserve it and because everyone who knows anything about politics says so. The voters know how hard you've worked for them and they're going to reward you for it."

"As long as this thing doesn't blow up in our faces, I agree." Still not quite convinced, the President knew he would feel much better after talking to his Attorney General.

* * * * * *

Portland, Oregon
Saturday, April 19

Don had awoken a little after six and couldn't go back to sleep, try as he might. Since more sleep wasn't in the cards, he'd gotten up, made coffee and sat down on the couch to watch CNN while he read the newspaper—all of which had become a Saturday morning routine for him. There was nothing particularly interesting in the paper, but then the CNN anchor's voice caught his attention.

As he watched and listened, Don found it increasingly difficult to focus on the television screen. He shook his head slowly, as if doing so might invalidate what he was hearing. Changing the channel to Fox News forced him to hear it all over again: "It appears that Michael and Sarah Niculescu—of Portland, Oregon—were killed very early this morning during what was apparently the first Collection raid on a 'Level Three' subject conducted by the ATF nationwide."

Don felt as though someone had punched him in the gut hard

enough to drive all the air from his lungs. He breathed deeply, swallowed hard, and dropped his face into his hands. Mike had been the best friend he'd ever had and Sarah was one of the sweetest women he'd ever known. This couldn't have happened...but it had. And, in some strange way, Don felt as though a part of him knew that it would.

He stood slowly and staggered down the hall to their bedroom. Seeing Jenny still sleeping peacefully, he almost turned around and walked back out; but putting it off wouldn't make it any easier—on either of them. Besides, he needed her now more than he ever had. He knelt down on the floor on Jenny's side of the bed and stroked her hair. Her eyes fluttered open and her mouth formed a sleepy smile.

"Good morning," she mumbled.

Don hesitated for a few seconds and then answered her in a shaky voice. "No honey...it's not."

* * * * * *

Washington, D.C.
Saturday, April 19

Attorney General Martinez had thought about calling the President early that morning, right after he got the call about the Niculescu raid. After considering the move further, however (there was *nothing* Charlie Martinez did that wasn't carefully evaluated beforehand), he decided not to. Knowing how nervous the President was about virtually everything, but especially the Collection process, the Attorney General was hesitant to make this seem like too big a deal. It was simply the kind of thing that was bound to happen from time to time when Presidents made tough decisions. The President of the United States wasn't notified every time there was a death due to a drug raid, armed robbery, or any other crime. Why should this be any different? He was to have lunch with the Boss today and that would be an appropriate time for them to discuss the matter.

Then his phone rang. It wasn't just a ring, but the distinctive ring that told him the leader of the free world wanted to speak with him. He *always* loved hearing that ring. Well, almost always. From time to time, Nichols really grated on him. *You've made your decision, now live with it and defend it like a man*, Martinez wanted to say.

"Yes, Mr. President?"

"Charlie, how early did you know about this mess out in Oregon?"

"Mr. President, I got a call a couple of hours ago, but I really didn't feel you should be bothered with something like this."

"How about letting me make that decision?"

It was time for Martinez to give the chief executive the reassurance he craved. "Look, sir, you've trusted me often in the past. I appreciate that trust and I'm asking you to do the same in this matter. Our HOT commander out there will be holding a press conference shortly and I have every confidence that he'll make both the press and the entire country see this as exactly what it was: a top-notch law enforcement agency going up against an obviously dangerous felon and getting the job done."

"I sure hope so, Charlie. I'm sure I don't have to tell you that if the Collection process turns into something different than what the voters expected, it could sink us both!"

It really did get a little old having to do this as often as he did. "Mr. President, this isn't going to sink us, it's going to re-elect us." And *that* was exactly the reason the President of the United States had called him.

* * * * * *

Portland, Oregon
Saturday, April 19

Payne stepped behind the lectern and arranged his notes carefully. It wasn't so much for the sake of being prepared, as it was *appearing* to be prepared. He needed to convey a sense of competence and soberness, without making the situation seem too much outside the routine. After all, this type of thing was likely to happen again. He wanted to set the stage for that probability and wasn't about to present what had happened as an anomaly.

"Ladies and gentlemen, at a little after one o'clock this morning, agents of the ATF's Hazardous Operations Team conducted a raid on the home of Michael Niculescu. Mr. Niculescu killed one of our agents and shot another before he and his wife were, themselves, killed. We were acting on information that indicated a large number of illegal firearms on the premises. Without divulging confidential information, I'll just say that Mr. Niculescu's background gave us cause to worry that he might indeed be a threat to his neighbors and to the community at large."

Without skipping a beat and without looking as though what he was about to say was anything other than cold, hard fact, Payne continued. "Additionally, significant amounts of homemade explosives were found on the premises. This may help explain his willingness to defy our laws governing firearms. It also fits a pattern. As is often the case, a person acting outside the law in one area does so in others. The explosives could indicate that Mr. Niculescu was involved in some type of conspiracy to overthrow the government, or to strike at a government building or some similar act. We just don't know. Unfortunately, it wouldn't be a first...we all remember the Oklahoma City tragedy.

"I hate to have to report this type of news, but it may, unfortunately, be necessary from time to time—until those who choose to defy the law cease doing so. Thank you for your time and attention."

Immediately, hands shot up and shouts for attention could be heard. Payne decided to take only a couple of questions. "Yes, in the back row."

"Commander, Mr. Niculescu's neighbors seem to be of the opinion that he was none of the things you are alleging. Can you comment on that?"

"Well, it's not unusual in this day and age for people not to know their neighbors very well, especially in relatively remote areas like that.

There were obviously things going on that were not only illegal, but also dangerous. He may have *seemed* like a good neighbor, but his actions spoke louder."

"Yes sir, in the blue suit."

It was Jim Schaefer, of *The Oregonian.* "Commander, what was it about Mr. Niculescu that called for HOT to be used in this case?"

"The specific criteria used to determine when HOT will be deployed are classified. I can only say that those deemed to be the most serious threats to society are given the most attention. Now, I'm afraid that's all the time I have this morning. Again, thank you for your time." As was his custom when he was finished with a room full of people, Payne turned quickly on his heel and exited, amid a chorus of shouted questions from his audience. The last question he clearly heard was "How many firearms did you find at the scene, Commander?" But Payne was already out the door by then.

His statement, as well as the answers he gave, left Schaefer and most of the other reporters unsatisfied. Payne had been too dismissive *and why was he in such a hurry to leave?* Unsatisfied or not, they'd been around long enough to know when a press conference was over. Picking up his notes from the chair next to him, Schaefer had an uneasy feeling about what he'd just heard. Though he'd personally been pro-Collection from the very beginning, something just didn't fit in this case. As soon as he got a chance, he'd look into it further.

* * * * * *

The press conference was over, but Don continued to stare at his television. He was absolutely seething. This man's arrogance was stunning and the picture he presented to the world was certainly *not* the Mike Niculescu that Don knew so well. *This guy's covering something up,* Don kept thinking.

The bit about explosives and being a conspirator was an absolute lie. Don had never seen one shred of evidence that would lead him to believe that about his friend—it just didn't fit. Don wondered why they would insinuate something like that and then he realized there was only one explanation for that blatant a distortion: the Commander was lying in order to justify his agent's actions. But the scary part was the *ease* with which the man had lied. *Where do people like that come from?*

Don had always trusted his government…to a fault, he now realized. At the opposite end of that spectrum was Mike. Don would never be suspicious to that extreme—in fact, he still wasn't ready to admit that Mike had been right all along about Collection. He didn't quite know *how* to feel. One thing he was certain of, however, was that he would never be spoon-fed anything by these people again. *How could both of them have been killed? Why did the ATF do it this way? There had to have been some way of pulling this off without anyone dying.*

Don knew he wouldn't be able to rest until he had the answers to these questions. The problem was that he had no idea what to do next. His best friend was dead and there was obviously more to the situation than was being reported. There was certainly no manual for this kind of thing. *Oh, God—the kids, George and Ana! How would any of them even want to go on now?* With that thought in mind, Don wondered briefly what might have happened if the kids had been in the house. He shuddered and put his head in his hands, rubbing his eyes harshly.

He knew they weren't in the house when it happened because Jenny had called there yesterday to see if Brett could sleep over. George and Ana weren't due back in town with the kids until tomorrow and Don knew there was no phone or television at the cabin. He and Jenny decided to go and tell them in person. The only other option was to let them find out via the radio on the way home—something Don couldn't even allow himself to consider. They'd be leaving within the hour to head up the mountain.

* * * * * *

Scott awoke shortly before noon. He hadn't had enough sleep, but he knew that his mind would allow him no more for now. He and Meg had talked only briefly about the raid before he fell asleep. Luckily, she'd honored his mood and let him have the peace he needed to collect his thoughts. Scott sat on the edge of the bed and stared at the wall. He was trying to put last night into some kind of perspective.

He had been involved in many tense and unnerving situations during his career and had been exposed to crime scenes that the average person would have been unable to look upon. He was usually affected by what he'd seen and often had difficulty letting go of the images in his mind. But there was something different about what went down last night, he decided as he brushed his teeth. The scene itself was pretty tough to take, but it wasn't just that. No matter *what* this idiotic "Collection" policy mandated, these people were no more felons than he was...but it wasn't just that, either. There was something more important bothering him.

Meg could tell that her husband was in one of those moods that caused him to turn inward rather than reach out for her. It was something that men in general tended to do, but Scott seemed to have a bigger dose of this particular character flaw than most. It drove his wife crazy—she so wanted to talk about this and everything else that was important to him.

"Hi, honey. I can't believe you're up already." Scott was ambling toward the kitchen table, craving a cup of coffee. Passing by her, he kissed his wife on top of her head and gently rubbed her belly.

"How are we?" he inquired, moving off toward the coffee pot.

"*We* are just fine. How about you?" No answer. "You know, Scott, I really hope you're going to talk to me about this. It sounds awful. I can't even imagine witnessing something like that!"

Scott sat down with his cup of coffee, looking as if he'd slipped into a trance. Staring down at the Saturday *Oregonian*, he was glad the story had broken too late to be included. He didn't even want to turn the television on, knowing that the local stations would be consumed by this for a while. "It *was* awful. We killed a man and his wife, in the house they'd probably worked and saved for, for years. They died in their own bedroom—both of them, lying there full of bullet holes." He didn't notice Meg's eyes begin to moisten. If he had, he probably wouldn't have continued. "And the worst part was the way *he* died… trying to protect his wife. He probably thought he'd saved her, too."

It was as if someone had opened the floodgates of Scott's emotions and Meg didn't want it to stop, painful as it was for her to listen. She closed her eyes and tried not to sob loudly enough for him to notice. "They have two kids. Don't know where they were…or are, but they had pictures of them all over the house—a girl and a boy." He closed his eyes and leaned his head back against the chair. He was so tired and emotionally drained that there didn't seem to be much else to say.

Dabbing the corners of her eyes with a napkin, Meg cleared her throat and said, "Not 'we'…you said 'we' killed a man and his wife. *You* didn't do anything."

In the strictest sense, she was right, of course, but he knew that just by being a member of the team, he'd played a part in their deaths. "Honey, I deserve just as much blame as the guys who pulled the triggers—which is to say, not much." Meg looked confused. "Listen, we went there with a shitty job to do. Now, I may have some questions about the way it was carried out, but ultimately the blame for this whole mess should be placed squarely on the shoulders of the President and every member of Congress who voted for this law. They're the ones who put us in that house last night."

Suddenly, Scott realized what was *really* eating at him. It wasn't Payne and Burke, or even the President and Congress. He realized that last night was the American public's fault. They were the ones who had voted for Nichols, largely *because* he said he was going to do something like this. They were the ones who had allowed themselves to be led along like sheep by politicians and the media. They were the ones who, in every poll taken, had given gutless politicians the temporary shot of courage they needed to pull off something like this.

What was really bothering Scott about last night was that what society told them to do to those people was a slap in the face to everyone who'd ever died, or been prepared to die, for this country and what it stood for. Even though there had been occasions in which the United States had failed to live up to its ideals, those ideals were always there as a guide—a track to run on. Whether a person wanted anything to do with guns or not, the effect of this Collection process was to tear up the track that we'd run on so well, for so long. He knew there would come a point at which the damage done was so extensive that the track couldn't be repaired. And that would be the end of the kind of life that made the United States unique and good. *Someone* was going to have to rise above the rabble and say "no more." There had to be a politician with the ability and the moral courage to shake us back to our senses.

Then he realized the futility of that kind of thinking. The President and virtually every politician of any consequence was fully in support of Collection—they were tripping all over each other trying to take credit for it! Speaking out against Collection made one more than politically incorrect; there was no surer way to become a pariah. No, if it were to be done at all, *this time* the United States would have to be shaken back to its constitutional senses by someone other than the "greatest and wisest" among us.

* * * * * *

Everyone's ears were starting to pop as the Williams family climbed slowly up Mount Hood in their SUV. This was always the kids' favorite part. They made a big deal of opening and closing their mouths to clear their inner ears as the pressure built. There was still a trace of snow up this high, though it had been a relatively light winter in terms of total snowfall. Regardless, to kids, any snow was cool.

Don, of course, was worried about more important things. What would he say to the Niculescus? What, if anything, was he going to do in defense of his dead friend? And finally, exactly where was this cabin? He'd driven to it only a couple of times, one of them in semi-darkness. Jenny had been there once and she generally had a better sense of direction than her husband (though, of course, he would never admit it). Between the two of them, Don hoped they could find their way.

What exactly *was* he going to say to George and Ana? "I've got some bad news—the government killed your son and daughter-in-law." Yeah, that was pretty much it, wasn't it? To say that Mike should have turned the guns in, that *he* was the one who placed his family in danger, while probably technically true, was too pat an answer—too dismissive of the complexity of this issue. Funny thing was, up until a few days ago (maybe even twenty-four hours ago), Don had felt that way himself. For the last couple of hours, he'd been wondering whether his mind would have been changed had two strangers been killed, instead of Mike and Sarah. Probably not, he decided, but that didn't make his change of heart any less legitimate.

This Commander Payne seemed like an arrogant bastard, but that assessment might not be fair. Don had seen him on television for, what, ten minutes? *He* may have been lied to about the explosives by one of his people. Besides, he was really just doing his job, wasn't he? There had to be a better way of reducing the misuse of guns. People like Mike obviously were not just going to roll over and take it. *Does that mean society has the right to come down on them with an iron fist…in the name of "safety?"* Don now felt the answer to that question was no. It was time for the politicians to step back, take a deep breath, and re-evaluate the entire problem. What were the odds that would happen, though, given the popularity of the new law?

"Honey, I think it's the next right."

"Huh?" Don answered, shaken from his pondering.

"Take the next right. I remember that little market we just passed. Are you okay?"

"Yeah. I've never been so nervous, though. You wanna tell them for me?"

"No, thanks. I *will* be right beside you, though," she promised. "I don't think it's the kind of thing you can really rehearse. Just be yourself and let your feelings come through. It'll be all right. We should have the kids go outside and play, though. They need to hear about it separately," she whispered, looking over her shoulder into the backseat at her own children and trying to imagine how they would be affected if something like this happened to her and Don. They didn't know about Mike and Sarah yet and she had no idea how they'd go about telling them.

Not surprisingly, his wife was correct again. The turn had been the right one and he found his own way from there with little difficulty. As soon as he turned off the paved road, there were sporadic patches of snow that crunched under the SUV's tires as the vehicle slowly rolled over them. The last fifty yards or so of "driveway" amounted to little more than a game trail and the overhanging tree branches scraped both sides of Don's lovingly waxed vehicle.

Pulling up in front of the cute little mountain cabin that George and Ana were so proud of, Don felt sick to his stomach. Their car was there, which meant that they were as well. Part of him had hoped they wouldn't be; he wasn't ready for this yet. The task before him was one of the most difficult he'd ever faced.

It didn't take long for the Williams kids to pile out of the car and run to the side of the cabin, where Brett and Lori were playing. Don and Jenny walked over to the children and greeted them warmly. Within seconds, though, Jenny felt tears begin to well in her eyes and both knew they'd better walk away. Looking at these beautiful kids and knowing what lay ahead of them was simply too much to bear at the moment.

Walking toward the cabin, Jenny reached for her husband's hand and squeezed it tightly. Don knocked on the door before opening it himself. "Hello…anybody home?"

Ana Niculescu came out of the kitchen, drying dishwater from her hands and George slowly removed himself from his recliner upon hearing Don's voice. Both looked upon their unexpected guests with a mixture of surprise and pleasure, with George moving over to them quickly to shake Don's hand and hug Jenny. Ana, who initially looked more startled than George, joined him in greeting their friends.

Obviously pleased to see them, George wondered aloud what he and his wife were both thinking; "What brings you way up here?"

Don looked at Jenny nervously before answering. "Uh, well…we need to talk to you for a few minutes," he stuttered.

"What is wrong?" It was Ana. Her intuition was legendary and she wouldn't wait a moment longer for whatever terrible news they carried with them.

"Please, let's go over here and sit down," Jenny suggested. As the group sat down on the couch and overstuffed chairs in the quaint little cabin's "great room," Ana repeated herself. "What is it, *please*?"

Don cleared his throat and promised himself that he wouldn't stumble. A deep breath. "Last night, there was an ATF raid on Mike and Sarah's home." He closed his eyes for a split second—it was enough for George to break in.

"Tell us, please, Don!"

"George, they were both killed." There, he'd said it. He only hoped it didn't sound as abrupt and uncaring to them as he feared it had. He expected to hear screaming and wailing from both of them. There was nothing imaginable more devastating than the death of a child, no matter how old that child was. Instead of the expected response, however, they both took on an odd, vacant look. Sitting there, amidst the most awkward silence of their lives, Don and Jenny desperately wanted to say *something*, but this was not their time.

Most of their acquaintances—even those who were considered close friends—found it difficult to read the Niculescus, and others from the "old country" as well. They were more private with their thoughts and more protective of their feelings and emotions than most who were born in *this* country. The two cultures were just different. No matter how long George and Ana lived in the United States, this aspect of their personalities would never change.

The few seconds it took George to speak seemed like an eternity. Finally, he looked at them sadly and spoke in a quiet, somber voice. "Is it...all over the news, Don?"

"Yes, George, it is."

"What are they saying about my son?"

Don closed his eyes momentarily and breathed a heavy sigh before answering. "Let's just say, uh...it's probably best you weren't watching television this morning."

"Don, I ask you because I need to know. Please."

"They talked about...George, they basically said he was a threat to the community and that..." Don didn't feel that he should be telling them this, but better they find out from him than from some talking head on the evening news.

"And *what*, Don?"

"They also said that they'd found homemade explosives on the property...and they hinted that Mike had planned to use them against the government."

George reached for his wife's trembling hand and squeezed it tightly. Though it was unimaginably difficult for her, Ana felt the urge to speak now. "It is not enough that they murder our son and his wife...the parents of our beautiful grandchildren. They also tell these lies, so that their souls cannot even rest! This is same as Romania. *Same!* They tell lies about good people to...make okay what they do." With that, she finally broke down and began sobbing heavily. George tried to console her and Jenny rushed over to help, but there was nothing anyone could say to mitigate the pain that she felt.

Dabbing his eyes with a handkerchief taken from his pocket, George asked the same question Don had asked himself, immediately upon hearing the same news. "*Why* would they tell these lies?"

"I don't know, George...I don't know." And he didn't...yet.

Eventually, Ana brought in the Niculescu children. At their grandparents' request, it was Jenny who told them that they would never see their parents again, though George and Ana were right there with them. Don went outside and broke the news to his own children. As he predicted, Clay took it the hardest. His son was nearly catatonic and it hurt Don greatly to watch.

Don and Jenny offered to take Brett and Lori back to their house, but the Niculescu clan—what was left of it—seemed to want to stay together for now, in order to find a way through this tragedy. That decided, Don and Jenny piled their family back into the SUV and said their tearful good-byes.

As they headed toward home, the two older children were silent. Don and Jenny talked in the front seat and Don went into detail about what was bothering him so much. The ATF was *lying*! He had no idea what to do about it, but he was sure that he was right.

Clay, having overheard his parents' conversation, finally broke the silence in the backseat. "Dad, why don't you just go tell those people they're liars. Tell 'em Mr. Niculescu never did anything wrong in his whole life. They have to know the truth. You know he'd do it for you, don't ya?"

It was all Don could do to maintain his composure. Through clenched teeth he answered his son. "Yeah, buddy, I know he would—and I'm going to do it for him, too...I promise."

******

Tired as he was, Scott wanted—no, *needed* to shake the cobwebs from his system. The best way he knew how to do that was to sweat them out. He called Bobby and they agreed to meet for a run. If he truly wanted to sweat, trying to keep up with Bobby was a surefire way to accomplish that goal. Both also knew that they would talk about last night and Scott needed that as much as the run. He was still asleep when Payne gave his press conference. Meg had watched it and filled him in on what he'd missed. Probably a good thing he hadn't seen it, Scott thought.

As he pulled into the gravel parking lot of the city park, Scott saw Bobby stretching. Scott got out of his car and thought he'd lighten the mood. "Hey, ready to get your ass kicked?" He was referring to their run, of course, but, as men are prone to do, he'd wondered how he might fare if he and Bobby ever went at it. Scott had trained in Brazilian Jiu-Jitsu for several years. He'd also wrestled, both in high school and at the Naval Academy. All the training, combined with his natural strength and aggressiveness, gave Scott a tremendous amount of confidence.

Bobby was extremely strong and tough-as-nails, though. He'd

also done a *lot* of boxing, Scott knew. It was probably a good thing the two men had become friends and developed a healthy respect for one another. Some things were better left undecided.

"Yeah, I haven't had a good whuppin' since the last time my wife did it," Bobby responded.

It would have been easier not to talk about last night, but there was no escaping the inevitable, so Scott finally began. "Heard anything from Payne or Burke today?"

"Yeah. Burke called a meeting of the squad leaders for today at 1630. Said it won't take long. Steve Anderson from squad three called to see if I had any scoop. As usual, I knew absolutely nothing. Said he'd heard they just wanted to reassure us all that last night was no big deal. You know: 'It was bound to happen sooner or later…part of the job,' that kinda stuff."

"Bobby, when was the last time they held a meeting on a Saturday afternoon to tell you that something *wasn't* a big deal?" Bobby nodded his head, conceding the point.

Scott had also been wondering about how things had gone with Bobby's team. "How did your op with the SEAL go down, by the way? I didn't hear about any fireworks, so I assume no news is good news?"

"Yeah, we knew where he worked, so we ended up pulling him over on his way home. I figured there was no need to let him get home where his family was and put him in a defensive mode. When we stopped him, he looked like he wanted to fight and he *was* carrying, but he didn't go for his gun…thank God," Bobby said with obvious relief. "So I guess it worked out okay."

"It worked out okay because you did it *right*, brother," Scott assured him.

"Or maybe we just got a lucky and drew a guy with some common sense," Bobby said dismissively before cutting to the chase. "Scott, tell me how things really went down last night." He knew that Scott would answer the question objectively and analytically, like the professional he was.

"Well, I didn't see it happen firsthand. I was with Sykes' group.

We entered through the back door, then moved topside. Heard shots downstairs. By the time we got down there, it was all over."

"I didn't ask you what you *saw*. I asked you how it went down. We're not in a courtroom, pal."

"The entrance was all wrong, Bobby. I hate to say 'I told you so,' but I did." Bobby conceded the point with a barely perceptible nod of his head. "Anyway, the subject didn't reach for the sky, like they figured he would. He came at 'em like John Wayne when they entered his bedroom. Had a Glock 34 with a laser on it that he knew how to use. Roberts never had a chance and Lynch would've been as dead as this picnic table if it hadn't been for his plates," Scott said, referring to the plates of body armor that were inserted in the vest that every squad member wore when conducting a raid.

"Anyway, basically, we tripped the alarm, the subject was armed when our guys entered the bedroom and he got Roberts right off the bat. Husband crawls toward the wife while shooting, then blankets her with his body. Lynch opened up on both of them. End of story."

The ATF agent was looking up at the sky, shaking his head. Scott wasn't quite finished, though. "When we got down there, it was a mess. I swear, Bobby, if that scene had been plastered across the front page of every newspaper in the country this morning, this dumbass law would be repealed tomorrow. Here's this guy, draped over his wife's dead body, with a bunch of holes in him." Scott paused for just a moment before going on. He didn't want to appear accusatory of the agents and he wasn't…necessarily. "I'm not saying it could've gone down much differently once we entered the house. I just think we were put in an impossible position by people like Payne, Burke, and the idiots in D.C."

"No argument here, man," Bobby said.

Scott hesitated before bringing up the explosives. The more he thought about it, the more *convenient* they seemed, especially in light of where they'd found them and what he'd caught Burke doing. "Did you see Payne's press conference?"

"Yeah. Brief and to the point, as always."

"So I hear. I was still asleep. Anyway, that business about the explosives? Well, I'm not saying it's impossible, but it just doesn't fit with what I saw in that house. They also found them out in the shop, where I caught Burke snooping around—after he ordered everyone else to stay inside the house. It didn't make sense, Bobby. The first thing he did was to go sneaking around in the shop—in the *dark*—where nobody else was. He didn't even go inside where the action took place until after he went into the shop! Why would he do that?"

"I don't know, Scott. Who knows what that guy's capable of? You think he planted 'em?"

"Beats me. I just think it's fishy as hell."

"No doubt," Bobby agreed. "Tough to prove anything though."

"I know. It's just bugging me. Also, you heard we found only two illegal guns, right?" Bobby nodded. "Well, I don't know whether the records were wrong or he sold them or what, but we cracked those safes and there was nothing but jewelry and a couple grand cash in them. The only other gun in the house was an 870 loaded with 00 buck in the closet."

Bobby Myers shook his head sadly. "I've got a bad feeling this isn't the last time I'll hear a debrief like this one." Scott just nodded and Bobby felt it was time to change the subject. "So, you gonna bail on me? Head back to that cushy-ass Marshals job?"

"Yeah, I am...probably next week. I heard back from Filson's office and they said the transfer's in the works."

"Well, this might be the last time I get to run you into the ground for a while, then. You ready?"

"No. But let's do it anyway." They didn't say a word on the run. Talking wasn't a priority anymore. Both men had a lot of thinking to do.

10

Portland, Oregon
Monday, April 21

WASHINGTON COUNTY SHERIFF'S Detective Walt Harris was knee-deep in paperwork on this particular Monday morning. Mondays tended to make him grumpy and this one was no exception. Don Williams had asked to come by and take a few minutes of his time and, though he felt there were more productive things he could be doing, the detective agreed. They hadn't seen each other in a while, but Don was a good guy and it wouldn't hurt to give him a few minutes. The paperwork would wait for him. They'd been neighbors until the Williamses moved away last year and their families, while not close, had gotten to know each other fairly well.

Walt was an eighteen-year veteran of the sheriff's office and he enjoyed his job very much. This, despite the fact that he got extremely frustrated sometimes at the ways the deck was stacked against a cop doing his job. He worked with some good people, though, and was proud to do what he did for a living.

"Lieutenant, Don Williams is here to see you," the department secretary notified him over the telephone. "Go ahead and send him back." Walt had been too busy to do so until now, but he began to wonder what Don wanted to talk to him about. His kids were too young to be in trouble (Walt hoped) and Don had never struck Walt as anything other than a law-abiding citizen. It had to be *something* out of the ordinary, though. There was no way he had come by the sheriff's office just to catch up on neighborhood gossip.

The two men had always liked each other. After a warm greeting, they discussed families, the neighborhood, and careers, but it soon became obvious to the detective that Don had something much more serious to talk about. Being a straightforward guy, Walt decided to cut to the chase. "Don, what's wrong? It's obvious there's something on your mind."

Don was glad to have Walt break the ice. "Walt, how much do you know about the ATF raid on Friday night?"

"Well, I know it was a damn mess. We had people on the scene over the weekend to assist. It's an ATF operation, though, and they're not big on asking us yokels for too much help. Haven't been over there myself or anything. Why do you ask?"

"I knew Mike Niculescu very well. In fact, he was my best friend."

"Really?" Walt was surprised. What little he'd learned about Niculescu didn't jibe with what he knew of his former neighbor.

Don sensed what Walt was thinking. "Yeah, but I'm not about to be the next ATF target. Believe it or not, I've never even owned a gun. Mike and I just sort of hit it off in general, I guess you could say."

"Don, I'm really sorry. Must've been tough for you to hear it on the news Saturday morning." The only answer was a nod. "Listen, I don't mean to be insensitive, but what can I do to help?"

"I'm sure you've gathered from all the news coverage that Mike was a real scumbag, right?" Walt had, of course, and based on his own experience, he tended to believe stories like that. He had the feeling that Don didn't really want to know what he thought about the case, though. So instead of answering the question as he normally would have, Walt simply nodded his head. "Well, nothing—and I mean *nothing*—could be further from the truth. This isn't a case of me not knowing him like I thought I did. I know for a fact that none of this stuff about him being reckless and a danger to the community is true. Ask any of his neighbors or anyone else who knew him. It's propaganda, pure and simple, Walt. The guy was as straight an arrow as you'll ever find. Extremely patriotic, a decorated Marine, you name it."

The charge caused Walt's alarm bells to start ringing. His natural reaction when law enforcement personnel were accused of wrongdoing was to deny and defend. They stuck together and for good reason. Still, Don had always seemed like a solid guy, so he made the decision to stay quiet for a little longer.

"And the business about the so-called 'homemade explosives'? Nothing less than an absolute lie, Walt. Not 'incorrect information' or anything like that. It's a lie! They *had* to have planted the stuff."

Walt had had enough. "Now wait a minute, Don. I know you're upset about this, but you're accusing a federal law enforcement agency of something very serious. What proof do you have?"

Don had expected this reaction. In fact, he probably would have reacted the same way if he were the detective. "Walt, how do you *prove* a dead man wasn't involved in something like that when a cop says he was?" The answer, of course, was "you can't," but Walt wasn't about to admit that. His silence motivated Don to continue. "Look, I don't expect you to jump over to my side and help me flush out the rats. In fact, I'm not sure I'm even going to go that far myself.

"The reason I came to you is that I need some advice. Whether you agree with me or not, I honestly believe everything I've told you and I don't take the implications of that lightly. That leaves me two options. First, I could just ignore it—try to talk myself out of believing it and go on with life. Or I could do something about it. This is where you come in. I've already decided I can't ignore it. It happened. My best friend and his wife are dead and the men responsible for their deaths are telling lies about them.

"All my life, I've pretty much taken the path of least resistance. But I want Mike's name cleared of this accusation about explosives and whatever implications that might bring with it. He was no 'menace to society,' and people need to know that. They have two great kids and Mike's parents love this country like no one else I've ever met. None of them deserves to hear what's being said about Mike.

"Walt, I need to know who to go see and anything you can tell me about talking to high-ranking cops would help. And ultimately,

I'd like you to try to put yourself in my shoes. Even if you don't buy what I'm telling you, if you were me and you felt the way I do, would you pursue it?"

This was some pretty heavy stuff for a Monday morning. The cop in Walt still wouldn't buy into Don's story. But he did have to admit that Don was a pretty sharp guy and *he* sure believed it. He was also definitely not the kind of guy to rock the boat unnecessarily. If he was willing to go to the mat on this thing, it was serious indeed.

"First of all, I'm assuming you're not denying the fact that your buddy held onto guns that he shouldn't have. Because of that, I don't think it's fair to pin a 'murder rap' on the ATF. I'm not even going to get into Collection itself. Let's just say I think it's a crock, but it *is* the law for now. I guess, if I were you...yeah, I'd push this a little. As a concerned citizen, you've got every right to do it. Also, *if*—and I'm not saying they are—but if anyone's lying here, that'll probably give them cause to think about it...maybe knock it off. You should go see the HOT Commander, Bill Payne. He's as high up as you're going to find without going to D.C., as far as I know. You should be respectful and polite, without being a wimp. Know what I mean?" Don nodded. "And that's it, pal. I hope it goes well for you. In fact, let me know how it goes, will you?"

"I will, Walt, and I really appreciate your help. Oh, and by the way, I'm not crazy. There's nothing I've told you today that I wouldn't bet my life on. I mean it."

"I believe you do, Don." Walt was thinking back over his almost two decades as a cop. There had been a few cases where crooked cops got caught and, in every case, he'd honestly believed that they would have done almost *anything* to keep from being found out. If they weren't already, they became vicious, conniving bastards...and *they* were small time compared to guys like Bill Payne. A man like that would have a lot riding on his success, especially in something as high-profile as this. You could bet he'd stop at nothing to see that a guy like Don Williams didn't get in the way.

"Don?"

"Yeah?"

"Be careful, okay?"

* * * * * *

Washington, D.C.
Tuesday, April 22

ATF Director John Mullin sat at his desk with a neutral expression on his hard-to-read face. His agency was front-page news again today and he was trying to determine whether that was a good thing or a bad thing. Yesterday's Collection operations had yielded the same type of results as Payne's had on Friday. HOT units in the Southeast and Southwest each had a fatality and one of ATF's Field Division Offices did as well—in addition to losing another ATF agent.

Regardless of what most politicians believed going into this process, Mullin knew from the beginning that Collection couldn't be accomplished without some bloodshed. In spite of that fact, he believed in what they were doing. There was absolutely no justification for civilians being so well armed. He was proud of the fact that the Attorney General was the driving force behind Collection. Martinez had favored Collection before it was politically correct to do so. That was the definition of leadership and he hoped his boss would be adequately rewarded for it.

Still, he was also aware of the fact that headlines such as these had an unsettling effect on many politicians. They would be full of resolve until a public opinion poll showed any slippage of support. To Mullin's knowledge, no polls on the subject had been conducted since last Friday, but he was sure they were in the works. He considered himself politically astute, but he veered away from conventional wisdom in this area: he believed that a leader should have strong convictions and stick to them, come hell or high water. That wasn't likely to happen in this case, though.

* * * * * *

Portland, Oregon
Tuesday, April 22

Don had made a call to Commander Payne's office immediately upon returning from his visit with Walt on Monday. The Commander's secretary put him on hold and (several minutes later) came back to ask specific questions about what he wished to discuss. The next time she returned, she was checking two to three weeks out on the Commander's calendar. When Don explained politely that it really was urgent and that it wouldn't take long, she placed him on hold yet again and returned with an offer of *today* at eleven o'clock—but only for a few minutes; the Commander was an extremely busy man.

So here he was, both impressed and intimidated by the building itself. He'd had to be buzzed in past two different armed guards just to get to the elevator! As Don was escorted down the hallway toward Commander Payne's office, he couldn't help but notice the photos on the wall. The same man (he assumed it was Payne) was in most of the photos, shaking hands with and putting his arm around the shoulders of various people that Don assumed to be powerful political types. Some he recognized, some he didn't. Finally making it to the end of the long hallway, he followed his escort through the open door leading into the reception area. The Commander's secretary looked up at him and smiled politely. She would notify Commander Payne that he was here. While the secretary was gone, Don took the chair she'd offered. Soon, she came back out to her desk and explained that Commander Payne was on an important phone call and would be a few minutes.

This gave Don time to stew in his own nervousness. Deciding he might as well make good use of the time, he mentally prepared for what he imagined he was about to go through. This included a quick rehearsal...for about the three-hundredth time. Maybe he shouldn't be so nervous. It was possible that Payne would turn out to be a good guy and make the whole experience a lot easier on him than he imagined.

Either way, Don *had* to speak his mind. He owed that much to Mike and Sarah. He had every right, as a concerned citizen, to be here and to question this man. Walt had verified that much for him yesterday. "Be respectful and polite, without being a wimp" was the way he'd put it. Don could do that. This was no different from meeting with one of the top executives from the huge insurance company he worked for, and he did that regularly. You simply had to demonstrate a quiet confidence, without appearing arrogant. That tended to impress them and engender sufficient respect to allow you to get your point across. He could do this, Don reminded himself once again.

The secretary's phone buzzed, visibly startling Don. He was sure that she'd seen him jump. A warm and friendly smile put him a little at ease as she told him the Commander would see him now.

As he knew would be the case, the man in the hallway photos was indeed Commander Payne. Swallowing hard, Don reached for the outstretched hand. "Good afternoon, Mr. Williams, I'm HOT Commander Bill Payne. Have a seat, please. Sorry about the wait, but I was on a call to Washington, D.C., with the ATF Director."

"No problem," came Don's dry response. He hadn't a clue what else to say, though he had to admit that it rattled him more than a little to know that Payne would be going from discussing official business with the Director of the ATF to listening to largely unsubstantiated ranting from a nobody such as himself. *Don't be a wimp!* "You have a very comfortable waiting area and I had some fairly heavy thinking to do concerning personnel issues at my office, anyway. I'm sure you can relate to that." Don hoped he sounded cooler than he felt. The truth was, his heart was in his throat!

"Management *does* have its responsibilities, Mr. Williams. Now, I understand you wanted to speak to me regarding a raid conducted by some of my people last week—a Mr. Nico…I'm sorry, I don't remember the name."

"It's Niculescu." *Like you've killed so many people in the last few days, you can't keep them straight?*

"Oh yes, that's right. I remember the case now. What was it, specifically, that you wanted to discuss with me?" Payne asked as he glanced rather obviously at his watch.

You ought to remember it. Do you hold a press conference every Saturday morning? "Ah, well, what I wanted to discuss with you, Commander, is the fact that I strongly object to your characterization of Mr. Niculescu. I saw your press conference and...well, the fact is...you said and inferred things about him that simply were not true." There. He'd said it.

"*Not true*, Mr. Williams?" The query was accompanied by a stare that could have frozen molten lava. "Why would I have said something that wasn't true?" Don was silent. Payne knew from experience that he had him on the ropes. "Exactly what are you implying, Mr. Williams?"

"I don't mean to imply anything, Commander. Perhaps you were given incorrect information by, uh, some of your people."

Time to move in for the kill. "So, now my people are lying—is that what you're saying? These are the finest law enforcement personnel this country has ever produced. Their bravery and character, as exhibited in the encounter with the felon you're referring to, are to be commended, not questioned. Is that clear?"

Payne's aggressiveness initially rocked Don back on his heels and his heart felt as though it would pound out of his chest. Now, though, another feeling was sweeping over him...a distinctly unfamiliar feeling. For the first time in his life that he could remember, Don Williams was angry enough about something that he felt compelled to fight for it.

"No, it's *not* clear!" Don answered. "The man your people killed was only made a felon by this ridiculous law. I've never owned a gun in my life, but even I can see how absurd this law is. *The words were coming easily and it felt good!* "And you want to talk about bravery? He had it in spades, Commander! He fought for this country and would have done so again if he were asked to. People like Mike Niculescu are heroes. They should be honored, not hunted down like animals."

Payne was stunned. He seldom misread people so completely. *So this guy has some guts and now he's fired up as well. Fine. The madder he gets, the easier he'll be to deal with.* "Is that right?" Payne finally asked. Don stared at him defiantly. "First of all, we merely *enforce* the laws, we don't create them. If you have a problem with this legislation, you'll have to take that up with the President of the United States and the Congress.

"Also, Mr. Williams, 'heroes' tend to *obey* the law, not ignore it—the *real* heroes *won* that fight. Besides, it's a good thing we got to Niculescu when we did, judging by all of the explosives we found on the premises. Lord knows what he would have blown up and how many people he might have killed otherwise."

Don was so mad he could barely focus. "Bullshit!" he screamed loudly enough that he surprised himself. "That's a lie and I'm going to make sure the whole world knows it."

A smile spread over Bill Payne's face. *Gotcha!* "Are you threatening me, Mr. Williams?" Payne asked, certain of the question's effectiveness.

Suddenly, Don wasn't so sure of himself. *Was* he threatening him? If so, what were the implications of threatening a federal agent? *It's another smokescreen and this guy's been blowing smoke up my ass since I got here.* No, he decided, he wasn't threatening Payne. "What I'm doing, Commander, is promising you that as many people as possible, by whatever means necessary, will know the *truth* about the kind of man Mike Niculescu really was. If the truth happens to be at odds with what you've said, the public will just have to draw its own conclusions."

Payne's eyes smoldered and his mouth fell into a crooked half smile. "Are you *sure* you don't own any illegal firearms, Mr. Williams?"

Don swallowed hard, but found that there was suddenly very little to swallow. "Who's making a threat now, Commander?"

A feigned look of innocence and shock came over Payne's face. "I don't know what you're talking about, Mr. Williams."

It was time to get out of there, Don decided. Standing slowly, without extending a hand, he looked Payne in the eye. "Have a nice day, sir, and thank you for your time." With that, he turned around and walked toward the door.

"Mr. Williams?" Don stopped to listen, still facing the door. "It's a dangerous sign indeed that upstanding citizens such as yourself have so little respect for the law enforcement officers who go into harm's way to protect them."

Don had no idea what to say in response, so he simply continued out the door. His hand was shaking as he reached for the brass handle and he felt beads of perspiration on his forehead.

******

Payne picked up his telephone and punched in Ray Burke's extension. He'd see just how tough Don Williams was.

******

Scott's heart certainly wasn't into what he was doing at HOT these days, but he wouldn't be heading back to the USMS until later in the week. These last couple of days would seem like months, he knew.

Eventually, each HOT squad would conduct a couple of raids per week. That would allow time in between for training and strategizing. For now, however, they were scheduling only one per week. Another was being planned for squad five to carry out on Friday—the same day Scott hoped to be back at the Marshals Service. Another Deputy Marshal would be coming in on Thursday to meet the necessary people and work with him on the transition. It was all a total waste of time. HOT didn't want a Marshal around any more than a Marshal wanted to be here, but Scott knew the decision wasn't his to make.

The bottom line was that Scott Keller was a short-timer. He was going through the motions and nothing more. Hatcher knew that as well. He had no more desire to involve the Marshal in planning the next raid than Scott had a desire to be a part of it. Though it wasn't in his nature to do so, for the next couple of days Scott would have to "find things to do." This was a euphemism for screwing off. He'd seen it done, but he'd never actually done it himself and he found he didn't enjoy it.

Today, he was "helping" Bobby and the rest of squad seven with tactical issues. At the moment, the most important of those issues was attacking the ham and cheese sandwich in front of him. Scott and Bobby were sitting alone at a small corner table in the cafeteria discussing nothing very important when Payne's secretary, Victoria, approached them, lunch tray in hand. "Mind if I sit down, gentlemen?" The two men looked quickly at each other, as if to ask permission. It was almost comical and she started to sit before Bobby stammered out his approval.

After exchanging some meaningless small talk, Victoria leaned forward conspiratorially to let the guys know she had something better to discuss. Reflexively, both of them did the same. It was no secret that Scott Keller didn't think much of her boss. It was also rather well known that many HOT personnel (Victoria included) didn't either. She knew she was among friends here. "Have you guys heard about the visitor Payne just had?" Both men shook their heads, indicating that they had not.

"Well," Victoria continued, "a man named Don Williams called yesterday for an appointment to discuss last week's raid with him. The Commander wanted me to press him for more details before I set up the appointment, so the guy told me he wanted to, quote, 'take issue with Commander Payne's characterization of Mr. Niculescu at his press conference.' So the Commander tells me to put the guy off, try to make the appointment three weeks out, that kind of thing—but Mr. Williams was pretty persistent.

"Anyway, long story short, he came in about an hour ago. He seemed like a nice guy. Real nervous in the waiting room, but I think he loosened up in the Commander's office."

"What do you mean, 'loosened up'?" Bobby asked.

"Well, the Commander's office is pretty soundproof, but I heard this guy's voice come through loud and clear a couple of times. And one of them was when he yelled, 'Bullshit!' I'm not kidding. Then he said, 'That's a lie and I'm gonna make sure everybody knows it'—something like that.

"Anyway, can you believe someone would talk to Payne like that, *in his own office*?" Neither man spoke, but it was obvious they were both suitably impressed. "That was really all I could make out clearly. They talked for a few minutes after that, but I couldn't hear what they were saying. When Mr. Williams walked out, though, he looked like he'd seen a ghost. I mean, he looked scared to death."

The two men glanced at each other and Scott turned back to Victoria. "So you have no idea what Payne could have said that scared Williams like that?"

"No idea at all," she assured him. "Sorry."

"Don't worry about it," Bobby answered. "What you *did* hear was pretty interesting stuff." After that, the small talk resumed until she finished her lunch and left to return to her unenviable position on the sixth floor.

"So?" Scott asked as soon as she'd left.

"Well, it's a first, I can tell you that," said Bobby. "Nobody's *ever* put it to Payne like that, as far as I know. Of course, we don't know everything that was said, but it's pretty obvious that *something* happened between the time this guy made his threat and the time he walked out the door—otherwise he wouldn't have looked so scared walking out of there."

Scott nodded his agreement. "Yeah, Payne said something to take the starch out of him." Then a thought came to him. "Why don't we go up to the squad room and run a check on Don Williams? You know Payne did before he came in to see him. Maybe we can find out if there's anything there for Payne to use against him as leverage."

"Why not?" Bobby agreed.

* * * * * *

Within a few minutes, the two men were sitting in front of the computer terminal in Bobby's office, running a background check on Donald Williams. Of course, there were a number of men named Donald Williams in the greater Portland area. More significantly, though, *none* of them were on any of the three ATF listings. Just to be sure, they ran the searches again and got the same results. This guy wasn't a target for ATF action of any kind. That figured, actually. Why would a potential Collection subject walk into the lion's den? But who was he?

"Where's your inter-office phone directory?" Scott asked.

"Right here," Bobby answered, grabbing it out of his desk drawer. Scott flipped through it and quickly found what he was looking for. As he picked up the phone and dialed a four-digit extension, Bobby looked at him quizzically. Scott just held up a hand: trust me.

"Hi, Victoria, this is Scott Keller…Yeah, long time no see, huh? Hey, I've got a question for you—just between the two of us, of course. This guy who came in to see Payne—Don Williams—you don't happen to have any more info on him, do you?" Scott reached for Bobby's notepad. "You know, a middle name or initial, phone number, address, that kind of thing…uh huh…really? Great. Could you give them to me? Awesome. Hey, thanks a lot."

The Marshal hung up and looked at the ATF agent. "Now, that's how it's done!" he jabbed, smiling. "It seems the Commander always wants a phone number for anyone he has an appointment with, in case he needs to cancel. Williams gave her his home and work numbers. Bingo."

An online phone directory gave them an address and from there they were able to access all pertinent information about Don Williams…of which there was very little. This guy was boring. No criminal record—not even a traffic citation. Married, good credit, pays his taxes on time. Squeaky clean. Nothing that would have connected him to Michael Niculescu in any way they could see. Oh well, at least it killed a little time for Scott, which meant that he was that much closer to getting out of there.

******

Ray Burke was in a small conference room near his office. He wanted a large, uncluttered table on which to spread out files and this room had such a table. It was also quiet. Burke was the kind of person who needed time alone in order to do his best work. He was taking advantage of that time and eating a sandwich, when one of the divisional secretaries opened the door nearly out of breath. When Payne couldn't reach him immediately in his office, he became frustrated and dialed several other extensions, eventually rounding up a small detail to search the building for his Deputy Commander.

Burke wondered what the emergency could be as he strolled past Victoria and waved. "Is he in there?"

"Oh, yes sir. You can go on in. He's been waiting rather impatiently for a while now," she added.

Payne was cursing his computer when his deputy walked in. "Ray, where have you been?"

"Eating a sandwich and working, sir. What's wrong?"

"We have a potential problem with the Niculescu case." He went on to fill Burke in on the details of Williams' visit. Burke considered his response. He didn't want to make Payne feel silly for being concerned, but he also didn't think it was smart to let him worry unduly.

"Sir, it may not be that big a problem," he answered honestly. "These issues are gray: whether or not someone's a menace to society or has ever been involved with manufacturing explosives, or is plotting against the government. How does anyone *prove* that things like that aren't true? What we've done is plant seeds of doubt about a man who defied federal law…and we've done that quite effectively, I might add. Williams can't prove anything."

"So your recommendation is to ignore him?"

"Nothing says we can't keep an eye on him. But I don't think we should do anything beyond that."

Payne thought about what Burke was saying. Burke was always cautious and that *was* one option. Payne's instinct, however, was to be proactive and history had usually proven him right. He was never comfortable waiting for something to happen *to* him. This case was no exception. Besides, Williams had pissed him off. How dare that insignificant little bastard come into his office and call him a liar! "Ray, I appreciate your input, but I'd like to be a little more aggressive in handling this one."

"Aggressive, sir?"

"Yes. Mr. Williams needs a dent in his credibility. I've checked all the Collection listings and he's not on any of them." Burke looked at him with no understanding of where his boss was going with this. "We need to add him to the list, Ray. Specifically, he needs to become a level-three subject. Can we do that?"

Burke did not even try to hide his displeasure. "Sir, that would be a mistake. He's not important enough for that. I think we should concentrate on pushing ahead with our operations. The headlines covering our success will overshadow anything Williams can do or say."

"Again, Ray, thank you for your input, but I've already decided what we need to do here. I'm asking you whether or not it's possible."

Burke knew the battle was lost. "Yes sir, I believe it's possible." That was all Payne needed to hear. His deputy went to work and within a relatively short time he'd created a well-documented record of firearms ownership for Donald James Williams.

* * * * * *

It had been a tough day for Don and no picnic for Jenny, either. She'd spent the day with five children—her own three and the Niculescu kids as well. As might be expected, they were having a tough time of it. The funeral was the next day and Jenny had serious doubts about their ability to handle it. Children were usually more resilient than adults gave them credit for being, but these kids had had an unusually close family and now both their parents were dead.

After all the kids were in bed, Don and Jenny sat at the kitchen table discussing a strategy for helping the Niculescu kids deal with the funeral. Afterward, Don went into detail about his meeting with Payne. The Commander's play at the end of their conversation had had the desired effect. Don had even found himself looking over his shoulder a time or two during the day. Now he had some idea of how Mike must have felt—for months!

"I'm sure he's just beating his chest, honey," his wife reassured him. "You've never owned a gun in your life. He wouldn't be stupid enough to make up stuff like that."

"You're probably right. Overall, I was actually pretty happy with the way the meeting went. Although, I'm not really sure where to go from here."

"How about your old buddy at *The Oregonian*?"

"Who, Jim Schaefer?"

"Yeah. A lot of people seem to pay attention to what he says."

"Good idea. I haven't talked to him in so long, I almost forgot about him. Maybe I'll call him for some tips on how to handle this." Now that he had a plan of sorts, Don needed to be sure that Jenny wanted him to push ahead with it. "You know, honey, this thing could get kind of ugly. I mean, there could be reaction from people we know who don't agree with me, or harassment from the ATF…or who knows what else."

Jenny was as proud of her husband as she'd ever been. "I don't think it'll get ugly, but if it does, I'm right here for you and I love you. We owe this to Mike and Sarah, no matter what."

11

Portland, Oregon
Wednesday, April 23

As it turned out, the weather forecast was all wrong. The clouds and likely showers that had been predicted hadn't materialized, at least not yet. Even in death, Mike Niculescu was in control of the situation, Don thought, smiling to himself.

Since he'd found out about Mike and Sarah's deaths Saturday morning, Don had thought a lot about his friend—and about how much he'd admired him. Mike never relied on anyone else for anything. His hard work and perseverance created a good life for his family and for the families of others who had worked for him over the years. He thought about virtually every issue first as a matter of freedom. He was a thoughtful, concerned, passionate, and patriotic United States citizen. People like Mike made this country work.

Again, he had to smile. Don had always considered himself to be a political moderate rather than an ideologue. He refused to be pigeonholed into any group, such as "conservative" or "liberal." He'd always been proud of the fact that he looked at each issue separately and determined his position rationally, refusing to be bound by a specific philosophy or set of beliefs. He wouldn't have said so, but he'd always felt that made him superior to those who held each issue up to a predetermined set of beliefs in order to decide how they felt about it.

Sitting here now, at his best friend's funeral, Don had serious doubts about his superiority. He'd fought it while Mike was alive, but had to admit now that his friend was probably right. If you didn't know who you were and what you believed in and stood for, how could you know—instinctively—whether something was right or wrong? Damned if Mike hadn't had an effect on him after all!

Don was fairly certain that none of those in attendance had ever been to a *double* funeral before and he was convinced that there couldn't possibly be a more depressing event. Both caskets were there, with photos of Mike and Sarah to the side of each. Most of the photos showed them together, just as they'd died. Don gave the eulogy, at George and Ana's urging. He'd had serious doubts about his ability to get through it, but he'd surprised himself. Most importantly, he didn't break down completely, which had been a real possibility. He used humor and conveyed the tremendous amount of respect he had for both Mike and Sarah. The love and sense of loss in the church was palpable.

Everyone handled their grief differently. Don had found that thinking about the positive effect Mike and Sarah had on the world around them was much more productive than drowning in sorrow. As he looked around at the others in attendance, though, he discovered that he was in the minority. Their daughter Lori was a mess. Sitting between her grandparents and Jenny, she was sobbing uncontrollably. Brett, on the other hand, looked angry, just as he had since Saturday. Don knew that he would require special attention in the coming months and was prepared to provide it. The young man's genes gave him a tremendous foundation on which to build a solid life, as long as he didn't give up.

Sarah's parents were inconsolable. Their daughter had been a very special person and it was virtually impossible to imagine them ever getting over her death. They lived over a thousand miles away, but made sure their grandchildren knew that they would be seeing them and hearing from them on a regular basis.

Knowing that the Niculescus would be there for the kids day in and day out was a great comfort to everyone. George and Ana were amazingly stoic, although both began to crack near the end. It was just too much—too tragic to bear. If Don needed any more encouragement to go on a mission, he was receiving it this morning. As he sat there and looked at young Brett, Lori, and their grandparents, he was more resolute and determined than ever to carry on...consequences be damned.

******

Burke sat in Commander Payne's office, feeling more than a little uneasy about the topic of conversation. Why, he wondered, wouldn't his boss listen to him from time to time? His opinion was often asked for, yet it was seldom heeded. It seemed that his only purpose was to validate what Payne already thought. This little meeting was a case in point. Once again, their direction had already been determined.

"I want him picked up tomorrow, Ray. The funeral's out of the way now. He hasn't begun his little media crusade yet and I want to keep it that way. Let's send Hatcher, Sykes, and Lynch to pick him up at his office tomorrow. That way, he'll experience a little public humiliation. After we've got him in custody, I want his house searched while his family's gone. Of course, when we do that, we'll find the contraband. Also, make sure they get the right guns from the lockup. The serial numbers need to match."

The firearms would come from an area of ATF's inventory of confiscated weapons where they'd never be missed. In fact, within a few days, all of the guns from that section would be destroyed. It should all work out perfectly.

******

Portland, Oregon
Thursday, April 24

This was a day that Scott Keller had looked forward to for...had it only been a couple of weeks? It seemed like he'd been here forever!

His savior, Deputy Marshal Carl Sheehan, was waiting for Scott when he arrived this morning, apparently excited about the whole thing. Sheehan was a young, hard-charging Marshal who'd volunteered for this assignment gladly. He saw it as a great opportunity to further his career and seemed to have no hang-ups about the issue of firearms Collection. Scott didn't know much about Sheehan, but was favorably impressed by what he did know. The young man had a bright future and, in the current political climate, he would certainly not hurt himself by volunteering for this assignment. Hatcher had already made it clear that Sheehan wouldn't be going on tomorrow's assignment with them, citing the fact that he was unfamiliar with procedures. It made sense to Scott, but Sheehan looked crushed.

The two Marshals were in squad room five reviewing the required inter-agency reporting procedures—yet another aspect of this job that Scott wouldn't miss. As they were talking, Scott couldn't help but pick up on a conversation Sykes was having with Deputy Commander Burke on the phone. His desk was adjacent to them and what piqued Scott's interest was hearing Sykes say, "Williams, Donald J., right?" After that, he wrote something down on his notepad, tore the page off, and assured Burke that he would get it right to Hatcher, who'd stepped out for a few minutes. *Williams?* About that time, Sheehan asked him a question and he forgot about the incident momentarily.

Hatcher returned a few minutes later. As soon as they saw him walk into the squad room, Sykes and Lynch followed him into his office, shutting the door behind them. Not ten minutes later, the three of them came out, grabbed their "assault gear" from the lockup, and headed out the door. Not a word was uttered, except for Hatcher mumbling to an agent as he passed that they would be out for a while. *What the hell's going on?* Scott was more than just curious; he was worried about what these guys might be up to.

"What was *that* all about?" Sheehan inquired.

"Huh? Oh, I don't know. Hey, why don't we take ten, okay?"

"Sure. I'll go look around a little, maybe get to know some of the folks around here."

As soon as he left, Scott walked over to Sykes' desk and inconspicuously glanced down at the pad he'd been writing on. It was one of those pads with a yellow carbon page beneath the top sheet and there, clear as a bell, was what he'd written: "Williams—office bldg—4800 W. 25th Ave—Ptld". He memorized that information and headed for Bobby's office, hoping he'd catch him there.

Scott walked down the long hallway at a brisk pace. He wanted to run, but figured that might attract too much attention. Upon arriving at squad room seven, he was informed that Bobby had left about five minutes before, but said he'd be right back. He wanted to go into Bobby's office and find what he was looking for, but thought better of it. Scott chatted with one of the squad members while waiting for his friend. Trying to make small talk was never easy for him and in this case it was even more difficult than normal. After twenty excruciating minutes, he heard the familiar voice behind him.

"Hey, what's up, short-timer?" Bobby joked.

"Not sure. Can I talk to you for a minute, *in your office*?"

"Yeah, sure." As they entered, Scott closed the door. "So, what's up?"

"Where's your notepad?"

"My *what*?"

"Your notepad…you know!" Scott was obviously excited about something. The request had caught Bobby off guard initially, but he finally realized what Scott was after and produced it. Scott flipped back a couple of pages until he found what he was looking for: Don Williams' home and work telephone numbers. Ripping both the top and carbon pages out of the book, he picked up the phone and dialed the work number that he'd gotten from Victoria. "Yes, uh, what's your address, please?"

At this point, Bobby noticed his friend's eyes grow wide and he knew something serious was up. Scott's mind was obviously racing and Bobby decided to let him think for a minute instead of interrupting him.

How can they justify this? Scott wondered as he hung up the phone. As he asked himself the question, a frightening possibility came to him. "Bobby, do me a favor and pull up the level-three listing for Portland."

"Okay, but I hope you're gonna tell me what the hell you're up to," Bobby grumbled as he turned around to his computer terminal.

"I will, brother. Okay, scroll to the W's...right about there—Look at *that!*" Scott stabbed his finger at the screen, pointing to "Donald James Williams."

"Scott, what's going on? That wasn't there yesterday."

Ignoring the question, Scott picked up the telephone and hit the redial button. "May I speak to Donald Williams, please?" Bobby wasn't sure he knew what was happening, but what he *suspected* made him sick.

******

Don was back at work...physically, if not mentally. For the first time in his working life, his career seemed insignificant and he was finding it difficult to do his job. He would try to call Jim Schaefer at *The Oregonian* later this afternoon, but for now, he needed to get his head back in the game here at work. He had to try to reclaim his life of two weeks ago. As he was reaching for one of the files he had to review from the huge stack in his in-basket, the phone rang. Don grabbed the receiver and cradled it between his ear and shoulder while thumbing through the file.

"Don Williams, may I help you?"

"Mr. Williams, please listen to me and don't ask any questions for a moment. My name is Scott Keller and I'm a Deputy U.S. Marshal." The tone of the man's voice caused Don to go limp. "Sir, there are three agents from the ATF on their way to your office *right now* to arrest you for the possession of illegal firearms."

Don stiffened. "But I've never owned a gun of *any* kind."

"Yeah? Well, you do now. Look, you don't have time to argue with me. Please trust me on this. I *know* you don't own these guns, but that's not going to do you a lot of good if you don't get out of there now. Take off. Go somewhere safe and lie low for a while, until this gets sorted out. You're in over your head, Mr. Williams. *Please* trust me."

The man sure sounded believable, but…this was too much! "Wait a minute—I don't even—where am I supposed to—" Don's office was in the front corner of the building on the ground level and, glancing out the window, he saw a black Suburban pull into a parking space near the front entrance. Out jumped three men in black uniforms… with ATF on the back! "Oh my God, they're here," he whispered.

"Get out of there now! MOVE IT!"

Scott's last words jarred Don, who felt numb. Grabbing his car keys, he ran toward the back of the building, drawing the attention of his employees. As he neared the rear exit door, a woman in the front of the office screamed. Three armed men entering a sedate office environment tended to do that to people. Don crouched low and ran as fast as he could for the door. He knew that opening it would not go unnoticed, but there were few options. Opening the heavy steel door as quietly as possible, he slipped out, but the pneumatic cylinder along the top hissed as the door closed.

The three agents, having just verified that Williams wasn't in his private office, heard the sound and knew where he'd gone. They started in that direction, but Hatcher stopped them about halfway there. "He's going to his car. Come on," he commanded his subordinates, heading back toward the front door and their own vehicle.

Don ran to his company car, which was parked a couple of rows back, and jumped in. Once inside, he fumbled with his keys, dropping them on the floorboard. Cursing his clumsiness, he reached down and found them with shaking hands. Finally, Don got the car started and jammed the accelerator to the floor. Now, where should he go? Turning right, he began to maneuver his way through the typically sluggish Portland traffic. *Better check the rearview mirror—that's what they always do in the movies.* The black Suburban was only a few cars back.

This was crazy…he was actually running from the cops! What if this was all some kind of setup and the guy who'd called him was in on the whole thing? What did he say he was—a Marshal? Why would a U.S. Marshal be helping *him*? How would he have known about the ATF coming to arrest him? There'd be time for those questions later—he hoped. Right now, he had to get away from the ATF guys.

Up ahead was a red light, with a dozen or so cars backed up in each lane. No way was he going to sit at that light. Whipping the steering wheel to the left, Don shot down a side street. He was headed into a fairly congested area, with a lot of commercial buildings on both sides of the street. The Suburban was behind him now, with no other cars in between, and Don was already driving a lot faster on a thirty-five-mile-per-hour street than he ever had in his life.

He'd decided where to go—for now. There was a huge linen processing plant several blocks ahead. Typically, a number of large trucks and cargo vans were in the parking lot and he ought to be able to lose himself among them. The downside to this plan was that he would be trapped in a fenced lot. Still, there were no other options that came to mind. It might work...*if* he could lose the Suburban long enough to pull into the parking lot without being seen.

At the next four-way intersection, Don made a hard right, barely slowing down. One block later, he turned left, then right again. *What the...?* A large delivery truck was backing out of an alley not fifty yards in front of him. A man was motioning for the truck to back out, but he hadn't seen Don yet. Flooring the accelerator, Don shot around the rear of the truck, scraping the driver's side of his car on a concrete pole as he flew by. The man directing the truck was waving his arms wildly for the driver to stop, but the driver didn't see him and the truck kept backing out.

******

Hatcher was so close to catching this guy, he could taste it. There was no way Williams was going to lose him with this type of lame-ass driving, even though the Suburban handled like a cruise ship. Making a tire-squealing right turn, he felt the rear end of the SUV slide out slightly. As soon as he was able to right it, the delivery truck was staring him in the face and he was unable to stop. Turning the steering wheel sharply to the left, he was heading for the gap between the rear of the truck and a building, which put him up on the sidewalk. The only problem was a concrete light pole a few feet ahead. He couldn't stop in time, but not for lack of trying. The anti-lock brakes worked well, they just couldn't slow the heavy vehicle down fast enough and it slammed into the pole. Both airbags deployed and all three agents were slightly dazed. The chase was over.

******

Don was relieved beyond words to no longer see the Suburban on his tail. He took the risk of slowing down a bit for a look in his rearview mirror and, though he couldn't make out the scene very clearly, he knew what had happened. *That pole got 'em!* Breathing a little easier now, he decided to abandon his plan of hiding in the parking lot. Instead, he kept driving until he was well outside town.

Finally, Don pulled over onto a narrow two-lane road as a drizzling rain fell. He had to stop and think. His hands were shaking as he put the car in park and leaned his head back against the headrest. What he'd just been through was by far the most harrowing thirty minutes of his life. The first thing that came to mind was his family. He couldn't go home to them. Certainly, they'd be waiting for him there. What were these people capable of? Could they somehow use his family to get at him? The thought seemed preposterous, but an hour ago he wouldn't have thought *any* of this was possible.

Reaching for his cell phone, Don still wasn't sure what he would say to her, but he had to call his wife.

******

"Damnit!" Bill Payne screamed, slamming his fist down on his desk. Burke hated having to be the bearer of bad news, but it came with the territory. "This was a one-shot deal, Ray. If he makes it to the press, or anyone else in a position to hurt us, we could be screwed. Don't you understand? We've committed an *overt* act of retribution here."

It wasn't the first time the Commander had pulled a stunt like this…going against the advice of others and then demanding that they share the blame when things didn't work out. Burke wanted to scream, *We?! Who was it who told you not to do this?*, but thought the timing was probably not quite right. "Yes sir, I do understand. We'll find him. He's not used to running and hiding. A guy like this *will* make mistakes and, when he does, our people will be waiting for him." Burke spoke the words with more conviction than he felt, but they were words his boss needed to hear. Having the Commander relax a little would make it much easier for Burke to do his job.

"What plan do you have for accomplishing that, Ray? Are you going to *wait* for him to make mistakes?"

"No sir, we're not." Burke didn't really have a plan yet and he didn't appreciate being put on the spot like this. "Sir, give me a couple of hours to meet with Hatcher and discuss strategy, okay?"

Payne knew he was right. "Sure, Ray. Let's give it top priority, though. Also, I don't want to put out an APB, or involve any other agencies. We need to keep this as quiet as possible. Oh…and one more thing. I don't want Hatcher or anyone else knowing *why* Williams is so important to us. Understood?"

"Yes sir. I understand completely."

* * * * * *

Don decided before calling Jenny that he would try to put on an air of bravery that he didn't necessarily feel. She was a strong person, but nothing in their life together had prepared them for a situation like this. Right or wrong, Don resolved to protect her as much as possible as he told her about what he'd just been through.

Jenny was incredulous. When all this was theoretical, she not only was supportive of her husband's decision to "take on" the ATF, she'd actually *pushed* him in that direction. Now that the harsh consequences of those actions were apparent, she was much less certain that this was the right thing to do. They had children to worry about and a future to plan. She couldn't imagine that future without her husband.

"Don, this is crazy! You need to turn yourself in and let the police sort this out. Go back and talk to Walt. He'll get to the bottom of it."

Don knew that was a bad plan. He *was* doing the right thing! That was clearer now than ever. The fact that Payne would set him up like this and abuse his power so blatantly meant that he was capable of virtually anything. It also probably meant that he was responsible for the explosives being "found" in Mike's home. No, he couldn't back off now. In fact, he was certain that he was doing not only the right thing, but also the *only* thing possible. Payne had to be exposed for what he was. How many other "Mikes" would there be otherwise?

"Look, honey, let's calm down for a minute, okay?"

That's easy for you to say, she almost replied. Then she caught herself. She knew he must be scared to death. Of all the wonderful things that her husband was, adventurous and fearless were *not* among them. "Okay. I'm calm," she lied. "What do we do?"

"First of all, I can't give up on this. It's more important than ever now that people know what's going on—If they'd do this to me, they'd do it to anyone. And I can't come home right now. I'm sure they'd expect that and be waiting for me. I've got to try to clear things up first."

"How are you going to do that?" she asked.

"I'm working on it, sweetheart. I've got some ideas," he lied. "But, for the time being, you and the kids can't stay there, either." He didn't want to alarm her unduly, but he needed her to do what he was asking. "I need to think clearly and I can't do that if I'm worried about you guys."

"What are you saying? Do you think they'd try to hurt us?"

"Honey, I don't know *what* these people would try to do. I wouldn't have thought they'd do what they've already done. I just want to play it safe, okay?"

"I understand," she answered with feigned calmness.

"I want you to take the kids and go to George and Ana's house. Stay there for...I don't know, a few days, I guess. Just take them out of school for the rest of the week. I really want you all to be together somewhere that I know you're safe."

"Don, how are we going to fix this?"

"One thing at a time, honey. Just go pick the kids up and tell their teachers that a family emergency's come up. They can give you some makeup work for them to do. We've done it before, right?" She didn't answer and Don knew that she was thinking about a lot more than the kids missing a few days of school. "I think George and Ana's house is the best place for you to go. They could use the company. I'll contact you as soon as I can and I'll have my cell phone on. You'll be safe there and I'll be fine...I promise."

"Honey, why don't you just turn yourself in to the police?"

"I can't yet. I don't want to do that until I have some kind of proof of what they've done to me. If I give myself up without it, I'm at the mercy of the system and it's my word against theirs. The odds wouldn't be in our favor. I *will* turn myself in, as soon as I've got a leg to stand on."

* * * * * *

Washington, D.C.
Thursday, April 24

Charlie Martinez absolutely loved giving press conferences. In fact, especially at this level, it was probably the single most enjoyable aspect of politics. Nothing else so perfectly showcased one's ability to think on his feet and Martinez had that ability in spades. He supposed others who didn't possess the same talent would prefer root canals, if given the option.

But press conferences were *not* optional. They were an essential part of modern politics. They gave leaders the opportunity to disseminate their ideas and points of view on a variety of important topics and that gave people like Martinez a huge advantage. Besides, the media were typically friendly to those of his political stripe. Martinez had called today's press conference to blunt any criticism of the Collection process that might be forthcoming. The last few days had seen the first deaths come about as a result of their bold policy. He would be proactive in reassuring those with a more delicate constitution that they were still on the right track.

Few people on the current American political scene had a brighter future than did Charles Martinez. No matter what it took to do so, he would see to it that the Collection process furthered his career. In short, he would be *credited* with overseeing firearm Collection, not blamed for it.

The hum of conversation in the room ceased immediately upon his entrance onto the stage. He loved that. Inconspicuously arranging what few notes he had, Martinez quickly looked up at his audience, flashing his trademark dazzling smile as he did so. "Good afternoon, ladies and gentlemen. I would like to give you an update on the firearm Collection process. In a nutshell, we've had extraordinary success to this point…far exceeding our own expectations. The men and women of the Bureau of Alcohol, Tobacco, Firearms and Explosives have performed exceptionally well and they deserve our appreciation."

The Attorney General wanted to stay away from specifics as much as possible. The truth about the results of their enforcement of the new law was somewhat different from what the press was hearing at the moment. Far fewer gun owners than they'd hoped for and expected had, in fact, turned in their firearms. Also, they'd expected to have significantly more arrests during this first week than it appeared they were likely to. The process was more labor intensive and less efficient than they'd thought it would be. For these reasons, Martinez decided to avoid specifics today. He would also be somewhat "misleading" about the level of success they'd enjoyed thus far. Everyone would be better off for it. They *were* doing the right thing.

"Now that we have a little experience under our belts, the number of Collection operations per week will gradually increase. Additionally, a steady trickle of gun owners continues to see the light without our, uh, direct assistance, shall we say. Collection stations across the country are still doing a rather brisk business. This combination of efforts will allow us to carry out the will of the American people. It's only a matter of time, ladies and gentlemen. We *will* remove these deadly weapons from our streets. I'll take a few questions now."

Hands shot up instantly. He always liked to start out with the *New York Times*, for a couple of reasons. First of all, they were usually friendly to the Administration's cause, and secondly, Amy Vandenhoff was a knockout. "Amy?"

"How long do you expect the process to take, Mr. Attorney General?"

"That's hard to say, Amy. It obviously depends on a variety of factors, but we're confident that within three to four years the bulk of these weapons will be off the streets."

Martinez next pointed to the *Washington Post* correspondent. "Yes, Ron."

"Sir, can you comment on some of the polling data released yesterday that seem to indicate a slippage of support for the Collection process?"

Martinez knew this would come up. Most of the papers weren't making much of the most recent data, thank goodness, but he was aware of the fact that it was out there. "Well, it's to be expected, I suppose. Bold leadership and popularity don't always go hand in hand. The President has shown us the way. Now it's up to the American people to stand behind him. I would remind those who might be wavering in their support that it was extremely popular just a couple of weeks ago. No one ever said this process was going to be easy or painless, but the majority of the American people understand the necessity of it."

Control the situation, Charlie. "Jerry?" CBS News had always been fairly reliable.

"Sir, the shift in the public mood seems to stem from the deaths we've heard about over the last few days, starting with the first one last Friday night out in Oregon. People weren't really expecting that to happen so soon and so…often. Did the Administration foresee this much resistance to the ATF's efforts?"

"As I just said, Jerry, we didn't expect it to be easy *or* painless. Yes, we had every reason to believe that those who would openly defy a federal law would put up a fight when confronted with the consequences of their actions. That shouldn't come as a surprise to anyone. It also doesn't mean that we can or should shirk our responsibility to enforce that law." *What's wrong with these people? Where are the softballs?* "Okay, one more question, please." He always had to be careful not to appear as though he was looking for a friend in the audience. This was no time to be accused of dodging the tough questions. Still, he could probably get away with picking CNN to close this thing out. "Catherine?"

"Attorney General Martinez, could you expand on the comments you made a moment ago regarding the anticipated timeline for the Collection process? People might be wondering how many deaths will be involved if the process does, in fact, take three to four years to complete."

Martinez knew as soon as he gave them a timeline that he'd made a mistake. *Avoid specifics!* "Catherine, that time period was in no way definite. Furthermore, I said 'within three to four years'…we could be looking at a *much* shorter period of time. As I said earlier, we expect the process to become more efficient and streamlined as we gain experience. In all likelihood, that will result in both more arrests *and* fewer casualties. Again, please remember that these people had ample opportunity to do the right thing, yet they chose to violate the law. Everything we're doing is on behalf of law-abiding citizens, who deserve to raise their children and live their lives without being paralyzed by fear. I'm sorry, but that's all I have time for. Thank you very much."

As he walked down the hallway back to his office—to sit and wait for the inevitable phone call from the Boss—it occurred to the Attorney General that he might have just held the worst press conference of his career.

12

Portland, Oregon
Thursday, April 24

Don felt a little better now that he didn't have to worry so much about his family's safety. Still, he wasn't quite sure where to turn next. Needing a quiet place to think, he went to a spot on the Willamette River that was a favorite of his. It never ceased to amaze him that places like this existed so close to a city the size of Portland. The rain had stopped falling for the moment and, as Don sat in his car looking out at the fast-moving water, he realized that the first thing he had to do was get a better handle on the predicament he was in. The only way he could think of to do that was to contact the Marshal who had called to warn him and now seemed like as good a time as any.

Directory assistance gave him the number to the U.S. Marshals office in Portland. Though he didn't know where Keller had called him from, this seemed the most likely place to start. Thus, his initial reaction upon hearing that Deputy Marshal Keller could be reached at the ATF's Hazardous Operations Team headquarters was one of total shock. *What was going on?* Don nevertheless managed to remain calm enough to ask for a phone number. The realization that he was stepping into Payne's world, even if only via telephone, caused the butterflies in his stomach to fly in formation as he dialed the number.

******

After giving Don a heads-up this morning, Scott realized there was little else he could do for now. He decided to go back and finish the transition work he needed to do with his replacement. Once that was done, he could leave this place for good. They were at Scott's—no, *Sheehan's*—desk in squad room five when the phone rang.

"Marshal Keller?" asked a nervous male voice on the other end of the line.

"Yes, may I help you?"

"This is Don Williams. Remember me?"

"Hold on a minute." Scott turned to his replacement. "Hey, Carl, could you give me a few minutes? This is kind of a personal call." The newest temporary member of HOT was only too happy to have a little time to walk around and "meet folks," as he put it. *This guy's way too chipper to be a Marshal*, Scott thought.

Watching him leave, Scott returned to his phone call long enough to say, "I'll call you right back." He hung up, pulled the number off of caller ID, and dialed it on his cell. Don answered nervously after the first ring.

"What are you doing calling me here?" Scott demanded.

"Well, where else am I supposed to call you? I'm trying to figure out why the ATF's out to arrest me when I've never owned a gun in my life and my only lead is a U.S. Marshal who's working *with* them. What would you do if you were me?"

"Okay, okay. Listen, first of all, in case this conversation gets interrupted, you cannot call me, or anyone else, here again. Every call coming in to a landline from the outside is recorded so they can trace any threats they receive. Today's my last day over here, so it's not that big a deal for me, but for your own good, don't do it again." Scott then gave him his home phone number, cell number, and direct line at the USMS.

"So, I assume you're okay. I mean, you're not hurt?" Scott asked.

"Yeah, other than being scared to death. Are you relieved or sorry to hear that?"

Scott knew how confused the poor guy must be. They didn't

know each other at all, a U.S. Marshal calls and tells him to run from the bad guys, then it turns out he's working *with* the bad guys.

"Look, Don, I know how crazy this whole thing must seem to you, but you need to understand that I'm about the only one on your side over here." He knew Bobby was too, but didn't want to drag him into it, at least not yet.

"I believe you, Marshal. But I'd still love to know exactly what's going on. How much trouble am I really in and why?" he asked, knowing the answers before he asked the questions.

"Don, you're in a ton of trouble. There's no other way to put it. As of this morning, not only do you have a felony record, complete with an extensive listing of illegal firearms that you failed to surrender, but you're also a high-priority target for one hell of an efficient Special Operations unit of the ATF." Keller wondered whether he should pause and let the man digest all of that, but decided against it. Better to get it all out in the open and deal with it. That's the way he'd want it to be done if the roles were reversed.

"Now, as to the 'why'…well, my friend, you went into the tiger's cage and yanked on his tail pretty hard. I'm not saying he didn't deserve it, but you *really* pissed him off. To tell you the truth, though, as much of a bastard as he is, I never thought Payne would go this far. Our only hope—*your* only hope—is to stay hidden long enough to prove that he did, in fact, create a dummy record under your name. You and I both know he did, but that leaves our word against his and I don't think that'll be enough. And if it's not, you could spend several years in prison, which I'm assuming you wouldn't be in favor of."

"Yeah, you could say that. So how do we go about *proving* that he did it?"

"Not sure yet. I'll work on it, though. Look, my real job is catching fugitive bad guys ('just like you,' he almost added as a joke, but decided against it). So I can tell you what they'll do to try to find you. First of all, your assets either have been or soon will be seized. That means your bank accounts are frozen and your house isn't yours anymore. Also, don't try using your credit cards. If they haven't already cancelled them, they'll use your purchases to track you."

"Well, what am I supposed to use to pay for all this hiding out, then?"

"Don, listen to me. You've got to try to calm down. There's no way you can think as clearly as you're going to need to otherwise. Go to friends and ask them for cash. It's your only option. The other thing is, they'll be watching your family closely. They won't hurt them, but they *will* use them to track you down if they can."

"I took care of that. They went—" Don stopped himself. He was catching onto this stuff pretty fast, he thought. "They went somewhere safe."

"Good. Good thinking," Scott said, meaning it. "Don, one thing we have going for us is the fact that it serves Payne's purpose to keep this quiet—at least for now. He's got a little inner circle made up of a handful of men here and I think he's going to want to confine knowledge of this situation to that group. That means city, county, and state law enforcement won't be all over you too."

"So, you're saying that as bad as it sounds, it could be worse?"

Scott allowed himself a chuckle. This guy was all right. "Yeah, I guess that's what I'm saying. Don, I'm going to help you out. I promise. I'm not sure exactly how yet, but I will. I'm taking a few days off before I head back to the Marshals office, so you can reach me at home or on my cell."

"Oh, and speaking of phones," he added, "you have to get rid of yours as soon as you hang up with me. They can zero in on your SIM card easily."

"My what?"

"Your phone's subscriber identity module. Basically, it's what links your cell number to your phone—and therefore to you. Anyway, throw it out the window and get far away from it. Go pick up a couple of prepaid cell phones at Walmart or somewhere. Use them only in an emergency and then throw them away after each call."

"Okay, I will." Don paused and then asked, "are you married?"

"Yeah. In fact, my wife's pregnant with our first child."

"Congratulations. I've got three of them myself. My family's the most important thing in the world to me, Marshal. I've *got* to get back to them."

"You will...I promise. And by the way, it's Scott."

******

That was it, then. He was supposed to sit tight until Scott Keller cleaned up this mess for him. Not likely, Don thought. He wouldn't get in the way and he wouldn't take any unnecessary chances, but he certainly wasn't going to sit around and watch television until Keller said it was safe to come out. What he *was* going to do was a little less clear at this point.

After getting rid of his cell phone, Don drove back into town, feeling more nervous with each passing mile. Seeing two police cars within just a couple miles of each other nearly caused his heart to stop beating. He'd have to trust that Keller was right about Payne not wanting to involve other agencies. He stopped by an ATM machine and confirmed something else the Marshal told him—the machine ate his card. It occurred to Don that he'd better leave quickly. Undoubtedly, they'd know very soon that he had attempted to use the card. As luck would have it, he'd cashed an expense reimbursement check yesterday for a little over five hundred dollars; it appeared that would have to last him for a while.

What to do next? Find a place to hide out, he thought. *Man, this is weird!* He felt like a character in any one of a hundred novels he'd read. Things like this didn't happen to people like him. Pulling up to a motel in a less than desirable part of town, Don was reluctant to even get out of the car. He had to do it sooner or later, though, and this was a fairly safe place to test the waters. While Don *did* stand out in this neighborhood, it wasn't because he looked suspicious. The police cruising this area were likely looking for drug dealers and hookers, not businessmen in wrinkled suits.

The desk clerk looked miffed at having to put down his book and get up from the tattered chair that he'd sunk comfortably into.

"Yeah, what can I do for ya?"

"I, uh, need a room for the night," Don stammered.

"Here, fill this out," the clerk ordered, turning a half-sheet form around to his guest.

Don looked it over. It was all the standard stuff: name, address, phone number, etc. He thought briefly about putting false information on the form. It would be the covert thing to do, but he decided against it. He envisioned the clerk asking him for ID and catching him in a lie, knowing all the while that the clerk didn't care about anything other than his paperback. He was tempted to try his Visa card, but Keller's warning rang in his ear. Feeling like a miser protecting his last few dollars, he peeled off the cost of a night's lodging and handed it to the clerk.

The place was a dump. There was no other way to describe it. Not wanting to stay in the room any more than necessary, after quickly checking the place out, Don turned around and left. There was a Walmart just down the street and he bought a pair of jeans, a couple of T-shirts, a sweatshirt, a cheap pair of sneakers, a pack of underwear, and a toothbrush and toothpaste. He also grabbed two of the least expensive prepaid cell phones they carried. That would have to do for now. On the way back, he stopped at a convenience store and picked up some food, if you could call it that.

Within forty-five minutes, he was back at the motel. Don wondered again how his life had come to this. There wasn't time to reflect on that now, though. Now, he decided, was the time to enact the first phase of his plan...the *only* phase of his plan so far, he had to admit. It was time to call Jim Schaefer. The two had been good friends in college and had kept in close touch for some time afterward. But, as so often happens, the realities of life became roadblocks to continuing the friendship. Both men had families now and lived in opposite corners of the city. That meant different sports leagues for the kids and different circles of friends.

* * * * * *

Jim Schaefer loved his job at *The Oregonian.* He liked to think of himself as a traditional reporter, in the best sense of the term. Unlike many in his business, Jim understood that editorials belonged on the editorial page, *not* on the front page. Members of the media were no different from others in society. They were no more capable of ignoring their biases than anyone else was. The difference was that, because of their occupation, they were *obligated* to put them on the back burner much of the time. Otherwise, credibility—the most important trait for a news organization to possess—was destroyed.

Despite his strong views on bias, few people held more passionate political beliefs than Jim Schaefer did. He was in favor of not only the Family Protection Act, but virtually everything else the Nichols Administration supported as well. He believed the federal government should be actively involved in improving the lives of American citizens. To him, it was an obligation, not an option.

At the present time, he was working on a story about a proposal to breach dams in eastern Oregon and Washington. In the course of his investigation, he'd gathered opinions on each side of the issue, from both politicians and regular folks. The story had also allowed him to travel into the high desert and rimrock country that he loved so much. Now it was time to wrap it up. As a result, he was at his desk putting the final touches on the story when his phone rang.

"Jim Schaefer," he announced, as if the call was an interruption.

"You sound just as friendly as ever."

"Who is this?"

"It's Don Williams. Long time no see, pal." They exchanged pleasantries and discussed their families. Don didn't look forward to going into the story. There was always the possibility that Schaefer would doubt what he said. After all, most people tended to *trust* the government. And why shouldn't they? It was Don's responsibility, for the first time in his life, to answer that question.

"Jim, there's something I've got to tell you. You're obviously up to speed on this gun Collection process, right?"

"Of course, Don. That's my job. Why?"

There was no gentle way to delve into the subject, Don knew by now. "Well, I've sort of been thrown right into the middle of it, you might say."

Just like anyone else who knew him would have been, Schaefer was genuinely surprised. Don had never struck him as a "gun guy." In fact, they used to agree about half the time when it came to politics. Sure, people changed over time, but he and Don had had a number of discussions over the years about things like this. Thinking back over those friendly debates made this revelation that much more of a surprise. "How so?" Jim asked.

Then Don began the story. Schaefer learned of a man who loved his country deeply—right up until the moment its government killed him. He heard about two children who would never see their parents again and about a couple who'd fled a communist country, certain that they'd never again have to experience that kind of terror, only to have their one child taken from them by an overbearing government. Jim mostly listened, just as a good reporter was supposed to do. By the time his old friend was finished, all of the reflexive objections that Schaefer would have raised under normal circumstances seemed lame at best. He'd never really had to consider how this or any of the federal government's other policies might affect real people in a negative way. That had always been Republican propaganda, as far as he was concerned. Now that the practical implications of governmental activism were being thrown in his face by a man he used to have—and, he had to admit, still had—a great deal of respect for, it was more difficult than he might have imagined to argue in their favor.

With all that being the case, he still had to try. "Don, I covered Commander Payne's press conference and I admit I had some serious questions that were unanswered when it was over. But I still think they're doing the right thing here."

Don expected this reaction. "Jim, last week I felt exactly the same way. I swear. But I've come to realize that this isn't about guns. When

I saw Payne's press conference, I knew the guy was lying. He was talking about my best friend and I was in a position to know he was full of shit. The bottom line is that he wouldn't have been in a position to lie without this 'war on guns.' It's all about control, Jim—not saving lives."

Just a few days ago, Don would have laughed at such a statement—and now the words were coming out of his own mouth. He could have come right out and started the conversation with a description of his *own* predicament, but wanted to give Schaefer some background first—knowing about Mike and Sarah was important. He'd done that and Schaefer (somewhat to Don's surprise) had offered little in the way of argument. Now it was time to bring the reporter over to his side.

"I'm in a lot of trouble myself now, Jim," he began, and proceeded to bring Schaefer up to speed on the events of the last several hours. When he was finished, there was nothing but silence on the other end of the line.

Jim Schaefer was stunned. In all his years as a journalist, he'd never heard such an unbelievable story. To him, it sounded like the plot from a conspiracy novel. But he didn't doubt it for a second. He knew Don Williams too well. Because of that, he wouldn't insult his friend by asking for proof. This was for real, he knew, and it would make a terrific front-page story. But that wasn't his primary concern right now.

"Don, there aren't many people I know who could get away with telling me a story like that without me thinking they're nuts…but you're one of them."

"Jim. I'm sitting here right now, scared out of my mind, and I've asked myself over and over again if this could just be a misunderstanding of some kind. It's not. I may be short on answers right now, but that much I'm sure of."

"Where do we go from here, Don? There's got to be a reason you came to *me* instead of another friend, or the police—and before you laugh at me, I hope you'd agree that not all cops are bad."

"*Of course* I don't think all cops are bad. In fact, the only real hope I have right now for a way out of this mess is the U.S. Marshal I told you about. Jim, I called you because you're the only reporter I know."

"That's what I figured. So, are you asking me to run with the story right now?"

"No, I'm not. There's not much we can prove at this point, so I'd like to wait a bit and see if Keller can scrape something up. That's our best bet. Payne set me up, Jim. He's trying to ruin my life to cover his own corrupt ass. I don't just want to embarrass him or make him call off the dogs, I want to bring him down…make him sorry he ever heard my name."

What he was about to say next pained him to even consider. "Jim, what I'm asking you to do is keep this under your hat for now. Obviously, if things work out the way I hope they will, you'll have one helluva scoop. If not…well, I'd like everybody to know my side of the story…if for no other reason than to make life a little miserable for the people who did this to me. I'm saying that if anything happens to me, I want you to run with this, Jim. I mean really give 'em hell. Will you promise me you'll do that?"

This was a first for Schaefer, as it would have been for most journalists. Frankly, it was a responsibility that worried him a little. If the worst-case scenario ever came to be, there would be an awful lot of pressure on him to do the story justice. Still, there was no way he could even consider turning down his old friend's request. "First of all, Don, It's *not* going to come to that, okay? But yes, I promise I'll run with the story—I mean *really* run with it—if need be. You can count on it."

******

"Man, I can't *believe* that sonofabitch!" Bobby Myers hissed. He and Scott were having a beer and trying to make sense of what had happened today. Never in his professional life had he been so ashamed. Neither he nor Scott had even met this Williams guy, but they both felt an overwhelming desire to help him any way they could. *Any* agency of the federal government was not something you wanted to have chasing you, but Bill Payne and his crew here at HOT would be particularly scary, especially for a regular guy who knew nothing about the game he was playing.

For all Bobby's talk a couple of weeks before about hanging around through the Collection process to make sure things didn't get out of hand—they had.

He also now questioned that whole rationale. Why *had* he stayed on, in spite of the fact that he was opposed to Collection? It wasn't mainly to keep his people safe and under control, he now had to admit to himself. It was, to an embarrassingly large degree, due to the same motivation he so freely attributed to others…self-interest.

He'd put a lot of blood, sweat, and tears into his career and his future was essentially limitless. That counted for a lot in this world. He'd watched his father work his whole life as a janitor. He was a good man—honest, trustworthy, and hard working. There was certainly much to respect in all of that; so many of Bobby's friends growing up didn't even *have* a father to teach them right from wrong. In his world, that was something to be proud of, and he was. Still, the thankless job and lack of achievement in the conventional sense had weighed heavily on his father. In the end, he'd "retired" on nothing but Social Security…with no pride at all in what he'd accomplished during his working life. That pride counted for a lot in a man and it was something that the elder Myers had never known. He'd never said so, but you could see it in his eyes. The memory wasn't lost on his son.

Bobby had always sworn that his kids wouldn't be able to say the same about him. He'd been determined to build a career that they could be proud of. Now those plans were circling the drain… *or were they?* Even though what had happened since last Friday wasn't his fault, there had to be something he could do to set things right. Bobby decided, then and there, that he would do so, even if it meant the end of his career—of *this* career, he reminded himself.

"So, how did our boy Williams sound when you talked to him?" Bobby asked quietly.

"Scared to death. Those are his words. Pretty sharp guy, though. I think he'll be okay if he can just lie low for a while."

"We've gotta help this guy out, Scott. We need proof that Payne set this thing up and we need it fast. If this goes on for more than a few days, Payne's gonna get desperate...maybe drag in local cops. This Williams dude's not gonna be able to run from every cop in town."

"I know, and I promised him I'd help. So, how *do* we help him?"

"I've been thinking about that. I'm no computer geek, but I think there's a way to check the records to see when they were accessed and what entries were made. They had some nerd from D.C. come by last week to tell us a bunch of stuff about the program we'd never need to know. Seems like he said something about that. Anyway, I couldn't remember how to do it if you put a gun to my head, but the little nerd left his card. I'll give him a call tomorrow to find out."

Scott looked relieved. He'd begun to feel as if he'd made a promise that he had no idea how to keep. *That* would have driven him crazy. "Thanks, man. You bailed me out on this one."

"Hey, I haven't done anything yet. Let's just wait and see how it goes tomorrow. We probably ought to work on a 'Plan B' just in case. Don't ya think?"

"Yeah. We probably should. I'll try to come up with something and give you a call. Meanwhile, if you stumble onto anything, call me at home, okay?"

"Yeah, yeah. Go ahead and rub it in. I know you're outta here." He looked at Scott with a sly smile.

Scott would miss Bobby. Oh sure, maybe they'd get together now and then, but realistically, not very often. They both knew that. "Bobby, why don't you apply to the Marshals Service? You'd be good at it and I'd have to think you'd be a top-priority candidate."

"I wasn't joking before when I told you I'd thought about it. I might do something like that; you never know. Would you put in a good word for me with Marshal Filson?"

"Of course!" Scott answered enthusiastically.

"Good. I'd appreciate it." Then the smile faded. "But first, we've got a little problem to solve at ATF, don't we?"

* * * * * *

Don knew he had to call his wife, for two reasons. First of all, of course, because he wanted to. She'd always been his primary source of inspiration when times were tough. Now, at what was undoubtedly the most difficult time of his life, he needed her more than ever. The other reason was more pragmatic. She needed to know that he was safe and that he had a plan to get out of this mess. This would all be over soon, he had to keep telling himself as he dialed George and Ana's number on the same cell phone he'd just used to call Schaefer. He'd need to get rid of it right after this call, Don reminded himself.

He was a little startled when George answered the phone, though he shouldn't have been. It *was* his home, after all. "George, it's Don."

"Yes, Don. Are you safe?"

"I am, George. How are you and the kids doing?"

"We are doing well, Don. The children are as strong as their father. It makes me very proud to see. Of course, they miss their parents. We all do. But we will live through this. We have no choice."

There, for all of his idealism, was the essence of George Niculescu's character. He was a survivor. One couldn't have gone through what he had without the innate desire to "make it," no matter what. Don hadn't thought about it before, but that just might be the children's saving grace. If their grandparents could instill in them that sense of survival, despite everything the world threw at them, they *would* make it. If that happened (and Don was suddenly sure that it would), they would go on to lead normal lives...maybe even extraordinary lives. Only time would tell.

"Don, I must say I am worried very much for you. It makes me happy that you risk so much for my son's memory, but I look at your wonderful family here and I feel that you should be with them. They need you…just as my son's children needed him and Sarah. I am thankful for all you do, but maybe it is time to go to this man from the government and tell him you mean him no harm. There is not shame in that, my friend. You must think of yourself and your family first. I believe that is what Michael would want.

"You must understand, he did what he did because of his beliefs. My son would never expect others to fight battles for him. He always did that himself. This battle he lost. It is that simple. After I have seen what happened in America in recent years, I think all governments are the same. You cannot win fight against them. All power is with them, not with people. Before, I did not think this way about United States. But I am afraid there is not much difference from Romania. I am afraid you will lose the fight too, Don…just as Michael and Sarah did."

All of this caught Don off balance. He would not have expected George to make more than a token suggestion that he give up. How could he do any more than that? Don was the only one capable of vindicating his dead son and daughter-in-law and it *had* to be done. *Didn't it?* He'd worked awfully hard convincing himself over the last couple of days that it did.

Now George was telling him otherwise and he was pretty convincing. Momentarily, Don's conviction wavered—but he quickly decided that he wasn't about to give up now. In fact, he reminded himself, he probably *couldn't* even if he wanted to. It was naïve for anyone to think that Don could simply walk into Payne's office, declare a truce, and go about his business. Payne had obviously taken steps that were irreversible.

Don would also always believe that the United States *was* fundamentally different from virtually every other country on the planet. An individual *could* make a difference here and, in the end, the good guys *did* win. No, he wouldn't take the easy way out that was being offered by this kind old man. But he also wasn't going to offer up a load of false bravado. "George, I appreciate your concern for me and my family. I really do. But I'm going to work on this for another couple of days. If things don't look more promising then, maybe I'll do as you say. In the meantime, though, I'll be fine. You've got enough to worry about there. Please don't worry about me too."

"Don...my son would be very proud of you. Good-bye for now, my friend," the old man said, choking back a sob as he handed the phone to Jenny.

"Hi, honey!" It was obvious by the tone of her voice that Jenny was going to try to lift her husband's spirits, which was fine with him. He needed a little of that right about now. "I miss you already," she continued.

"I miss you too, baby. How are the kids?"

"Oh, they're fine. They're having a blast playing with each other. It's like a vacation for them. Clay looked at me real seriously and said he wants to talk to you, but I don't think even *he* knows what's really going on."

"This is going to be over soon, I promise. I talked to the Marshal who called to warn me. He knows all about what Payne did and he's gathering the proof right now. I really think he'll get it done." It wasn't a lie, but he was far less confident than he hoped he sounded.

"I hope you're right. We need you with *us*, Don. I want to be clear about this. I was in favor of you helping Mike out even before...well, you know, before last Friday. I still feel the same way. What happened to him and Sarah was one of the most disgusting things I've ever heard about. And what they've done to you is even worse, in a way. These people need to be stopped and you might be the only person in a position to do it. No offense, honey, but if someone had told me that a couple of weeks ago, I would have laughed in their face—but it's true. Still, I'm begging you not to get carried away. This isn't some action-hero movie. Don't take any stupid chances. You're a good man and you don't have anything to prove to anyone...or to anyone's memory. Do you understand where I'm coming from?"

"Yes, I do. Don't worry, I haven't turned into Jack Bauer all of a sudden. I'll be okay." Don gave her the motel's address and phone number. He then told her about ditching his cell phone, while assuring her that he'd stay in contact. "Now I'd better talk to Clay, don't you think?"

As they exchanged the usual conversation-opening pleasantries, Don could tell that his son knew more about what was going on than Jenny gave him credit for. It wasn't what he said, but what he *didn't* say, that told the story. When Clay was bothered by something, he tended to become quiet rather than throw a fit like so many kids his age.

"Dad, are you in trouble?" He finally asked.

He was smart and Don didn't want to insult the young man by lying to him outright. He'd never buy it anyway. "A little bit, yeah. But you know what, I'm gonna be okay, buddy. I promise. I've got a really good man helping me out. He knows what these guys have done and he's working real hard to help me."

"Who is he, Dad?"

"He's a U.S. Marshal. That means he's a really good police officer."

"But the guys that…that killed Mr. and Mrs. Niculescu were police officers too."

"Yes, they were. But, you have to understand that most police officers try really hard to help people—not hurt them." That was important for Clay to understand. It was also true, Don believed. What he didn't want to go into with his twelve-year-old son was his belief that it was certain powerful politicians and a couple of loose cannons within the ATF who had killed Mike and Sarah. They—and Don—were the victims of a relative handful of power-hungry individuals, not a huge web of conspiracy.

"Dad, I just want you to know that you're making me really proud of you, okay?"

"Thanks, buddy. That means a lot to me." And it did. Don spoke briefly with his two younger children before hanging up. Those conversations were much easier on him. Troy and Stephanie obviously didn't yet understand what was going on, nor should they. Their lives would become complicated enough in just a few short years. Clay was proof of that.

Talking to his family was a brief distraction from the things that had been occupying his mind, but not necessarily a welcome one. It was hard to hear their voices and not choke up. He hoped that knowing people cared so much about him wouldn't make it more difficult to do what he had to do, to take the chances that he might have to take.

Don realized that he'd spent his entire adult life subconsciously sidestepping issues that might force him to take an irreversible stand. He hadn't even *chosen* to do so in this case. Or had he? It occurred to him that he might have welcomed the opportunity to prove to himself that he was capable of more than simply maintaining the status quo. Certainly, he would rather have had a different issue to deal with—losing one's best friend was hardly the kind of thing any sane man looked forward to. Still, he could have taken the easy way out after it happened. But he hadn't, he thought, somewhat proudly.

Why *was* he doing this? Was it to prove something to himself, or because he felt he owed it to Mike? No, he didn't owe his friend anything. The two of them were good friends, but not blood brothers. And he had never longed to risk life and limb to prove something about his character to himself. That left a third possibility. Maybe an issue that was larger than him, or Mike—or anyone else, for that matter—had finally confronted him. He remembered Mike preaching about this kind of thing right to the very end. And of course, history was replete with examples of people attempting to advance a cause for the greater good. How many of those people had stumbled into their fight the way Don had?

His boring life of just three weeks before was now history and while he felt a sense of pride in his willingness to tackle this issue, the predominant emotions flooding his consciousness were fear and uncertainty. He was absolutely scared to death, with no idea how to proceed from here. It just didn't feel right to wait for Scott Keller to fix things for him, but what could he do? George *had* to be wrong about not being able to win a fight against the government.

13

Portland, Oregon
Friday, April 25

NICK LARSEN WAS glad to finally have something constructive to do, after spending the last several weeks essentially marking time. His pager had gone off very early that morning—much to his surprise, since only a handful of people had the number. It was George Niculescu, his old friend's father. Nick hadn't spoken to him in a long time, but he'd always had a high degree of respect for the elder Niculescu.

Nick had been at Mike's funeral, though not conspicuously. He didn't buy every conspiracy theory that came down the pike, but he'd spent enough time around high-level decision makers in the federal government to know that nearly anything was possible. Not wanting to fall into what could easily have been an ATF trap, he'd steered clear of anyone who might know him, hanging around the fringes of the very large gathering. He had also changed his appearance slightly. Nick was a bit paranoid these days, he had to admit. The bottom line, however, was that nothing—not even the fear of imprisonment—would have kept him from paying his respects to one of the men he'd admired most in the world.

Nick felt like a hunted man. Even though there was no indication that he actually *was* at this point, he was sure that at the very least he was one of thousands on ATF lists who would eventually be targeted for Collection. That knowledge had taken its toll. Previously, Nick had viewed a little paranoia as healthy—a good thing, for the most part. It had served him well and had kept him alive on more than one occasion. Living that way required a strong constitution, however. These days, Nick was less sure it was healthy. He was older now and had been a civilian for a few years. Maybe he'd gotten soft.

Regardless, it seemed more than a little ironic that the last time he'd felt this way was when he was fighting for the same government that now persecuted him. Several times over the last few days, Nick had wondered whether his old friend had felt the same sense of irony.

They had known each other since they were roommates at The Basic School, which all Marine officers were required to attend. Mike and Nick then went on to the Infantry Officer Course together, as well. During those eight-plus months, the two young men became fast friends. They had a lot in common, from personality type to mannerisms to likes and dislikes. They were even both from the same state, Oregon. Their buddies joked that they must be brothers and just didn't know it. They hung around together whenever possible and developed a bond that would grow only stronger over time.

After all the required training, Mike was assigned a reconnaissance platoon to command and Nick became a Ground Intelligence Officer in the same battalion. The two of them served together for the next three years. Both were very good at what they did and were well regarded by the enlisted Marines they commanded, by their peers, and by their superiors.

As they neared the end of their initial obligations, Mike told Nick of his decision to return to civilian life. They discussed going into business together and the idea appealed to Nick, but in the end he decided that he wasn't ready to leave the Corps. He also wanted a new challenge.

So, when Mike reentered the civilian world, Nick extended his service obligation and went to a Force Reconnaissance company. In those pre-MARSOC days, Force Recon was considered the tip of the spear within the Marine Corps. They were the "sneak and peek" Marines, who could get behind enemy lines in small teams, gather intelligence, and get out without being detected.

During Nick's second Recon deployment, he was selected to work with a CIA Paramilitary team. The mission went well and the CIA boys were impressed enough with the young Recon officer that they encouraged him to apply to the Agency. Once again, young Nick Larsen had a decision to make that would dramatically alter the course of his life. The CIA piqued Nick's interest as nothing else ever had. He thought a lot about it and decided that although he loved the Corps, the Central Intelligence Agency fascinated him enough that he had to give it a try.

After a lengthy application and evaluation process, Nick was hired by the CIA as a Paramilitary Operations Officer in the Special Operations Group, which gave the President of the United States a covert option for use when overt action was not feasible. The unit's missions included everything from subversion of foreign governments, to intelligence gathering in hostile environments, to the rendition of prisoners.

Over the next several years, Nick traveled the world as a CIA officer, learning the tricks of the trade and loving every minute of it. The missions were usually challenging, exciting, and potentially dangerous—all things he had come to crave as part of his daily existence. He fully intended to stay with the CIA until he retired, but another unexpected twist of fate changed the direction of his life.

Nick's parents had for many years operated a very successful import/export business. He'd always been close to them and had tried to keep in contact, though that was often difficult. He was just a couple of weeks away from a vacation that he planned to use for a rare visit with his parents when he received a phone call in the middle of the night. Nick would never forget sitting up in bed, the fog of a deep sleep still clearing as he listened to his younger brother Danny tell him that their parents had been killed in a traffic accident. As a result, the "vacation" came a little earlier than it was supposed to and was dominated by a painful and emotional funeral.

Nick and his brother had a couple of days after the funeral to discuss the future. Both young men had just inherited a very large sum of money, but more importantly to them—and, according to the will, their parents—they'd also inherited a vibrant business. By the time the two of them boarded their flights home, they knew that they had to honor their parents, not only by keeping the business running but also by growing it and fulfilling its potential.

Though it was difficult to do, Nick turned in his resignation to the CIA and moved back to his hometown of Bend, Oregon. Over the next few years, Nick and Danny proved to themselves and everyone else that they had the same aptitude for entrepreneurialism that their parents had. The business thrived and expanded, including overseas, Nick's specialty. The contacts he'd made while in the CIA came in handy at times and he loved to travel abroad.

Nick had no family of his own, whereas Danny was married, with two young children. Nick was never jealous of his brother, but from time to time he wished he'd found the right woman and settled down. The life he chose just never seemed to allow for it, though. There'd been relationships, but nothing lasting—and more than once, Nick had felt himself engaging the familiar defense mechanisms that he'd used so many times before. *Some people just aren't cut out for long-term relationships*, he'd told himself over the years, never really believing it.

Nick also had hobbies that kept him busy when he wasn't working and traveling. Primary among them were shooting and hunting. He shot both long-range rifles and handguns competitively and hunted all over the world. The trophies from both competition and his many memorable hunts adorned the comfortable log home he'd built in the hills of central Oregon. He'd also assembled an extensive and very impressive collection of firearms, many of them custom-made by some of the finest craftsmen in the world.

The arrangement between the two Larsen brothers worked out perfectly and the value of their business skyrocketed. Over the last couple of years, however, Nick had become consumed by the state of political affairs in the country. In particular, the passage of the Family Protection Act had really affected his mood—and his outlook on life.

He became restless and had to fight the urge to disengage from his responsibilities. Danny saw this coming and offered to buy his older brother's share of the business. This made sense to both of them and the timing was right. Nick had no idea what he would do, but knew that he needed to establish a new direction in his life.

As a result, at the age of forty, Nick Larsen was both independently wealthy and unemployed. This was a great combination; it allowed him the freedom to do things he couldn't otherwise have done...such as hide from the federal government. He had spent his entire adult life trying to stay one jump ahead of his opponents. This situation would be no different.

His course of action was never in doubt. Having no one but himself to be concerned about, Nick never even considered compliance with this absurd governmental proclamation. He'd leave the country if he had to. There were plenty of places he could go and plenty of people he knew around the world. The final step in preparation for whatever actions he would have to take was to sell his house and most of his personal belongings...except his firearms, of course. Those had been preserved and hidden where no one but Nick would ever find them.

He transferred a large portion of his wealth into a numbered Swiss bank account, and then moved to a furnished apartment in Portland. Despite what many people thought, it was actually easier to hide in a heavily populated city than in the boondocks. The apartment was rented under a business name. There was no landline telephone and he used a post office box for receiving mail. His pager and prepaid disposable cell phones were his only communication links to the outside world and his SUV had false license plates, which he acquired through an old friend from his Agency days. Nick was as close to being a nonentity as was possible—yet he still didn't feel safe.

His mind was awash in these thoughts as he drove to the Niculescus' home. George had summoned him that morning without divulging the reason, which was fine with Nick. The man deserved his attention, regardless of the subject to be discussed.

******

It had been a while since Sykes and Lynch were on an all-night stakeout and both of them had thought more than once over the last several hours about how much they hated doing it. Occasionally, they'd start the vehicle, drive around the block, and park in a different spot along the street, in order to keep neighbors from becoming overly suspicious. That was always a risk in a residential area like this one.

The subject of this stakeout wasn't home—that much they'd verified the night before. So, why were they watching this house, waiting for somebody to arrive? A search warrant should be a piece of cake for any level-three subject. Why not just serve it and then send in an HOT squad? This made little sense to either of them and they were both bright enough to question things that didn't make sense. After the way the last Collection had gone, they were also more than a little nervous about tackling a "three" by themselves. Some of these gun nuts were serious dudes! There was little need to worry about that at this point, though. The house was still just as empty as it had been when they'd arrived last night. Either these people were on a family vacation, or they'd cleared out.

It was a little after 7:30 a.m. when Lynch ended a call on his cell phone and started the vehicle. "Man, I don't get this," he complained after pulling away from the curb. After reporting in to Burke about thirty minutes before, the Deputy Commander had just called back with instructions. "You know the guy we took down last week?" Lynch asked his partner. Sykes nodded. "Burke wants us to go over to his *parents'* house and see if this Williams guy's car is over there. Not do anything, just look for the car!" Both of them were dead tired and in no mood for this.

"He didn't tell you what this is all about?" Sykes wondered.

"Nope. I don't think Hatcher knows anything, either."

******

Neither the Niculescus nor Jenny had slept well. By 5:30 a.m. they were all wide awake, drinking coffee and discussing possible ways to help Don. George had come up with the idea of contacting Nick Larsen. Mike had given his parents Nick's pager number sometime back—long before he had any reason to fear for his own safety. He wanted them to have someone to call if they ever needed real help and their son wasn't around to provide it. That time had clearly arrived. George and Ana had complete confidence in Nick. Their son had trusted this man more than anyone he'd ever known and every contact they'd had with him over the last fifteen years had validated that trust.

The soft knock on the front door at 7:30 told them that Nick had wasted no time in coming to their aid. After exchanging pleasantries, they spent a few minutes catching up before finally discussing the reason for the early morning page. Nick listened patiently, asking only a few questions for clarification. He soon understood the depth of the trouble Don was in and was surprised to learn that Don had put himself in that position in spite of the fact that he'd never even owned a gun. Nick admired that kind of friendship.

He wasn't sure how far he wanted to go, however, to help this man he'd never met. His own ass was very much on the line already and helping Don would likely make matters much worse. On the other hand, the man *had* been a friend of Mike's—a very good one, it seemed. Many of the decisions Nick had made in his life were made quickly, usually out of necessity. The decision was made. He *would* help Don Williams. He would do it for Mike.

"Okay, I'll do what I can, but you all need to understand that I may not be able to save him. These people after him have tremendous resources and manpower. They're pros and they've got the law on their side, whether we like it or not." Nick realized how tough that must have sounded, especially to the man's wife, but he had to be honest. "Where is he?"

Now it was Jenny's turn to make a difficult decision. She didn't know this man and she was more paranoid than she'd ever been.

Right now Don was safe—as far as they knew—primarily because no one knew his whereabouts. Once that was no longer the case, all bets were off. Besides, he had that Marshal helping him; maybe that was the safer way to go. Normally, the fact that George and Ana knew and trusted Nick would have been enough to wipe away any doubts she might have had. *But these aren't normal times, are they?*

"Mr. Larsen, there is a U.S. Marshal helping my husband already. He knows about everything that's gone on and he promised Don that he would take care of it. Do you think we'd be better off waiting to see what he can do?" It was as much a plea as a question.

"Mrs. Williams, understand where I'm coming from. I'm here because Mike Niculescu was the best friend I've ever had. With all due respect, I'm not doing this for your husband. You see, my own life is pretty important to me as well. What I'm telling you is that it won't take much to talk me out of this." Jenny looked into his eyes. They were sincere, trustworthy, and serious—just as Mike's had been. As she was evaluating him, Nick continued. "Having said that, I've got to be honest with you. I wouldn't trust *any* federal law enforcement officer with your husband's life if I were you. But of course it's up to you."

"May I call you Nick?" He nodded. "Nick, I don't mean to insult you by hesitating. I'm just scared. Really scared." The tears streaming down her face confirmed the words she spoke. "I love my husband very much and if anything happened to him, I don't know what we'd do. It's that simple." She paused and dried her eyes with a paper napkin that Ana handed her from the kitchen table. "I do trust you." With that, Jenny proceeded to tell the stranger all she knew about her husband's predicament, including where he could be found. Her instincts said he was their best hope.

After some discussion, they all agreed to call Don before sending Nick to the motel. Though Don might object, the fewer surprises the better. As it turned out, they need not have spent time debating the matter. Attempts to reach him through the motel phone were unsuccessful and Jenny was terrified by the implication. Nick left within minutes. They'd know soon enough whether she was right.

Jenny felt the need to go for a run, as she did most every morning until her routine was interrupted by the events of the past few days. It helped her relieve stress and she needed that in a big way. The Niculescus understood and assured her that they'd give the kids breakfast if they woke up while she was gone.

* * * * * *

Because of the Portland rush hour traffic, it was almost 8:30 by the time Lynch and Sykes reached the Niculescu home. They drove past it, then parked across the street a few houses down, not noticing the dark blue SUV that had pulled out of the driveway only seconds before their arrival.

"There it is, sitting right in the driveway," Sykes noticed. Just to be sure, he checked the license plate with a pair of binoculars. "Yep."

"No sign of the other one…the one Williams got away from Hatcher in." Lynch was thinking out loud as he scanned the area. "It could be in the garage, though."

"How about I pretend to be a meter reader or something? You know, go up there and take a look in the garage window?"

Lynch considered the idea for a few seconds. "I don't think we ought to risk it. For some reason Burke and Payne are super uptight over this one. Let's give 'em a sit rep first and see what they want us to do." He dialed the number to headquarters.

It was the same nonsense as the last time he'd called: Burke had to check on something and would call back in a few minutes. That wasn't exactly what they wanted to hear. Both of them were starting to get bedsores from sitting still for so long.

"Hold on." Lynch was staring at the front door. "Woman coming out of the house." They watched as Jenny jogged down the street.

"Wonder if that's his wife," Sykes muttered.

"Don't know. Either way, looks like she's going out for a run, not running away. Nothing for us to do but log it and wait."

* * * * * *

Burke went into overdrive after Lynch's call. He didn't want his men nosing around and tipping the subjects off unnecessarily. Something told him that Williams wouldn't be hiding out in the same place as his family. He wouldn't endanger those he cared about, but he probably would keep in touch with them.

A call to the telephone company brought him the break he was looking for. Within minutes, he had a PDF on his computer consisting of all incoming and outgoing calls from the Niculescu residence over the past forty-eight hours. There had been two the night before. One of them was a call to Florida and the other was an incoming call from a Portland number that turned out to be a motel inside the city limits. *Bingo.*

* * * * * *

The annoying ring of the cell phone jarred Lynch and Sykes out of a sleep-deprived trance. "Lynch, this is Deputy Commander Burke. Hatcher and I are going to meet you two across the street from the Parkview Motel on Martin Luther King Boulevard. We believe Williams is in hiding there. I repeat, meet us across the street from the motel. Do *not* attempt to close in on your own. Do you understand?"

"Yes sir, I do."

"Good. Now get moving."

* * * * * *

For the first time in his life, Scott Keller had more on his mind than achieving the next goal in front of him. There had always been at least one, whether it was winning a football game, completing a mission as a MARSOC Marine, or apprehending a fugitive as a U.S. Marshal. Now—though many other things were still on his mind—his wife and the child she carried were uppermost in his thoughts.

There was very little he could do to help Don Williams directly right now and he was convinced that Bobby would come through. That certainty allowed him to actually look forward to a little time off. It had been a while since he'd taken a vacation without having a specific purpose in mind; it wasn't in his nature to not have a plan. But Meg had insisted they not have an agenda for today. They'd wake up when they wanted to and do whatever came to mind, she'd told him last night.

Though he promised himself before falling asleep that he would lie in bed until Meg woke up, by 5:45 he was wide awake and certain that she would sleep for at least another hour and a half. That was just too much of the day to waste. He'd let her get the sleep she needed while he got up and read the paper over a cup of coffee or two. At about 7:30, he heard sounds in the bedroom that told him she was awake. Scott was just about to go in and give her a proper 'good morning' when the phone rang.

* * * * * *

A nice hot shower was just what Don had needed—one of the things he needed. He hadn't slept at all and he had to be able to think clearly. The hot water removed at least some of the cobwebs. As he dressed, he decided to call the Marshal at home.

"Hi, uh…Scott?"

"Yeah."

"It's Don Williams."

Scott was a little shocked. Though he'd given Don his number, he hadn't expected a call quite so soon. "Morning, Don. Are you okay?"

"I'm fine. Didn't sleep a wink last night, but at least nobody's chased me or shot at me in almost twenty-four hours. I'm sorry; I probably shouldn't have called so early, but I just wanted to know if anything turned up yesterday."

It was amazing how fast Scott's mood changed. Suddenly he felt lazy for not being somewhere right now, doing something—*anything*—to help this guy. "Don, there's an ATF agent working on your case today. He's a friend of mine and he's solid. He'll come through for us."

"What's he doing to help?"

"This 'record' of yours is obviously false. Bobby's working on getting proof of that from the computer system that it was created on. He thinks that's the best angle to work from—*maybe the only angle*, Scott thought—and I'd have to agree with him."

"I guess I've got no choice but to trust you guys. I feel like a puppet, though, sitting here waiting for people to pull the strings. It's a pretty helpless feeling."

Scott didn't know what to say. He didn't want to give the guy false hope. Something could always go wrong and it usually did. Because of that risk, Don was better off having only realistic expectations. "I can only imagine," he finally said.

"Just promise me one thing, Scott. If it looks like you guys aren't going to be able to get what you need, please let me know as soon as you can, okay?"

"You bet I will. Bobby and I are both taking this whole thing very personally. We really are both on your side…you need to know that. This kind of thing makes the whole federal government look shady and we're part of it. Like I told you before, I'm taking a couple of days off, but I'll still be working on this. I want you to call me anytime you need to. I'll let you know as soon as I find something out."

"Thanks, Scott." Don thought about bringing up his contact at the newspaper, but decided against it. Schaefer was his ace in the hole and, though he trusted the Marshal, one never knew when a secret weapon might become useful.

******

Scott walked back into the bedroom as Meg was brushing her teeth.

"Who was that on the phone?" she asked.

"It was Don Williams. He wanted to know whether we'd found anything out yet. Poor guy doesn't know what to do with himself while he's waiting for us to bail him out. He's a sharp guy, but he's not used to this kind of pressure and I'm afraid it'll cause him to do something stupid if we don't nail Payne soon."

Meg came over and lay down on the bed beside her husband. "Honey, I can't imagine how he must feel. If this were happening to me, I wouldn't have any idea how to deal with it. How do you know what to do and who to trust?"

"Actually, I think you'd do pretty well and I believe Don will too. Something happens to people when they're thrown into a situation like this. They find out what they're really made of and they generally do all right, even if they've never experienced anything like it before. Don's going to be okay…if we can get what we need before Payne finds him."

******

Although Nick had what he thought was a better idea for a safe house, this place wasn't bad. A shabby motel on the wrong side of the tracks wasn't the first place anyone would come looking. With some trepidation, Nick knocked quietly on the dingy motel room door, hoping this guy would have his wits about him. After all, he could have gotten his hands on a gun. Nick certainly would have. Then again, he never would have allowed himself to be *without* one in a situation where his life might be on the line.

"Yeah?" came the nervous response from inside the room.

"Don, my name's Nick Larsen. I was a friend of Mike's and your wife asked me to try to help you. Can I come in?"

Nick Larsen. Don remembered Mike mentioning the name many times. He was an old Marine buddy of Mike's. What should he do? *Make sure it's really him.* "What was Mike's dog's name?"

Nick smiled on the other side of the door. "Patton. Now open up." Don unlocked the door and slowly opened it.

Before him stood a man who reminded him a lot of his deceased friend. About the same age, very fit, and a little menacing…the kind of guy most people wouldn't choose to tangle with. Don shook the stranger's hand while looking around outside nervously. They sat down and began the somewhat awkward conversation. Don learned how Nick had been talked into helping him (something he clearly was not altogether comfortable doing). He also began to understand just how much the man stood to lose by doing so—his own freedom, for instance. Before long, it was clear to Don not only that he *could* trust Nick, but that he had to. Regardless of what Scott Keller and "Bobby" from the ATF were able to accomplish, Nick could make him a lot safer in the meantime.

That was Nick's goal for the moment. He didn't yet know enough about the situation to offer anything in the way of a solution to Don's predicament. That would change soon, he hoped; but in the meantime, his apartment would be a safer place than this motel. Nick looked at the bundle of nerves in front of him. "We tried to call you to let you know I was coming."

"That must have been while I was out getting rid of the prepaid cell phone I used to call Jenny last night," Don said, choosing not to mention his call to Schaefer at this point.

Nick was impressed. "Good move. Where'd you get that idea?"

"From Scott Keller...the Marshal who's helping me."

"Uh huh," Nick responded with distrust. "Let's get out of here. They've probably had enough time by now to pin down your location one way or another." Don quickly gathered what few belongings he had and the two of them walked out into broad daylight, feeling vulnerable. As they covered the short distance across the parking lot to Nick's waiting vehicle, Nick scanned the area. On each side of the lot across the street, a plain-looking Chevrolet Suburban was parked. The professional in him also quickly noticed a few other important similarities. Both had the driver's side spotlights common to law enforcement vehicles, were occupied, and were parked pointing in the direction of the motel. This was no coincidence!

"Hurry up and get in," Nick muttered harshly as he thumbed the key fob in his hand to unlock the doors. Don did as instructed without asking any questions about the sudden change in his new friend's sense of urgency. His thinking had become much more "tactical" in the last few days, obviating the need to ask questions before taking action. Nick saw the Suburbans begin to move as he started the vehicle. *Here we go.* "Buckle up and hold on."

The motel consisted of three rectangular buildings arranged as three sides of a square, with an exit at each of the two junctures in the back of the complex. As Nick accelerated toward one of the exits, he glanced into his rearview mirror just in time to see one of the SUVs barreling across the street and into the parking lot. *Where the hell was the other one?* The sight of a ponderous vehicle heading directly toward them from the left answered his unspoken question. Nick saw a flash and heard his left rear window explode. He and Don were under fire—if he'd needed any more convincing about how serious these people were, that did it!

Nick's hand was a blur as he reached under his left armpit and extracted a Glock Model 21. The .45 ACP pistol held a total of fourteen rounds and was his trusted companion—this particular specimen having fired over fifty thousand rounds of full-power ammunition during the last few years. Nick switched the pistol to his left hand and opened fire on the Suburban as it bore down on them. The SUV's windshield shattered and the driver swerved hard to the right and into a concrete fence. *Now it's a fair fight.*

As Nick started to make a right turn, his truck's rear window was blown out. He cut the steering wheel sharply, mashed the accelerator and sped forward. All else being equal, his Dodge Durango handled slightly better than the huge Suburban behind them. Even more important, however, was the person behind the wheel. During his time in the CIA, Nick had received extensive training in vehicular evasion. He'd also put that training to good use more than once. As a result, Nick was convinced the ATF driver was not his equal in that regard.

He opened up the gap between them, then made several more turns as the sporadic gunfire behind them continued. One of their pursuers was firing away while hanging out of the passenger-side window—not exactly conducive to accuracy. Still, Nick knew they had to be neutralized quickly before they eventually connected. "Here, Don, take this pistol and climb into the backseat. I want you to take aim out the back window and keep squeezing the trigger until you're out of ammo. All you have to do with this thing is point and shoot."

"I've never fired a pistol in my life," Don objected.

"Well you're about to. Now go!"

******

Sykes loaded a fresh magazine into his handgun, while breathing heavily. He was sure he could disable the Dodge one way or another this time. Firing at a moving target while hanging out of a car window had proven to be a lot tougher to do than he would have imagined, but he was starting to get the hang of it. These guys meant business—that much was certain. He and Lynch had seen the exchange of gunfire between them and Burke.

******

Don did as Nick had ordered him to. While bracing himself against the backseat to avoid being thrown about, he pushed the strange-feeling handgun forward and toward the gaping hole in what was once the rear window. Don squeezed the trigger time after time. He hardly noticed the noise or the empty brass flying around inside the SUV as he followed Nick's instructions. The last round caused the Suburban's windshield to shatter and the vehicle ran headlong into a car parked on the side of the road.

"Good work, Don. Climb back up here," Nick said after seeing the results of the firefight in his mirrors.

Once again, Don did as he was told, shaking like a leaf. "Jesus, what if I killed one of them?"

Nick didn't take Don's concern lightly. "You did what you had to do. These people are out to kill *you*. Make no mistake about that. You were defending yourself—nothing more and nothing less. Try to sit back and relax. We're okay for now."

Don looked at him as he might a madman. How could this guy be so cool and matter-of-fact about what they'd just been through? Nick seemed to know what he was thinking. As he took the empty Glock from Don, inserted a fresh thirteen-round magazine, and closed the slide, he spoke quietly. "I'm not saying you should ever take shooting at another human being lightly. It's serious business, but sometimes it's the only option you have. It was either them or us, Don."

* * * * * *

It was late in the day on Friday and Bobby Myers sat staring at the HOT computer screen. The place was virtually empty and he felt safe doing what he was about to do. There were no Collection operations scheduled for tonight—a welcome departure for the worn-out members of this organization. Bobby was armed with information about the computer system he'd gathered earlier in the day, knowledge he hoped would allow him to accomplish his mission. Computers were one of the few things in life that scared him. He didn't trust them and he had serious doubts about his ability to do anything constructive with them. For this Williams guy's sake, Bobby hoped he could overcome his sense of inadequacy.

The process didn't seem too complicated, really. He had in front of him a step-by-step guide to find what he was looking for, in an area of the system he'd never had reason to venture into. Following the instructions dictated to him over the telephone earlier, Bobby began to carefully enter the proper access codes. As he did so, he was struck by the fact that what he was doing was at least somewhat disloyal. He didn't think much of Payne, Burke, and others like them. Still, they *were* his people. He was an ATF officer and, in spite of the current wrong direction in which his organization was headed, Bobby was proud of that fact. It was all that he'd known for a long time and, growing up the way he had, it was more than he'd ever thought he'd achieve.

If the instructions he'd received were correct, Bobby was only a few keystrokes away from answering the big question. It was at this point that the hair stood up on the back of his neck. He swiveled around in his chair to see who was behind him. There, not ten feet away, was HOT Commander Bill Payne.

"Hello, Bobby. I thought I saw a light on in here," Payne said as he began to move closer. As Bobby's mind raced, he wondered for a few seconds whether he might actually be in danger. "What are you doing here so late on a Friday, Bobby? The purpose for suspending operations tonight was to give you and your people a break."

"Uh, yes sir, I realize that. I was just finishing up some work here. I'm just about ready to take off." Sitting directly in front of the computer screen, Bobby tried to make himself even larger than he was in order to obscure it, while Payne seemed to be working just as hard at seeing around him.

"Good. It's late, Bobby. You've been working your tail off and I'm sure your family would like a little time with you. Go ahead and finish up. I'll wait and walk out with you."

Bobby reluctantly turned back around to face the screen as Payne sat on the edge of the desk, getting a clear look at the terminal as he did so. "We could all use a bit of a break, actually. I'm sure you heard about the close call we had this morning."

"Uh, yes sir, I did. Sounds like it was pretty hairy," Bobby replied, trying to concentrate on the task at hand.

"It was. These people are maniacs, Bobby. They'll stop at nothing to prevent us from carrying out our mission. Thankfully, none of our people were hurt this time."

Bobby wanted to tell his boss that he was full of shit, but said nothing.

He backed out of the system one screen at a time, as he had to in order to complete the shutdown. There…it was done. He shut the system down, no closer to proving what he now *knew* Payne was up to than he had been when he'd sat down in the chair twenty minutes earlier.

The two men took the elevator down and walked out through the security checkpoint on the first floor. "You and Keller became pretty close during the short time he spent with us, didn't you, Bobby?"

"Oh, I don't know. I guess we hit it off okay."

"You *do* know that you have a very bright future at ATF, don't you?"

It was a thinly veiled threat and so typical of Payne. "I guess so, sir." Bobby just wanted to get back in there and do what he needed to do. Unfortunately, he realized that wasn't going to happen…at least not this night.

"Well, I can guarantee that you do." As he was saying this, Payne stood in the doorway of the last security door on the way out. "I just remembered something I need from my office, Bobby. I'll see you Monday morning," he added, as he turned and walked back into the building.

Payne approached the guard inside. "I'm going to be up in my office for a while. I want you to call me if *anyone*—including Agent Myers—enters the building tonight." The guard assured him that he would.

Once in his office, Payne picked up the phone and punched the speed-dial button for Burke's home number. "Ray, I need you to get in here ASAP. I found Myers snooping around on the computer in an area he had no business being in. I think he's up to something."

"Did he find anything out, sir?"

"I don't know, Ray. I just want to make sure that if he didn't, he won't in the future. There have to be access codes or passwords that we can change."

"Yes sir, there are. I'll be right in." Burke's wife closed her eyes and lowered her head. They were just sitting down to their first dinner together in almost two weeks. He probably should have told his boss that he'd be there in an hour or two. After all, what difference would a couple of hours make? Burke wouldn't do that, though, and both he and his wife knew it.

14

Portland, Oregon
Friday, April 25

DON AND NICK sat across from each other at Nick's very plain kitchen table. The apartment had come furnished and it showed. No matter, though—Nick didn't plan on being here much longer. They knew they had to work on a strategy, but for the time being, the topic of conversation was their mutual deceased friend.

"He was one hell of a Marine," Nick recalled. "He led by example and his men loved him."

Don listened intently as Nick filled in the blanks about Mike. He'd always thought he knew his friend well, but he'd never heard about this part of his life before—Mike had certainly never been one to talk about himself. What he learned further galvanized Don's resolve. He would do more than just save himself. He would make them pay for killing his friend.

Nick decided it was time to turn to the more immediate problem confronting them. "Don, we need a strategy to clean up this mess. Eventually, we have to find a way to allow you to get your story out. That would create enough space between you and the ATF to put the pressure on *them* for a change."

"Yeah, I've thought about that. I have a connection with Jim Schaefer at *The Oregonian* and I've already talked to him about running a story." After what they'd just been through, there was no sense in holding anything back from Nick.

"*The Oregonian*?" Nick asked incredulously. "I'm pretty sure every one of their reporters is in favor of Collection, based on what I've seen on their editorial page."

"I know. But we spoke a couple of days ago and, when I told him my story, he was furious. Whatever he thinks of this policy, he's completely on *my* side in this fight. Besides—and I hate to admit this now—*I* was in favor of Collection, too."

"All right, fine," Nick conceded, still unconvinced. "Obviously, Schaefer can't print that story with you on the run, though. It would allow the ATF to spin it their way. You'd look like a fugitive doing something desperate to help his own cause and that wouldn't do us much good."

"I agree. We *do* have help, though. There's a Marshal who—"

"I know," Nick interrupted him. "Your wife mentioned him. But like I told her, I wouldn't trust *any* federal agent to save you." Hearing those words come out of his own mouth sounded odd to him in light of his not-so-distant past.

"Nick, I understand what you're saying. I felt the same way at first, but I've talked to him a couple of times now and I really do trust him. He's got an ATF agent working on getting the proof we need and they're pretty sure they can do it."

Nick couldn't believe what he was hearing. "An *ATF* agent? That's just great. Now not only are we expecting two Feds to help us out; one of them is an *ATF agent*!"

Don felt a little foolish, but decided to stick to his guns. "It's just a gut feeling, but I really do think we can trust these guys."

Nick decided to relent for the moment, but his doubt was obvious. "Uh huh," he answered skeptically. "Well, I guess we'll go with your 'gut feeling' for now, but they're going to have to *earn* my trust. There's one thing I'm going to insist on, though: if you happen to speak to one of your fed buddies, don't mention me by name, or even my existence. They don't need to know you've got help and I don't need the exposure.

"Also, I don't feel comfortable waiting for *anyone* else to take care of things for us. We need to come up with a 'Plan B' in case your boys don't come through." Nick paused and walked over to the counter for a fresh cup of coffee. "I've been thinking about this since I spoke to your wife this morning. We need to draw Payne out."

"What do you mean?"

"Well, regardless of what these two guys might be able to do for us, we need to make Payne *think* you have proof that he doctored your record—whether it actually exists or not. That way, we'll still have some leverage even if they're not able to help."

"How would we do that?"

"First of all, we'll give these guys a little more time to come up with something concrete. If they can't do that, we need to find a way to put enough fear into Payne to make him wonder. If he thinks there's a chance that you have proof of what he did, he might be willing to do something stupid—like meeting with you alone." Don's eyes widened, but Nick continued. "If he agrees to do that, I can wire you and record the conversation."

Don couldn't take any more. "*What?!* Are you kidding me? You know damn well he'd bring his men with him and I'd probably be killed."

Nick had expected that reaction. "Try to calm down. What I'm talking about is a last-resort strategy if your fed buddies don't get anything. There really aren't any other options that I see. You've got to understand that guys like Payne have huge egos. If you go head to head with him and rub his nose in the fact that little ole' you has him scared, I think you'll piss him off so bad that he'll not only admit but also be *proud* of what he did! When he does, we'll have it on tape. And you'll run faster than you ever have in your life…with a carefully planned escape route and some help along the way."

Don knew Nick was probably right. If Marshal Keller and his friend didn't come through, extreme measures would be necessary. "You really think that would work?"

"It's definitely worth a shot. I've known a lot of guys like him. They can't stand having their authority questioned, especially by someone they have no respect for...and, I'm sorry, but I think you fall squarely into that category."

Don laughed nervously. "Yeah? Well, I'll wear that as a badge of honor."

"You should. So what do you think of my plan?"

"I think I hope Keller and his buddy find what we need. But if they don't, I guess your idea makes sense. How are we going to make him think we have the proof, though?"

"Don't know yet. Besides, if I had everything figured out, we wouldn't have anything to do today."

Don smiled weakly. "Yeah, I wouldn't want that. My life's been a real snooze lately."

******

Walking down the long hallway toward Payne's office, Burke began to wonder when this would end (or at least slow down). Having spent over two hours last night changing access codes to certain areas of the HOT computer system, he was now back at work at 8:00 on a Saturday morning. Payne had called him early this morning and "asked" Burke to come into the office for a while. Apparently, his boss had been struck by a fresh idea during the night and didn't want to discuss it over the telephone. Burke didn't at all look forward to hearing about any new ideas at this point. He'd come to believe that Payne was more than a little out of control. They would be better off letting things develop on their own, but Burke knew that wasn't Payne's way.

"Morning, Ray, come in." Burke sat down, uncharacteristically slumping in the chair. He was tired and it showed. Payne, on the other hand, thrived on this type of conflict and the pressure it created. This exemplified the difference in their relative mental toughness, Payne believed. Ray Burke was a loyal deputy and a great technician, but the Commander had serious doubts about his ability to lead. Leadership required the ability to thrive—not wilt—under pressure.

"Ray, we've got two problems." *Only two?* Burke thought. "First, we need to figure out what to do with our own Bobby Myers. It's safe to assume that he's trying to bring us down. Obviously, that can't be allowed to happen. Secondly, I'm fairly sure that Myers is working with Keller to undermine us. If that's true, we need to find out how much Keller knows and what he plans to do about it. From the time he got here, Keller's attitude was confrontational and accusatory. I'm not saying Myers couldn't have come up with this idea on his own, but it seems to have Keller's name written all over it. I think it's worth finding out whether or not I'm right."

Burke was a bit groggy, but the Commander's statement caught his attention. "Sir, I don't know of anything that we could 'do' with Myers. As to Keller, how would we find out for sure whether or not he's involved?"

"Well, that's a tough one, especially now that he's no longer attached to our unit." Payne ignored the first issue raised by his deputy—for now. Ray might not be ready to consider the thornier issues yet. "Still, there's a way. I want to put a wiretap on his home phone."

What? Burke couldn't believe what he'd just heard. "Sir, with all due respect, that would be a bad idea no matter *who* you did it to, but Keller's a federal law enforcement officer. Are you sure you want to do that?"

"You bet I am!" Payne was growing tired of his subordinate's lack of resolve. "Listen, if you don't think these guys can ruin *both* of us, you're kidding yourself. Our only way out of this is to find Williams and then keep anyone else who knows about it quiet. We've already committed ourselves, Ray. Now it's a matter of perseverance.

"I want you to have it done—today—and don't use Hatcher, Sykes, or Lynch. The more they're involved, the more complicated things become. Use our tech people and don't let them know anything you don't have to. We've got to start tying up every loose end very quickly, Ray. Our careers are on the line and I, for one, am not about to let it all end over something like this!"

What could Burke say? There may have been a time for him to say "No—enough is enough!" but that time was past. As much as he hated to admit it, Payne was right. From here on, very little would be over the line. "I guess we'll figure out what to do about Myers later, then?"

Hearing Burke come back to that issue on his own was a pleasant surprise for Payne. "Yes. We will indeed," the Commander answered.

As he stood, Burke wondered, once again, what he'd gotten himself into. "I'll get a team on the wiretap right away, sir."

******

The three-man crew had just set up the surveillance on Scott Keller's phone line. They'd done the same thing many times in the past and the mechanics of it were always the same. This job seemed different, however. Though it was seldom, if ever, necessary for them to know whom they were listening in on and why, they usually asked anyway—and were told. In this case, the orders came directly from Deputy Commander Burke and their casual inquisitiveness went unsatisfied.

Burke's reluctance to divulge what should have been less than exciting information, along with his demand that the results from the wiretap come *only* to him, led to a burning curiosity in these men. It was easy enough to obtain the homeowner's name and from there to find out what he did for a living. After doing that, none of the three could conceive of a legitimate reason for their actions. Still, orders were orders.

Maybe not, thought Tim Murdoch, who supervised the small crew performing the task. It was proper and even mandatory to question certain orders. Did these orders fall into that category? Who knew? Maybe there *was* a good reason for doing what they'd just done. Maybe this Keller was involved in some kind of gunrunning or black market operation. There had been rumors about that becoming a real problem now that prohibition against gun ownership was in place. Obviously, there would be a ton of money to be made in that case. Was a federal law enforcement officer with the "inside track" immune to such inducements? Of course not.

Besides, Murdoch had the feeling that crossing Burke—or, God forbid, Payne—would do little to further his career...especially if he were to accuse them of doing something illegal. No, he decided, he wouldn't question this order, but he sure was curious about what, exactly, was going on. He had always wondered whether there was a limit to what Payne and Burke would do to reach an objective. This situation might provide an answer. He'd have to keep an eye on it.

With that in mind, Murdoch made the decision to do something else highly irregular. He would see to it that *he* also had access to the results of Keller's wiretap—just to answer the nagging questions that he had. Technology had progressed to a point where that was easily possible. Murdoch would be setting up a monitoring device for Burke and it would be a simple matter to do the same for himself.

15

Portland, Oregon
Saturday, April 26

Payne's stomach growled audibly. It was late in the morning and neither he nor Burke had had breakfast, but they had a more important task before them at the moment. Who *was* the guy that helped Williams get away? It was an important question, not only for the obvious reason that he was now an escaped felon but also because of the fact that he could undoubtedly lead them to Williams. The two men had begun the process of determining his identity earlier that morning, but were no closer to a name now than they were then. The most obvious avenue to try first was the vehicle's license plate, which was a fake.

The Commander began to grow impatient. "Look, the guy's likely to be a level-three, right?" Burke nodded. "He's also probably local."

That was an assumption Burke didn't necessarily agree with. "Sir, we can't assume that. To do so could lead us on a wild goose chase that we don't have the time for."

"Well, we've got to do *something* to narrow the search," Payne objected.

"I agree, sir. But it won't do us any good to head off in the wrong direction." Burke's eyes narrowed as a thought came to him. "How about a military connection?"

"A military connection to *what?*"

"Between this mystery man and Niculescu," Burke answered as he moved toward his boss's computer.

"What are you doing, Ray?"

"I need a phone number in D.C. from your e-mail directory, sir." After working his way through the system, Burke scribbled a ten-digit number on a scratch pad and turned to Payne.

"This might be a long shot, but we have a couple of photos of our new subject walking out of the motel with Williams. Granted, they're not exactly studio quality, since they were taken from across the street and he was walking pretty fast."

The Commander still looked puzzled as Burke continued. "First of all, it would take a very good friend to risk as much as this fellow's risking to help Williams. The fake license plates tell us that he's gone to a great deal of trouble to remain anonymous. Why would he literally put his life on the line now?

"There aren't too many ties strong enough to bind people that tightly, but I think one might be military service—especially combat. We've assumed that this guy is helping Williams because he's a friend of his, right?" Payne nodded. "Well, maybe they're friends, but it's a lot more likely that *Niculescu* would have a history with a guy with this kind of skill set. What I'm saying is that it's likely they were mutual friends of the deceased and there's a good chance this guy might have served with Niculescu in the Marine Corps."

"I guess it's possible. Is that the reason you're calling D.C.?"

"Yes, sir. I think I can find someone at the Pentagon to dig up the records we need, even on a Saturday. If we can obtain a list of men who might have served with Niculescu, we can cross-reference it with the level-three listing to come up with a fairly limited number of names for us to run down."

Burke punched in the long-distance number and waited patiently through the extended number of rings. It was, after all, Saturday and the crews manning the building were much thinner than during the week. Finally, a rather harried sergeant answered. "Hello, Sergeant. This is Deputy Commander Burke of the ATF's Hazardous Operations Team in Portland, Oregon." Burke went on to inform the duly impressed enlisted man of what he needed. It shouldn't take too long, he was promised. The results would be e-mailed to HOT as soon as possible.

* * * * * *

It was nearly impossible for Jenny Williams not to think about her husband every minute of every day. They were soul mates, best friends, and deeply in love. In fact, throughout this ordeal, Jenny had begun to realize how lucky she was. As in every marriage, no matter how strong, the numbing details of everyday life had accumulated to dull the feelings that had brought the two of them together in the first place. It was an unfortunate side effect of real life. But Jenny could honestly say that their current troubles had re-ignited the love she'd always felt for Don and she promised herself that, when this was over, she would resist falling ever again into the trap of monotony.

The kids were all outside and Jenny was sitting on the edge of a bed that wasn't hers. Their life was in the strangest place it had ever been. Soon, she told herself, this would all be over. What if…? *NO*, she wouldn't allow herself to think about it. Don *would* come back to her and their children. *Now get up and go do something—anything—to keep your mind from exploring every possible negative scenario.*

* * * * * *

The information that Burke had requested from the Pentagon came through much faster than he could have hoped for. Experience told him that the Pentagon was no more efficient than any of the other bureaucracies he had to deal with on a regular basis. Maybe it was simply a case of a dedicated sergeant doing his job well. He had always been of the opinion that you got results by dealing one-on-one with *people*, not organizations. That didn't mean you had to be a "people person" or well liked to be successful. In fact, Burke was under no illusion that he was either. Still, he was consistently able to get results.

Though his boss would never have admitted it, Burke was sure that the Commander realized this fact as well. It was no accident that, despite Payne's obvious air of superiority, it was *he*, Ray Burke, who always got the call when something had to be done both quickly and correctly. He just hoped that when he needed it (and he knew the day would come), the Commander would show the proper level of appreciation for all that he had done. There were few traits that Payne seemed to attach more importance to than loyalty. If that was true, Burke thought, then he ought to be in good shape when payback time rolled around.

Burke's first step would be to check the Pentagon's list against the level-three subjects in the state of Oregon. The guy might have come in from another state, but they had to start somewhere. The ATF listing was searchable, but this had to be done one name at a time, checking off each name that didn't match.

Payne paced the floor behind him, something he did every time his deputy undertook a project in his presence. This always irritated Burke, but he had never spoken up about it. This time, however, because his nerves were completely shot from the unusual level of stress and lack of sleep over the last few days, he stopped and turned around to face his superior. "Sir, it would be a lot easier for me to concentrate if you would just relax." Payne stared back blankly, so Burke spelled it out for him. "I know the past few days have been very stressful for you. Why don't you go get a cup of coffee and maybe take a walk? I promise I'll let you know as soon as I find something."

Payne wasn't used to anyone being assertive with him. At the same time, he realized Burke was right. He needed a break and Burke needed to do his job. "You're right, Ray. I'll get out of your hair for a little while." Stopping at the door of his office, he turned around. "Ray, I want you to know how much I appreciate your loyalty and hard work. The fact that I can trust you completely means more to me than you can imagine." It was both awkward and unusual for Payne to speak those words. He was typically unemotional and rarely spontaneous, but the statement needed to be made. To see this through would take an extraordinary amount of determination and loyalty from a handful of people. No one among them was more crucial than Ray Burke.

"Thank you, sir. It really means a lot to hear you say that."

"You deserve it, Ray. I'll be back in a little while," Payne answered as he walked away.

Wow! There were few things that would have surprised Burke more than what he'd just heard. Feeling overworked and underappreciated had become a part of his psyche. It made a world of difference to know that Payne thought of him as an asset. With a renewed sense of purpose, Burke went to work on the task before him.

It was slow going, but when he was about three-quarters of the way through the list, a name leapt off of the screen. Burke put that name through the wringer, checking for a criminal record and looking up his last known address, occupation, and whatever else he could find.

To narrow the search as much as possible, Burke went through the remainder of the list and found exactly what he'd hoped to find. This guy was the only former Marine living in Oregon who was likely to have served with Niculescu in combat. *Bingo!* There was no greater feeling than when the tumblers clicked into place. His concentration was interrupted briefly when Payne re-entered the room after being away for a surprisingly long time. "Sir, I think I just found something."

Payne hurried over to Burke's side, dragging a chair along with him. "You've got a name?"

"Well, yes. I'm not sure it's the *right* name yet, but it's a great place to start. Captain Nicholas Larsen, USMC. He served with Niculescu. And…" Burke's voice trailed off as he studied the information on the screen before him.

"What is it, Ray?"

"He was a non-military employee of the United States government for several years after being discharged from the Marine Corps. The lack of details makes me think CIA or something similar." Burke hesitated. "That bothers me, sir."

"It is what it is, Ray. Besides, we don't know that your assumptions are correct."

Burke continued. "Last known physical address was in Bend, Oregon. The only thing on file now, though, is a P.O. box number in Portland. I checked the DMV system and there's no driver's license number on file for him, either. He surrendered it last year. I'll check on a couple of other things through the Department of Defense, but I'd be very surprised if anything else turned up. It's pretty clear that our man made a conscious effort to disappear and it looks like he did a good job of it. I'm pretty sure this is the guy we want, but at this point I'm not sure how to go about finding him."

Payne had an unusually thoughtful expression on his face while his deputy was speaking. "I think I do. There's got to be a reason he kept a P.O. box." Payne paused as he stood and walked behind his desk. "Maintaining contact with the outside world was obviously important enough for him to take that risk, right?" Burke indicated his agreement with a nod. "That means, sooner or later, he's likely to visit the post office to check the box."

"Maybe. But he's probably less likely to now than he was twenty-four hours ago. Besides, sir, we can't station someone to watch the post office around the clock."

"No, we can't. But how about going *into* the box and planting a tracking device on a package? In fact, we could even plant our own package in there if we had to." Burke was thinking about it. This just might be the only workable option they had. Payne knew he was onto something and pressed on. "Access wouldn't be a problem. We clearly have grounds for a search warrant, due to his status as a level-three subject."

"That's a good idea, sir. I'll set things in motion and we'll get it done right away."

That was a switch, Payne thought. He usually had to drag Burke, kicking and screaming, into agreement with him. "Looks like we put the fear of God into this Larsen guy, huh?" Payne asked smugly. "Now that we know who we're looking for, let's go get him, Ray. If we can find him, there's a good chance we'll be able to kill two birds with one stone."

Somehow, Burke thought as they began shutting things down in preparation to leave, it wouldn't be that easy.

* * * * * *

Bobby Myers was feeling paranoid. He'd driven by headquarters twice earlier and seen the Commander's and Deputy's cars in the parking lot. Both times he went back home and tried to find something else to do. The third time, however, the cars were gone. After circling the compound twice, he satisfied himself that neither of them was there.

The guard at the building entrance didn't quite seem himself, leading Bobby to wonder if he'd been told to be on the lookout for him. Would there be a call placed as soon as Bobby passed through the heavy steel door? He'd have to hurry—though he really didn't need much time. The information he was looking for would either be there or it wouldn't.

Settling in before his computer, he fidgeted as he waited for the system to come online. The two minutes or so seemed like fifteen to him. One by one, Bobby knocked down the electronic barriers in his path by entering the correct alphanumeric combinations. It was smooth sailing, until he came to the final step. The first time his code was denied, he thought he must have made a keystroke error. The second time caused him to sit bolt upright in his chair and rub his palms together to alleviate their sweating. He carefully reread the instructions he'd scrawled on a piece of scratch paper the day before. One more incorrect code and he knew his system would be frozen until at least Monday, when he'd have to beg a bureaucrat back in Washington D.C. to "thaw him out."

It was with this unsettling thought running through his mind that Bobby very slowly and deliberately entered the code a third time. Doubting himself, he erased it before hitting the "enter" key and repeated the process. It was now or never. Bobby carefully pressed the key and closed his eyes, hoping he'd gotten it right for Don Williams' sake. When he looked back up at the screen, his heart sank. "Password is incorrect. Access suspended. Please contact your systems division for assistance." *Damn!* He would have been out of options at this point even if he were a computer genius, which he most certainly was not.

Forgetting about the proper way to shut the system down, Bobby simply turned the power off. Any complications that action might have caused would be the least of his worries come Monday morning. Instinctively, he checked his office for belongings to erase the fact that he'd been there at all. This was, of course, unnecessary, but he was on autopilot now. He felt that he'd not only failed in his mission to help Don but also might have exposed his actions to Payne and Burke.

There was absolutely nothing else he knew of to do at this point. The same guard who had eyed him suspiciously on his way in said good night with a smile. Bobby hurried across the parking lot to his car, which was parked behind the building and near the fenced area containing the HOT trucks and vans. He'd hoped that parking there would make his presence less obvious to curious passersby.

Bobby closed the car door and sat for a moment before putting his key in the ignition. He *had* to have entered the code correctly—at least by the third try. Maybe his informant had given him the wrong information. That was a possibility, but the guy was one of those anal-retentive super nerds who double and triple-checked everything and demanded that Bobby read every code back to him before they ended the conversation. Still possible...but not likely.

That left only one other possibility. Payne—or, more likely, Burke—must have changed the codes, which meant that Bobby no longer needed to wonder whether or not they suspected him. He had called Scott last night to tell him about being caught in the act by Payne and they'd both agreed it was likely that their efforts to get the proof they needed had come to an end.

Bobby punched in Scott's home phone number as he pulled out of the parking lot. Meg answered and informed him that Scott was out running errands but he did have his cell phone with him. Bobby was glad to hear his friend's voice—the sooner they figured out their next move, the better off everyone would be. "Hey, it's Bobby."

"Any luck?" asked a hopeful Scott Keller.

"No. It looks like they know what I'm up to. The only other possibility is that my little nerd in D.C. screwed up." Bobby went on to relate the specifics of the last hour's events.

"We're through, then, Bobby. I'm sure the codes he gave you were right, at least as of yesterday. We both know that Payne's no dummy—he had you figured out last night. I hate to do it, but I've got to call Don to give him the bad news. I just talked to him before I left the house a little while ago and I'm not looking forward to calling him back."

"No other ideas?"

"I'm fresh out of 'em, pal. I take it you don't have any either?"

"Nope. I feel like a real turd, though. I should've been able to find *something*. Maybe there's another way—"

"I don't see what it could be. Looks like we're not going to be able to *prove* it now. It's time we admit that and come at it from another angle. The only thing I can think of is for you and me to go to the mat for Don and back up everything he says. Payne still holds a lot of the cards that way, but we might at least be able to create enough doubt to cause some serious problems for him."

"Scott, he's too good for that. We'll be left twisting in the wind and that bastard will come away without a scratch."

Scott considered that, but couldn't let it go. "I know we're in a tight spot, but I don't know of anything else to do. We can't leave Don all alone out there. We're pretty much committed at this point, don't you think?"

To Bobby, it seemed that doing what Scott had suggested would amount to giving up and he wasn't ready for that yet. There had to be something else they could do, though nothing was coming to him at the moment. Maybe they *could* let Williams run with it briefly. That might at least buy them another day or two to figure something out. Would that really do any good, though? Probably not, he had to admit. "Yeah, we're committed. Let's go ahead and tell Williams he's on his own for now. Tell him we're not gonna give up, though. Maybe he'll come up with something we couldn't. Sometimes we're not as smart as we think we are, Scott."

* * * * * *

Burke entered the post office and went immediately to the room number he'd been given over the phone. He'd decided to plant the device himself. It was hardly rocket science. Hatcher and Lynch were parked several blocks away in a van, with equipment on board that would allow them to track any movement of the package from a very safe distance. This capability allowed them to stay far away from the post office. Larsen was likely to scour the area surrounding this public building before entering and nothing stuck out more than a government-issue cargo van parked alongside the road.

The post office supervisor on duty was extremely cooperative. Burke had a search warrant and she was only too happy to help a federal law enforcement officer. She handed the key to Burke and asked him to drop it off at her desk on the way out. That was perfect. The last thing he needed was to have her looking over his shoulder while he worked. In order to insulate himself from as many prying eyes as possible, he would open the box from the *inside*—just as employees did when inserting mail. This would also allow him a few additional seconds to react, in the event that he saw Larsen coming.

The tracking device was of the newest generation, both tiny and flat. Burke had brought a small, plain shipping box along with him, though he hoped he wouldn't need it. He really didn't want to risk Larsen being suspicious of the parcel that they had their hopes pinned on and a package from someone he didn't know might have that effect. He was in luck. As he opened Nick Larsen's post office box, he noticed an oversized, heavily padded envelope.

Burked worked as quickly as possible, without being sloppy. Striking the proper balance between speed and quality was always important, but especially so in this case. Based on what he'd come to know about Nick Larsen, it was obvious that the man would be no easy target. Installing the tracking device would need to be done carefully, because Larsen was trained to notice the little things. It would need to be done quickly for another reason: the last thing in the world Burke wanted was to be caught pilfering through *this* guy's mailbox. Though the two men had never met, Burke had the feeling that his target was a dangerous man indeed. Besides, they didn't need a confrontation here. Larsen was basically just another level-three subject at this point. The real target was Don Williams and they could get at him only with the help of an unsuspecting Nick Larsen.

Burke checked over his shoulder to see that no one else had entered the room. Satisfied, he moved the package over to a tall table across the hall and opened up the small kit that he'd brought with him. He selected a scalpel from it and began to carefully separate the two layers of the flap at the bottom of the envelope. Then he placed the tracking device inside the flap and added an extra layer of packing tape from the roll on the table. The entire operation took only a few minutes.

Turning the package around and inspecting it carefully, Burke admired his work. There was virtually no way anyone could tell that the envelope had been tampered with, he decided. He then replaced the package and closed the box. The final step was to call the guys in the van to make sure they had a good strong signal. No problem there. This had all been much easier than he'd expected, but he was smart and experienced enough to know that a number of things could still go wrong.

******

Tim Murdoch closed the door of his condo behind him and threw his keys on the kitchen counter. After this morning's assignment, he'd needed to clear his head and a quick eighty-mile loop on his favorite road always did the trick. He was still wearing his riding suit and, as always, felt a little like Frankenstein. It was worth it, though. He'd been riding motorcycles—fast—for a long time now and there had been a couple of spills over the years. The last one had been pretty bad and Tim promised himself on the spot that he'd never get on a bike again without wearing the best gear he could find.

As he peeled off the heavy protective clothing, he remembered that he was supposed to call his girlfriend as soon as he got home. She had plans for the afternoon that included him, like it or not. Sometimes he just wanted to relax on the weekend, but that was rarely acceptable to Sherry. They'd been dating for a little over six months now…which might actually be a new record for him, now that he thought about it. He grabbed a beer from the refrigerator and headed into the bedroom. After a quick shower, there would be at least a little time to relax.

As he walked past his bedroom closet, he thought about the receiver on a shelf inside. He'd put it there yesterday, wanting to keep it out of sight as much as possible. What he was doing was illegal, something unfamiliar to him. Tim was thankful that he worked on the right side of the law. It was obvious after this experience that doing otherwise would quickly turn him into a nail-biting wreck.

He took the actions required by his job very seriously. Basically, he got paid to eavesdrop on people. Those people were virtually always guilty, though—a wiretap authorization being notoriously hard to come by. In this case, however—if Tim's hunch turned out to be right—he would be listening in on *innocent* people and that was a violation of their privacy that he wasn't comfortable with.

Still, he had to listen to the calls, didn't he? No, he didn't have to and under normal circumstances, he wouldn't have. The difference this time was that he had a strong suspicion that high-ranking federal law enforcement officers were committing crimes of their own and that couldn't be allowed to stand. He was using *his* power and position to uncover what he was afraid might be criminal activity. If he was right about his superiors, they were using theirs for…well, he wasn't sure yet, but it wasn't likely for the good of anyone but themselves.

Tim pulled the machine off the shelf and pressed the "play" button. There had been three calls so far. The first two were made by Keller's wife—one to her mother and another to a friend. Then, an incoming call from some guy named Don that Keller answered almost caused Tim's heart to stop beating. It was all there. He had enough circumstantial evidence recorded to convince him that his fears were justified. It wouldn't be enough to convince anyone who mattered, though. That would require the same thing that Keller and his friend were apparently after. He'd have to talk to Keller. The guy deserved to know that he was being spied on.

It also occurred to Tim that Payne and Burke now knew what they must have only suspected before. How long would it take before they did something about it and *what* would they do? They obviously had no legal recourse and the possibilities that remained gave him a chill.

******

Scott waited a little while before calling Don. He had errands to run anyway and he wanted time to think about how he was going to say what he knew had to be said. Don was on his own—at least until Scott and Bobby could come up with another idea. There was little he could do to sugarcoat that message.

The last time they spoke, Don had given Scott the number for his current prepaid cell phone. Hoping he was still using the same one, Scott made the call.

"Don, this is Scott Keller."

Don's heart skipped a beat. "Hi, Scott. I assume you heard something?"

No need to beat around the bush. "Yeah, I did. Bobby had a roadblock thrown in his way. It looks like they changed the passwords on him, so he wasn't able to get the information he needed."

"Why would they have done that?"

"Well, Payne wandered into Bobby's office last night before he could find anything out. We were afraid he might have suspected something and it looks like we were right."

Don said nothing, so Scott continued. "The bottom line is that we've shot our wad at this point. I'm not saying this thing is over by a long shot, but we've got to regroup. Do *you* have any ideas about what to do from here?"

Though he probably should have been prepared for it, Don felt a little like a guy thrown into the middle of the ocean without a life preserver. Nick's words rang in his ear. He didn't want to let Scott know about his new partner. "Yeah, I've got a couple, but they need work. For us to have any leverage, Payne needs to *believe* that we can prove what he did. I'm not sure how to achieve that yet, but I'll get to work on it."

"I think you're right about that and we're not giving up either, Don. I called you this afternoon because I said I'd let you know as soon as I heard something, not because I think it's over."

"I realize that, Scott, and like I told you this morning, I appreciate your help. Let's keep in touch. I'll let you know when I've got a plan put together."

"Okay," Scott answered. "Don, I want you to be careful. We're playing in the big leagues here. I know you can handle it and we'll help any way we can. If you get in trouble, I want you to promise you'll call me immediately—anytime, day or night."

"I will. After all, it's not like I have a long list of volunteers." Don's instinct was to trust Marshal Scott Keller, but there was absolutely no doubt in his mind that Nick Larsen would lay it on the line for him.

* * * * * *

Nick had already driven past the post office once, just to make sure there were no law enforcement types in the vicinity. He wouldn't describe himself as completely paranoid yet—but he was sure getting there. At this point, "appropriately cautious" might be a more accurate term. Nick had always carried himself in a manner that suggested he was prepared for any situation, an attitude he believed was prudent for anyone to have.

Satisfied that there were no obvious traps waiting to be sprung, Nick parked his Durango and got out. The weather had turned downright nasty again. Nick pulled his collar up, both to protect himself from the wind-driven rain and to obscure his face. He'd gotten everything else done this afternoon that he'd set out to do. The final stop was to pick up his mail. He visited the post office only every few days, but it was important to him to do so. He may have been extraordinarily disciplined, but he was still human. As independent as he was, he needed *some* contact with the outside world.

As usual, his mailbox was overflowing, with three days' worth of letters and junk mail stuffed into the relatively small box. Nick had brought a medium-size paper bag with him for exactly that reason. Checking over both shoulders, he quickly scooped all his mail into the bag, then locked the box again and turned to leave. Scanning the area on the way back out to his vehicle, Nick once again felt pretty sure that there were no surprises waiting for him. His caller I.D. showed that there'd been no calls placed to his cell phone since he entered the post office. Don would probably be getting a little nervous and stir crazy by now, though. He was stuck in a strange place with nothing to do and with strict orders not to venture outside. Time to get back, Nick decided as he pulled away from the curb and headed for his apartment.

******

The sudden movement of the tracking device startled Dennis Hatcher. He verified the signal strength and location, and then slapped Wayne Lynch on the shoulder. Lynch had been reading a book—the current shift was Hatcher's. "We've got movement. Let's get out of here."

"Which way?"

"He's heading west on thirty-eighth right now, but we don't have to get very close, so don't take any chances." Hatcher dialed Burke's number on his cell phone. "Sir, this is Hatcher. The package is on the move."

"Which way is he headed?"

"West, at this point. We're hanging several blocks back."

"Good work." Hatcher was as good as they came. That was why Payne wanted him in that van. Lynch and Sykes were good together, but neither had the judgment of the more senior officer. "Let me know as soon as you have a firm location, Dennis."

"I will, sir." Hatcher ended the call and returned his attention to the screen in front of him. Another thirty minutes passed and he began to wonder whether their subject was heading home or to some other destination. Why would someone use a post office box so far away from where he lived? There must have been at least a couple of other locations more convenient. Then the answer hit him: This is exactly the kind of thing a guy with Larsen's background would do. Hatcher would take this particular subject very seriously, which should guarantee him a safe trip home at the end of the day.

Each time Larsen stopped, Hatcher told Lynch to slow the van down. He wanted to get no closer than they already were. Now Larsen had been stopped for nearly five minutes. "Pull over, Wayne." Satisfied after another fifteen minutes that their target was staying put for a while. Hatcher instructed his subordinate to drive toward the device. Doing so brought them alongside a large brownstone apartment building. They drove past it and made a circle a couple of blocks wide. As they got close to the apartment building again, Hatcher was as certain as he could be that Larsen was inside that building, based on what he was seeing on the screen. Lynch stopped the van a block and a half away from the building's entrance. This still allowed them line of sight to the front of the building.

As soon as they stopped, Hatcher dialed his boss's number. "I think we've got him, sir."

After writing down the location, Burke wanted to make himself perfectly clear. "Do not do *anything* unless he takes off again. I mean don't even roll down a window. This case is of the utmost importance, Dennis."

Why? Hatcher wondered. They'd devoted an inordinate amount of time to the pursuit of this Williams guy. Granted, he suddenly had help from someone who *did* get Hatcher's attention, but what was this all about? "Yes, sir. I understand. You can count on me."

"I know I can. Commander Payne and I will track down Sykes and meet you there ASAP."

Now Payne is coming along? This is getting to be too much. Why would the Commander be part of this? What IS it about Williams that gives them such a hard-on? Another hour passed and the tracking signal never changed. This was either home base for Larsen or he was visiting someone. Either way, they could get to him.

16

Portland, Oregon
Saturday, April 26

THE SACKS OF groceries and mail that Nick had returned with not long before still sat scattered on the kitchen table as Don related the details of his phone call with Scott Keller.

Nick listened quietly as Don spoke. By the time he was finished, there were as many questions left as there had been before he started. "So, he called you just to say they struck out and that you're on your own?"

"Yeah. What are you getting at?"

"I don't know. It just seems strange. It's almost like he wanted to get some kind of reaction from you. How long did he keep you on the phone?"

The unspoken but obvious implication was that Don was being duped. Scott's credibility was also being questioned again and that bothered Don for some reason—probably because he'd come to really trust the Marshal and, if that trust was misplaced, what else could he have been wrong about?

"I don't know, maybe five minutes or so. Why is that important?"

"It might not be."

"Look, Nick, I know you don't trust anyone with a badge, but my instincts tell me that Keller's okay. And if he is, the other guy he's working with probably is too. I think we'd be better off working on our 'Plan B' than debating his motives."

Nick didn't want to insult the guy, though he wouldn't walk on eggshells either if he thought they were being compromised. So, even though the 'logic' Don had just used was absurd and even though Nick had very little respect for Don's instincts at this point, he would let it go—for now. "Okay, you're probably right. I'm just being careful. You didn't tell him about me, did you—or did he ask you if you had anyone else helping you?"

"No, of course not. We didn't talk about anything other than what I've already told you."

Nick decided to give up. Don was right about one thing: whether his fed buddies were on the level or not, he and Don were on their own now. That meant their time was more precious than ever. They needed to flesh out the details of the plan he'd been working on in his head for the last couple of hours.

******

By the time Payne, Burke, and Sykes arrived, it was well past sunset. The darkness gave them a sense of security, though they were all aware of the fact that it could aid their subject as well. Hatcher and Lynch had been monitoring the equipment in the van and there had been no movement of the tracking device. Each person entering or leaving the apartment building was examined through binoculars and compared to the grainy photo they had of Nick Larsen. They'd also been able to obtain a couple of pictures of Don Williams. As best they could tell, neither man had entered or left the apartment building through the front entrance. One or both of them could have done so through the back, of course, but in following Burke's conservative instructions, the two agents could keep an eye only on one entrance or the other. It was a matter of playing the odds. Besides, the parking lot for the complex was on the left side of the building and most people seemed to use the front entrance to access it. This gave the HOT team an opportunity to see each person's face as they walked to their vehicles.

Burke had come to his boss earlier in the afternoon with the recording of Williams and Keller's phone call. Neither was surprised by the confirmation of Keller and Myers' involvement, but actually hearing them speak the words put Commander Bill Payne into overdrive. He would see to it that this matter was put to rest *conclusively.* As always, Burke was slower to grasp the severity of the situation. In the end, though, Payne believed his deputy was finally coming around enough to understand that drastic steps had to be taken.

The feel of the situation changed as soon as Payne came onto the scene. Unlike many of his peers, Hatcher had no real problems working with the Commander, but the dynamics of a mission were different when he was around. Hatcher was confident of his own abilities and he was pretty sure that Payne and Burke thought highly of him as well. Why couldn't they leave him alone and let him do his job *this* time? *What is so special about Williams?* Once again, the question gnawed at him. There was something different about this case.

Whatever it was, there was little doubt as to who was in charge now. Payne was characteristically impatient. "Okay, let's get something straight. I want to hit them hard and fast."

As was often the case, it was time for Burke to rein his boss in tactfully. "Of course, we also want to be careful about injury to innocent bystanders. Remember that this *is* an apartment building. There could be someone directly on the other side of the wall from your target. So, if you have to shoot, don't do so indiscriminately."

Payne sneered at his deputy. "Thank you, Deputy Commander Burke," he said sarcastically. "As always, we will exercise due care when discharging our weapons." The Commander wanted the two men inside that building *dead*, though of course he couldn't actually say those words to his men. But just to make sure things turned out the way he wanted, he would be inside the building with his team. "Is there a handheld version of that?" Payne asked as he pointed to the monitoring screen.

"Yes sir," Hatcher answered, reaching for the portable monitoring device and holding it up for the Commander to see.

"How close can it get us to their exact location?"

"I can nail it, sir. It may take a couple of passes to verify, but we can pin the device's location down to within a few feet."

That was exactly what Payne wanted to hear. He'd always liked Hatcher for that very reason. There was nothing wishy-washy about him. The man was decisive and Payne would see that he was rewarded for it someday. "Good. We may as well get going, then. There might be less chance of attracting attention if we all go in through the rear entrance. We can spread out once we determine which floor they're on." There were nods all around. "Keep in mind that Larsen is a highly trained individual. As a result, there's a greater than average chance that we'll be met with aggression." Payne wanted to prime his team to shoot first and ask questions later. For that to actually happen, though, their subjects would need to do something to precipitate a firefight. Based on what he knew about Nick Larsen, Payne was sure he wouldn't let them down.

All of them were wearing undercover clothing—jeans with sweatshirts and jackets. Sykes and Lynch had on baseball caps as well. Burke had relayed that requirement to the team before they left headquarters. Once again, the men wondered why they were handling these subjects so differently. As Hatcher surveyed the group, he thought to himself that Burke and especially Payne would never be able to pull off an undercover job. Maybe it was just the way *he* saw them, but for some reason they never seemed to blend in with their surroundings.

As Hatcher sat there waiting to charge into yet another situation where they hadn't done their homework beforehand, he couldn't help but wonder again, *Why the rush?* Both the Commander and Deputy Commander wanted to storm the place, but in Hatcher's opinion they'd failed to consider a couple of important tactical issues. This left him feeling the need to take charge.

"Uh, sir," he began, looking at Payne, "in view of the fact that we're at least semi-undercover here, I think we should leave the M4's in the van." The M4 was normally a part of virtually everything HOT did. As relatively compact as they were, though, they were still a lot bulkier and more conspicuous than a handgun and might prove to be a liability in an apartment complex. This situation was a far cry from the raid they'd performed on Niculescu's place. The last thing they needed was for some old woman to see a bunch of shady-looking characters coming up the stairs with automatic weapons and let out a scream. The potential for over penetration of the M4's 5.56 mm round was another consideration—apartment walls tended to be paper-thin. As in every other tactical situation, planning for this one called for striking the proper balance between aggressiveness and prudence.

"Negative." It was Payne and his one-word reply convinced Hatcher that more was going on here than met the eye. "This is too important and Larsen is too dangerous for us to limit our options. Like I said before, we'll hit them hard and fast, using all necessary force. We've discussed this enough. Now let's get moving!"

******

One of the first things Nick had done after moving into the apartment was to install tiny motion-activated cameras at both the front and rear entrances to the complex. He'd installed the cameras very early on a Saturday morning, in order to minimize the number of explanations he might have to give. He'd worn coveralls and integrated the small devices into the heating vents in the ceiling. There had been only one tenant who'd exhibited anything resembling curiosity and he'd seemed satisfied by Nick's cover as a heating system technician. The vents were at the base of the stairway and about fifteen feet from the doors—a perfect location. The wiring was then fished up through the ductwork and into Nick's third-floor apartment. He'd wanted a unit on the ground floor, but none were available. Looking on the bright side, he'd figured that if he did see someone coming in who looked suspicious, he'd have more time to prepare while they climbed the stairs.

Two small television sets acting as monitors were mounted side by side on a wall of Nick's "family room" and were also visible from the kitchen. The makeshift surveillance system did not record anything, but it did give him a live feed whenever anyone entered or exited the building. Each time the cameras were activated, the monitor emitted a faint beeping sound. As a result, Nick and Don spent much of their time looking up at the monitors, which served only to heighten their paranoia.

* * * * * *

The team members entered through the rear door and began to file slowly up the stairs, with Hatcher in the lead. Payne was directly behind him, followed by Burke. Lynch and Sykes brought up the rear, carrying the compact battering ram that was used so often in these types of situations. Hatcher stopped momentarily on the landing outside the doorway to the second floor. The handheld monitor showed him that they weren't yet level with the tracking device. Turning around to face Commander Payne, Hatcher pointed upward and Payne nodded.

The building's layout was more like a hotel than an apartment complex. The stairs were carpeted and quiet. There would be no noise to warn their subjects, barring some unforeseen accident. Hatcher, Sykes, and Lynch carried their M4's as inconspicuously as possible on single-point slings under their jackets. Payne and Burke, on the other hand, didn't feel as comfortable with the automatic weapon, so they'd stuck with their handguns, which they had each unholstered and were carrying in their right hands.

Hatcher froze on the last step before reaching the third floor landing. He was surprised, especially on a Saturday night, that they hadn't encountered anyone else on the stairway, but he didn't want to push their luck. Showing the monitor to Payne, he pointed at the door leading to the hallway and then gave the entire team the "hold fast" sign. Hatcher then stepped up by himself and looked through the narrow rectangular window in the door to make sure that no one was coming toward them. The coast was clear.

He motioned for the other four men to join him on the landing. The only thing he was certain of was that the tracking device was on this floor and he felt he could safely assume that their subjects were as well. It was now simply a matter of moving down the hallway until the two red dots on the screen lined up. Then the fun would really begin, Hatcher thought sarcastically as he reached for the door handle.

******

Since the day he moved into the apartment, Nick had done several things that any "normal" person would have considered completely over the top. First, he kept all of his essential belongings in a black ballistic nylon rucksack next to the door. Everything he owned that mattered was in it. When he was inside the apartment and awake, that's where it stayed. When he left, it went with him. Known as a "bug-out bag," the backpack became a matter of habit. That way, if he ever needed to leave in a hurry, muscle memory alone would force him to grab it on his way out the door. Or, if he had to leave by one of the apartment's two windows—using the rope ladders that he kept stowed and covered on the floor beneath each window—he would at least know where his pack was. For the same reason, unless he was sleeping, he always wore shoes and remained fully clothed.

Sleep was not something that came easily to him these days, but when it did, he slept more soundly knowing that he'd wired his apartment door with an alarm that would emit a shrill sound through a speaker on his nightstand—right next to his Glock. The rucksack followed him into the bedroom at night as well and to its contents was added a shirt and a pair of shoes. Nick slept in either shorts or sweatpants, depending on the season. If he awoke during the night to the sound of the alarm, he could be gone with everything he needed in less than thirty seconds. And if that wasn't fast enough, he had one hundred and thirty rounds of .45 ACP ammunition already loaded into ten spare magazines with which to protect himself and slow down the invaders.

It was a hell of a way to live, but there were no other options at the present time. Nick looked forward to the day that would change, but for now he would survive the only way he knew how to—by being more careful and thorough than those who might come after him.

He had gone into the bathroom and was on his way back to the family room when he heard Don scream his name. "What is it?" Nick demanded as he came around the corner.

Don was pointing at the camera monitors. "Look!"

Two men were entering the building through the rear door. They appeared to have weapons hanging down under their right arms: Nick could see bulges under their jackets and what looked like muzzles protruding below the jackets. They were also carrying something that could very well be a battering ram. "Did any more go up the stairs before them?"

"Yeah, three."

"Right in front of these two?"

"Yeah…just a few seconds."

It wouldn't take long for them to climb two flights of stairs. Nick realized that he and Don *had* to be their targets. This place wasn't fancy, but it wasn't a crack house, either. In fact, he'd never seen a cop around here.

He put on his backpack and instinctively checked for the Glock in its Blade Tech holster on his right hip. "Let's go!" Don started to look around for his belongings. He would be in denial, Nick knew. There was no time to be gentle. "NOW—MOVE!" Don snapped out of his trance and followed Nick to the door.

Nick decided to try the door before resorting to the window. *If* they had time, it was preferable. The stairwell on the opposite end of the hallway from the one the ATF was using was only three doors down and he was worried that if the intruders had help on the perimeter of the building, they might be waiting for them directly below the window. If he and Don could make it to the stairs and get to another floor, they could decide where and when to exit the building rather than having the choice made for them.

If they were going to use the door, they'd have to be quick about it, though. Nick grabbed Don's arm and pulled him close, whispering, "If I say go, you stick to me like glue—got it?" Don found himself unable to speak, but nodded his head rapidly. Slowly, Nick cracked the door open a few inches.

* * * * * *

The five ATF agents were just starting to come out of the stairwell into the hallway. Hatcher—his eyes darting back and forth between the monitor in his hand and the doorways in front of him—was in the lead. He kept expecting one of the doors to fly open at any moment. No possible good could come of that. If their subjects were responsible for it, a firefight of epic proportions would ensue. If it was a little kid chasing his brother...well, he wasn't ready to consider that one. Tension in the team was thick—a situation made worse by Payne's and Burke's presence. Hatcher had complete confidence in his own men, but the Commander and Deputy worried him. They had probably *never* been very good at fieldwork and several years away from it would hardly have made them any better.

The two red dots on the screen were moving ever closer to each other and Hatcher's heart rate increased commensurately. Judging from the rate of closure, they should be no more than four to six units away from their target.

Hatcher was about to have Sykes and Burke move ahead of him to the far end of the hallway and close in on the subject's door from the opposite direction when he suddenly stopped in his tracks, as did the four men behind him. A door up ahead on the right opened slowly and the agents instinctively began to raise their weapons. A man stuck enough of his head out to see them and then shut the door quickly. The team began to move forward at a brisk pace and Hatcher dared to take his eyes off the door for a few seconds to check the monitor. The last thing he wanted to do was knock down the wrong door while the men they were after escaped.

* * * * * *

Nick closed the door quickly, without slamming it. The men in the hallway would be on top of them in seconds. Turning around to face a still shocked Don Williams, Nick realized they had no other option. "Go to the window, open it all the way, and throw down the ladder—NOW!" Don started to move. They'd gone over the "window escape" last night and Don remembered thinking it was a little over the top. Right now, however, it seemed anything *but!*

The men in the hallway had to be slowed down. *These guys picked the fight—and killed my best friend.* Nick opened the door again quickly. As he did so, he saw the M4's and handguns that the team now openly brandished. His reflexes took over at this point and he raised his Glock and leveled it at the lead attacker. The man had his head down looking at something in his hand. That would be a mistake he'd never make again.

Two shots rang out in the narrow hallway as all of the aggressors put the brakes on. The lead man crumpled to his knees and fell face down onto the carpeted floor—a victim of two shots to the head. Seeing the other four stop their advance, Nick closed the door and locked it with the two deadbolts he'd installed.

Don had just finished lowering the rope ladder and was spending far too much time making sure it was untangled completely. "Go! Get out of here!" Nick hissed. Don began to do as he was told, turning around to back out of the window. At that instant, the door came partially off its hinges as the battering ram struck its first blow. Nick had installed pins in between the hinges to slow down a forced entry. Just as he began to think that strategy might have worked, a second blow struck and the door spun inward.

Don had just taken his first step onto the shaky ladder. Two more steps and he'd be below the windowsill—and safe. Though it was the last thing he *should* have done, the inexperienced "felon" stopped and looked up at the sound of the splintering door. Nick was crouching off to the side and saw the M4 coming up toward Don. Raising his own pistol, he squeezed off two shots just as the attacker let loose a burst from his automatic weapon.

Nick began firing in an attempt to give Don a chance to escape. He hit one of the attackers in the chest and the man lunged backward out of the doorway. As Don quickly began his descent, a sharp pain shot down his left side each time he grabbed onto a rung.

Nick didn't want to go out the window the same way that Don had; it presented far too great a target. He'd anchored the rope ladder into the floor with heavy lag bolts and was about to find out just how good a job he'd done.

A head flashed past the edge of the doorway and was then pulled back. It was a tactic used to draw fire and Nick wasn't falling for it—he needed a little more time. Don was most of the way down the ladder when Nick reached down with his right hand and grabbed the first rung under the windowsill, looking back at the doorway as he did so. He saw one of them begin to enter the apartment again and opened fire left-handed. The man backed off just as Nick's pistol ran dry. This was his chance and there were only a few seconds to act.

Without hesitation, he shoved the Glock into his belt and went headfirst out the window. His body came around in an arc and, as his back slammed into the side of the building, the strength of his grip was tested as it hadn't been in years. The wind probably would have been knocked out of him if it hadn't been for the cushioning of his backpack. Immediately, he turned around on the ladder to face the wall and started down. He used only his hands on the rungs, keeping his legs spread slightly so that his feet wouldn't catch on the ladder. That method required more strength, but was much faster. When he was still almost a full story up, he'd had enough and jumped. As he hit the ground, he rolled forward and into the thick shrubbery that lined the perimeter of the building. Instantly, his Glock was out and a fresh magazine was inserted.

Don was already halfway to the vehicle and Nick could hear one of the intruders above him barking orders. He hoped there weren't others waiting for them at his SUV in the back parking lot. He took a deep breath and jumped out of the bushes, aiming his handgun up at the open window as he did so and opening fire. Satisfied that he'd bought as much time as he was likely to, he took off toward what he hoped was the safety of his vehicle. The ground to his right erupted, ripped up by a hail of 5.56 mm bullets. Nick weaved left and accelerated—to stop and return fire would be suicide.

Fishing the keys out of his pocket as he ran, Nick could see Don waiting for him by the passenger door. He punched the button on the remote to unlock the doors and Don jumped in and slammed the door. Nick opened the driver's door and threw the rucksack over to his passenger as he started the truck and sped out of the parking lot. There were no headlights in the rearview mirror.

Neither man spoke for a couple of minutes. When he was sure that no one was following, Nick looked over at Don. "Do you have the cell phone that Keller called you on last?"

"Yeah…oh shit!" Don blurted out, rolling down the window as he spoke.

"Good boy, get rid of it."

Don threw it out the window as if it were a poisonous snake.

"You did okay back there, Don. I mean it."

"Thanks."

"Are you all right?"

"Yeah, except for the fact that I've been shot."

"You're kidding me! Where?"

Don raised his left arm above his head and pointed to an area about six inches below his armpit, grimacing as he did so. He could feel the blood soaking his shirt. Nick turned the overhead light on and slowed down just enough for a cursory examination.

"Looks like it's stopped bleeding. Must have just grazed you," he decided, reaching up and turning the light off. "That's a good thing. I think there's a wad of napkins in the glove box. Hold 'em on the wound with some pressure. I'll take a look at it as soon as I can, but first we've got to figure out where we're going to go."

"You don't have anywhere in mind?"

"No, not really. Do you?" Nick shot back, tired of always having to be the one with all the answers.

"Yeah. Head up to Mount Hood."

******

How could we not have nailed these bastards? Payne wondered as he looked out the window through which their two subjects had escaped. Sykes and Burke had gone down the rope ladder after them, but were already on their way back from the parking lot wearing a look of failure on their faces. There should have been another half-dozen men covering the perimeter of the building, but that would have meant expanding the circle of HOT personnel who might have reason to suspect something.

Payne had a sense that Lynch and Sykes would have a few questions on their minds following the death of their squad leader. Their loyalty could not be taken for granted. Still, he and Burke obviously couldn't do this on their own. His men were as good as they came and yet these two nobodies had beaten them—again. That brought Dennis Hatcher to mind. Payne knew he was dead the moment he fell. Hatcher was a good man. He'd be missed.

Lynch had returned to Hatcher's side as soon as Sykes and Burke went down the rope ladder after the subjects. There was no way they'd catch them—not without backup watching the building perimeter. Lynch was glad he'd worn soft body armor. The bullet had struck him at an angle, so the blow wasn't as bad as it might have been. He'd be fine. A good friend of his lay dead in the hallway, though. The two of them had been very close. They'd respected each other's abilities and worked well together. One could always trust the other to do exactly what he was supposed to do. In Lynch's opinion, Dennis Hatcher was the perfect boss. He wasn't afraid to do anything that he'd ask someone else to do and he stood up for his people. *What are we doing here and what did Dennis die for?* Lynch wondered as Commander Payne stepped out into the hallway.

"Don't worry, Wayne. We'll get those bastards."

Lynch looked up at the Commander without understanding at first. There was a disconnect between what Payne had just said and what was going through Lynch's mind. It hadn't occurred to him that he should feel a primordial hatred for the men they were after—the men who'd just killed his boss and friend. Maybe he should, but right now he wasn't sure *whom* he should hate. "Uh, yes sir. I know we will" was all the enthusiasm he could muster at the moment. Someone else would have to be pissed; Wayne Lynch was confused.

"It's all right, folks. We're federal agents," Payne announced as he held up his badge. A few curious souls had begun to crack their doors open to see what was happening. To them, it was probably like watching a television cop show…until they looked down and saw the man lying face down on the floor, with an increasingly large pool of blood under his head. Lynch took off his jacket and covered Hatcher's upper body and head with it.

Burke and Sykes worked their way through the growing number of onlookers as they returned from what Payne knew would be a fruitless chase. Sirens could be heard now. It wouldn't be long before this place was an absolute madhouse, Payne realized as he ordered Lynch and Sykes to keep the crowds back. "No sign of them?" he asked an out-of-breath Ray Burke.

"No, sir. We saw the taillights of their vehicle, but that was all." Burke looked down at Hatcher's lifeless body. "Now that's a shame. Thank goodness Lynch was wearing body armor, or we'd have two of them down."

Payne grabbed Burke's arm and walked a few feet down the hall. After he'd put some space between them and the small crowd that had formed near Hatcher's body, he stopped walking and leaned close to his deputy. "They got away from us *again*, Ray. One way or another, we *will* take these two out. We *have* to."

"Yes, sir. I'm well aware of that."

"Good. Now make sure we get an ambulance here to go along with the hundred or so cops that are about to descend on us."

* * * * * *

The drive up the mountain seemed to take forever, but at least Nick felt safe under the cover provided by darkness and the huge fir trees lining the winding highway. It may have been only false security, but right now he would take comfort in any modicum of refuge that came his way, real or false.

"It's the next right, Nick." Don was thankful for remembering the turn. Of course, it had been only a week ago that he was here breaking the life-changing news to what was left of the Niculescu family.

"You're sure it's safe up here?" Nick asked.

"I can't imagine a safer place for us to be right now," Don answered. "The only way the ATF could find out about this place is to question George, Ana, or Jenny, and they'd never tell them."

"Well, that's good, because there's something I want you to think about. Doesn't it seem a little odd to you that shortly after you had a chat with your friend Keller, we were attacked?"

The question hit Don in the pit of his stomach. He hadn't even considered the possibility of betrayal. Scott Keller was the one guy besides Nick whom he'd really felt he could trust, even though he'd never met the man.

Could he have been *that* wrong about the Marshal? If so, it would mean Mike and Nick were right about more than he wanted to give them credit for. On the other hand, if they *were* right, Don had reason to be even more scared than he was now. If Scott had done this to them, it meant that they weren't fighting just a few "bad apples." If Nick was right, they would truly have nowhere to turn. Just how much was he—were *they*—capable of doing on their own to protect themselves? As confidence-inspiring as Nick Larsen was, he was only one man.

"Yeah. I guess I can see how you would think that," Don conceded.

"How *I* would think that...what about you? Don, what's it gonna take to snap you out of your little fantasy world? These people almost killed us—twice."

He was right. Or at least he *could* be. That had to be enough for now. "You're right. It sure looks like those guys had the inside scoop tonight, huh?"

"Yeah, it does," Nick answered.

As they started down the long drive leading to the cabin, Nick began to survey the surroundings for pros and cons. That was the way his mind worked. As he had been back at the apartment and on so many other occasions throughout his life, Nick Larsen was in condition red, survival mode. Actions would come without thinking. It had to be that way, or you didn't see the next sunrise.

"What do you think?" Don wondered. He was proud of himself for coming up with an idea. It had been his first one.

Nick pulled around behind the cabin and put the Durango in park. "Not bad, but there's one glaring problem."

"What's that?" Don was shocked. He'd thought for sure that this idea would rate an "attaboy."

"The thick timber is great in one sense, but it also creates a problem. Think about it."

Don did for a few seconds, but he wasn't in the mood for guessing games. "Nick, I don't know what you're getting at. I just hope that someday my life returns to normal, so I won't need such sharply honed jungle survival skills."

Nick laughed out loud and it felt good. "I can't say I blame you and I hope to get back to 'normal' someday, too. Until then, though, we've got a little problem to deal with. I'm just trying to help you do that."

"I know. I'm just kidding...I think. Without you, I wouldn't stand a chance. I want you to know I really appreciate what you're doing, Nick. You saved my ass back there for the second time in the last thirty-six hours."

"Don't mention it," Nick answered as he opened the door and grabbed his rucksack. "Let's get inside."

Don was relieved to find the hidden key where he expected it to be and opened the front door of the cabin. Having stayed here a few times with his family, he knew there were a couple of important chores to be done upon arrival. Don tackled the chores while Nick familiarized himself with the cabin and its surroundings.

After a few pulls, Don got the large Honda generator started. It was amazingly quiet and efficient, and sat in an insulated box twenty feet from the back door. The next task was to get the woodstove inside the cabin fired up. As the sole source of heat, this was a high priority. It was cold at this elevation and the cabin always took a while to warm up.

Both men were now back inside and Nick sat down on the couch. "Come over here and take your shirt off. I need to clean that wound."

Don hadn't forgotten about it; in fact, it was beginning to hurt more as time passed. The problem was that he was a wimp. He remembered all the old Westerns he'd seen where some grizzled old cowboy heated up a rusty skinning knife to "sterilize" it and then used it to dig a lead slug out of his buddy. By this time, the patient had usually had several gulps of whiskey and was told to bite down hard on a leather belt or something.

Nick sensed Don's reticence. "Oh, come on. I'm not gonna hurt you, sweetheart." Don laughed nervously and did as he was told. Nick had surmised correctly when he'd glanced at the wound earlier. The bullet had just grazed Don's side, several inches below his armpit. Another inch to the inside could have resulted in substantial damage; Don had been lucky.

Nick went to work quickly, cleaning the wound and bandaging it with gauze and tape that he'd found in a first aid kit in the cabin. He had a small kit in his rucksack as well, but wanted to keep it intact. Nick was efficient and relatively careful and Don was impressed with his skill, though he couldn't keep from yelping on occasion. Nick rolled his eyes and shook his head each time it happened. However efficient he was, Nick lacked anything resembling a bedside manner.

"You're really lucky, you know that?" Don just nodded his head. "You've got to promise me that you won't stop to look the next time you hear a loud noise, okay?"

"Yeah, I know. That was pretty lame, huh?"

"Pretty lame," Nick agreed, as he packed up the first aid supplies. "I'm going to go outside and take another look around."

"You don't really think we're in danger here, do you?" Don wondered.

One of the differences between Nick Larsen and most other people was that he understood that a person was *always* in danger, simply because they never knew for sure what life would throw at them next. He would always be ready for whatever it was and if he didn't win the fight, he'd go down swinging. "No, I'm sure we're fine. I'd just like to have the advantage if we're surprised."

As soon as Nick stepped outside, the darkness nearly enveloped him. There were no exterior lights on and the drawn curtains obscured much of the illumination from inside the cabin. The tall trees combined with just a sliver of a moon and overcast skies created a sense of almost liquid blackness, exactly the kind of condition that made Nick most comfortable.

The temperature was in the upper thirties and there was still snow in some spots. As he used his Surefire flashlight to carefully pick his way through the thick, damp underbrush, Nick wondered whether Mike had had any influence on his parents' choice for a retreat. It must have suited his desire for solitude well, although Nick was certain that his friend never could have imagined this place becoming what might be a last line of defense.

Nick continued to explore and came across a fairly large area where the soil had recently been worked up. As he moved some of the brush away from the area, he also noticed faint tracks remaining from what must have been a very heavy piece of equipment. It was difficult to tell in the darkness—even with a flashlight—but it looked as though someone had dug a large hole and attempted to disguise it.

Nick thought about Mike again and wondered if this was the place he'd chosen. If so, the items he'd buried could come in handy. He'd keep that in mind.

Before leaving the cabin, Nick had scoured the interior of the place for potentially useful items. As he worked his way around the property, he used many of them to construct a makeshift alarm system. At a height of just a few inches above the ground, he strung fishing line in a continuous circle around the perimeter, to which he attached glass jars at various points. In each jar he put several pieces of gravel, which, when rattled forcefully (as would happen if a person tripped on the fishing line), made a surprisingly loud noise. It wasn't infrared, but it would have to do.

Nick was glad to see that a shallow gulley bordered the south end of the property, about fifty feet from the cabin. Such contours in the terrain often provided an escape route where none otherwise would have existed. He made a mental note of it and moved on. After spending another twenty minutes or so scouting the area, Nick realized that there really wasn't much else he could do tonight. At least now he had some semblance of a warning system in place and that would allow him a sounder sleep.

Nick closed the cabin door behind him and walked over to the woodstove. It was cold out and he wasn't dressed for it. Don was rummaging through the cupboards, looking for food, but stopped as soon as Nick came back in. "Hey, I think I've got the answer to your question."

"Huh?" Nick was caught off guard.

"Your little quiz about what was wrong with this place?"

"Oh yeah. Well?"

"The timber does a good job of hiding us, but it might also allow someone coming after us to get too close before we can see them."

Nick was impressed. It wasn't rocket science, but the answer showed a certain sense of tactical awareness that he hadn't noticed before in this guy. Still, he couldn't let him off that easily. "Are you asking me, or telling me?"

"Oh, come on!"

Nick laughed. "Actually, you're exactly right. I'd prefer another twenty or thirty yards of clearing all around the place, but we'll have to play the cards we've been dealt. Besides, I don't think we're going to make our last stand here anyway. I've got better ideas than to wait for them to come and get us."

"Like what?" Don wondered.

"Well, we talked last night about Plan B. You know, being proactive?"

"Yeah."

"We need to work on that some more, but it can wait till tomorrow."

The possibility of Scott's betrayal had been nagging at Don since Nick had brought it up earlier. "Nick, do you really think Keller was behind that attack?"

Nick rubbed his eyes and considered the question. "Yeah, I do. Now that we know about it, though, we may actually be able to use it to our advantage." Don wasn't getting it. "What I'm saying is that, the next time you talk to Keller, we can use him to launch our own little counterattack."

Don nodded his head, apparently resigned to the fact that a man he'd come to trust had betrayed them. That potential phone conversation with Scott wasn't the first call on Don's mind, though. "Nick, I'd like to call my wife tomorrow morning, too. If she hears about what happened last night and doesn't hear from me...well, I just can't let that happen."

Nick almost blurted out what he believed to be the truth: if they didn't get out of this mess *soon*, she might have to deal with her husband's death for real. He sighed deeply instead and admitted to himself that he would feel the same way if he were in Don's position. "I understand. We'll get a message to her tomorrow, somehow. For now, though, let's get some sleep. I'm sure we'll both be able to think a lot more clearly in the morning."

Sleep sounded good. Don couldn't remember ever being as worn out as he was right now.

17

Portland, Oregon
Sunday, April 27

Don't make any messes you can't clean up. The Director's words had come back to haunt Bill Payne more than once since Mullin had spoken them a couple of weeks ago. "I'm tired of being delicate about this, Ray. These four men will *not* mark the end of my career. I want them out of the way *permanently*—all of them. Got it?" Burke nodded slowly. "There are no other options. Williams made the decision to stick his nose into this and the other three put their lives on the line to help him. They've asked for it and, by God, they're going to get it!" Payne eyed his deputy carefully. "Am I wrong about any of this?"

Burke knew that his boss wasn't looking for an honest answer, so he couldn't tell the Commander that his premise was absurd—or at least it would have been had Payne not already pushed things as far as he had. Unfortunately, Burke was bound inextricably to this man he'd once respected, but who was now becoming more out of control by the hour.

Burke had slept very little last night. His wife wanted to know all about what had happened after seeing it on the news, but he wasn't in the mood to talk. Then again, he rarely was these days. She would never know the truth, of course. He could never tell her, because she would have tried relentlessly to talk him out of going along with this insane plan to kill two men—*or was it four now?*—who didn't deserve it. His wife had always been his conscience and she could tell that something was eating her husband alive these days. "Why seven days a week all of a sudden, honey?" she'd asked this morning. It was only temporary, he'd assured her. It was temporary because, at this rate, he would either end up dead or in prison, he didn't add.

"No, sir. You're not wrong."

Payne was happy not to have to explain himself further. He needed Burke on board in order to pull this off. He also needed Sykes and Lynch to at least follow orders without asking questions, though he doubted they would present much of a problem. The subjects had gunned down their friend and leader last night. That should be enough to convince them of the need to shoot to kill. "Good, Ray. I know this isn't easy—no one ever said it would be."

"Yes, sir. I'll just be glad when it's over."

"Me too, Ray." Clapping his hands together like a high school football coach, Payne's eyes began to light up. "Okay, let's stay tight on Keller's phone line and send Sykes and Lynch back over to the Niculescus' house, where Williams' family is. If his wife leaves to go anywhere, have them follow her. He might even show up there himself.

"After we get them set up, let's work on running down some of the possible contacts that Larsen might have. There must be a ton of them. After all, he played a pretty rough game for a long time."

"You don't plan on bringing Sykes and Lynch in on this, do you?" Burke asked. They were good young officers, with bright futures ahead of them, and Burke had worried from the beginning about their being dragged down into the mud along with him and Payne. He'd worried about Hatcher too…for all the good it had done.

"No. I don't see any advantage in doing so at this point."

******

It was Sunday morning and Scott had promised Meg that they would go to church. The service didn't begin until 8:30, which gave him time for a short workout beforehand. He was finishing up his workout in the garage when Meg came out to him with his cell phone in hand.

Being pregnant, she slept in whenever possible these days and Scott smiled at her as she stumbled toward him in her pajamas and fuzzy slippers.

"Bobby's on the phone," she mumbled, handing it over.

"Sorry he woke you up, sweetie," he whispered. She dismissed his concern with a wave of her hand as she turned back toward the warmth of the house.

"Hey, what's up?"

"Sorry to call so early, but I assume you heard about what happened last night?"

Scott had no idea what his friend was talking about, but gathered from the tone of his voice that he should have. "No, I didn't hear anything. We went out to dinner and a movie. We got home late and I haven't even seen the paper yet this morning. What happened?"

"More of the same, I'm afraid. Our boys found Williams and some other guy in an apartment building downtown and shot the place up pretty good—you know, in Payne's typical low-key style. It's front-page stuff. Anyway, sounds like Williams and his buddy got away without a scratch, but Hatcher wasn't so lucky."

"How bad?"

"Dead."

"Seriously?"

"Yep. Two shots to the cranium, within a couple inches of each other."

"Williams couldn't have done that," Scott replied.

"Doubtful."

Scott was wondering how Williams had managed to find someone so capable to help him. When he'd talked to him just a few hours before last night's raid, he'd sounded as helpless as ever. He probably just didn't want to tip his hand. Scott couldn't blame him for not trusting anyone with a badge these days. "Well, it sounds like whoever he's got helping him probably saved his life. That's a shame about Hatcher, though. You know, I can't say I really liked the guy, but he sure did know his stuff."

"Yeah, he did. Actually, Dennis was a good man. It's easy to get distracted by a guy's personality, but I gotta tell you, I'd have taken him on my side in a fight any day." Hatcher was, after all, a brother agent and when one of them went down, they all felt it.

Scott understood this completely. "Yeah. Based on what little I knew of him, I'd agree with you a hundred percent." He was about to end the call when he thought of something else. "Hey, how did you find out about the specifics of last night? I'm sure they didn't go into much detail in the paper."

"I called Sykes this morning. Why?"

"So, it's not like Payne called HOT together and made a big deal of it, right?"

"No. What are you getting at?"

"Oh, I'm just trying to figure out how desperate he's getting. The more desperate he gets, the deeper the shit Williams is in."

"Scott, there's not a whole lot of doubt about how deep it is for Williams. Payne just lost one of his best men and that's going to turn the heat up on *him*, which means big trouble for our boy Williams."

Scott walked into the house and found Meg in the kitchen, stirring a cup of tea. "What's wrong?" she asked as her husband closed the garage door behind him.

He related the details of the conversation he'd just had. "I don't know, honey, I'm beginning to think I should just go find the guy and bring him in. We could hold him in custody and at least keep him away from Payne. From there, I'm not exactly sure where we'd turn, but I can work on the rest of the plan as I go."

"You guys still wouldn't have any proof of what Payne did, though. And when it's just your word against his, are you even sure that *Bobby* would stick with you? He's an ATF guy, after all, and he's going to have to live with them when all of this is over."

She may be right. "I really haven't thought about that too much, but I think Bobby would be there to the end. I haven't known him very long, but he seems to be the kind of guy you can count on to do the right thing first and worry about the consequences later. The problem is there's no perfect solution. If I *don't* bring him in now, the guy could end up dead and that wouldn't do anybody but Payne any good." Scott looked up at the ceiling and sighed. "I don't know what the right thing to do is. The only thing I *do* know is that I need to talk to Don face to face. If I can do that, I'm sure we can work something out."

"You're probably right. What a mess! Can you imagine what Don's family must be going through? They're not used to this kind of thing like we are," she added with a sarcastic smile. Meg had spent many a night as a little girl wondering whether or not her father would come home and many a night since marrying Scott Keller doing the same.

As his wife was making her subtle dig, Scott had a thought. "What if he doesn't want me to find him?"

"What do you mean?"

"Well, soon after I talked to him yesterday, he was almost killed. What if he puts two and two together the wrong way and thinks I set him up?" Scott's first reaction to his own idea was that it was ridiculous, but then he thought about it again from Don's perspective. They'd never met before and Scott was a federal cop, working with the ATF. What happened yesterday could easily be seen as a perfect example of cause and effect. That realization hardened his resolve. "I've *got* to find him."

Ironically, Meg felt the baby move at that exact moment, but she decided against telling Scott. It was a new phenomenon and they both became giddy whenever it happened, but now was not the time. "Scott, promise me you'll be careful." He almost rolled his eyes. "I don't mean that the way I usually do, either. These guys don't know you like I do. To them, you're just another cop that's out to get them... and they killed a cop last night. Don't assume anything, honey."

* * * * * *

Don was surprised that he'd slept like a rock. Though he was dead tired, he'd been sure that his fear would keep him awake all night. It hadn't, and even the pain from his bullet wound hadn't overcome his body's need for sleep. *I was shot yesterday!* It was nearly impossible for him to believe—except when his left side throbbed, as it did right now. It was a completely foreign concept to him. Of all the things he would have thought might happen to him during his lifetime, being shot wasn't even on the "outside possibilities" list.

Nick, it appeared, hadn't been so lucky as far as sleep was concerned. Though he just grunted when Don asked him about it, the man looked as if he hadn't slept a wink. That would have to change soon, or they were both in trouble. Then again, Don hoped this nightmare wouldn't last *too* much longer.

Nick scratched absentmindedly at the stubble growing on his face. They'd found some canned peaches and granola bars for breakfast and he was just finishing his. "Let's go ahead and contact your wife. We've got to get some things figured out ASAP, but you probably won't be able to concentrate until she knows you're safe, right?"

"Right. What's the best way to do it? Is it okay to just call her?"

"No. I wouldn't be surprised if the ATF had George and Ana's phone tapped, so that's out. And if they're able to pick up her cell signal, they could get you that way, too. If they do, one phone call could have them here in twenty minutes by chopper."

"What am I supposed to do, then, send smoke signals?"

"The only thing I feel comfortable with is using one of your prepaid cells to text her. Do you have any left?"

Don nodded. "Yeah, I've got one. I'd sure like to hear her voice, but you're probably right. We don't have a signal here, though."

"Yeah, I know. Let's go find one."

* * * * * *

Nick drove while Don held the cell phone and checked the signal strength. About four miles farther up the road, they had a signal and Don sent the text, wishing he could hear Jenny's voice. That would have to wait, though. For now, at least she would know that he wasn't dead and that he was somewhere safe.

* * * * * *

Scott showered and dressed. He'd decided to head down to USMS headquarters to do some digging. As he backed out of his driveway, he remembered Don telling him that his family had gone "somewhere safe." He had to find out where that might be. There was no other way he could think of to find Don in a hurry. Regardless of how clever Don thought he'd been, Scott was sure that he had underestimated HOT's ability to find his family. That meant it shouldn't be too difficult for a U.S. Marshal to do the same. Scott also knew it was likely that, wherever they were, they were being watched and that the phone line might have been tapped. In that case, if Don's wife *did* know where he was, there was a good chance that Payne and his boys did too. That meant Scott would have to beat them to the punch—no simple task, he knew.

Scott was deep in thought as he drove. Even so, he was still able to spot the incredibly inept person tailing him in a red BMW. He remembered seeing the same car down the street from his house as he drove away, but hadn't thought anything of it then—the car could have belonged to someone visiting a neighbor. Instead, his mind simply made a mental note automatically, as it had so many other times over the years. It was what he was trained to do and he was good at it. *Who is this?* Whoever it was now had his undivided attention. Just to make sure he wasn't being paranoid, he made several quick and unnecessary turns. The guy was still on his tail. This was almost funny. Not only was this person clueless, but he was also driving a bright red sports car!

Scott parked along the curb and got out of his car quickly. He stepped up onto the sidewalk and kept walking in the direction his car was facing. Looking in a plate glass window as he passed by a department store, he noticed that the BMW had parked right behind him and a guy in a baseball cap was getting out. As soon as he was past the storefront, Scott turned right. The side entrance to the store was just a few feet ahead. He ducked into the brick entry and waited.

It didn't take his pursuer long to catch up. Scott knew the man had been close behind him as he turned the last corner and now he could hear footsteps. *Just a couple more steps…now!* He reached out just as the bill of the black baseball cap came into view and grabbed the man by the collar of his windbreaker. Turning quickly, he swung the hapless character around a hundred eighty degrees to his right and up against the brick wall in the entry from which he'd sprung his trap a split second earlier. Now he was looking into the very frightened eyes of someone he'd never seen before, with his forearm putting pressure on the man's throat to the point of severe discomfort. Scott Keller was in a bad mood and this seemed like the perfect opportunity to vent.

Tim Murdoch was sure he'd just pissed himself and would have looked down to check but for the fact that this guy was about to crush his larynx. Just before he thought he would pass out, his attacker let up—not completely, but at least enough to let a little air through. Something told Murdoch this wasn't the first time Scott Keller had done this to another human being.

"Talk fast. Who are you and why are you following me?"

Gasping for breath, Murdoch managed to croak out, "my back left pants pocket…my I.D. and badge…go ahead and check."

Moving his left hand up to the man's throat in place of his forearm, Scott removed the leather pouch and opened it. "Tim Murdoch…ATF, huh? Who the *hell* does Payne think he think he is, having a U.S. Marshal tailed?"

"No. That's not it." Murdoch was shaking his head back and forth vigorously. "Please take your hand off my throat and I'll tell you what's going on."

Scott did so, but not before putting the man's credentials in his own pocket, just in case the guy decided to bolt. "Okay, talk to me."

"As you know, my name's Tim Murdoch. I'm ATF, but I'm a tech guy. I set up surveillance, that kind of thing. Anyway, my crew and I got an order yesterday morning to do a phone tap. No big deal, except Burke was real tight-lipped when it came to talking about the subject. That made me and my guys real curious. Sometimes we know who we're snooping on and sometimes we don't, but the way Burke acted made us—"

"I know—'real curious.' Now get to the point." Scott was losing patience and his tone caught Murdoch off guard.

"Okay. Anyway, we found out who our subject was and, well…it was you." Keller's eyes narrowed and Murdoch thought for a minute that he was going to beat the hell out of him, or worse. "Uh, and as soon as we found out who you were—I mean, you know, a Marshal and all—well, we thought something might be wrong. We couldn't figure out a legitimate reason to tap you."

Scott never broke eye contact with the guy. He was telling the truth, that much he was sure of. "Did you complete the tap?"

"Yeah, we did." Murdoch felt himself getting a little defensive. "Hey, it *was* an order and we thought maybe you were involved in some kind of black market operation or something." Keller shook his head slowly, but remained silent. "I know, I know—I never really believed that." The young man knew he was on thin ice and paused before going on. *Just tell him.* What he had to say was a lot more important than what he'd done. In this case, the end definitely justified the means. Keller would see that. "Anyway, I set up a way for me to hear your calls also—I mean, in addition to Burke." Keller was getting that look in his eyes again. "I kind of felt like it was my duty to follow through on my suspicion. So I did, and I heard your conversation with Don Williams yesterday. I heard everything." Keller's expression didn't change one bit. Murdoch wondered what kind of guy lived behind those intense eyes.

"Did they have you do anything else—like put some kind of a tracking device on my car?"

"No. Nothing like that. Just the phone line."

"Marshal, I didn't know what to do," Murdoch continued, "so I slept on it last night. But when I woke up this morning, I knew I had to tell you what was going on. I was parked on your street for almost two hours before you finally left the house. I was about ready to knock on your door, but I was afraid there might be someone from HOT watching the house. Anyway, that's it. That's why I was following you. I figured, wherever you stopped, I'd flag you down and give you the scoop. It might be lame, but I'm pretty new at this stuff."

As mad as he was, Scott almost laughed. "Don't worry, you did fine. I'm glad you gave me a heads-up. I'm just mad at myself for not seeing this coming—I really should have known." The hardest part for him to swallow was the realization that, even though he and Don hadn't talked about Don's location, he might have somehow played a part in what happened last night. No sense in worrying about it now, though. He *had* to find Don's wife.

******

Last night's news had nearly ripped Jenny's guts out. There must have been a hundred police officers and the apartment was bullet-riddled from top to bottom. They said that the "subjects" were wanted by the ATF's elite Hazardous Operations Team for unspecified crimes, but the HOT officers present declined to comment. They could have been after anyone, but something told her that their target was the man she loved. The only consolation was the fact that they apparently had been unsuccessful.

Jenny glanced down at her cell phone as she walked by the Niculescus' kitchen counter and noticed an unread text:

> *U probably saw what was left of Nicks place on news last night. Don't worry. We r ok. Sitting in same place u and I were one week ago yesterday. Love u and kids so much. Don't worry. Will all be together soon! No need to text back. Won't be able to get it.*

The same spot they were sitting in a week ago yesterday? It seemed as though the last week had been a year. Time had ceased to be important. *Where were we last Saturday that would make a good hideout? The cabin! That had to be it.* Jenny didn't know how much more of this she'd be able to take, but at least she knew her husband was safe for now. *I sure hope Nick Larsen knows his stuff.*

* * * * * *

Scott knew that he was going to have to do some digging to find Don. He didn't bother going to the Williams' house. Don had said that he'd sent his family somewhere safe and though he could have been trying to throw the Marshal off track, Scott was sure that the Williams clan wasn't sitting in their living room waiting for Dad to come home.

So, where were they? There was likely a connection between Don's wife and what remained of the Niculescu family. Both families were clearly affected by this mess and the two men had obviously been very close. You didn't go to the mat for a guy the way Don had without good reason. With that in mind, he further assumed that their families were close as well. Maybe not, but it was at least *something* for him to go on. He would start where it all began for Don Williams—with his friend's death.

Scott pulled up in front of the coroner's office. A quick call had confirmed what he'd suspected: even though it was Sunday morning, there was a good chance that someone would be there. The door was locked, but as they'd agreed over the phone, a loud knock brought someone to open it. "Hey, Larry, how's it going?"

"Not bad, Marshal. Just as exciting as ever around here. Come on in. What was it you needed to look at?"

"Well, there was a case that would've come in here a week ago yesterday...name was Niculescu." The man nodded his head slowly. "I need to check on a couple of items like next of kin, who identified the body, that kind of thing."

"Yeah, that was the first Collection death, wasn't it?"

"That's the one."

"How come the Marshals are mixed up in it?"

Curiosity among cops and those who worked with them was a real pain sometimes, but there was no way to avoid it. "Oh, a couple of the guy's cronies fled and guess who gets to track 'em down?"

Larry gave him a knowing smile. "Guess that's why they pay you the big bucks, huh, Marshal?"

"Oh yeah, they're always throwing money at me." The two of them had been walking down a long, sterile-looking hallway and finally arrived at a room with several computer terminals in it.

"Marshal, I hope you don't mind if I leave you on your own from here on out. I've still got a ton of work to do and I'd like to get home before I have to be back in the morning. You know how to navigate the system, right?" Larry asked as he led Scott over to one of the small desks and powered up the computer.

"Absolutely. Thanks for letting me in; I can handle it from here." Larry nodded and ambled off down the hallway. Scott settled in and scrolled down until he came to April 19th and clicked on it. The cases were listed alphabetically within the date they came in and Scott quickly found what he was looking for. He was shocked for a moment to see two under the same name…he'd almost forgotten that Niculescu's wife had been killed as well. He clicked on "Niculescu, Michael" and waited for the images to load.

The photographs were not very different from hundreds of others he had seen during his career, but they rocked him nonetheless. There was something about black-and-white photographs that amplified the macabre aspects of a crime scene. Scott remembered being fascinated by "Old West" photos of dead outlaws as a kid. He could never understand why they held his attention so and he wondered now what his fascination said about him. Nothing that wouldn't also be true of millions of other kids, he hoped.

It wasn't the pictures themselves that bothered him—it was his knowledge of the details. He'd been there to witness the killing. These weren't exactly Bonnie and Clyde in front of him. Here lay an innocent man (and a damn good one, by all accounts), killed because of an idiotic law. That law had been enthusiastically enforced by mostly well-meaning cops. It wasn't their fault. It wasn't even primarily Payne's fault, Scott had to admit. Initially, even *he* was just doing his job—albeit with too much joy. In the end, it was society's fault. We were getting exactly what we deserved. Busting Payne might not mean much in and of itself, but Scott began to hope that it would focus enough national attention on the issue of Collection to put pressure on Congress to reverse course. It would also save lives, if he did it soon enough.

Scott quickly scanned the coroner's report. Most of it was useless to him. Here was what he'd come for: the deceased's parents, Mr. and Mrs. George Niculescu, had identified the body. Their address was right in front of him. Now he just had to hope that they had houseguests.

* * * * * *

Washington, D.C.

Attorney General Martinez strode confidently down the West Wing hallway toward the Oval Office. The surroundings in this building always impressed him more than any other place he'd ever seen. Power seemed to ooze from the walls. To occupy the office in front of him was the ultimate goal of every politician worth his salt and it was one that he himself would someday achieve—regardless of the cost.

It was Sunday and the place was almost empty. Martinez loved it this way. He felt an even greater than usual sense of exclusivity, being one of so few who could possibly have a reason to be meeting with the President of the United States on a Sunday afternoon. The Secret Service agent escorted him into the Oval Office. The room was arranged with two armchairs flanking the fireplace, above which hung a portrait of George Washington. The President and Vice President normally occupied these chairs when there was a formal meeting. This hardly qualified as such, however, so the President was sitting on one of the two much more comfortable overstuffed couches that faced each other, with a large rectangular coffee table between them.

The President looked up from a briefing paper and motioned Martinez to take the other couch, across from him. "Have a seat, Charlie. Can I get you anything?"

"No, thank you, sir."

The President looked nervous. There had been several more deaths during ATF raids over the last week and what at one time had looked like a surefire express ticket to re-election had now begun to faintly resemble an albatross. Polls were showing slippage in support for the policy as people saw their neighbors hauled off to prison or heard about Collection deaths on the news. "Charlie, we need to take a look at the way we're handling Collection. Another one of our people was killed last night. Hell, the *Wall Street Journal*'s editorial page is keeping a body count...they're projecting more dead Americans in the first year than we lost in Desert Storm and Bosnia together!"

"Mr. President, the press is going to sensationalize everything, you know that. All we can do is our job. The American people and Congress have entrusted this to us and we can't let them down."

"Charlie, this issue isn't like anything else we've ever dealt with. Everything else, you get it through Congress, make a speech or two, and claim victory. Usually you don't know for years—if ever—whether or not what you did actually had any effect. This one's been in our face almost from day one. Even when things were going well in the beginning, it was hard for people to be comfortable with what they saw on television."

Martinez knew the man in front of him very well. This wasn't just another moment of doubt and the Attorney General was afraid of what Nichols might do. Collection was still a popular and necessary policy. There was no way he would let this fall by the wayside like so many other grand ideas this President had supported when it was popular to do so, then abandoned when he couldn't take the heat. Martinez would head this off at the pass.

"Mr. President, I'll have Director Mullin call in the Division Directors within a few days. I'll chair the meeting myself and we'll find ways to improve the process. Until then, though, we've got to stay the course. The American people knew from the beginning that this policy couldn't be implemented without some loss of life, yet they still supported it."

"Well, we'd better hope they don't develop amnesia because of these body bags, or you and I'll *both* be out of work on January twenty-first of next year!"

18

Portland, Oregon
Sunday, April 27

SCOTT WAS UNFAMILIAR with the area, but it wasn't unlike so many others in Metro Portland—a middle-class neighborhood full of row after row of single-story ranch-style homes. It wasn't much to look at, but it gave the greatest possible number of people a slice of the American dream.

As he slowed his car, Scott wondered whether or not Payne's boys might be watching this place as well. There wasn't much he could do about it now; he had to find Don ASAP and he could always lose a tail if he had to.

Scott never parked in anyone's driveway but his own. Parking on the street made his presence less obvious and allowed a quicker getaway should he become suddenly unwelcome. He thought about that as he approached the house. How welcome would he be here? How welcome *should* he be? A group of children playing in the street provided what he was afraid might be the answer.

They stopped what they were doing as Scott came closer. A boy of about twelve held a ball under his arm and eyed the Marshal suspiciously. Pretty intense for a kid that age, Scott thought. He considered talking to the kids for a moment, to alleviate some of the awkwardness, but decided against it.

He rang the doorbell and a sturdy-looking older man answered within a few seconds. "Mr. Niculescu?" The old man's eyes narrowed.

Was it Scott's imagination, or was everyone staring at him as if he had horns growing out of his head? He was dressed in jeans and a leather bomber jacket, but he felt as if he had "Fed" written all over him. Maybe there were some things you couldn't hide.

"Yes. I am. Who are you, please?"

"Sir, my name is Scott Keller. I'm a Deputy United States Marshal," he explained, resisting the urge to produce his badge. "Mr. Niculescu, I would appreciate a few minutes of your time."

Jenny had told George and Ana about Scott, so his name was familiar—but federal agents had killed his son and daughter in law. George was conflicted and that was obvious to Scott.

"Sir, this is about Don Williams…it's about *helping* Don Williams," he corrected himself. Not wanting a confrontation on the front porch, Scott didn't want to come right out and ask if Mrs. Williams was inside. He held his breath and waited for what seemed an eternity as the old man studied his eyes. The truth was always in the eyes, Scott knew. Hopefully, the man before him understood that as well.

A part of George Niculescu still reacted with fear when confronting someone in a position of authority. Old habits were hard to break. It was *never* good news when a representative of the Romanian government knocked on your door. How different had it been in this country lately? The man looked honest, though.

"Excuse me. Please come inside."

Two women were at the other end of the foyer. They gave Scott a look that said they'd heard the conversation. The younger one was likely Don's wife, but he didn't want to assume anything. He didn't have to.

"Hello, Marshal. I'm Jenny Williams. What can I do for you?" she asked, stepping forward but not extending a hand. Her approach was businesslike without being rude. Jenny decided that she wasn't going to force the Niculescus to deal with whatever lay ahead; they'd been through enough already. It was time that *she* handled something, she thought, not giving herself any credit for the load she'd been carrying for the past three days.

Scott wasn't taken aback by her attitude. In fact, he admired it. She was obviously under a mountain of stress, yet she gave the impression of being cool and collected. It was something Meg would do. "Mrs. Williams, I'm glad to meet you. I've heard some good things about you from Don." It was meant to be an icebreaker and it worked.

"Why don't we have a seat?" Jenny asked, looking at Ana as if for permission. The older woman was wearing a scowl, but nodded her head and began to move toward the kitchen table.

Never one to beat around the bush, as soon as the four of them sat down, Scott began the conversation. "Look, Mrs. Williams, I assume you know who I am and that I've been in contact with Don." A nod in response. "I won't waste your time by being anything other than completely straight with you. I want to find your husband."

"Why?"

"Because I think he needs my help—especially after what happened last night."

"Marshal, I don't mean to be rude, but don't you think that he would have asked for your help after last night if he wanted it? They—uh, he—might have something else in mind." Jenny knew she hadn't caught herself in time, but she figured they probably already knew that Don had help.

A fair question. *Did* Don think Scott had set him up? And if so, had he told his wife? Those weren't questions he wanted to ask right now. As much as he hated to, Scott would have to use fear to motivate her. "You may be right, Mrs. Williams, but I'm not sure you or Don realize how much trouble he's in."

"Oh? Well, I think we're beginning to get the idea. It looks like they've tried to kill him a couple of times now and that's just a little out of the ordinary, wouldn't you say?"

"Yes, I'd say so. What I'm trying to tell you, though, is that the man who's after Don—HOT Commander Bill Payne—has become *obsessed* with finding him…and I don't use that term lightly. Let me be a little more blunt. He *will* find him and he *will* see to it that Don is unable to cause him any trouble. Do I make myself clear?"

Jenny could only nod. As strong as she'd been up till now, she was out of her league here. Her eyes welled up with tears and she looked down at the table. After a deep breath, she bit her lip and looked up. "Now I'll be completely straight with *you*, Marshal. Why should any of us trust you? I'm not sure of the specifics, but I know that you were working with the ATF. Now, all of a sudden, you're not and we should just buy all of this without question?"

"No. I wouldn't if I were you."

"Thanks for admitting that. I mean, how do we know you're not *still* working with them? Maybe they sent you here to talk us into handing Don over to them."

Trust me! Scott took a deep breath. "Mrs. Williams, I love my wife more than anything in the world. If she were in serious trouble, I don't know that I'd trust *anyone* to help. We're expecting our first child and since the day we found out Meg was pregnant, I've understood that there is nothing more important than family. My first conversation with Don was a little…rushed, you might say. But the next time we spoke, we talked about your family and I realized that you and your kids are the reason he has to get through this mess in one piece."

Jenny was bawling now. Ana had fetched a well-used box of tissues and set it in front of her. She pulled them out three at a time as she listened to Scott, but he wasn't finished yet. "I said I wouldn't trust anyone to help me if the tables were turned. There's a difference, though. I'm trained to deal with situations like this. I've spent almost every day of my life since I was eighteen years old learning how to win a fight when the odds were against me. My guess is that Don hasn't."

He paused and then continued. "I know he has someone helping him and judging by the results of the two encounters they've had, I'd say the man knows what he's doing. Still, they can't know the people they're up against the way I do." Jenny was staring at him, listening carefully to every word. "I can help him if you let me."

Scott thought he was getting through, but he also knew that this might be his last chance to allay their fears. "I wouldn't blame any of you for not trusting me. I can't even begin to understand the pain that the federal government has caused your families. But it's important for you to know that we're not all bad.

"Some follow orders a little too blindly for my taste and a very few actually *do* have less than honorable intentions. Those are the ones we need to flush out and expose for what they are…criminals. We can do that in this case, but we're going to need each other's help. I want to do my part, Mrs. Williams. Will you let me help?"

After gathering her composure, Jenny asked the one question that Scott had hoped he wouldn't hear. "How do you plan on helping him, Marshal?"

Scott knew that he should have a detailed plan worked out by now. But he didn't and that would make him look like a fool to these people whose trust he was begging for. *Be honest. That's all you've got.* "I'm not sure yet. But I *am* sure that I can."

It was enough. Here in front of Jenny Williams was a young, hard-charging U.S. Marshal, who appeared to be as honest as anyone she'd ever listened to. He was telling her a story that seemed believable on its face and she knew that she had to make a decision quickly. *God, please tell me I'm doing the right thing.* "Okay, Marshal, I'll tell you where you can find him."

Scott put a finger to his lips, telling her not to speak the words, as he reached into his jacket pocket for a small notepad and pen—there was no such thing as being too careful. He put the pad down on the table in front of her and handed her the pen. Jenny began writing the detailed instructions necessary to find the Niculescus' cabin.

******

Scott had been very careful to make sure that he wasn't being followed before heading east out of town. Even so, he stopped a couple of times on the way up the mountain to verify that no one was behind him. Leading Payne and his men to Don would be inexcusable under any circumstances, but especially so after Jenny Williams had placed her trust in him. Though Murdoch had assured him a tracking device hadn't been planted on his car, there was no such thing as being too careful.

As Scott drew closer to the turnoff, he was surprised at how nervous he felt. Why? He was accustomed to closing in on bad guys. But that description didn't fit these two, did it? Technically, it did. They *were* fugitives—wanted by a federal law enforcement agency. And, though Scott knew that Williams' "record" was false, there was a good possibility that his partner's was not. But that wasn't the reason he was driving up the mountain today. No matter what else happened, he wouldn't end up hauling these guys in. He'd collaborate with them on the best course of action to take. If they came back with him, it would be because they'd all agreed there was no other choice. Was he crossing a line that he shouldn't be crossing? This might well be the strangest thing he'd ever done in his life.

Scott blinked his eyes hard to clear the unwelcome thoughts. There wasn't time right now. Now was the time to put his game face on. The two men he was coming to help might very well try their best to kill him. Now, *there* was a comforting thought.

Scott pulled the car off to the side of the soggy gravel road after he turned off the highway. He would walk in the rest of the way. Driving right up to the front door was likely to send these guys into full barricade mode and that wasn't the reaction he was after.

* * * * * *

Nick had been out for a walk, exploring the area around the cabin. The place looked different in the daylight. It *felt* different, too—less secluded and he didn't like it one bit. They'd stopped off at the market on the highway for some supplies on the way back from sending the text to Jenny. Had the young woman behind the counter studied their faces a little too closely, or was it just his imagination? He felt sure that the ATF wouldn't have plastered their pictures all over the place; the last thing Payne wanted was to have them caught by anyone other than him.

As he munched on a banana, Nick sat down in George's favorite chair, though he didn't know that fact. He had a small notebook and a pen in his hand. "Okay, we've put it off long enough. Time to figure out exactly how we're going to nail these bastards before they nail us."

Don sat on the couch across from him, in exactly the same spot he'd sat one week before, when he'd had to break the news to George and Ana. The coincidence was not lost on him. "It seems to me the first thing we have to do is convince Payne that we actually *do* have proof that he set me up. Without that, he's not going to be in a big hurry to do anything."

"Right," Nick answered. "That means we need something realistic to show…" His voice trailed off as Nick slowly pushed himself up out of the chair. He stood and held his left forefinger up to his lips. Don hadn't heard a thing, but he trusted Nick's senses enough to heed the order. Then they both heard the gravel rattling in the jars. *Something* was caught up in Nick's alarm system.

They'd discussed the strategy last night. Nick grabbed his rucksack and fished out his spare Glock 21 for Don. "Here. The chamber's loaded. Keep your finger off the trigger until you need to shoot and make sure of your target." They both slid out through the back door and toward the gulley bordering the property on the south end.

* * * * * *

Scott was furious with himself. He'd come ditty-bopping in here like he owned the place and gotten tangled up in some jury-rigged alarm system. *MARSOC, my ass!* He quickly freed himself from the fishing line, checking around to make sure he was clear of it. He hoped they hadn't heard the racket, but that was unlikely. The plan *had* been to approach the front door with his hands in the air, calling Don's name. Scott wasn't in uniform and he'd hoped that approach would be sufficiently nonthreatening to get him inside the cabin. From there, he felt pretty sure, he could win them over.

That was probably all out the window now, since he couldn't even see the cabin yet from where he was. Williams and his buddy were probably already out of there. Scott thought for a second about picking his way slowly around the edge of the timber to a point where he could observe the cabin. That would allow him to survey the situation before approaching, but he probably didn't have time for it. Instead, he moved into the trees just off the trail. At least that way he wouldn't be as likely to run into punji sticks, or whatever else these guys might have cooked up. Not worrying too much about being quiet, he pushed ahead, through the wet tangle of underbrush. It shouldn't be too much farther to the cabin.

* * * * * *

Nick and Don crouched down in the depression that served as a ditch to carry excess rainwater away from the cabin. It was running a few inches deep at the bottom now and they clung to the brushy bank. Nick had been listening intently for the couple of minutes or so that they'd been there. "Not much commotion at all. Can't be too many of 'em…sounds like they're coming straight up to the front door."

Nick looked over his shoulder at Don, who was shivering and too scared to say a word. "Okay, here's the deal. I want you to take off that way," he said, pointing west. "Stay in the ditch as long as you can. This thing empties out into a creek. Head north when you come to it. I didn't follow it all the way out earlier, but I'm pretty sure it'll lead you all the way up to the highway. There's a little turnout about a hundred yards west of the market. I'll meet you there."

"Where are *you* gonna go?"

Nick didn't feel like spending a lot of time explaining himself at the moment. "I'm going to take out a couple of these assholes, right here and right fucking now."

"No way," Don hissed. "Let's just get out of here."

"Don, I'm gonna take out as many as I can so we don't have to keep running from them. Don't you realize there's only one way back down this mountain? Do you really think we can outrun them all the way back to Portland?"

Don knew that Nick was right. "Okay, but be careful."

"Always. Now move it." As Don followed his orders, Nick crawled up out of the ditch. He low-crawled through the wet grass, Glock still in hand, toward a huge half-rotten stump about twenty feet from where the "driveway" opened up into the clearing around the cabin. The stump would provide great cover. Nick knew there was a good chance that this bunch was operating on its own and that there weren't many of them. If he could take a couple more of them out, the number of problems they faced would be greatly reduced. And if he could take one of them alive, so much the better. He would love to have one of them to interrogate. Nick had had enough of being on defense.

* * * * * *

Scott was at the edge of the tree line. He reached back to his right hip for his pistol, but thought better of it. If they saw him coming forward with a gun, they just might shoot first and ask questions later. He took a deep breath, stood straight up, and slowly walked into the clearing.

* * * * * *

Where's the black ninja jumpsuit and the M4...and where are his buddies? Nick wondered. This guy wore civvies and was walking in on them, apparently *unarmed*, like he didn't have a care in the world. Nick had to decide quickly whether to try to stop the intruder at gunpoint, or to incapacitate him first. The former option could be more dangerous than the latter, he realized. Though the man appeared to be unarmed, he couldn't be sure. If Nick yelled "Freeze!" the man could raise an unseen firearm and things might end very badly. He made a snap decision as the stranger crossed less than ten feet in front of him. There wasn't much time to think about it. If it was a mistake, he hoped it wouldn't be the last one he'd ever make.

Staying low, Nick sprung from his hiding place, covering the distance between them in three steps. By the time Scott turned to face him, Nick had his shoulder planted squarely in the younger man's chest. The blow took Scott off his feet and drove him down hard onto the ground.

Nick quickly scrambled to get on top of the intruder. Straddling the man, he reached back for the Glock, which he'd shoved into his waistband in the small of his back. The only problem with doing so was that he momentarily left himself defenseless. Just as he felt the familiar plastic grip of his Glock, the man beneath him bucked his hips and almost simultaneously shot his left fist up into the bridge of Nick's nose as he fell forward. The timing between the hip thrust and punch was nearly perfect.

Scott then reversed positions and sat atop a very dazed Nick Larsen. Now Scott was reaching for his own pistol, in a distinctly worse mood than he'd been in less than thirty seconds before. He didn't make it all the way there, though.

"Hold it. Put your hands up…*NOW!*"

Don had decided to work his way back toward the cabin before getting too far. It might have pissed Nick off, but he had a bad feeling about leaving his partner to face whatever he was up against alone. As it turned out, his fears were well-founded.

Scott did as he was told, then got off of Nick, stood up, and turned around slowly. The man holding the gun on him was obviously new at this sort of thing. "Hello, Don. I'm Scott Keller."

Nick rose unsteadily to his feet and drew his Glock with one hand while he wiped blood out of his eyes with the other. When he walked around to face the man who'd bested him, he felt a little better. The guy was a horse and quite a bit younger. Nick was pretty good at hand to hand combat—or at least he used to be—but Keller was obviously better, as much as it bothered him to admit.

Scott noticed that Don still had the gun on him and that his finger was inside the trigger guard. Glocks were great handguns, but threat management in the hands of the uninitiated wasn't their strong suit. More than one cop had "let one fly" while holding a suspect at bay. Tension did strange things to the body. "Uh, Don. I'd feel a whole lot better if you took your finger off that Glock's trigger. I'm not going anywhere…I promise."

Nick reached around to Scott's side and pulled his pistol from its holster. "It's okay, Don. You can put it down. I've got him."

Don lowered the gun without taking his eyes off the Marshal. "Yeah, nice to finally meet you. You didn't bring any of your friends along, did you?" He was surprised by how sarcastic he sounded.

"No, I didn't. I think you both know that if anyone besides me was here, you'd have met 'em by now."

He was right, of course. "Come on," Nick said as he motioned toward the cabin with the muzzle of his pistol.

Once inside, Nick kept an eye on their guest while soaking a dish-cloth with cold water from the faucet. His head was starting to throb, but a look in the mirror gave him hope that at least his nose wasn't broken. He dabbed at the blood gingerly, finally just holding the rag in place and letting the cold ease the pain.

"Sorry about the nose, uh…?"

"My identity's not important at this point." Nick was pretty much convinced by now that Keller was on the level, but he was also a little pissed. "Why don't you just tell us what the hell you're doing here?"

Scott was starting to get a little irate himself. It had been a while since he'd been knocked around *and* held at gunpoint in the same afternoon. "I'm here to try to help you two, damnit!" He was looking directly at Don as he spoke the words and they seemed to get Don's attention.

"I believe you. How did you find us?" Don asked.

"Your wife told me where you were. I don't lie well, Don. So, instead of trying to, I've got this funny habit of talking straight to people and letting the chips fall where they may. I think she sensed that and I hope you do, too…both of you," he added, looking over at

Nick. "I really *am* sorry about the nose. Had it happen to me a bunch of times. It sucks."

Nick nodded and even half smiled. He couldn't help but like this guy and that was something he never thought he'd say again about a federal cop. Finally, Scott started talking and the other two mostly listened, interrupting only occasionally to ask questions. They found out a lot about the raid that took Mike and Sarah's lives and about Payne, Burke, and Bobby. They heard about Scott's MARSOC background (which made Nick feel better about losing the fight), listened to his ideas on Collection, and learned that these bastards from HOT had even wiretapped the Marshal's home telephone. The last piece of information struck Nick as potentially useful and he filed it away for future reference.

After thirty minutes, the Marshal was no longer an adversary, but a partner. The skeptical Nick Larsen felt as though he shared a bond with the fellow Marine sitting across the table from him. Besides, he'd learned firsthand just how useful Keller was in a fight.

Scott asked a few questions of his own. He now understood how close the two men had come to being killed the day before. The most important thing he learned from talking to them, however, was the quality of the man who'd been killed by governmental decree just over a week ago. Their friend was not only worth avenging, but Scott now understood why it *had* to be done. Mike's death represented everything that was wrong with Collection and it was clear that the world had to be made right again. They couldn't do this by simply bringing Payne down. They would need to go much higher. Scott had already decided that he wouldn't ask Don and Nick to come back with him and be placed into custody. That would be ridiculous. Sure, the Marshals Service could protect them, but they had to be able to *prove* what Payne had done in order to achieve their ultimate objective.

"So, how do we go about turning all of our grand ideas into reality?" Don asked. "I know we want to force Payne to admit what he did and the best way to do that is to piss him off. I'm pretty good at that part." Nick and Scott smiled.

"Yeah, and when he does blow his top, we need it on tape. Keller, can you get us the equipment we need to wire our friend here?"

"No problem," Scott assured Nick.

"Okay, okay," Don broke in, "I can see there's no way around me having to come face-to-face with Payne, but I'm worried about what we're going to do for proof. If he doesn't buy into the fact that we've got something on him, he'll just shoot me and it'll all be over. Please tell me I'm missing something here."

Nick had been thinking. "No, you're not missing anything."

"Great, I feel a lot better now, Nick."

Nick continued. "Let's keep in mind that Payne's listening in on Keller's phone calls. It seems to me that since we don't actually have any proof, we've got a little bit of a credibility problem with the Commander. He knows—or at least suspects—that he stopped Myers short of getting what he needed." Nick was thinking out loud and began to pace the floor. "That being the case, anything we *tell* him is not likely to be real convincing."

The light went on for Scott just before Nick finished the thought. "But if he overhears us talking about it, there'd be no reason for him *not* to believe it, right?"

Nick studied the Marshal with a straight face. "Now, Keller, tell the truth. It had to be the *Marine* in you that figured that one out—not the cop, right?"

Scott laughed. "Bet your ass. Semper Fi."

******

After spending some time working on the details of their plan, Scott headed back into town—and straight for Bobby Myers' house. He needed to talk to Bobby and it had to be in person (he wondered whether he'd ever trust telephones again). The ATF agent had to be in on the plan, even if he wouldn't play a big part in it. Scott was conscious of the fact that this was Bobby's organization being indicted and although he'd want to help do it, Scott knew it had to be tough on him.

Driving slowly by his friend's house, Scott saw his car in the driveway. He wondered whether HOT had Bobby's house under surveillance, too. Probably so, but he really didn't care. Still, as he walked up to the front door, he decided that it would be a good idea for the two of them to take a walk to discuss the morning's revelations.

"Hey, man, what's up?" Bobby asked when he opened the door and saw Scott staring back at him. "How did you get so dirty?"

Scott hadn't noticed the dried mud on his knees and face. "I've already been in a fight today, how 'bout you?"

"Only with my old lady. And I *still* don't look as bad as you do."

Scott laughed. "Hey, grab a coat and let's take a little walk around the block." Bobby did so without asking questions; Scott wouldn't have made the request without a good reason.

As they walked, Scott filled his buddy in on the day's events so far. Bobby could hardly believe his ears. "Man! You *have* been a busy boy today."

"Yeah. So, what do you think of our little plan?"

"I think it's about the only kind of thing that might work. Only problem I see with it is my role—or lack thereof."

"You've done enough, Bobby. We hung you out to dry looking for the proof until Payne caught on. You don't need to be any closer to this when it hits the fan than you already are."

"To hell with Payne! I'm tired of him thinking he can ruin anyone's life he wants to, just to save his own ass. Besides, *you* didn't hang me out to dry. I wanted to do it…just not bad enough, I guess. This whole thing would be over by now if I'd have come through."

"Oh, don't give me that, Myers. There wasn't a thing you could've done differently. Besides, this whole thing *will* be over by Tuesday morning—at least for Payne."

"I'll believe that when I see it."

19

Portland, Oregon
Monday, April 28

Soon after Scott left the day before, Nick and Don made the decision to vacate the cabin. They drove down the mountain until they found an inconspicuous little motel and paid cash for one night's lodging. It wasn't that Nick didn't trust the Marshal—in fact, to his amazement, he actually *did.* The reason for his paranoia was the healthy respect he had for the tenacity of their pursuers. He was sure that if Keller could find them, HOT wouldn't be far behind...and out in the woods, no one would hear them scream.

They got an early start and were now officially working on "phase one" of their plan. After all the hours spent worrying and wondering how they would get out of this mess, it felt good to finally *have* a firm plan—and even better to be taking action. Offense was always preferable to defense.

The first order of business was meeting a man outside the city limits to exchange vehicles. Nick greeted him in a businesslike manner, chatted with him for less than a minute, flipped him the keys to the Durango, and slid in behind the wheel of the maroon Jeep Grand Cherokee.

Being an inveterate rule-follower, Don wondered about such things as a bill of sale, title transfer, and proper registration. Then again, this was Nick Larsen and Don had learned in the last few days that there was more to him than met the eye. Nick noticed his passenger's confusion. "It was time to ditch the Durango." No further explanation was offered and Don didn't ask any questions. He really *was* getting better at this.

Nick parked along the street and he and Don walked a couple of blocks up to Pioneer Square, in the middle of downtown Portland. They'd thought long and hard yesterday about the location for their encounter with Payne and it was Don who finally came up with the idea. The place had to be public, easy to get in and out of, and "observable." Pioneer Square was perfect. He and Jenny had taken the kids to a concert there about a month before. It was essentially an old-fashioned public square in the middle of a large, modern city. There would be a lot of people around, yet there would still be room to maneuver ("you mean 'run'," Don had corrected them). There were also elevated points on the outskirts from which Scott and Nick could keep an eye on things. Perfect.

As they walked around, Don remembered the concert and how much fun his kids had had there. He missed them more right now than he had since this whole mess started, but he knew he couldn't let himself think that way—not yet. It wouldn't be long now, though. By this time tomorrow, they should have what they needed to put Payne out of business.

While Don's mind wandered, Nick was as focused as he'd been in a long time. This situation that he'd been pulled into a few days ago had provided him with both a diversion and a purpose, but it was time to end it. While he disparaged them on a regular basis, he actually had tremendous respect for ATF's abilities—especially those of the Hazardous Operations Team. He knew that he and Don couldn't outrun them forever and he didn't want to push his luck.

Nick studied the layout of the Square carefully. It had the feel of a sunken amphitheater, constructed of red brick with huge white stone pillars lining the north and south sides. It was an impressive structure.

The four city streets forming the square were designated one-way. Three of them had a lane dedicated to a light-rail tram system, though none of the three trams stopped at Pioneer Square. Nick noticed that the trams ran regularly and almost simultaneously. They were programmed so that one would narrowly miss the other where the tracks intersected.

The primary question on Nick's mind was precisely where Don should be when he and Payne came face-to-face. It was the most important decision they had to make. If given half a chance, Payne might very well put a bullet into Don and solve his problem. After making a few rounds of the likely spots, he kept coming back to the area in front of the Visitors Center. It was almost directly in the middle of the huge square and could therefore be easily watched by Keller and him. Don would also be able to see anyone coming after him and (hopefully) have time to react. There should be enough people around to make Payne think twice about doing anything crazy and there were a handful of possible escape routes for Don to use. It felt exactly right.

There was a large round brass placard laid into the brickwork about thirty feet directly in front of the doors of the Visitors Center. That would be the meeting spot.

* * * * * *

George had slept on it for the last two nights. He didn't want to jeopardize anything that Don, Nick, and the Marshal were trying to do and he had doubts about whether it would do any good anyway. Still, it seemed like the kind of thing that his son might have done. It was a decision based on faith in a political system that, even after all that had happened recently, still represented the finest system of government ever created.

Though he'd never before contacted his congressman or senator, now was the time, George was sure. If Don and Nick were unsuccessful, or if—God forbid—they'd been wrong about Marshal Keller, at least *someone* with power would know about what had gone on out in the Pacific Northwest. Besides, he knew that Congressman Skiles was sympathetic to their cause.

A phone call to his office in Washington, D.C., revealed that the Congressman was in town, but currently unavailable. George left a message with a member of his staff, but then felt foolish. He realized that he probably sounded like a crazy old man, upset over the death of his son. That was probably true, he thought, but there was much more to it than that. George wanted what was happening to Don exposed for what it was: a gross abuse of governmental power. Now, after he'd spoken with the congressional staffer, his natural self-doubt took hold and told him that one man's voice couldn't possibly make a difference.

Though George would always have doubts about his ability to communicate verbally, he had no such doubts when it came to the written word. That confidence helped him decide to follow up the phone call with an e-mail. It might do no more good and the Congressman himself might never see it, but at least the Romanian-American would have done what he considered to be his civic duty. He would also be exercising one of the constitutional rights that he so cherished. George spent over an hour on the content of the e-mail before taking the irreversible step of clicking the "send" button. Once he'd done so, a strange calmness came over him. He'd gotten it off his chest now and in a way that he thought would make sense. There was nothing more he could do at this point. The rest was up to God and a few good men.

******

They'd decided that Don should place the call at an odd time. A call coming in at exactly 10:00 was more likely to be staged than one coming in a few minutes before or after. It was always the little things that tripped you up, Scott and Nick both knew. This call was critical to the success of their plan. Payne would have to be convinced that they had proof of what he'd done for it to work. He also needed to believe that Don wanted nothing more than to have his name cleared. That way, the HOT Commander was less likely to come out swinging or shooting. Finally, if Payne felt he'd won with a simple transfer of information, Scott was convinced that Don could get him to admit (and maybe even justify) what he'd done—their definition of complete victory. It was now 10:12 a.m. and he sat staring at his phone… knowing it would ring any second.

After leaving Bobby's house the night before, Scott had gone to the USMS office. He needed to pick up the equipment to wire Don with, as well as communication devices for all of them. They'd need to be able to communicate with each other during the entire operation. He also wanted to pick up one more little gadget as well. Ever since hearing that his phone line was tapped, he'd become paranoid. What if they'd planted other listening devices that Murdoch wasn't even aware of? Hatcher and his boys could have slipped into the house when it was unoccupied and left all kinds of little goodies behind. It wasn't likely, but it was certainly possible. He'd "sweep" the house just to make sure.

The last chore on his list was to dummy something up that would pass for the proof Payne was looking for. It had to be only good enough to buy a little time and Scott was pretty sure that Payne wouldn't know shit from Shinola without Burke's help. He'd thought about how he would do it all the way down the mountain yesterday and felt pretty good about the end result.

As soon as Scott got home last night, he'd swept the house for bugs. As it turned out, he *had* been imagining things. That made both he and his wife feel much better. Meg, in particular, was relieved to find out that every word they'd uttered in the last few days hadn't been recorded for some dark purpose—or for *any* purpose. A person's privacy was sacred and the federal government ought to be very careful about invading it.

Still, their phone calls *were* now a matter of record and that gave Scott a chill as the phone beside him started ringing. He had to keep reminding himself that he was the hunter again—no longer the hunted. *Act natural!*

"Hello?"

"Hi, Marshal. It's Don Williams." If Scott was nervous, Don was almost physically ill. Nick was staring at him as he talked and that didn't help. Don knew that the next twenty-four hours were going to be absolutely miserable—at best. This was just the beginning. "Did you have any luck?"

"Yeah. We did, actually. We've got proof that Payne falsified your record."

"Are you sure it's solid?"

"Don, listen to me. It's the real deal, I promise. Everything the bastard did to you is right there in black and white. I still think we should nail him to the wall, though. We've got everything we need to do it with now."

"No! We've already talked about that. I just want my life back. I don't want to be testifying in some courtroom against a guy like Payne, who'd probably win in the end anyway."

"Don, he wouldn't—"

"Look, Marshal, this is *my* life, okay? I appreciate your help, but I just want this to be over."

"Okay. Fine, we'll do it your way. I dropped the envelope off and your buddy said he'd be there the rest of the day."

"Good. I'll go over and pick it up right now."

"When are you going to call Payne?"

"As soon as I have the proof in my hands. I hope he's around this afternoon—maybe he's out of town or something."

"No, I don't think so. Just tell whoever you talk to that it's real important. They'll hunt him down for you. Where are you going to meet him?"

"Don't know yet. I'm still working on that. You know, I really do hate this, Marshal."

"Yeah, well, it'll all be over soon and you'll have your nice boring life back."

"Good. I can't wait."

* * * * * *

Washington, D.C.

Congressman Tom Skiles was furious after reading the email he'd just been shown. An enterprising young staffer had printed it out and personally tracked her boss down. This one couldn't wait, she'd decided. Skiles had been railing against Collection from the beginning and had become almost apoplectic since the death of Mike Niculescu. He *knew* that something like this would happen! The ironic thing was that it had happened in his district. What were the odds that one of the most vocal critics of the Collection process would have his warnings borne out in his own backyard? It certainly gave him no satisfaction, but it *was* quite a coincidence.

Though his gut told him to believe every word of the e-mail, he asked the helpful staffer to verify its authenticity. He wanted to make sure that George Niculescu was the father of the deceased and that this Don Williams actually existed. The last thing he needed right now was to go ballistic and be made to look foolish.

On the other hand, his marginalization would serve certain people well. It was amazing how many in his own party had made it known that they'd rather lose his seat to a Republican in November than see him re-elected. For that reason, Skiles wanted to make sure that this wasn't a setup (a possibility he would have scoffed at before coming to Washington).

An hour's worth of digging had verified the authenticity of the e-mail. That was entirely different from proving the allegations, Skiles had to remind himself. Besides, he wasn't sure what he was going to do with the information anyway. The Speaker of the House wasn't taking his calls anymore and he'd been assured that the votes were not there to repeal the Family Protection Act. The only bit of heartening news lately was that polls had begun to show a shift in the public mood regarding Collection. Skiles was afraid, however, that it was going to take a lot more Mike Niculescus before that shift would translate into congressional action.

Actually, there *was* one thing he could do, if for no other reason than to make himself feel better. The Congressman leaned forward and punched a button on his phone. "Lucy, will you please try to get me ATF Director Mullin on the phone?"

"Uh, yes sir, but…do you really think he'll take the call?"

Skiles laughed. "Your guess is as good as mine, but we'll never know till we try, will we? Tell him that I've got some very important information for him."

"Yes, sir."

This issue had been more than divisive on Capitol Hill. It got in the way of almost everything else that Skiles felt was important. His unpopular stand on Collection had made him a pariah among members of his own party. If it wasn't for the fact that it would give those people exactly what they wanted, there was no way he'd run for re-election this year. He could go back to Portland and make more money practicing law, and his family didn't like D.C. anyway. The fighter in him wouldn't let him do it, though. Skiles could handle running and losing, but his pride wouldn't let him bow out because the other kids were being mean to him. He planned on calling it quits in two years anyway, but he wanted one more term—just to show the bastards!

"Congressman, I have Director Mullin on the line for you."

Skiles could hardly believe it. He'd expected to hear that Mullin was unavailable—either because he really was, or because he didn't want to talk to a man whom he probably considered a traitor to his party. Skiles had heard that term used more than once in reference to him.

"Director, thank you for taking my call."

"Not a problem, Congressman. What can I do for you?"

What, no chitchat? "Well, I'm calling about contact that my office has had with a constituent in Oregon. It's related to the first Collection death." The Congressman could almost *feel* Mullin's eyes rolling. "We haven't had a lot of time to check the story out yet, but our preliminary findings indicate that there's some truth to it."

"The way you use the term 'preliminary findings' would seem to imply that you're conducting an official investigation. Is there something I don't know about?"

"No, there's no official investigation…yet." Skiles had had about all the nonsense he was willing to put up with.

"Congressman, will you please get to the point? I have a lot of important things to do."

You arrogant sonofabitch. "It appears that we have a case of overzealous enforcement of the Collection laws in the Portland area—again. Do you think it's a coincidence that we've had trouble there twice in the last ten days?"

"Congressman, with all due respect, I don't have time for this. Now, if you've got a point to make, please make it."

Skiles then did exactly that—telling the Director all about the allegations in George Niculescu's e-mail. Mullin was silent for several seconds afterward. "Congressman Skiles, in my opinion the whole story sounds like an angry old man looking for vengeance. Nevertheless, I'll look into it."

"Director Mullin, I have to say that your attitude doesn't give me a great deal of confidence that you'll look very hard."

"As I said, I'll look into it. Have a nice day."

Skiles had come to Washington a little more than five years before as an idealistic young man. He was afraid that he would leave—perhaps very soon—jaded and cynical, his energy and idealism eaten up by a town known for doing that to people. For now, he would give Mullin a couple of days to look into this, knowing full well that nothing would come of it. The only chance that Skiles had was that he might have just disturbed the ATF Director enough to have him call off the dogs. It wouldn't be enough to satisfy Skiles long term, but it might provide some temporary relief to his constituents. He wasn't sure that there was much else he could do at the moment.

* * * * * *

Portland, Oregon

Burke had just listened to the recording for the third time. His boss wanted to make sure that he hadn't missed anything. The eighty-six-second phone call made it pretty clear to both the Commander and his deputy that they had real trouble on their hands. The two of them were in Payne's office, which had become something of a war room. Time was of the essence now. The fewer people who knew about the proof—whatever form it was in—the better.

"What could they *have*, Ray? You told me there was no way Myers could get back into the system."

"I didn't think there was, sir. Maybe he had someone helping him who knows more about the system than I do, or maybe they came at it from a different angle."

"Like what?"

"I don't know. Maybe they were able to do something with the firearms themselves. I don't think they're scheduled to be destroyed until tomorrow. I suppose they could have cross-referenced serial numbers or something and found out that the same guns were listed under two different names."

"Is that possible?"

"Sir, I don't think so, but I can't say for sure."

"Well, I guess it doesn't matter now. We've got to assume that they have what they say they do." Payne's intercom buzzed. "Yes?"

"Sir, there's a call for you from Don Williams." Victoria's voice didn't betray the fact that she remembered the man very well from his visit the week before.

"Go ahead and put him through." Grabbing a legal pad and a pen, the Commander put the receiver to his ear and pushed the flashing button on his phone. "I assume this is the same Don Williams who's responsible for the death of a federal agent?"

With Nick's help, Don had psyched himself up as much as possible before making the call. This conversation would begin the biggest—and in reality, the first—showdown of his life. He wanted to start riling Payne right away. "Oh, don't give me that bullshit, Payne. I'm getting a little tired of your boys taking potshots at me."

"I'm afraid that a couple of the things we don't put up with are the violation of federal laws and the killing of our brother officers. You've done both, Mr. Williams, and you *will* pay for it."

"You and I both know the truth, Payne. Here's the deal: I've got proof that you set me up and all I want in exchange for it is for you to undo what you've done. I've got no desire to pursue this any further. I just want to go back to my family."

"Mr. Williams, I don't know what you're talking about."

"Don't play stupid with me. I don't expect you to admit it over the phone. I just want it erased."

"Like I said, I don't know what—"

"Yeah, whatever. Bring proof that you've cleared my record to Pioneer Square tomorrow morning at nine a.m. There's a round brass placard near the middle of the square, right in front of the Visitors Center. I'll be in the vicinity. Come alone, bring the proof, and we'll exchange evidence. Like I said, I'm not looking to push this. I just want my life back—the life that you took away from me."

"For the third time, I don't know what you're talking about, but I *will* be there tomorrow morning…to place you under arrest." At that, Payne slammed the receiver down in its cradle and turned to face Burke.

"Let's get set up for tomorrow, Ray. Have Sykes and Lynch up here in an hour. Call Myers and tell him to meet us at the staging area tomorrow at 0630. We'll 'explain' the situation to him then."

"Myers too?" Burke asked, with a pleading look in his eyes.

"Absolutely. Ray, don't you understand? There are three people alive besides us who know about Williams' record. Each of them has both the ability and the credibility to ruin us. I want all of them at Pioneer Square tomorrow morning. We'll bring Myers with us, Williams is a given, and you know Keller won't be able to keep his nose out of it. That'll take care of every real threat we face. Larsen will be a bonus."

"But where will it stop?" Burke wondered out loud. "What about their wives? They must know the whole story too."

Payne was in preservation mode now. "I've thought about that," he assured Burke as he paced the floor. "Anything they say could be dismissed as second or third-hand. It would be easy to spin as an attempt by grieving widows to lash out at anyone they can for their husbands' deaths. We can set things up so we can win that one."

Burke closed his eyes. There really was no good way out of this.

"Now let's get moving, Ray. We've got to come up with something to give Williams tomorrow, just in case I need to buy some time."

Burke left and Payne sat down in his huge leather chair and leaned back, staring up at the ceiling for a moment. As he closed his eyes to think, his cell phone rang.

Payne answered brusquely and then heard Director Mullin's voice on the other end of the line. He sat up quickly and felt his throat go dry—the timing was terrible. "Hello, sir. How are you?"

"Bill, let's cut to the chase. I just spoke to Tom Skiles and he has a lot of sordid details about the first Collection deaths, as well as certain 'abuses' by you regarding some guy named Don Williams. Bill, I want you to level with me completely. We need to figure a way out of this mess. Now what's going on?"

Unexpectedly, Payne felt himself relax. Mullin's attitude was actually refreshing, after having to deal with Burke's hand wringing. The Director had always been a man of action and Bill Payne liked to think the same about himself. He also knew from experience that Mullin would be on his side and would want to put the matter to rest, once and for all.

The Commander filled his boss in on all the pertinent details, including the phone call he'd just received from Williams and the plan for tomorrow. Mullin listened intently, interrupting only a few times for clarification. He was particularly interested in the others who were helping Williams.

"Bill, I think you're on the right track. I do think we need to end this thing tomorrow, but I wonder if we shouldn't ratchet up the pressure on Williams a little."

"I'm afraid I don't follow, sir."

"He's an amateur, which means he'll respond to fear. I want to leave no doubt in his mind that he's to give us every shred of proof that he has. I also want him to be fully aware of the consequences of *not* doing so."

"I think that makes perfect sense, sir, but I don't—"

"Bill, I'm going to send four men to see you. They're in the Spokane area right now, so it won't take them long to get there. "

"Uh, who are they, sir?"

"They're problem-solvers, Bill—good ones and completely trustworthy."

"Sir, I really think that my men—"

Again, Mullin cut him off. "Bill, I'm not going to negotiate with you. With men like the Marshal and Larsen helping him, you're up against something entirely different than you're equipped to handle. These men are experienced and reliable. They'll be in Portland in a few hours to meet with you and firm up the plan for tomorrow. I'll brief them on the details prior to their arrival, but understand that these four gentlemen will be running the show from here on out."

"Yes sir," Payne answered, not at all comfortable with the implications.

"Bill, I told you before that Collection *has* to succeed. I won't allow something like this to jeopardize it."

* * * * * *

Scott was winded. He'd been running at nearly full speed for almost a mile now—mostly along jogging paths, but he'd also taken a few strategic detours through the bushes to throw off anyone who might be following him. The Marshal's destination was a secluded picnic area near a large parking lot. He could have parked in that lot and walked in, but he would have been less comfortable with that option.

Scott, Nick, and Don had debated whether to meet face-to-face again to finalize their plan. Though Scott was admittedly a bit paranoid, he also was pretty sure he was being followed and that presented a certain level of risk. Still, it made sense to meet, they'd decided. The use of the Marshal's home phone was obviously out and they were nervous about having cell phone signals flying around.

Nick and Don found the spot with no trouble, using a map that Scott had drawn for them. Nick was as meticulous as ever in his preparation for the next day's encounter. He had a detailed map of downtown Portland with various notes and highlighting on it, as well as a number of individual sketches he'd made. His and Keller's placement could very well determine whether or not Don would live through this thing tomorrow.

"I hope you're not running *from* anybody," Nick said as Scott slowed to a walk.

"Not as far as I know. Doesn't matter anyway...they never could've kept up," the Marshal said, smiling. "What did you think of Pioneer Square?"

"It looks like things are going to work out okay."

"Good." Scott unzipped the fanny pack he was wearing. He hated the things and didn't wear one unless there was no other alternative. In this case, the need to carry his handgun and the other gear he'd brought made it necessary—gym shorts tended not to have cargo pockets. "Here you go, Nick. You know how to set one of these rigs up, don't you?" Scott handed him the gear that Don would be wearing.

Nick looked at the wiring equipment for several seconds. "Yep. Looks like pretty standard stuff."

"It is. You can just wear the recorder on your belt." Scott was referring to the wireless device that would, hopefully, record everything Don's microphone picked up when he confronted Payne.

"Actually, I was thinking about stashing the recorder somewhere near the Square, as long as it's within range. That way, if anything happens to me, Don will be able to come back for it."

Scott nodded. "Good idea. The range on that thing is at least a mile; so a few blocks away should be no problem. If that happens, Don…if Nick and I get separated from you…for any reason, you get to the U.S. Marshals office and turn yourself in with whatever proof you can gather. Understand?"

Don looked stunned as the weight of Scott's words fell on him.

"Okay, but I want to make it clear that we are *all* walking away from that place tomorrow morning."

The other two men laughed nervously. "No question about it," Nick promised.

Scott thought now was as good a time as any to bring up something he'd been thinking about since the first time he spoke to Don a few days before. "Guys, you need to know that there's another option." The other two men looked at him strangely, not understanding. "What I'm saying is we can avoid this showdown tomorrow by going straight to Marshal Filson, laying our cards on the table, and asking him to help us build a case against Payne."

Nick glanced over at Don and then down at the maps they'd spread out on the weathered picnic table. But no one spoke for several seconds. It was obvious to Scott that the other men—or at least Don—had also considered some version of the plan he'd just offered.

Don looked at Nick first and then at the Marshal. "I've thought about doing something like that too…I mean, you know, ever since those guys started shooting at us," he added with an awkward smile. "But it just doesn't seem right, does it? Besides," he added before either could respond, "Do you really think it would work?"

"No," Nick answered quickly. "Hell no. We don't have any evidence that would come *close* to convicting a guy like Payne. Isn't that true, Scott?"

"Yes it is," Scott answered. "Our only hope would be to get Burke to testify against Payne, but that isn't likely. What *is* likely is that the case would never even make it to trial. Exposing Payne like that might make him back off, though," he said, looking at Don. He wanted to offer a way out and, if Don accepted it, then there was a good chance he never would have followed through with their plan for tomorrow anyway.

Nick bit his lip, but remained silent. He felt certain Scott didn't favor this alternative, but he understood why he'd brought it up. He just hoped Don wouldn't take what the Marshal was offering him. This was about something bigger, Nick believed.

Don shook his head slowly. "That's not enough," he responded after a few seconds. "Mike and Sarah's deaths would have been for nothing if we did that. Mike would want some good to come out of what happened. That's the kind of guy he was."

Nick nodded but said nothing.

Scott was relieved. "I think that's the right call, Don. I just wanted to give you the option."

Some stands *had* to be worth taking—and all three men had just decided this one was.

Getting back to the task at hand, Scott produced a small manila envelope. "Okay then, here's what I came up with to give Payne. It's the best I could do on our computer system. I think it'll look close enough to fool him—at least for a little while." He saw the sick look on Don's face.

"It'll do the job, Don. It's not like he'll have a team of attorneys there to authenticate it." Don nodded his head, but didn't say a word. "Now, what do the X's and O's look like for tomorrow?"

Nick sighed heavily. "Well, first of all, we need to be up front about the fact that there's no way this guy is going to show up alone, right?" Both of the other men nodded, but Don was forcing himself to hold out hope that he was wrong. "That means our location is critical," he pointed out, looking at Scott, who nodded in agreement.

Scott dug into the fanny pack again and withdrew three small plastic boxes. "Each of us needs one of these. They'll allow us to hear and talk to each other. Be careful handling them—they're very sensitive. I've already made sure all three of them work, but we'll test them again tomorrow as soon as I see you guys enter the Square."

They went through the plan in detail. Scott had a few suggestions and some changes were made. They discussed the most likely avenues of approach by Payne's men and the best ways to deal with them, as well as the firearms and other equipment that each would likely be carrying. They would each acquire two prepaid cell phones and exchange the numbers in advance. If things went awry, the ability to communicate would be critical.

Finally, all three felt about as comfortable with the plan as was possible and decided to stop beating a dead horse. They shook hands and prepared to go their separate ways.

Scott looked each of them in the eye and then put his hand on Don's shoulder. "It won't be long now. We're going to fix this tomorrow—I guarantee you. Oh, I almost forgot. Here's the keyless remote for the getaway car. A buddy of mine rented it today. It's a white Dodge Intrepid and it'll be backed into a parking spot two blocks away…right here." He marked the spot on Nick's map and circled it. The keys will be in the ignition and the doors will be locked. If we're not *right behind you*, jump in and head straight for the Marshals office. Got it?"

"Yeah, I think so. Thanks, Scott. Thanks for all you've done. I know everything's going to work out."

As the Marshal turned to run back the way he'd come, he couldn't help but think that Don didn't believe a word of what he'd just said.

* * * * * *

The four men had the rough, unmistakable look of operators who'd "been there and done that," Bill Payne thought. They'd called the Commander a couple of hours ago and told him (there was no asking and no pretense of respect, he'd noticed) to meet them in his office at 4:00 p.m. As he'd been instructed to do, Payne made sure that the guard at the HOT building entrance had strict orders to call him upon their arrival and to allow them up without having to show any identification.

As they walked into Payne's office, he noticed that all were of roughly average height and very fit. Two were considerably stockier than the others. One of the two "weightlifters" had short, almost jet-black hair and the other was square-jawed and blond. The third man was a redhead, while the fourth had brown hair and was fairly nondescript. Payne walked around his desk and extended his hand. The men shook it without enthusiasm. "Gentlemen, I'm Commander Bill Payne. I—"

The smallest of the four men cut him off. "Commander, we're here to get a job done, not exchange pleasantries."

"I would hardly call that an exchange of pleasantries," Payne asserted. He wasn't used to being treated like this and didn't plan on putting up with it. He continued, "It would help if I at least knew what to call you."

"You can call me Mr. Brown. That would make the rest of these gentlemen Misters White, Black, and Red," Brown said, gesturing at each member of his team as he described their hair color.

"The Crayon Gang—perfect," answered Payne sarcastically.

"Let's be clear about something, Payne: I don't care what you think of us. We're not here to be your buddies; we're here to finish what you couldn't."

Payne clenched his teeth and stared at the man, but didn't say a word. He'd been under tremendous stress since long before the first Collection and especially for the last couple of weeks. He didn't need this at all, but there was nothing he could do about it.

Brown—who definitely appeared to be the leader of the four-man team—went on. "We've been briefed, but we have a few questions for you." Payne filled in the blanks for them about the involvement of Keller and Myers. The men paid particular attention when Larsen's name came up. What they learned of the man's background—both from Director Mullin and now Payne—didn't give them comfort.

"So, we have to assume that both Larsen and Keller will be helping Williams tomorrow," Brown said. "And you think Myers will come along with us willingly?"

Payne squirmed in his chair. He hated the thought of killing Bobby. He was a good man and he was ATF. Still, Payne was very much a realist. He knew that Bobby had to be taken out and had planned on doing so even before these men became involved. "Yes, I do. He won't be happy about being put in that position, but he'll want to be along for the ride to try to do what he can to help the others."

"Yeah, well, we won't give him the chance to be much help," Brown assured him. How many others, besides you, are aware of the situation?"

"Well, there's only my deputy, Ray Burke. He's, uh…fully aware of everything."

"That's it? Are you sure? What about the others involved in your two prior failed attempts to apprehend Williams?"

The question stung and Payne began to despise the men who'd been sent to "help" him. "There are two men—Sykes and Lynch—who have been involved. But they don't know any…specifics."

"You're sure?" It was Black (the dark-haired weightlifter) this time, just when Payne was beginning to wonder whether any of the other three were capable of speech.

"Yes, I'm sure. They might suspect something, but they haven't been privy to the truth, if that's what you mean."

"Uh huh," Brown answered skeptically. "I don't want them involved any further. We'll let you know tonight what role you and Burke will play tomorrow."

"Okay, but you understand that I'm supposed to meet Williams at—"

"I understand completely. That will still happen. *We* will worry about what happens from that point on. By the way, have you done any surveillance on Williams' family?"

"Yes. Just to be sure he didn't make contact with them. They're staying with the parents of Niculescu, who was the Collection subject—"

"We know," Brown interrupted. "We'd like to see the observation logs from the surveillance. You do have them, don't you?"

"Uh, yes, I'm sure we do," Payne answered without certainty. "But, uh, why do you—"

"Good. We'll wait while you have them brought up. I also want the entire file on the Niculescu operation," Brown added, thinking there might be something useful in it.

The Commander called Burke and asked him to retrieve the requested information and bring it to his office. His deputy wanted to know why. "Just bring it, Ray," Payne said in a defeated tone and hung up the phone.

"We'll wait outside for it," Brown said as he and his men walked toward the door.

Payne wanted to know more. He felt he *deserved* to know more. "The Director mentioned this morning that he wanted to increase the pressure on Williams," Payne began.

Brown raised his hand abruptly and turned around to face him. He was the only member of the four-man team who knew *for sure* that Mullin was the one giving the orders—though all of them suspected as much. That gave the other three men some degree of deniability. This was a common practice, he'd learned, with operations such as this. Sometimes not even the team leader knew the identity of the person ordering the mission. Making it clear that Payne was not to speak another word along those lines, Brown gave him a cold stare. "As I said, we'll talk this evening." With that, he turned and walked out of the Commander's office.

As the four men left, Payne felt more confident than ever that this problem would be resolved tomorrow. At the same time, however, he knew that he wasn't the least bit in control—an uncomfortable feeling for a man like Bill Payne. Then again, he was fully aware that the Director hadn't sent these men to comfort *him*.

******

Don and Nick had driven up into North Portland looking for the kind of motel that had an uninquisitive desk clerk. The place was an absolute dump and the surrounding area was the kind in which you had to watch your back. That was okay, though. They were used to doing that by now.

"You really think they were able to pin down where I made the call from?" Don wondered.

"Sure," Nick replied nonchalantly. "They were expecting the call and technology's made it pretty easy to do, but we got out of there right away and we're sitting clear on the other side of town now. Don't worry about it."

Strangely enough, Don *didn't* feel worried. If anything, he was more fatalistic about what might happen tomorrow. As much confidence as he had in the two men helping him, Don had a bad feeling about what lay ahead. He really wanted to call Jenny and the kids… just in case, but was afraid that he wouldn't be able to pull it off without losing it. Besides, at this stage, any carelessness would *ensure* their failure tomorrow.

Instead, he'd gone down to the motel office and bought a couple of envelopes and a stamp from the disinterested clerk. When he got back, Don asked Nick for a few minutes alone in the tiny room and Nick understood completely. Then, kneeling on the floor in front of a decrepit nightstand, Don wrote a letter that he hoped and prayed his family would never have to read. In doing so, he cried as he never had before. *God, I miss them!* He put the letter in one of the envelopes and then put that envelope inside the other, with a note to his secretary:

> *Jean, if you haven't heard from me by the time you receive this, please make sure that Jenny gets it ASAP. Thanks for everything, Don.*

He'd find a mailbox in the morning.

Nick didn't want to discuss the plan anymore tonight. They'd gone over it enough for now and there would be plenty of time in the morning for brushing up. Tonight they needed sleep. It was barely dark outside, but they were both exhausted enough not to care.

As worn out as he was, though, Don found that his mind wouldn't rest. Lying on his back, he noticed that there was enough light filtering in through the yellowed curtains to highlight the water stains on the sagging ceiling. How did he get here? *How did we all get to this point?* After conjuring up every "slippery slope" argument he'd ever heard, Don knew that the answer was complacency. It was a mistake he would never make again.

* * * * * *

"Yes, I understand," Bill Payne said as he hung up the phone. Brown had called, as promised, to describe the roles that Payne and Burke would play tomorrow. The Commander was not the least bit surprised to find out that their roles would be minor. That was fine, Payne reminded himself. *This will all be over soon.*

He then dialed his deputy's cell phone number. "Ray, I've got some info for you about tomorrow," Payne began, and then filled him in on what little he knew. "All they told me was to follow through with the first phase of our plan exactly as we intended to. I'll meet Williams where I told him I would at nine a.m. After you drop me off, you and Myers are to wait in the vehicle one block east of Pioneer Square for further instructions."

"That's not much to go on, sir."

Payne's patience was wearing thin. He didn't blame Burke for asking questions—the same questions that *he* had asked, or had wanted to. The problem was that there were no satisfactory answers. In a matter of a few hours, the two of them had gone from being fully in control, as far as they knew, to having no control at all over the outcome of this situation.

"Ray, I'm as frustrated as you are about it. These guys were sent by Mullin, though, so there's no arguing with them."

"I don't feel good about this at all, sir. Why wouldn't they fill us in on the details?"

"I don't know, Ray. The good news is that this will all be over tomorrow."

* * * * * *

Bobby Myers picked up the ringing cell phone off of his kitchen table. "Myers here."

"Agent Myers, this is Deputy Commander Burke."

"Yes sir, what can I do for you?"

"We have a special operation scheduled for tomorrow morning that we'd like your help with. Commander Payne would like you to be at the staging area tomorrow morning at 0630."

"Uh, yes sir. I'll be there. What kind of—"

"We'll go over the specifics tomorrow. Don't worry; there'll be plenty of time to do so prior to the operation. See you then."

Bobby hung up the phone with a puzzled look on his face. *Why would they want me there?* Probably just so Payne could keep an eye on him, he thought. It was actually a pretty smart move—keeping him from helping Scott and Williams. At least now, Bobby had an excuse to be there.

He thought about calling Scott, but with all the phone tapping that had been going on, decided against it. He *could* drive over to his house, but that was probably just what the boys upstairs expected. Sykes and Lynch would be on him like bloodhounds as soon as he left his driveway. He'd keep this to himself.

Bobby hated not having a plan for tomorrow, but without knowing more about what Payne and Burke had in mind, he really couldn't formulate one. He knew that if he could take the edge off any element of surprise that Payne and the boys might otherwise have... well, at least he'd be doing *something* to help.

20

Portland, Oregon
Tuesday, April 29

SCOTT LEFT HIS house at 6:00 a.m. He and Meg had had their "be careful" pep talk the night before and it hadn't gone well. This morning when he'd bent down to kiss her good-bye, she'd hugged him tightly and hung on longer than usual. She was becoming more emotional as the pregnancy progressed and Scott was unable to convince her that he'd be home for dinner.

This wouldn't be the first time his life had been on the line, but Meg acted as though it was. Right now, though, he was more worried about Don's safety than his own. Scott was a stickler for details and wanted to get moving early this morning. He'd grab breakfast somewhere and go over every aspect of the plan one more time.

*****

Bobby walked toward the staging area at HOT headquarters. As he got closer, he saw Payne, Burke, and another man he didn't recognize.

"Good morning Agent Myers," Payne blurted out strangely.

"Morning, sir. Who's this gentleman?"

"This is, uh, Mr. White."

"Hello, White," Bobby said as he walked toward the large blond man and extended his hand. "Bobby Myers. Sorry, I didn't catch your first name."

White shook hands reluctantly. "No need for it."

Bobby stared into the man's eyes as they continued the *very* firm handshake for an uncomfortably long time.

Payne broke the ice. "Agent Myers, Mr. White will be joining us this morning. He's here to lend us assistance and is very experienced in these matters."

"What matters are you referring to, Commander?" Bobby pressed. He'd had about enough of this.

"Bobby, we're ready to go. Put your gear bag in the back and get in the passenger seat up front."

Since when doesn't Payne ride shotgun? Bobby pondered. *Easier to keep an eye on me if I'm up front. This could get hairy before it's over.*

* * * * * *

Something was nagging at Nick as he rigged the equipment for Don to wear. He couldn't help thinking that Payne knew he was being set up. *But if so, why would he go through with it, unless…he's setting up an ambush? What are we walking into?* All they could do was recon the area thoroughly and stick to their plan. Nick certainly wasn't going to discuss his fears with Don. If *he* got spooked, he might not follow through with the plan and that could spell the end for all of them.

Nick wished he'd had the chance to talk to Scott about his concerns, just to be sure the two professionals were on the same page as far as contingency planning was concerned. That was the weak point in their plan, Nick thought. There wasn't a solid alternative in the event that things went wrong—and things always seemed to go wrong.

"Don, I want you to make it count, okay?" A confused look forced Nick to explain. "Whatever happens to anyone else this morning, you get your ass out of there and get your proof to the Marshals Service. You got it?"

"Yeah, I hear you."

"I mean it. Mike and everyone else who's ever died for this country deserves that much. I'm in this thing to see that you get what you need to bring these bastards down. That means you do *whatever it takes* to save yourself—no matter what. If I'm on the ground bleeding to death, you jump over me and run to that white Dodge. Understand?"

Don swallowed hard. "I understand."

"Remember, you've *got* to get Payne to admit what he's done."

"What about the recorder? Where's it going to be?"

"Well, assuming Keller's buddy comes through, our getaway car ought to be in place by the time we get there. I think the perfect spot for it would be under the driver's seat. What do you think?"

"Perfect. That way, there's no coming back to Pioneer Square for it—it'll be with me."

"Right. Now, let's get out of here. I want to be there early to check things out."

******

The tension inside the HOT Suburban was palpable. Bobby had glanced back a couple of times at White. Each time, the man met his eyes with a cold stare. Burke had said last night that the details of the plan would be explained to him. That hadn't happened and Bobby wasn't holding his breath. What they had in mind, however, was becoming crystal clear.

Payne's motives had often been questionable, but Bobby never would have believed that his boss was capable of something like this. *And if he was capable of setting up and ordering the death of an innocent man like Don Williams, what else might he be willing to do?* Two questions from last night resurfaced in Bobby's mind. He wondered why else *he* would have been invited and whether or not Payne would really go that far. It was hard for the dedicated agent to believe that his boss would, but the presence of the fellow in the backseat convinced him otherwise. Bobby had to tell himself to wait for the right opportunity to do something about it.

They dropped Payne off a couple of blocks west of Pioneer

Square, then drove around to a spot a block east of it and parked along the street.

"Is this where we get out?" Bobby asked.

"No. We wait here until further notice," Burke answered as he looked over at Myers with an odd expression on his face.

"Burke, what's going on?" Bobby demanded.

"Don't worry about it, Myers," White answered from the backseat.

"I didn't ask you," Bobby shot back as he turned around to stare at the man. White stared back without saying a word and Bobby turned back around. *I hope I get the chance to break this motherfucker's neck before this is over.*

* * * * * *

The morning was chilly and overcast, but at least it wasn't raining at the moment. Nick stopped a few blocks south of Pioneer Square to drop off Don. "The car should be one block north of here," he told Don. "Find it, plant the receiver, and head on to the Square."

He thought Don might actually throw up, judging by the look on his face. "You'll be fine, Don. And Scott and I will both be there… now let's go do this thing."

Walking toward the Square, Don found the white Dodge parked exactly where Scott had said it would be—a good sign. He planted the receiver under the driver's seat and continued on.

Not knowing where Payne's men would be or what surprises might be in store for them, they thought it prudent to enter the Square in disguise. Nick had gone to a secondhand store the day before and purchased some rather bulky and nondescript clothing for the two of them. The clothes, baseball cap, and enhanced facial hair made Don almost unrecognizable. In addition, he'd been working on an uneven gait with a limp that he was rather proud of. Nick, on the other hand, would look significantly more "homeless." He even had a folded "will work for food" sign in his coat that he'd use after getting to his assigned spot.

Nick drove north of the Square a few blocks and parked the Jeep. Not wanting to be seen getting out of a brand new vehicle looking homeless, he grabbed his gear bag and headed into a nearby alley to change. A few minutes later, he emerged from behind a dumpster in full disguise, shuffling toward his assigned spot.

* * * * * *

As he entered Pioneer Square, Don glanced in the direction his partner was supposed to be. Though he couldn't see him, Don had no doubt that Nick was stationed in the Square's northeast corner.

If everything went according to plan, the two men wouldn't meet again until after all of this was over. Slowly, the feelings of despair and loneliness that he'd had before Nick snatched him from his hiding place a few days ago began to creep back in. Gritting his teeth and holding his breath, the insurance executive turned off the street into the Square and kept going. Nervously shifting his eyes around, Don told himself to slow down and remember the walk he'd practiced. He knew where to go and what to do. The coast appeared clear for now—there was no reason to panic.

* * * * * *

Scott had arrived forty-five minutes earlier than his two partners. Now, settled in as comfortably as possible, he would sit and wait. He'd spent some time Sunday afternoon checking out the area and settled on a high-rise retail and office building across the street from the southwest corner of the Square—diagonally across from where they'd decided Nick would be. There was a large unrented space on the third floor that was high enough to allow a clear view of the entire Square. The door was locked when he tried it, but getting in didn't present much of a problem—Scott often thought he'd have made a top-notch burglar in another life.

With his Swarovski binoculars, he scanned the area, looking for anyone and anything that appeared out of place. He could clearly see the meeting spot in front of the Visitors Center. Thousands of surveillance hours had given him the ability to keep a watchful eye out while letting his mind wander a bit. Unintentionally, he was doing that now.

Scott had no doubt that he was doing the right thing. Of all the choices presented to him since he'd reluctantly accepted this crazy assignment, helping Williams out of this mess—in this manner—was by far the least ambiguous; it *was* the right thing to do. Always one to consider every angle and possible outcome, though, Scott realized that his career could be over if this went down the wrong way. He was freelancing and that wouldn't be looked upon favorably. He also had a wife and, soon, a child to think about... *Knock it off! You're here now and you've got a job to do!* People like Payne had to be stopped—for the good of everyone who'd ever put on a badge, as well as the public at large.

* * * * * *

Nick set up on his assigned corner, looking for all the world like a homeless man. He was certain the disguise would work—an important consideration, since he was sure that they'd have photographs of him by now. He couldn't allow himself to be taken off the dance floor before the music even started. Don needed him and, besides, Nick enjoyed his freedom.

The way their communication system was set up, everything was routed through Scott. He could talk to both Nick and Don, either separately or at the same time, with a small switching unit that allowed him to choose who he wanted to talk to, but the two men on the ground could communicate only with Scott. The goal was for Don to act as naturally as possible. With that in mind, Scott and Nick wanted to keep the amount of chatter that came through his earpiece to a minimum.

"Larsen, you look like a natural," Scott joked. The voice in his earpiece startled Nick for a second. He'd almost forgotten he had it in. It had been a while since he'd conducted ops like this.

"Yep, just another down-on-his-luck fella mumbling to himself. Can Don hear us," Nick asked.

"No. It's just you and me. Why?"

"Scott, you know this thing isn't likely to go down exactly the way we want it to, right?"

"Yeah," Scott admitted. "I've been thinking about that, too."

Nick knew it was too late at this point to add any new layers to the plan. "We'll adjust on the fly if we have to. Just make sure you get Don out of the area. I'll deal with these guys."

"I don't feel right about that, Nick. We don't know how many of them there are. Don can get away on his own," Scott objected.

"You've got to make sure he gets out of here in one piece, Scott. It's not up for debate." Keller also had a career and a family, Nick knew, and he had neither. It wasn't that he considered himself expendable, or some kind of martyr. It just made sense that he be the one to cut off the pursuers. "Don't worry about me, Keller. I'm pretty good in a gunfight."

"I have no doubt. Okay, I'll get him out of here if the shit hits the fan. Let's hope we don't have to cross that bridge, though. I'm going to contact Don now. Good luck, brother."

"You too," Nick answered. "Semper Fi."

"Semper Fi," the former MARSOC officer replied.

Don was stationed north of the brass placard by about fifty feet, sitting on a bench and pretending to read a paperback. Strangely enough, Don's bullet wound hadn't bothered him much—until now. As he sat waiting for Payne to show up, the wound throbbed terribly with each beat of his heart.

"Don, you're looking good. I don't see Payne or any of the rest of them yet. Just stay calm. This will all work out." Scott knew that Don would be more scared than he'd ever been in his life. They needed him to perform well, though, and for that he had to be as calm as possible.

"Thanks for the vote of confidence," Don mumbled, tilting his head down as he did so, in order to let the bill of his cap obscure his face. He and Nick had discussed the importance of that this morning. "I'll be fine."

"We know you will."

"All right," Scott continued, "I've got clear com with both of you. As soon as I see any of them, I'll—" he cut himself off. "Okay, guys, here we go. I've got Payne coming out of the Visitors Center right now. Don, you're on, buddy." He looked at his watch. Payne was right on time.

******

Don took in a deep breath, exhaled slowly, and then stood. As he made his way toward the brass placard, he felt two very different emotions. Without a doubt, the stronger of the two was a nearly incapacitating fear. He wondered whether, by the time he reached his destination, he would still be able to breathe (much less speak), due to the golf ball–size lump in his throat. The other emotion was more subtle. In spite of the fact that he was about to walk into the most dangerous situation he'd ever faced, Don felt a strange sense of relief that this nightmare was about to come to an end.

As he approached the meeting spot, Don could see Payne looking around…almost nervously, it seemed. This surprised him and had a strangely calming effect. It also gave him a little more confidence as he approached the high-ranking federal agent. The task was not an easy one. He had to provoke the man before him into admitting that he'd done something both illegal and immoral. Don's only hope was to infuriate him—something he appeared to have a unique talent for.

"Well, Payne, there you are. I was wondering whether or not you'd show up." Don stopped about fifteen feet away, determined to keep that much distance. It was enough room so that people would occasionally walk between them and that was ideal. Payne's demeanor hardened a bit as he focused on Don.

"You seem so sure of yourself, Mr. Williams. I can't help but think that it's false courage, though. You appear to be a very intelligent man, who's in *way* over his head. I really do pity you. I think you've allowed yourself to be manipulated by others whose agenda is different from your own. You've been thrown into the middle of something you had no business being involved in."

With his confidence suddenly ebbing, Don couldn't hide his fear. Payne was right—he *was* in completely over his head and the only thing keeping his knees from buckling right now was his certainty that Scott and Nick were *not.*

* * * * * *

Scott was methodically covering the scene with his binoculars. Don had made contact and they were talking. Everything had gone as planned, so far. Still, he knew that the HOT squad would be armed to the teeth and would stop at nothing to achieve its objective. If they *did* have more in mind than a simple transfer of information, he had serious doubts about their ability to protect Don. Payne could solve all his problems here this morning and Scott had no doubt about his resolve to do so.

None of that really mattered, though. All he could do now was stick to the plan. That meant he was to observe the exchange of "evidence" and communicate anything he saw to his two partners. The timing would be critical. It was now 9:03 a.m. Whether or not Don was successful in provoking Payne, by 9:08 he was to start walking toward the east side of the Square. At precisely 9:09, if it was on time, the northbound tram would cross his escape route. It was important for Don to get across the street just before that happened. That would allow him to use the tram to create a screen and buy some time. From there, he would need to make it only a couple of blocks southwest to the car—and freedom. Scott was to give him a heads-up at 9:06 and then again at the one-minute and thirty-second marks.

* * * * * *

Don knew he needed to get a lot out of Payne. So far, he had nothing…and the clock was ticking. "Did you bring proof that you cleared up my record?"

Payne was about to answer as he'd planned to all along, when Brown's voice came through the earpiece he was wearing.

"All right, Commander, it's go time. Tell him that he's to come with you without a struggle, or we'll kill his wife. Do *not* turn and look, but I've got her right here with me, over your left shoulder at the edge of the Square."

Payne had a strange look on his face, as if he hadn't heard Don. "Well, did you bring the proof, or not?" Don asked again.

"Uh, actually, there's been a change in plans."

* * * * * *

Scott was just starting another scan of the area when he froze. "Nick, there's a guy about fifty feet to your right who looks out of place. Something about him, I don't know—stocky, wearing a tan windbreaker, sunglasses, dark hair."

"Got him. I'll keep an eye on him."

"Okay…oh shit!"

"What is it?"

"Not good. They've got Don's wife."

"Where?! Are you sure?"

"Yeah. Another hundred feet or so from you beyond the guy I just told you about—same direction."

"Can't see all the way over there; these pillars are in the way."

Scott glanced down at Don and saw that he and Payne were still talking. He didn't recognize either of the two new players, but they obviously planned on using Jenny as leverage. They also clearly had more in mind than an exchange of information.

"Nick, this thing's going to go down fast. They wouldn't have brought her here unless they planned on forcing Don to give himself up. Nothing else makes sense. I'm headed down there now to help him get away. I'm going to bring Don on now and tell him to run. If he knows she's here, there's no telling what he'll do."

"Roger that," Nick agreed.

* * * * * *

"What do you mean, 'a change in plans'?" Don asked Payne.

Then he heard Scott's voice. "Don, listen to me. Don't say a word. Things have changed. You need to trust me. I want you to turn around *right now* and run as fast as you can."

"But I don't have—"

Scott was already close to the ground floor. "NOW. RUN!" he screamed at the top of his lungs as he hurled himself down the last flight of stairs.

Don knew he had to trust Scott. He looked at Payne and back-pedaled a couple of steps, then turned and ran toward the east side of the Square.

Payne hesitated and looked over his left shoulder. He saw Brown at the same time he heard him over the earpiece. "Go after him, Payne!"

He took off after Don, who had a decent head start by this time.

* * * * * *

Brown looked around him for any sign of a police officer and was glad there was none. He knew there was a possibility that Don would run. That was why he'd brought along his wife. Now he just had to let Don know she was here.

Jenny Williams had been told to be completely quiet and motionless. Now Brown pressed the barrel of his handgun against her ribs and gave a very different order, just as Don started running.

"I want you to scream your husband's name as loud as you can, right now."

Jenny knew they didn't want Don to get away and she didn't want to help them. She was sobbing and shaking her head.

"I said RIGHT NOW, or I'll kill you both!" Brown seethed as he jammed the gun barrel deeply into the terrified woman's ribs.

Almost involuntarily, she complied. "Don!"

"Again, NOW!"

"Don!" she screamed again while crying uncontrollably.

* * * * * *

Don thought he heard a woman's voice scream his name. *Jenny?* He slowed down and heard it again—behind him, he was sure. He stopped and turned around just as Payne was coming up on him. From his left, Scott was running toward him at full speed.

"Get away from him, Payne!" the Marshal yelled as he came up and grabbed a very startled and confused Don Williams by the arm. "I said back off, or I'll kill you where you stand," he warned, reaching under his jacket with his right hand and finding the grip of his Sig P229.

Payne was just catching his breath enough to speak. "Maybe you should let *him* make the call, Keller," indicating Don with a nod of his head.

Then Don saw her across the square. "Jenny—my God, what have you bastards done!"

Scott knew he had to take control of the situation. "Come on, Don. We're getting out of here now to regroup."

"Don, if you come with us, she will *not* be hurt. I give you my word," Payne offered.

"Shut up, Payne. Don, we're leaving NOW. Come on."

"No, I'm not letting them take her. I don't give a damn about myself. They're not taking her..."

Scott doubted that Payne would draw his gun in this setting, even though they'd already attracted plenty of attention. He kept an eye on the HOT Commander and began pulling a terrified Don Williams backward while whispering in his ear. "Listen to me. They will NOT hurt her as long as they don't have you. If you give yourself up, they'll kill you both. You've got to trust me."

Don hadn't taken his eyes off his wife. He quit fighting Scott and began walking backward with him.

"Don, when I say run, you turn and follow me, okay?"

Don nodded his head.

"Payne, I swear I'll kill you if you follow us."

"They're not going to let him get away, Keller."

Scott ignored him. "Run!"

The two of them turned and headed south, toward the car that was waiting for them. They hadn't gone far when Scott heard Nick's voice through his earpiece.

Nick had heard everything up to this point. "Scott, the dark-haired guy is on the move, headed in my direction. He's definitely part of this thing. I'm going to follow him and find out where they're taking her. I'll be in touch on my number one cell."

Scott slowed down so that he could hear Nick clearly. When they'd exchanged their new cell phone numbers last night, they'd assigned a "one" and "two" to each person's phones, in case they had to go back and forth between them. That would come in handy now.

"Roger that, Nick. By the way, it looks like some new players might be involved. I don't think the guy you're going after is HOT and Payne said something that made me think he's not really in charge anymore. Just be careful."

"Roger that. Out," Nick replied.

"What do mean, 'new players'?" Don wanted to know—glancing behind him to verify that no one was chasing and then stopping to put his hands on his knees for a rest.

"Don't know for sure. Looks like Payne might have brought in some new muscle. We don't have time to talk about it now, though. Come on," Scott ordered. "We're almost there."

* * * * * *

Brown clenched his jaw as he walked quickly toward the waiting vehicle. He was trying not to attract undue attention, while maintaining a viselike grip on Jenny Williams' arm. Dragging a crying woman along the streets of downtown Portland was likely to interest *someone* eventually, however.

Brown had spent several years in the military and a couple more afterward as a private security contractor. In neither case had he fit in very well. He'd often thought that he wasn't cut out to play well with others; but not everyone was. The same could certainly be said for the other three men on his team. Most would probably call them misfits—and Brown wouldn't argue with that characterization.

On the other hand, they were all very good at accomplishing certain tasks in the short run—the one before them being a prime example. Their training and experience had prepared them well for the types of situations they faced in their current line of work. Thinking outside the box was often necessary in order to survive and succeed. This mission had turned out to be one of those situations.

Brown had made more money in the last two years doing this kind of work than he had in the eight years prior—and it was off the books, which had tremendous tax advantages. White had served with him in the military and was reliable. They'd worked well together and his was the first name that came to Brown's mind when he had to come up with someone he'd be comfortable working with on freelance operations. White liked the idea as much as Brown did and a two-man team was born. They were good at what they did and they enjoyed being on call for a handful of very powerful men within the federal government. They were problem-solvers, pure and simple.

This mission, in Mullin's opinion, apparently required two additional team members. Brown hadn't worked with either Black or Red previously, but they seemed solid enough. Still, you didn't trust new guys the way you trusted the ones you'd been under fire with.

Director Mullin himself had come up with the idea of grabbing Williams' wife. It was an obvious and effective method of increasing the pressure on a man—especially one who wasn't used to doing this kind of thing. The HOT surveillance records showed that she'd gone for an early morning run. Most runners were creatures of habit and, though they didn't have a lot of prep time for this mission, it seemed like a prudent use of time to watch the house for an opportunity to pick her up.

Things had worked out perfectly. After about an hour of waiting, she'd come out of the house and began jogging down the street. It was a simple matter to grab her and throw her into the car. Unfortunately, things at Pioneer Square hadn't gone down as smoothly. It was time to adapt. They'd planned for this contingency, of course. Now they'd just have to bring Williams to them by other means.

They'd obtained two cars the day before and parked them four blocks apart this morning—just in case. Black would take the second one and meet Brown and Red at their prearranged destination. White was with Burke and—more importantly—keeping an eye on Myers. They knew that Myers could present a problem if not handled correctly. Whatever happened, Brown was sure that White could deal with it. White was to rendezvous with them as well, if things didn't work out at the Square.

Red was stationed in the Visitors Center to keep an eye on things. The plan was for him to return to the vehicle with Brown, the woman, and hopefully Williams. Obviously, that hadn't worked out. Red had started out of the Visitors Center when Williams took off running, but Brown called him back. They'd be better off moving on to their contingency plan now, especially with Keller at Williams' side. A shootout with a Marshal in the middle of Pioneer Square would be hard to explain to Mullin.

The car was only a little over a block away now and Brown noticed Red trailing him on the other side of the street. The woman he was dragging along was becoming a major annoyance. "Quit crying," he whispered harshly. "If someone stops us, I swear I'll kill them *and* you. Do you understand me?"

Jenny, obviously terrified, nodded her head and tried to compose herself. She desperately hoped she'd have a chance to do something to help her husband, but this wasn't the time or place.

* * * * * *

Nick figured the guy would be good. As a result, he'd have to be cautious, yet still aggressive. He also had to remind himself that he hadn't done this kind of thing in a while. His tussle with Keller a couple of days ago had made that painfully obvious. Ingenuity, not brawn, had always been Nick's most effective weapon, anyway. He hoped that trend would continue.

He assumed the man was heading for a vehicle. The big guy wasn't running, but he was walking down the sidewalk fast enough that Nick would have to run to catch up to him before he got to his car. Not wanting to attract any more attention than necessary, Nick ducked behind the row of cars parked along the street, crouched down, and moved as fast as he could in that position. Every now and then he'd look up to keep tabs on his target. He was getting close now and decided to slow down. His guess was that the man's car was one of the many parallel parked along the busy one-way street. About fifty yards later, the dark-haired man turned off the sidewalk and walked up to the driver-side door of a gray sedan.

Nick was within ten feet of him, his Glock out of its holster and tucked inside the heavy coat he was wearing. He quickly came up behind the man, grabbed his left arm, and jammed the barrel of the .45 ACP handgun into his ribs while pressing him against the vehicle. He knew the man wouldn't be easily intimidated, but hoped he was smart enough to be reasonable.

"It won't take much for me to pull this trigger. Now listen to me—you and I are going to walk around to the other side of the car and you're going to get in and climb over to the driver's side. Got it?" The man gave no indication that he did. Nick pressed. "Don't think for a second I won't gut-shoot you and throw you in the backseat. We can do this more than one way, I promise you."

"Okay," was the only response he got, but it was enough.

Nick pushed the man in front of him around the back of the car, keeping him within reach. "Now open the passenger door, get in, and climb behind the wheel. Oh, and keep your fucking hands where I can see them at all times."

The man did as he was told. Nick climbed into the front passenger seat and turned toward his captive. "Look straight ahead and put both hands on the wheel," he ordered. "You carry on the left or right side?" The man turned to look at him. Nick screamed, "I said look straight ahead! Now, for the last time: Do you carry on the left or right side?"

"Right."

"Okay. Take your *left* hand off the wheel slowly and grab your weapon with *two fingers* only. Then slowly hand it to me." The man did as he was told and reached across his body with the handgun. Nick grabbed the Sig P226 from him.

"Good, now slowly reach down and pull up both pant legs." Again, the man complied, satisfying Nick that he had nothing in an ankle holster. He'd pat him down completely after they got to where they were going.

"I see the earpiece in your right ear. Where's the transmitter?"

"Front shirt pocket."

"Slowly grab both and hand them to me."

That done, it was time to get moving. "Now you're going to start the car and pull out into traffic slowly. Head south on this street until I tell you otherwise. Got it?"

"Yeah," Black grunted as he started the car.

"Oh, and you *really* don't want to do anything stupid," Nick warned.

As soon as they were moving, Nick put his Bluetooth in his ear and punched a saved number on his cell phone, without ever taking his eyes off the man to his left.

"Yeah?" answered the voice on the other end.

"It's Larsen. I need another favor."

The man's name was Randy and he'd known Nick for years. They'd had a complicated relationship, but the bottom line was that Nick could count on him to come through when needed. "Jeez, Nick,

I don't hear from you for months and now twice in twenty-four hours? What's up? Something wrong with the Jeep?"

"No, but you can come pick it up. It's near Sixth and Alder downtown. Doesn't look like I'll need it anymore."

"Okay. Is that it?"

"No. I need a place to go for an hour or so that's close to downtown."

"I assume you're looking for a place where you won't be bothered?"

"Yeah—you could say that."

"Well, I have a warehouse space west of town that I keep a couple of old cars in. It's only about fifteen minutes away from where you left the Jeep. Does that work?"

"Perfect. What's the address?" Nick committed the address and lock combination to memory. "Great. Can you meet me there and bring a few things?"

"Sure, but it'll take me a while to get there. What do you need?"

"I need a laptop with a wireless card so I can get online, my spare bug-out bag, and one of the rifles you're holding onto for me."

"The HK?"

"No, the quiet one. The case is marked number seven and there are ten loaded thirty-round mags in the case with it."

"Got it. Anything else?"

"Nope. Thanks, I owe you."

"Come on, Nick. We're still not close to even and you know it. Let me know if there's anything else."

"Thanks," Nick said and ended the call. "Turn right at the next light," he ordered the driver.

* * * * * *

As Scott drove, Don sat beside him, fuming. "How could it have come to this, Scott? They have my *wife*, for God's sake! Now we know for sure that there's nothing they won't do. I actually wondered this morning whether or not Payne would really go as far as killing someone to solve his problems. Now there's no doubt in my mind that he will."

Scott agreed, but knew that it was even worse than Don realized. The guy that Nick followed didn't look familiar to him and Payne's words rang in his ear: *They're not going to let him get away*. Scott was afraid that their little problem had been kicked up the chain of command. If so, they'd have their hands more than full.

He considered again calling in the Marshals Service for help, *if* Nick was able to find out where they were taking Jenny. He decided against it, though. If these new players were as good as he feared they were, they'd sniff that out and be gone before the cavalry got there to help.

Scott had to be sure that Don could handle this, however it was going to go down. Whatever they ultimately came up with for a solution, Don would have to play a pivotal role once more.

"Don, I can't argue with you one bit. We have to do everything we can to get Jenny away from them and solve this problem once and for all."

"How are we going to do that?" Don asked in a voice that rang of despair.

"Nick's working on it," Scott answered without certainty. "He followed one of the men from Pioneer Square. He'll find out where they're taking Jenny and we'll work on a way to get to her. All we can do right now is sit tight until we hear from him…or *them*."

"Scott, you need to understand that I won't hesitate to give myself up to save my wife."

"I do. That's why I had to get you away from Pioneer Square. They won't be satisfied with just one of you…or probably with one of *us*, at this point. And I don't think they'll be looking to take anybody into custody."

Don turned away and stared out the window at the gray skies. "They really *have* gone too far now to stop short of killing us all, haven't they?"

"I'm sure that's what they're thinking…but we've got something to say about how this thing ends, too."

21

Portland, Oregon
Tuesday, April 29

THE SMALL WAREHOUSE was exactly what Nick wanted. It was a dreary place—dimly lit and surrounded by vacant buildings. After making sure there were no vehicles in the parking lot, or any other signs of activity in the complex, Nick instructed his captive to park behind the building that Randy's unit was in.

He took the keys from the ignition and ordered the man to keep his hands on the wheel. Nick got out and walked around to the driver's side of the vehicle. He then ordered the man out and told him to walk toward the back door of the metal building in front of them.

As he got out of the car, Black sensed his best opportunity to escape. As soon as he exited, he feigned doubling over and then immediately launched himself toward Nick.

The man was very quick for his size and that caught Nick a little off guard. He sidestepped the lunging man just in time and his Glock came crashing down on the back of the big man's head. That made up for what could have been a disastrous lapse in judgment on Nick's part. It had been a long four days since Nick had joined this fight, but he suddenly realized that, regardless of how exhausted he was, nothing less than complete awareness would allow him—or Don and Jenny—to survive. He wouldn't make the same mistake again.

"Get up and do what I told you to, or I'll blow one of your damn feet off," Nick threatened. The man did as he was told this time.

Nick locked the door behind them and surveyed the interior of the warehouse unit. The lack of proper ventilation resulted in a heavy smell of motor oil and general mustiness. The place desperately needed to be aired out for several hours, but that wasn't practical at the moment. Nick knew he had to work quickly.

He was operating under the assumption that the men who had Don's wife would contact Don eventually and the most sensible thing for them to do would be to try to draw Don to *them*, at a place of their choosing. They would want to control the situation and be sure that nobody followed. Nick also assumed that his adversaries were very good. He usually made that assumption anyway, but, if Keller was right, the stakes may have been raised. That made it all the more important to get accurate information from his captive.

Nick's mind had been in overdrive since picking the guy up at Pioneer Square. He knew what he had to do. In order to have anything more than pure luck on their side, he had to find out where they took Jenny and how many of them there were—as quickly as possible. He also had to get there before they expected Don to arrive. Otherwise, there would be very little chance of saving Don and Jenny, or, for that matter, himself and Keller. If the four of them walked into the trap as expected, they'd all be killed.

During his time in the CIA, there had been occasions for Nick to use what were now known as "enhanced interrogation" techniques. He found the term hilarious, frankly. Another example of political correctness run amok. Torture was torture, pure and simple. There *were* different levels of it, however, and the variety of methods available was limited only by one's imagination. Also, contrary to what some people talked themselves into believing, torture was sometimes necessary in order to serve the greater good.

Nick often wondered to what lengths the president of the ACLU would be willing to go if his child was kidnapped and buried alive. If Nick ever got the chance, he'd ask that person one question: If we caught the kidnapper and there was only so much time left before your child ran out of oxygen, what would you be willing to do to find out where the child was buried?

The answer was obvious and no amount of equivocation he'd ever heard had convinced Nick that the equivocator actually believed what he or she was saying. The "torture is never justified" crowd hated the *idea* of torture and they had the luxury of not being forced to go any further than that. Others, like Nick Larsen, had been put in the position of actually having to deal with the issue—more than once. He'd leave pontification to others.

The other argument that he knew held absolutely no water in the real world was that torture didn't work. That was a fashionable line these days, but the truth was that anyone who said that had never been tortured. Obviously, some were capable of withstanding it for longer than others, but, eventually, everyone broke.

Highly trained individuals were not only capable of holding out longer, but also skilled in giving false information—initially. That's where a well-trained interrogator came in very handy. Information had to be verified prior to acting on it. Usually, there were ways to do so.

Nick had never enjoyed torturing another human being; only a psychotic person would. What he *had* always been able to do was justify it and detach himself enough for it not to affect him. His personal definition of torture was the forcible extraction of critical information from a person who had done, planned to do, or knew about the impending occurrence of something horrific. Based on that definition, he'd never tortured anyone who hadn't deserved it—and today would be no exception.

Black sensed what was coming. Having been around the block a time or two, he was starting to become visibly nervous, despite trying desperately not to. The less obvious that was to his captor, the better off he'd be. Regardless of Black's efforts to conceal his emotions, however, Nick noticed. Before this was over, he would exploit every one of the man's natural human weaknesses.

A blow to the back of the head had stunned the man long enough for him to be easily subdued and Nick always carried a pair of handcuffs in his pack. Those, plus a length of rope found in the small warehouse allowed him to put the guy in a serious bind—literally. There was a large water pipe running from floor to ceiling that he handcuffed the big man to, with his hands behind his back.

A hard knee to the gut then dropped him to his knees after asking him to get there nicely hadn't worked. Part of the rope was then used to bind his feet to the water pipe and, as a final touch, Nick tied a piece of rope around his neck, with the other end around a bracket further up the pipe. This would ensure that the man didn't slump while being "worked on."

Nick looked around the area for equipment he could use and quickly gathered a few implements that he thought might come in handy. He assembled them on a workbench behind him and then knelt down so that he could look directly into the man's eyes.

"So, here's the deal. I've got nothing against you personally, but I assume you know how these things work. I won, you lost. Now I get to make the rules." The man stared at him with pure hatred and defiance, the makeshift noose around his neck tightening every time he attempted to lower his head even slightly.

Nick stood up and continued. "I'll get right to the point. I need some information from you and you're going to give it to me…one way or the other." He paused for effect and slipped on a pair of heavy leather work gloves that he'd found. "All that stuff about the 'easy way or the hard way' that we've seen in the movies applies here, too. I just want to give you a taste of the 'hard way' so you'll have a reference point."

With that, Nick hit him with a left cross to the jaw, followed immediately by a savage right. The man moaned loudly and blood dripped from his mouth. Nick went on, nonchalantly. "I'm a little rusty at this stuff, to be honest with you. In another life, I used to do a lot of it, but not so much lately." He pulled a chair up and sat down. "I don't really care who you are, so I won't bother with that. What I want to know is where—exactly—are your partners taking the lady that you kidnapped?"

"Fuck you!"

"Buddy, that's a huge mistake," Nick replied calmly. "You see, I'm in a bit of a hurry and you're wasting my time with that stuff, which pisses me off. The downside of that for you is that I enjoy doing this a lot more when I'm pissed."

Nick got up and walked over to the workbench, grabbed a pair of Vise-Grip pliers, and returned to his chair. The man's eyes widened when he saw the pliers, the defiance replaced by something far different. *This guy won't be that hard to break*, Nick thought.

"So, again, where are they taking the lady?"

"Man, I—don't even know," came the shaky reply.

"There you go again, wasting my time," Nick said as he pushed the chair out of the way, reached over to the man, and lifted his shirt up. He then adjusted the Vise-Grips for an extremely tight grip, grabbed the skin on the man's belly, attached the pliers, and squeezed until they locked shut.

The man screamed loudly and Nick stuck a shop rag in his mouth to muffle the sound. He let go of the pliers and they hung there, attached to the dark-haired man's skin. Nick then removed the rag from his mouth. "You've got another chance to save yourself a lot of pain. Tell me exactly where they're taking her, how many of them there are, and what their plan is, or you ain't seen nothing yet—I promise."

The man's breathing was rapid and he appeared to have a hard time focusing. Nick grabbed the pliers, which caused Black to yelp. "Answer me!" Nick pressed him.

"I…don't…"

And with that, Nick slowly pulled on the pliers until a chunk of the man's skin was ripped loose.

The scream this time brought back memories that Nick had tried to suppress over the years. Again, he jammed the rag in the man's mouth, just in case the warehouse complex wasn't completely deserted, as it appeared to be. He opened the pliers and the torn piece of skin dropped onto the concrete floor. The wound was bleeding profusely. Nick walked back to the workbench. He lit a propane torch, went back over to the bleeding man, and held the blue flame to the wound long enough to cauterize it.

The stench of burning flesh filled the dank room and the man howled through the rag. Nick was worried that the guy might pass out. He grabbed the man's hair and slapped him in the face a couple of times.

"Stay with me, dude. We're not finished yet." The man's eyes half-focused on his tormenter. "This is the last time I'm going to ask you. If you don't give me *everything* I need, I will keep this up until you're dead. Got it?"

Black's eyes were blinking rapidly. His mind was spinning. He knew he had to give this man something to make him stop, but it couldn't be the truth. He searched his memory for locations that Brown had discussed with them last night. There'd been two that they looked at in detail before deciding on a third. Black was unfamiliar with the area, which didn't help his recollection process. He at least needed a legitimate street name. Finally, the tumblers clicked into place just as Nick was growing impatient again.

"Okay, okay…I…I'll tell you where."

Nick studied the man's eyes. His experience told him that he was about to lie. "I'm listening."

Black gave him an address and Nick reached for his cell phone. While dialing Randy's number, he studied the man in front of him carefully. There was no doubt in his mind that he'd been lied to. Nick had thought about having Randy check out the location and let him know whether it was legit, but there were problems with that course of action.

First of all, for absolute verification, Randy would have to get close enough that he might not make it back out if they were, indeed, there. Secondly, and perhaps more importantly, it would take him the better part of an hour to get there from where Nick suspected he was now—and they didn't have that kind of time. After quickly considering every option, Nick decided on a bluff of his own.

After three rings, Randy answered. Nick spoke quickly. "Yeah, it's me. I need you to check out an address. It's 51723 Green Valley Road. That's close to you, isn't it?"

"Come on, Nick. That's almost an hour away with traffic, you know that. I mean, I'll do it, but—"

"So, about ten or fifteen minutes, then? Good, that's what I thought. Check it out, look for any sign of activity, and let me know ASAP." Nick paused and Randy started to speak. Nick cut him off again. "I expect to hear back from you within fifteen."

"Uh, yeah, Nick. I'll call you back in fifteen."

"Perfect." He ended the call and looked at his prisoner.

"Okay, my friend, in fifteen minutes or less, we'll know whether you've been straight with me." Nick paused for effect. "And if you haven't, you'll have a whole new understanding of pain."

Black was scared to death. His eyes darted around the room, looking for something—anything—he could use to free himself. Any semblance of a plan would provide comfort…but there was none.

Nick used the next several minutes to very methodically collect more tools. He dragged a small stainless steel table next to his prisoner and carefully laid out a variety of instruments. He knew that the mental aspect of torture was far more important than the physical. Once the man was convinced that there was no way to avoid the pain and that it would be worse than anything he'd ever experienced, Nick knew that he'd be much closer to getting the truth out of him.

Exactly fifteen minutes after Nick had asked him to, Randy placed the call. "Nick, I'm not sure what you're up to, but I knew you wanted me to call back in fifteen minutes."

"That's what I thought. I *knew* he was lying to me. Get over here ASAP, okay?"

"On my way now. I'll be there in about twenty and I've got the gear you asked for."

"Perfect. See you then."

Nick put his phone away and stared at the bloody and sweating man before him. What he was about to do actually required a lot of courage on his part, though the average person would never understand that. Nick was built to help others and that's what he'd spent most of his adult life doing. The methods he used were often indirect and usually more gray than black and white, but that was just the reality of the world he'd operated in.

The issue before him now was as clear-cut as any he'd ever faced, though. If he didn't get the truth out of this man very soon, it was highly likely that an innocent man and woman would die. What compelled him even more, however, was the fact that the same men would also get away with having killed his best friend. He had to save Jenny and Don and also make those responsible pay for Mike and Sarah. These bastards picked the fight and they deserved everything they were going to get. With that in mind, he walked over to the stainless steel table and picked up the pipe cutters.

Black was shaking his head. "I'll tell you the truth. I swear."

"I know you will. But first, there's a price to pay for wasting fifteen minutes of my time." He approached the man and hammered his right elbow into his left cheekbone. The big man moaned loudly as Nick walked around behind him. His hands were cuffed around the water pipe, behind his back. Nick grabbed the man's left hand and put the pipe cutters around the thumb, ratcheting them down until the blade just made contact with the joint closest to the hand.

Black couldn't see what Nick had done, but he was fully aware of the predicament he was in. He began to try desperately to pull free. He was panicking—exactly what Nick wanted.

Nick moved back around in front of him, letting the pipe cutters hang, attached to the man's thumb joint. "You know, I find it interesting that most of us take opposable thumbs for granted. Just think about the stuff you can't do without them...holding a handgun, a fork...even wiping your ass would be pretty tough to do without thumbs, don't you think?"

"Get those things off my hand...I'll tell you."

"Bet your ass you will," Nick answered as he reached around behind the man and squeezed the handles of the pipe cutters partially together. As the razor-sharp implement ratcheted down, the blade cut into the man's thumb joint, but his hand was still intact. A couple more squeezes, however, and the severed thumb would fall to the floor. Nick jammed the dirty rag into the screaming man's mouth again and bent down so that his face was within a few inches of the mercenary's.

"As you can see, I don't fuck around," Nick said. "Now, unless you want to lose the thumb completely, as well as a lot of other body parts, you'd better tell me what I want to know. Otherwise, my guess is that about the time the pile of meat in front you is bigger than what's left of you, you'll die. But there's a *lot* of pain between that point and where we are now."

The broken man glanced down at the piece of his flesh on the floor in front of him and nodded his head quickly. When Nick removed the rag this time, it was as if a dam had broken. In between choppy breaths, he gave Nick everything he asked for. Further questioning and a couple of well-placed threats satisfied him that the man was telling the truth, although Jenny's location surprised him.

A knock on the door startled Nick. He jammed the rag back into man's mouth, jumped to his feet, and drew his Glock. "Yeah?"

"Nick, it's Randy."

Nick opened the lock and slid the heavy steel door open to let the man in. As requested, he had a Hardigg Storm Case, a small black backpack, and a laptop with him.

"Damn, Nick!" Randy said as he looked at the bound man in front of him.

Nick was moving fast now. "Fire up the laptop and get online—quickly," he ordered. Randy removed the computer from its case and powered up both it and the MiFi device that would allow them to get online.

While his partner was doing that, Nick opened the heavy-duty rifle case and checked to be sure everything was as it should be. Ten spare loaded thirty-round magazines were tucked into a pouch that could be slung over his shoulder. There was also one shorter twenty-round mag in the case. Nick purposely left that one empty and stuck it in his jacket pocket. He verified that the batteries in both the EoTech holographic sight and Crimson Trace vertical fore-grip were good to go and snapped the EoTech 3X magnifier back into place behind the sight. The setup allowed the operator to rotate the magnifier out of the way for close-range work, or lock it in place behind the sight to engage targets further out. The Crimson Trace fore-grip was a combination tactical light and green laser aiming device that could come in very handy.

The short-barreled carbine itself was unique. It was an Advanced Armament Corporation AR-15, made with some of the best components available. The barrel was only nine inches long and chambered for the 300 AAC Blackout cartridge. Although capable of ballistics comparable to the very effective 7.62X39 AK-47 round, when loaded to its maximum powder capacity with lighter bullets, Nick preferred a subsonic load, firing the 220-grain Sierra MatchKing bullet at about 1,000 feet per second—just under the speed of sound. An AAC suppressor completed the rig. Even with the "can" attached, the overall length was about the same as the typical un-suppressed 16-inch barreled carbine.

Contrary to what some believed, "silent" weapons did not exist. Set up the way it was, however, the combination in Nick's hands fired about as quietly as a center-fire weapon was capable of, while remaining very effective on the receiving end—at least at short to moderate ranges. The sound from the firing of the cartridge itself was so well-suppressed that the noise of the semi-automatic action cycling could be clearly heard. This was a small price to pay for self-loading capability, however, and there were ways to mitigate that downside. A bolt-action rifle chambered in the same cartridge would have been even quieter, but not nearly as flexible.

"Okay, we're up and running," Randy announced.

"Good, pull up Google Earth. I know where I'm headed, but I want to find the best way in." The two of them developed a plan and Nick prepared to leave.

"Sorry about the mess," he said as he looked at the blood and flesh on the floor.

"I'm sure you only did what you had to do," his friend assured him.

Nick had a vacant look in his eyes. "I've got to go. Help me get this guy into the trunk of his car."

* * * * * *

Scott had been changing locations every fifteen or twenty minutes, just to be safe. Even though it stood to reason that Payne would try to draw him and Don to wherever they had taken Jenny, he didn't want to be a sitting duck. The unfortunate fact was that they would have to allow themselves to be drawn in eventually, in order to have any shot at saving Jenny. He was about to put the car in drive to move again when his phone rang.

"Yes," he answered, wondering who was calling.

"Hey, it's Nick. Are you guys okay?"

Scott was relieved to hear their partner's voice. "Yeah, we're fine. How about you?"

"I'm good. More importantly, I've got some useful information. Our dark-haired friend turned out to be very helpful when properly motivated."

Scott's mind wandered a bit as he pondered the implications of that statement. He'd been on the receiving end of a couple of "standard" torture techniques during some of the advanced training he'd had in the military, but he'd never had to apply them to others.

During his career in law enforcement, he'd had to play by a set of rules that didn't allow for anything like what he suspected Nick had just done. Torture was distasteful and hard for most people to even acknowledge the existence of. Still, he knew that the tactics were necessary and justified in certain cases…like this one.

"What did you find out?" he asked.

"First of all, there *were* a total of four new players—now three. All of them are former Spec Ops guys. Other than them, there's

Payne, Burke, and Myers. Myers wouldn't be helping them, would he?" Nick asked, knowing the answer before he asked it.

"No," Scott responded, "he wouldn't. Did you find out where they took her?"

"Yeah. They took her to Mike Niculescu's house."

Scott was shocked. "You're sure?" he asked, as he noticed Don staring at him intently from the passenger's seat.

"Yeah, I'm sure. I can tell when I'm being fed something. Believe me, this dude was in the mood to tell the truth, the whole truth, and nothing but the truth. I'm sure you'll be hearing from them soon, so I've got to move it. By the way, how are they going to contact you? As careful as we've been with phones, there's no way they have the number you're using now."

Scott had thought about that, too. "I was waiting till I heard from you. Then I figured I'd call Bobby's cell phone and tell him to give them my number."

"Makes sense. I'm headed there now. I'll get set up and work on a plan. Scott, you need to know that I'll do everything I can to save Don's wife. Let him know that too, okay?"

"I will," Scott assured him.

Nick went on. "We may not be able to communicate once we're both on the premises. In fact, we probably shouldn't try to. My only advantage will be the element of surprise." He hesitated, not really knowing what to say next. Both men were professionals, trying to protect two others who were not. Nick was sure that their instincts would kick in under pressure and, from what he knew of Scott Keller, that thought gave him comfort.

"We're going to have to wing it, Scott. I've acquired some good equipment and I'll neutralize as many of them as possible. I'll try to find out exactly where and how they plan on springing their trap and either take them out or wait for you to show up—depending on the situation. Stay on your toes and trust your instincts."

"Will do, Nick. See ya soon."

Scott filled Don in on the details and he was both stunned and infuriated to find out where they'd taken his wife.

"Bastards," Don mumbled through gritted teeth. "These people deserve to die, Scott."

"Can't argue with that, my friend. Let's make the first priority getting Jenny out of there safely, though."

"I know. I just want to see them pay."

"They will, buddy. They will."

As he dialed Bobby's cell number, Scott thought about his friend. The big man had to hate the fact that he wasn't able to do anything to help. It took four rings for him to answer.

* * * * * *

They were only a couple of miles from Mike Niculescu's house when White heard Myers' cell phone ringing. As Bobby reached into his pocket for the phone, White issued a warning: "Just don't say a word about where you are or what you're doing, Myers."

Bobby held up his middle finger in response and answered his phone.

"This is Myers."

"Hey, buddy, it's Scott."

"Yeah?" was the only response.

To Scott, that meant he was under duress. "Bobby, I know you can't talk. The reason I'm calling you is to make sure they have my number. Go ahead and give it to them, okay?"

"Who is it?" White wanted to know.

Bobby proudly displayed his long middle finger once again, but otherwise ignored the man.

"Yeah, I got it," the ATF agent assured his partner.

"Bobby, we're going to do everything we can to end this thing our way and make these bastards pay, okay?"

"Roger that," Bobby answered, before ending the call.

"Who was that?" White asked, highly annoyed.

"Your fuckin' mom."

******

Brown had started formulating his plan as soon as they pulled up in front of the large shop at the end of Mike Niculescu's very long driveway. His mind worked quickly and he had a knack for details. As a result, it didn't take long for him to get the lay of the land and begin to finalize a plan.

The idea to use this property as a fallback position came to him last night as he was poring over the file on the Niculescu operation. They needed to come up with a suitable location and none of the four members of his team was familiar with the area. They also had very little time available for research.

A computer search for properties that had been foreclosed on (and would therefore be vacant) revealed two decent possibilities. They examined both in some detail and decided that either might have worked in a pinch, but Brown hated the idea of using a place that they knew so little about.

He was almost ready to reluctantly consult Payne when the perfect solution presented itself. The relatively remote nature of Niculescu's property was ideal for what they'd have to do. He also knew that the place was still vacant. Most importantly, though, using Niculescu's house ought to give them a mental advantage over Williams. Forcing the man to come to his dead friend's house to try to save his wife was a stroke of genius, Brown thought proudly. For all these reasons, this was their predetermined Plan B when things went wrong at Pioneer Square.

Payne had grumbled when Brown called him very early this morning and told him to bring the keys to the Niculescu property. They were in the lockup with a lot of other evidence and Payne would not have had the patience to search for them. The natural thing for him to do was to call Ray Burke and make sure that he arrived early enough to find them. Once again, his deputy had come through. Though both wondered why Brown would need the keys to that property, Payne's questions to that effect went unanswered.

The first thing Brown did upon their arrival was to personally check out the house itself. The surveillance system mentioned in the file could be helpful if it was still operational. He verified that there was still electricity coming to the property and fired up the system. It would take a little while for all the cameras to come online. While he was doing that, he ordered Red to take the keys and unlock every door in the house and shop. Coming and going freely could become very important if things went down the wrong way—as they already had once today.

The team leader then walked out to the huge six-bay shop, checking to be sure that Jenny Williams was still in the backseat of the car as he passed by. Inside the shop were various motorcycles and ATVs. The shop was neat, clean, and well-lit. Tools were strewn around on the benches and floor, but Brown doubted that was the case prior to ATF's search of the premises. His sense was that Niculescu had been a squared-away dude. Beyond simply being impressed, though, Brown liked the shop for another reason.

"Red?" he shouted.

"Yeah," the man answered as he ran in from outside.

"We're going to use the shop to do this thing. Let's get the toys off to the sides, so the middle is clear."

Soon, the shop was set up to Brown's satisfaction. The two men walked back outside, just in time to see the Suburban pull up. White, Burke, and Myers got out of the vehicle. Brown knew which one Myers was and that meant the other was Burke. Handling Myers presented a bit of a problem. They'd decided to initially maintain the charade that he was part of the team and Brown knew that White probably could have handled the situation if things had gotten out of hand. Now that they had him here, though, that was no longer necessary.

Bobby's mind was a blur as he processed his surroundings and tried to determine the best time to make a move. He still had his gun, but had to be careful choosing the time and place to do whatever he would end up doing. These guys were well-armed and there would be only one chance.

Brown stared at Myers. He was an intimidating figure and it made no sense at this point to allow him to remain armed and free. "Myers, right?" he asked.

"Good guess. Who are you?"

Brown didn't hesitate. In one smooth motion, he brushed back the right side of his jacket, drew his handgun, and shot Bobby in the left thigh. The big man fell, clutching his leg and screaming.

"Take his gun and search him for anything else," Brown ordered. Payne and Burke appeared to be in shock as White and Red searched Myers.

White removed Bobby's handgun and cell phone. "He took a call a couple of minutes ago and we're pretty sure it was Keller."

"Okay, get the number off of it, take him in the shop, and tie his hands."

"You want us to slow down the bleeding?" White asked, looking at the blood already pooling on the driveway.

"Yeah. Get him inside the shop and pack it with QuikClot. There's some in my bag."

Brown didn't want the man dead—yet. If he had, his shot placement would have been far different. Flexibility in an operation was important. He knew that Myers and Keller had become buddies and that relationship might become useful at some point. When the time came, Myers would die like the rest of them.

By now, Brown knew exactly how he would handle things when Williams and Keller arrived. The next step was to call them and get them here. He was worried about the fact that Black hadn't shown up yet and had to assume the worst—though he wasn't sure what the worst might be. There was a better than even chance that it had something to do with Larsen, though.

He figured he was down one man and didn't trust Payne or Burke to be of much help when the balloon went up. Brown walked over to the door of the shop and stuck his head inside. "Red, grab an M4 and patrol the perimeter of the property. Be sure to take a radio with you, too."

* * * * * *

Scott had just pulled into a county park when his cell phone rang. He looked at Don and answered it. "This is Keller."

"Is Williams with you?"

"Yes. Who is this?"

"Don't worry about that. How about Larsen?"

"I don't know who you're—"

Brown cut him off. "Don't waste my time, Marshal. Is Larsen with you or not?"

"No. We got separated at the Square and I haven't heard from him since," Scott lied.

Brown didn't believe him, but there wasn't much he could do about it at the moment. "Okay. Here's the deal. You and Williams are to make your way to Mike Niculescu's house, ASAP. You remember how to get here, don't you?" Brown asked sarcastically.

Scott knew he needed to act surprised by the location. "*Niculescu's* house? Why would you—"

"You don't need to worry about anything but getting here quickly. How far out are you?"

"I don't know for sure. Maybe thirty to forty-five minutes."

"Then I expect to hear from you in a half hour or so. You're to call me back at this number when you're outside the gate to the property. I'll give you further instructions at that time. Oh, and Keller?"

"Yeah?"

"You'd better not bring anyone else with you. I'll have people watching the route in and we'll know if you do. We can be cleared out of here in a matter of minutes and Williams will never see his wife again. Do I make myself clear?"

"Yeah, I understand," Scott replied. He knew the man was lying about having enough bodies to cover the route in, but he had no plans to bring anyone else anyway. Scott knew that, if he did so, regardless of how well things went otherwise, it was a near certainty that Jenny would die. Their "plan," imperfect though it was, was their best chance.

Don was demanding that Scott give him the phone. "Williams wants to talk to you," he told Brown.

Scott had the mouthpiece covered as he handed Don the phone. "Be calm," he whispered.

Don took a deep breath and spoke into the phone. "Who are you?"

"None of your business."

"I want to know that my wife's all right before we come to you. I want to talk to her."

Brown didn't answer him, but walked over to the car that Payne was guarding, opened the back door, and handed his phone to Jenny. Hearing her voice might actually ensure that Williams would do what he was supposed to, Brown thought. "Here, your husband wants to talk to you."

Her hands shaking violently, Jenny put the phone to her ear and spoke. "Don? Are you really there?"

His emotions almost overcame him and he found it hard to breathe, but Don knew he had to be strong for her. "Yes, baby, I'm here. And we're coming to get you. Don't worry—this will all turn out okay. I'm so sorry that—"

"If you ever want to hear her voice again, you'll make sure Keller does *exactly* what I've told him to," Brown threatened before hanging up.

Don handed the phone back to Scott. The Marshal studied his face and was surprised that he'd kept himself together. He continued to be impressed with this man. "Let's go get her, Don."

"Scott, you know they're going to try to kill us all."

There was no sense in sugarcoating the situation. "Yeah, I do. We'll figure something out...and Nick's pretty good."

******

Nick turned onto a gravel road. He was about a mile away from Mike's property and would go the rest of the way on foot, approaching from the back. Making sure no one was around, he got out of the car, draped his jacket over the rifle, made sure the Glock was ready to go, and walked around to the trunk. He'd thought about burning the car, but the fire would present problems as well. After considering his options, Nick simply wiped it down for prints, as best he could. If he made it through this thing alive, he planned on using the car to get out of the area. If not, his fingerprints wouldn't matter. Nick Larsen always covered his tracks, though. On the off chance that he made it out alive but got away by other means, he'd prefer to not leave his prints all over the vehicle. *Wipe away every trace.*

Then there was the matter of the fellow in the trunk. Obviously, he could either kill him or let him live. He wasn't worried about being implicated by him. In fact, the thought of this guy in the hands of the cops brought a smile to his face—he would present a lot of problems for whoever gave the orders.

Nick had put the man through hell, though, and he didn't like the idea of a guy like this coming after him to get even—just the kind of thing a guy like this was likely to do. He also knew that the man would have killed *him* in an instant, if given the chance.

Nick had been operating in a different mode these last few days. He was using instincts and skills that he wasn't sure he still had and was glad to find out that he did. He seemed to be thriving on the adrenaline and wondered briefly what that said about him. Then he stopped wondering. He reminded himself again that these bastards had brought the fight to him. You either played the game by the same rules they did, or you lost—and he wasn't about to let that happen.

He calmly flipped the carbine's safety off and opened the trunk. Not surprisingly, the bound and gagged man stared at him with eyes full of hatred. That made it easy. He put the muzzle a foot away from the man's face and pulled the trigger twice. The minimal sound was further muffled by the trunk and his jacket. He calmly picked up the two pieces of hot spent brass, put them in his pocket, and closed the trunk.

Moving at a fast pace, the walk to the back of his old friend's property took only about fifteen minutes. Nick decided to enter along the northern boundary of the property. Mike's thirty acres was bordered by a neighbor's parcel of about the same size and both were planted in Christmas trees—which would make fantastic cover from which to approach the buildings. His primary concern was the surveillance system that, ironically, he had talked Mike into installing and helped him design a couple of years before. Assuming that the electricity hadn't been turned off, the cameras could present a problem.

Nick remembered that there were cameras at each of the property's four corners, but that none of them allowed a view of the entire fence line that stretched between them. That gave him the opening he needed to get onto the property undetected. The plan was to enter the back corner of the neighbor's property to the north and then come down the fence line till he was directly across from Mike's house. At that point he hoped to have some sense of where Don's wife was being held.

Nick had started to move down the fence line on the neighbor's side when he heard a twig snap. He froze and heard a whispered voice and then a response. The man was talking on a radio. He'd apparently stopped, but was now moving again—toward Nick's position. Nick readied himself. The EoTech magnifier had already been rotated out of the way. The man should pass within fifteen yards of his position if he stayed on the perimeter trail. As soon as he came into the EoTech's field of view, Nick saw his target's M4, put the red dot on his ear, and squeezed the trigger once. The suppressed round dropped the man without even a twitch.

Nick was pretty sure that he was in a blind spot for the cameras. He crawled over to the dead man, grabbed his radio, and continued on. A few minutes later, he was looking at the back of Mike's house and allowed his mind to drift—for only a moment. The last time he'd been here, Mike had grilled steaks for them on this same porch, while the two friends sipped good bourbon and reminisced. *This is for you, buddy.*

Taking in the scene, he noticed that there appeared to be no activity inside the house. The shop, on the other hand, was clearly occupied and a couple of times during the few minutes that he observed, men came and went through the side door. It looked as if whatever they had planned would take place in there.

The first thing Nick wanted to do was get inside the house, because he knew that there was a camera feed from the interior of the shop. Before he could, though, he had to do something about the camera that looked directly at the back of the house. If anyone was monitoring the system—and he had to assume one of them would be—that camera had to be taken out before he could get inside.

Having eliminated the threat posed by the red-headed man on the perimeter, Nick was fairly certain that the rest of them were inside either the shop or the house. With a round already chambered, he quietly replaced the thirty-round magazine in the carbine with the empty twenty-round version from his pocket. His reasoning was simple: doing so would cause the short-barreled rifle to lock open on the empty magazine after the round was fired, eliminating the sound of the bolt slamming home and chambering another cartridge. Sure, the bullet's impact would make a sound as well, but he had no control over that.

His target was mounted to the top of a light pole at the edge of the trees. Nick took careful aim and squeezed the trigger. The small camera exploded with a slight metallic clank that seemed much louder to Nick than it probably was.

He quickly replaced the empty magazine with a fully-loaded thirty-rounder and waited for a couple of minutes to see if anyone came running—no one did. He eased the bolt closed and used the forward assist to be sure the round was fully chambered. Taking a deep breath, he broke into the clearing and approached the back door of the house.

* * * * * *

Bobby was lying on his side in a corner of the shop, largely ignored by his captors as they came and went. Several minutes before, he'd been able to work his way a few feet over to a small gardening spade that was on the floor under one of the workbenches. Using his good leg, he was able to move it enough to reach it with his hands, which had been tied behind his back. Now, sawing back and forth with the spade, he could feel the rope starting to give.

He'd lost a lot of blood before the QuikClot had done its job and Bobby was afraid he might lose consciousness—one more reason he had to act quickly. Brown, White, and Payne were putting things in place and it sounded as if Scott and Williams would be here any minute.

The big man had worked his hands free and White was walking his way. *Perfect—I've been waiting for this!* Unsure of how quickly he'd be able to move, Bobby waited till the man was just a few feet away and rose as quickly as he could when White turned around to say something to Brown.

The blond man caught Bobby's arm just before the spade sank into his throat. They spun around and Bobby slammed him against the wall. Even in his weakened state, Bobby was still bull-strong, especially with an extra dose of adrenaline.

Brown had to be careful about shooting, for fear of hitting his own man. The tip of the spade was just starting to puncture the skin of White's throat. Realizing that he was about to die, the big blond man pushed back on Bobby's arm with all he had and turned his body quickly to his left—away from Bobby. That was the opening Brown had been waiting for. He fired three quick shots into Bobby's back and the ATF agent slumped to the ground. White felt the gash on his neck and stared down at Bobby's body. "Sonofabitch!"

Brown was running out of what little patience he'd had to begin with. "You're fine. Now let's get everything ready. They'll be here any minute!"

* * * * * *

Burke was sitting at the desk in Niculescu's study. He'd been monitoring the cameras from inside the house for a half hour or so—a task that was just fine with him. He'd doubted their course of action from the very beginning. And now that Mullin's boys were involved…well, things could only end horribly. He knew he couldn't wash his hands of what was about to happen, but he also knew that he couldn't pull a trigger on Myers or Keller…much less Williams or his wife. Inside the house and away from the rest of them was probably the best place Burke could possibly be.

The large computer screen that he was viewing the camera feeds on could be set up to see four of the eight cameras at once, on a split screen. He could then toggle back and forth, so that with one keystroke he could cover all eight of them. Switching back to the inside of the shop, Burke stared intently as he watched Myers attack White. Then came Brown's three gunshots. It was surreal to watch it happen in such a detached way.

After a minute or so, Burke forced himself to check the other four cameras. *That's odd.* One of them—the one covering the back of the house—was dark. He clicked on the main security system screen to check its status and then tried to pull it up again. Still dark. *What was that noise?* Burke turned to face the door while fumbling for his handgun.

He was way too late, however. Nick's rifle coughed and Burke's head flung violently back against the executive chair he'd been sitting in. Moving with real purpose now, Nick kicked the rolling chair out of the way. As he did so, Burke's lifeless body slumped to the side and fell onto the floor.

Nick checked his watch and looked at the computer screen. It took a couple of minutes for him to recall how to toggle between cameras, but he finally was able to pull up the one with a view of the shop. He could see a man he assumed to be Bobby Myers lying motionless on the floor and he got a sense of where the other three men would be stationed. Then he saw Jenny. *Crude but effective*, he thought.

Now that he had some idea of what he would face inside the shop, his course of action was relatively clear. There was a small apartment unit above the shop, which Mike had finished off a few years before to use as a guest room. They used to joke that it would make a great mother-in-law unit if you wanted to get her as far away from the rest of the family as possible. The three bad guys left were all inside the shop. Two stairways led up to the apartment. One was inside the shop—obviously not a possibility. The other was at the back of the building's exterior. Nick looked quickly through the desk drawers for keys, to no avail. He'd have to hope the door to the second floor apartment was unlocked, or break in somehow.

******

As he'd been instructed to do, Scott called Brown when they got to the gate. It opened by remote control and he was told to park in front of the shop and walk in through the side door on the south end.

As they drove down the long driveway, Don remembered the last time he was here, when he and Mike had walked along this same path. They hadn't agreed on much that night. Now, Don thought about how wise his friend had been. The fact that this kind of nightmare could take place in this country meant that Mike had been right about virtually everything. Don shook his head vigorously. He needed to concentrate on Jenny. He'd give himself up in a second for even the slightest chance that she could get away, but he knew he'd have to be smart about it. They assumed that Nick had put a plan into motion and Scott had warned Don not to do something stupid that might jeopardize that plan.

Scott's mind was in tactical overdrive. He considered several options. One of them involved his getting out of the car along the driveway and sneaking up through the trees. Another was to ram one of the three huge roll-up shop doors with the car. There were problems with both courses of action, however. First of all, they had to assume they were being watched—with cameras, if nothing else—and if he rammed the car through a door, he could easily hit Jenny. He decided, in the end, to trust that Nick would come through.

******

Brown wasn't particularly happy with the state of things. He'd lost contact with both Red and Burke. That meant Larsen was probably running around unaccounted for.

On a brighter note, however, in a matter of seconds, Williams and Keller should be walking through the door that his M4 was trained on—directly across from him. Brown hunkered down behind two huge stainless-steel toolboxes and waited. White was just twenty feet away from the door, along the same wall and Payne was diagonal to him, in the far corner. They had the shop well covered.

Brown didn't think much of the HOT Commander and wouldn't have trusted him to do anything complicated. As things had turned out, though, he might actually come in handy. If he was required to do it, the one job Payne had been given would be a simple one.

Brown's idea was to take out Keller, and Larsen, if he showed up, and then leave with Williams and his wife. He'd kill them and get rid of the bodies where they'd never be found. Director Mullin wanted a story for the press that at least had the appearance of a reasonable explanation. It wouldn't take much, but he had to give them something.

If everything went according to plan, Payne would be having a press conference tomorrow, at which he would announce that ATF agent Bobby Myers had received information leading him to believe that an associate of Niculescu's (Larsen) was on his way to recover hidden firearms from the home of the deceased felon. Tragically—the story would go—Myers and his friend, Deputy Marshal Scott Keller, who was assisting him, were killed in a shootout with the highly trained Larsen. The story wasn't perfect, but they could make it work.

******

Nick was greatly relieved to find the upstairs apartment door unlocked. He hoped all three men were still downstairs in the shop as he carefully pushed the door open. As quietly as possible, he entered and closed the door behind him. The door on the other side of the small apartment led down to the shop. It was cracked open slightly and Nick could clearly hear a man's voice. "They'll be coming through that door in a matter of seconds. Payne, if I give you the signal, you know what to do."

Nick crept across the room, his soft-soled boots not making a sound, and peeked out through the doorway. From that angle, he could see nothing in the shop. He started down the stairs slowly, thankful that his friend had overbuilt everything he'd ever made—so far, there hadn't been a single squeaky board.

The stairway was a two-section affair, with a landing halfway down, after which the stairs went in the opposite direction. Due to this layout, Nick was concealed all the way down to the small landing. He made it there and peeked over the railing—still a half-story above the people in the shop. Nick had the advantage: the three men were all concentrating on the side door rather than looking up.

Payne was the only one of them directly in his line of vision. He would have to expose himself in order to shoot, but that didn't matter. Once he pulled the trigger, all hell would break loose.

* * * * * *

Don and Scott had no idea what they would find inside the shop, but there was no choice except to open the door. Scott would go in first. He looked behind him at Don, nodded, and slowly pushed the door open.

"Both of you come in and close the door behind you," Brown ordered. He'd considered shooting Keller as soon as he was inside the shop, but he had a feeling that Larsen was sneaking around and thought Keller might be useful as an additional hostage. As long as Brown disarmed the Marshal, he wouldn't present much of a problem—so there was no real risk in keeping him alive, for the moment.

Don followed behind Scott and was about to close the door

when he froze, staring at his wife. She was perched precariously on the top rung of a tall stepladder—hands tied behind her and a gag in her mouth. What rendered him unable to move, however, was the fact that there was also a noose around her neck. The other end of the rope was tied to a rafter two stories high, with very little slack in it.

She was situated on the far side of the shop. The farthest two bays were the only ones with exposed rafters, due to the apartment above the other four. Mike had wanted to leave some rafters exposed so that he could mount a hoist for working on his machinery.

"If you both do what I tell you to, she'll be fine, and the two of you can walk away from this, Don," Brown lied.

Then both men noticed the rope tied to the bottom of the ladder and followed it to the corner, where Payne stood.

"Payne, you sonofabitch!" Scott said through clenched teeth.

"Shut up, Keller." Brown again. "I want you to slowly remove your handgun from its holster, put it on the floor, and slide it toward me."

Scott did as he was told, while keeping an eye on Brown. He also glanced quickly to his right and saw that a big blond man had an M4 aimed at him as well. He put his pistol on the floor and stood, then kicked it toward Brown. It hit one of the shop's support beams and stopped several feet short of him.

"Lift up your shirt and your pant legs," Brown ordered.

Scott exposed the Scandium-framed Smith and Wesson revolver that he always carried in an ankle holster. "That one, too." Once again, he complied.

"Now get on your knees and put your hands behind your head." Scott hesitated. "NOW, or Payne yanks that ladder out from under her!" Scott knelt on the ground and locked his hands behind his head. *Any second now would be nice, Nick!*

Brown checked Don for weapons in the same manner and was satisfied that he was clean. Then came the moment of truth. "Don, I want you to walk toward me slowly."

"No! You let her down and I'll go with you without a fight!"

"Get over here, or I'll hang her and shoot you where you stand,"

Brown countered in a firm but eerily calm voice.

Don started slowly walking toward the man.

* * * * * *

Nick shouldered his rifle and raised himself to the point where he could just see over the railing. He leaned forward enough to have a clear shot. With Payne holding the rope that was attached to the ladder, there was no margin for error. If Nick's shot was even slightly off the mark, Payne could flail about and pull the ladder out from under Jenny. Nick would have to "rag doll" him.

As Don started to walk toward Brown, the red dot in Nick's Eo-Tech settled on Payne's temple and the slow squeeze began. At the shot, Payne dropped as if the floor had been pulled out from under him.

Though the report from Nick's rifle was very quiet, it was loud enough inside the enclosed shop to cause Brown to focus on his position. Nick knew this would be the case and began to quickly move down the stairs. At this point, there was nothing to do but react to what the bad guys did and shoot back. His plan had run its course.

Brown cut loose several rounds in his direction and the 5.56 mm bullets ripped through the drywall that was shielding Nick. He was hit and rolled the rest of the way down the stairs to the concrete floor. He lost his rifle on the stairs, but began returning fire with his Glock—keeping Brown behind cover for the moment.

Scott started running toward White, whose attention had been drawn to the stairs when Nick fired. White turned just in time to get off a shot that tore through the Marshal's midsection. Scott's guts felt as if they were on fire as he fell on top of the man who'd just shot him, knocking him to the ground. White threw him off, got up on a knee, and was about to finish him off at powder-burn distance when two shots from behind White came ripping through the large blond man's chest. Scott rolled over onto his hands and knees while reaching for the dead man's carbine.

Don grabbed Scott's handgun from off the floor, where it had stopped at the base of a support beam. Brown was firing at Nick, who'd squeezed in behind two ATVs for cover, but couldn't hold out much longer. Then Brown noticed Scott going for White's M4 and began to swing his rifle toward the Marshal.

Gripping the pistol tightly, Don approached Brown from his blind spot. He raised the pistol and leveled it at Brown just as the mercenary was putting pressure on his M4's trigger.

"Put the gun down and get your hands in the air," Don ordered. The words sounded strange to him. *That couldn't have come out of my mouth.*

Brown whipped his head to his right and then smiled. He couldn't believe he'd taken his eye off the prize.

"Now settle down, Don," Brown said in the same eerie-calm voice he'd used before. He also started to slowly rotate the M4 to his right. "You and I both know you don't want to shoot—"

Don squeezed the trigger once, and then again and again, until the man fell backward. Then he ran toward the ladder, put the handgun on the floor, and climbed up to his wife. He slipped the noose off and helped her down. They stood wrapped in each other's arms and she sobbed.

"It's all right, baby. I'm here," he assured her.

The smell of gunfire was thick in the enclosed shop, but it was surprisingly quiet. After a few seconds, it occurred to Don that he and Jenny were the only two left standing. Thirty feet to his right, Scott was trying to crawl toward where Payne lay dead. Then Don noticed the other man next to Payne.

As Scott crawled toward Bobby's body, Nick was extricating himself from the twisted steel that had been two ATVs a few minutes earlier. "You okay?" Scott asked him.

"I'm gonna need repairs, but I think I'll make it," Nick answered. "How about you?"

Before Scott could answer, he dropped the rest of the way to the floor while still trying to crawl. Nick reached into his coat pocket for his cell phone and slid it toward Don. "Here, call 911! They're probably on their way already, but tell 'em we need an ambulance."

Nick limped over to Scott. He knelt down, rolled the Marshal over, and looked at the wound.

Scott knew it was bad. "Through and through?" he asked.

Nick nodded his head. "Yeah."

"Well, that's good," Scott answered through clenched teeth. "Help me over to Bobby."

Nick looked over and saw Bobby Myers lying on his stomach, in a huge pool of blood. As they got closer, Scott could also see that there was a handgun in his right hand. Thinking back, he knew that Nick couldn't have been in a position to shoot White. Bobby had multiple gunshot wounds, but apparently had still been able to drag himself over to Payne and grab his pistol.

Bobby's head was turned toward him and his eyes were barely open. He was trying to whisper something that they couldn't hear.

"What's that, buddy?" Scott asked as he lowered his ear to Bobby's mouth.

"Payne got off easy."

Scott and Nick looked over at Payne's lifeless and nearly decapitated body. "I don't know about that, pal." As much blood as Bobby had lost, Scott couldn't believe he was still breathing.

Scott sat up as much as he was able to, looked down at Bobby, and then at Nick—as if to ask, "What do you think?" Nick shook his head and Scott cleared his throat. "We've got help coming, Bobby. Just hang in there."

Nick reached down and closed the big man's eyes. "He's gone, Scott. And if we don't get you taken care of fast, you will be too."

"Nick, you didn't shoot that big blond guy, did you?" Scott asked, just to be sure.

"No way. I was pinned down over there," indicating the corner behind the ATVs. Then it occurred to him as well. "It had to be Myers. But how…in that kind of shape?"

Scott just nodded and smiled. Nick looked down at Scott's wound again and ordered Jenny to grab all the clean shop rags she could find.

"Keep pressure on this thing, Scott. You'll make it. The ambulance is almost here." They could hear the sirens wailing in the distance.

"Where are you going?" Scott asked Nick, his voice very weak.

"You know I can't hang around here."

Scott understood. "Take care of yourself, brother."

"Roger that. You too."

Nick limped back up the stairs and grabbed his rifle. On the way back down, he noticed the single shell casing from the shot he'd fired at Payne. He picked it up and put it in his pocket. *Cover your tracks, Nick.*

It was time to go. The bullet wound in his side was starting to bleed heavily. He grabbed a handful of rags and headed for the same door that Don and Scott had come through a little earlier.

Don looked up from Scott's side. "Where are you going, Nick?"

Nick turned and looked at him. "I don't want to be around when the good guys get here. Just tell 'em you've never heard of me, okay?"

Don got up and ran over to him. "Nick, you're hurt...bad. You're going to need a doctor."

"Don't worry—I know a couple."

"Nick, I'll never be able to thank you enough for all you've done. I owe you my life, several times over."

Nick looked over at Jenny, then back at Don. "You don't owe me a thing. Just promise me you'll enjoy the rest of your lives together."

"I can promise you that," Don said, sticking his hand out.

Nick shook his hand. "Don, you did well. You really did. Not just today, but from the beginning. You should really be proud of yourself. I know Mike would have been proud of you."

"That means more than anything to me, Nick."

"I know it does. And I mean every word of it." The sirens were getting very loud now. "I need to get out of here," he said, wincing as he turned and walked out the door.

******

The paramedics went to work on Scott immediately. They had to get him into surgery ASAP and Don and Jenny demanded to ride to the hospital with him.

There was some explaining to do, of course, but Don's friend, Detective Walt Harris, showed up at the scene and took control. He put Don and Jenny in his unmarked car and followed the ambulance to the hospital. There would be time for questioning at the sheriff's office later.

* * * * * *

Nick turned onto a narrow road and drove until he saw the large gravel pit up ahead. He made sure nobody else was in the area, pulled the car down into the pit, and got out. There was a can of gasoline in the trunk that he'd brought from Randy's warehouse and he doused the car inside and out.

Nick was almost in a trance as he reached into his pack for one of the butane torch-type lighters that he always carried. He pushed the button to light it, then slid the catch that locked it in the on position. Nick stared at the small blue flame for a few seconds, then opened the door and tossed the lighter inside. *Wipe away every trace*, he thought as the car was almost instantly engulfed in flames.

As he turned and began limping out of the gravel pit, he knew that, although he could never bring Mike and Sarah back, he had avenged their deaths—or at least had begun the process. He'd also played a major role in keeping Don and Jenny Williams alive.

It had been a long time since Nick Larsen had felt so useful.

Epilogue

"I am persuaded myself that the good sense of the people will always be found to be the best army. They may be led astray for a moment, but will soon correct themselves."

—Thomas Jefferson

Washington, D.C.
Thursday, June 13

THE SOUND OF their footsteps echoed loudly off the polished sandstone and marble of the House corridor. As they made their way out of the Capitol Building, Don realized that he was experiencing one of the best days of his life. He hadn't merely been privy to the inner workings of the greatest republic ever created—that experience could be replicated by a tour and a night spent watching C-SPAN. More importantly, he'd witnessed it actually *working.*

As it had in relatively few instances throughout U.S. history, today the United States Congress had put the Constitution *first*—not subjugating it to the political whims of the moment. It had listened to the people that it represents and sided with them against the squealing and entrenched bureaucracy. Some people saw everything the government did as evil, while to others it could do no wrong. Neither perspective was correct, of course. Several weeks ago, Don had witnessed the seamy side of the most powerful institution in the Free World. Today, he had seen that institution live up to the expectations of Jefferson and Madison.

The last six weeks had passed Don by in a blur. *The Oregonian* ran a story the morning after the shootout, of course, and the phone calls began shortly after the paper hit the stands. Initially it was treated as just another regional ATF bust turned violent (of which there had been so many that people had grown numb to them). In the days that followed, however, his story grew into front-page news across the country. Investigative journalists representing entities ranging from the *New York Times* to the *National Enquirer* began to contact Don and he spent hours turning down requests for interviews. As far as he was concerned, Jim Schaefer could do whatever he wanted with the story. He'd promised him that much and Schaefer had held up his end of the bargain by keeping quiet when it was necessary. Besides, Don was tired of the subject.

There had also been multiple questioning sessions with both local and federal law enforcement personnel. Don had, after all, been unsuccessful in obtaining any real evidence to prove that Payne had falsified his record. Ultimately, however, the hard-to-explain presence of the mercenaries' bodies and an interview conducted with Deputy Marshal Scott Keller from his hospital bed had been enough to convince the U.S. Attorney's office that pursuing a case against Don Williams was not in the federal government's best interest.

Then, a little more than a week after the shootout at Mike's house, Don received a letter asking him to testify before a congressional committee. That trip was made on short notice and there had been little pomp and circumstance about it. He was one of many witnesses—albeit the most important one—regarding ATF excesses committed as a result of the Collection policy's enforcement.

To their credit, most members of the committee from both sides of the aisle seemed genuinely interested in what Don and the others had to say. Of course, there was a handful who insisted that he *must* have done something wrong to attract the attention of the ATF in the first place, but they were insignificant in the end.

The result of the hearing was a suspension of all Collection activity until the matter could be debated by the full House. It was determined that this particular law could not be enforced without an "unreasonable" number of casualties—within both the civilian and law enforcement communities. Though obviously pleased with that outcome, Don wondered cynically what a "reasonable" number might be.

Additionally, further registration of firearms and licensing of their owners would cease. Collection and registration/licensing—laws passed a couple of years apart—would be debated together, as they should have been in the first place. Having witnessed how one policy led to the other, the American people demanded that both policies be reviewed, which ultimately led to the laws being repealed.

There were other repercussions as well. Heads usually rolled when the federal government overreached and this time was no exception. *Someone* had to take the fall for what had happened. The question was, how high up the chain of command would the sacrifice be made? It turned out that when the music stopped playing, the last one standing was ATF Director John Mullin, who made the decision to resign, "for the good of the country as well as this great organization."

Attorney General Martinez managed to save himself and the President deflected all criticism with aplomb, but it really didn't matter. The country was only a few months away from an election and it wasn't looking good for the incumbent. It seemed the American people blamed the President for talking them into supporting Collection—a cop-out, as far as Don was concerned.

Scott Keller had recovered fully and was looking forward to becoming a father. He and Don were keeping in touch.

Nick Larsen was a different story. Don tried every way he could think of to contact him, to no avail. Then, a couple of weeks after the shootout, he received a letter. It was short and to the point—typical for the ex-CIA man. "All is well on my end. Say hi to all the fancy people in D.C. for me. Enjoy life, Nick."

Though he would like to, Don doubted that he'd ever see Nick again. Whether or not he did, though, he would never forget the man who had saved his life more than once.

Over the last month and a half since the shootout, the most substantive and important thing Don had done was to immerse himself totally in his family. *That* was where he belonged and where he would spend as much time as possible. He'd learned that life truly was too short and he vowed never again to take for granted the people that he loved. His career was important, but his family was infinitely more so.

When the second surprise invitation to Washington came two weeks ago, Don knew that it had to be a family affair. The kids had just finished school and they decided to turn it into the family vacation that they hadn't had in a long time.

"Thanks again, Congressman, for asking us to be a part of this. It really means a lot," Don said as he put his arm around Clay's shoulders. "Besides, it was the best history lesson these guys will ever get." Don, Clay, George, Ana, and the Niculescu children were walking down the Capitol steps with Congressman Skiles. Jenny had decided to take their two little ones to do something more befitting their ages.

The Congressman had called Don at home the day after the shootout, just to make sure he was all right. Skiles promised him he'd be back in touch soon and he had kept his word.

"I wouldn't have had it any other way, Don. I firmly believe that your perseverance and guts had more to do with the outcome today than anything I or anyone else in Congress did." Skiles wanted Don and the Niculescu family to be present when the vote was taken to repeal both pieces of legislation. It seemed appropriate.

Don shook his head. "Oh, no. If it hadn't been for Marshal Keller and—" He caught himself before Nick's name slipped out. It wasn't the first time he'd come close to saying it when he shouldn't have and it probably wouldn't be the last. "If it wasn't for Scott Keller, I wouldn't have stood a chance." Then Don's eyes got a faraway look. "And Bobby Myers, of course. I wish I'd gotten to know him. He died trying to help me and I never even got to shake his hand." The entire Williams family, along with George and Ana and the Niculescu children, had attended Bobby's funeral and it had occurred to Don that Bobby and Mike had had a lot in common.

Don shook his head, as if to clear his mind of such serious thoughts for the moment. "Funny thing, though. Marshal Keller wasn't at all excited about coming to D.C. with us," he said with a smirk on his face.

Skiles laughed. "Well, this town certainly isn't for everyone, but it's really not a bad place. Believe it or not, there are actually a bunch of us around here who come to work every day and try our best to do the right thing, even if we disagree about what that is."

Don knew that he might never again have the chance to speak his mind in so ideal an environment, so he couldn't resist the urge. Once again, he was aware of the effect that Mike had had on him and he wanted to get in a parting shot for his dead friend.

"You know, Congressman, that brings up something that I've been thinking about in all my spare time over the last few weeks," he began. "Don't you think that the more comfortable Congress gets with the idea of doing things *for* us, the more natural it feels to do something like this *to* us?" Don wondered if that sounded as confrontational as it felt. But then he thought about what Mike would say. *These guys are no better than we are. They were sent here by us to do a job on our behalf—that's all.* "What I'm saying is that this is really about more than gun control, isn't it?"

Skiles stopped at the bottom of the steps and turned to face his constituent. He'd been thinking along the very same lines since the debate over Collection first began, though that was a tough thing for him to admit. The lawmaker smiled. "The thought has crossed my mind a time or two as well." He paused and looked carefully at Don. "You know, even if I manage to get re-elected this time, I can almost guarantee that there'll be an open congressional seat in our district the next time around. You ever think about running for Congress?"

Don laughed. "Not even for a second," he answered.

The Congressman held up his hands. "Okay, but never say never. Now, if you'll excuse me, I've got an appointment across the mall in about fifteen minutes. I really appreciate you all making the trip out, though."

George hugged Ana to him with one arm and stuck the other hand out to the Congressman. They were both busting with pride at having witnessed the wheels of their adopted country's government turning. "Sir, I must say you are very good man. My son would have like very much to meet you. Thank you. Thank you for everything."

"You're welcome. Once again, I'm very sorry for your loss. I know your son and his wife were wonderful people. I suppose the only consolation is that the country has learned a very important lesson from this tragedy."

I sure hope so, Don thought as he watched the Congressman walk away. The United States had just passed the kind of constitutional test both envisioned and feared by its founders—barely and not without a huge cost. *How many more tests can it stand?* he wondered.

* * * * * *

Chesapeake Beach, Maryland
Late June

It was an absolutely perfect early summer night on Chesapeake Bay. A light breeze was coming off the water and it was warm enough for only a sweater. John Mullin twirled what remained of the brandy in his snifter and took a smooth draw on the Cuban cigar. His wife was out for the evening and he was taking full advantage of the peace and quiet.

Although his world had changed dramatically in the sense that his law enforcement and political careers were over, it was not as if he had nothing to live for. He'd received numerous invitations for speaking engagements since his resignation and he was set financially, thanks to a very large inheritance that his wife had received a few years earlier.

His future would be far different from what he could have imagined just a few months back, but it would remain perfectly tolerable,

Mullin thought as he drained the last of the brandy.

As he reached to put the snifter on the small glass-top table beside his chair, Mullin heard the voice.

"Nothing like fine brandy and a good cigar, is there?"

The startled former ATF Director dropped the glass. It rolled off the table and broke on the deck.

"Don't turn around," the man said, calmly but forcefully.

Mullin froze. "Who are you?"

"That's not important. What *is* important is that you understand there are consequences to your actions."

"What are you talking about?"

"Let's just say that justice wasn't fully served by your resignation."

"Look…I–I can give you money—a lot of money. Whatever you're talking about, we can make it right," Mullin stammered. He was starting to become hysterical.

"I don't want money. Haven't you heard that money can't buy happiness?" The man wanted to toy with Mullin a little. He wanted him to beg—and it didn't take long.

"I'll do whatever you want…anything at all!"

The man standing behind him had been trying to decide how to do it. There was the suppressed .22 handgun in his right hand and the garrote in his pocket. Either would be sufficiently quiet. But then he looked down at the broken brandy snifter on the deck. A jagged portion of it was still attached to the stem. He returned the handgun to its shoulder holster, reached down, and picked up the razor-sharp piece of glass. He'd thought from the beginning that he'd prefer to make the death look accidental, if possible.

"Just name it. I–I'll do anything. I'll pay for whatever I've done," Mullin pleaded.

"You're damn right you will," the man assured him as he quickly grabbed Mullin's hair with his left hand and plunged the jagged glass into his carotid artery with his right. Blood began spurting immediately from the gaping wound and the assassin pulled Mullin's body to his right, until the chair tipped over and the glass-top table broke under his weight. The dying man flailed about in futility. It would be only a matter of seconds until he drew his last breath.

The killer walked downstairs and slipped out the back door. The police would investigate the death as a homicide, of course, but it would be as difficult to prove as Mullin's involvement with the mercenaries.

Trying not to attract any attention—even in the darkness—Nick Larsen walked casually down the stretch of beach on Chesapeake Bay, the hood of his sweatshirt up and his hands shoved into its pockets. In the course of his interrogation of Black, he had discovered that the man was pretty sure it was Mullin who'd ordered the four mercenaries in. It made sense—and that was enough for Nick. Obviously, that kind of information wouldn't be admissible in a court of law, however, which was just fine with him. Justice came in more than one form.

As Nick walked, he told himself that the loop was now closed. Every debt had been collected and this chapter of his life was mercifully over. He still had the rest of his life to live—whatever that meant. Uncharacteristically, he had been pondering that a lot lately. He'd told Don to enjoy life and it occurred to Nick that maybe it was time for him to try to do the same. The two men lived in entirely different worlds, though—especially now, after what he had just done. Though he would always believe that he was morally justified in killing Mullin—and that it was necessary—Nick was enough of a realist to know that he was operating at least on the edge, if not over it.

He stopped and turned around, looking back at his trail of footprints in the sand. The tide was coming in and some of his tracks were already being washed away. Before long, they would all be gone. *Wipe away every trace.*

Nick turned back around and continued up the beach. Maybe he wasn't meant to enjoy life, he thought. Maybe he had been put on earth to be useful…to do things that *had* to be done, things that others couldn't—or wouldn't—do. And maybe that was enough.

Acknowledgments

The list of those to whom I'm grateful is extensive. First and foremost, I'd like to thank God, because without Him I am nothing. Among earthly beings, none is more important to me than my beautiful wife, Amy. You've been a rock for me and have supported my writing endeavors from day one. You've also provided wise counsel and valuable literary criticism. Thank you, baby. I love you!

I would also like to thank the following people:

My sons, Mitch, Ben, and Jack—You inspire me to push on and not be deterred, even in the face of daunting odds. Without you guys, life would not be worth living.

My father and mother, Bob and Sheila, and my stepmother, Pat—Your encouragement and support sustained me. And my stepfather, Fred—Thank you for believing in me in the "early years." God rest your soul, I miss you.

My brothers, Todd and Ross, and the many other relatives and friends who convinced me to not give up.

David Keene, President of the National Rifle Association—Your vote of confidence inspired me. Thank you for reading my manuscript. I know how busy you are.

Donna Keene—Thank you for your willingness to introduce me to Pam and for your helpful advice.

Pam Leigh—Thank you for your guidance and honesty. You are a true professional.

Michelle Lovi of Odyssey Books—Thank you for laying it out so that it makes sense.

Joe Verbanac—Thank you for the phenomenal cover design and for your insight. You were right...it's perfect!

Eric Blehm, *New York Times* bestselling author—Thank you for your support, advice, and friendship...and for introducing me to Rita. She is amazing!

Rita Samols, my talented and insightful copy editor and cheerleader—Your herculean effort made my manuscript readable and your encouragement gave me confidence. You're a true friend and I appreciate you very much!

A certain active-duty U.S. Navy SEAL—Your insight was invaluable and much appreciated...it made a huge difference.

Billy, former MARSOC Marine—Semper Fi and thank you for your help with so many of the technical aspects of the manuscript. It is much better as a result of your input. What your buddy says about you is true: you ARE a "boy genius"!

Rick Stewart, Host/Executive Producer & Senior Military Advisor, NRA *Life of Duty* Television and NRA *American Warrior* Magazine—What can I say, brother? Without your encouragement, I might never have begun to rewrite the manuscript. Without your valuable input, the book would be of lesser quality. And without your friendship, my life would be far less rich and enjoyable than it is. Thank you from the bottom of my heart!

All of the other "advance readers" over the years who provided important input. I sincerely appreciate you taking time out of your busy lives to read my manuscript.

About the Author

Rob Olive enlisted in the U.S. Marine Corps fresh out of high school and served four years. He holds a bachelors degree in history from Oregon State University and has operated an insurance agency for over two decades. He lives in Oregon with his wife and three sons.

Essential Liberty is Rob's first novel. The concept grew out of his fascination with the one characteristic that distinguishes the United States of America from every other country in history—the importance its Founders placed on individual liberty.

CPSIA information can be obtained at www.ICGtesting.com
Printed in the USA
LVOW060617120613

338133LV00001B/102/P